The Lost Gold
An Elegy for Santa Fe

The Lost Gold

An Elegy for Santa Fe

Tori Warner Shepard

Tori Warner Shepard
4 Camino Pequeño
Santa Fe, NM 87501
victoriawshepard@aol.com

Cover photo by Mrs. XX. Frank
Author photo by Kim Kurian
Book Design by Molly Bradbury

"Los robados faltan sus dueños"
"Stolen things yearn for their owners."

AN OLD SPANISH *DICHO*

For David, my ever patient and gracious husband, thank you for so much.

I also want to thank Morgan Farley for her superior editing and encouragement, and Bruce Moss and Mari Graña from the Santa Fe Writer's Workshop for their help. To Lorna Calles and to my readers, Beth Shepard, Elise Phillips, Jonathan Carleton thanks with a special gratitude for Joan Crowley who combed for typos three times. I am full of appreciation too for my warm years among generous and welcoming Hispanic families and to Marie and Jim White for adding their charming stories of growing up in Santa Fe. I am humbled by and indebted to the vast collections of writings, memoirs and research from hundreds of scribes and authors who over the last four hundred years have immersed me in the fascinating historical background so necessary to this story.

To Page Stegner, Ken Lincoln and Sally Denton, it is ever my joy to read and to know you.

CHAPTER ONE
Santa Fe, New Mexico, 1930

The Blessed Virgin never spoke to his wife. She, or rather Her statue, spoke only to Faustino, answering his prayers in Spanish with a highborn Castilian lisp: "Pay attention, Faustino, my faithful servant. The restoration of your legacy is at hand. Join the Saturday *monte* table at the Elks Club. You will win the map that was taken from you."

Never questioning the Blessed Virgin's promise, this devoted family man led his burro five miles up the Santa Fe river canyon and headed for the Saturday card game in the speakeasy under the tall trees on the side of the mountain guarding the small town. It was July and the remote saloon had opened for the season well before the snowmelt had dried on the dirt track winding up along the river In those buoyant Prohibition days, the bar was crowded with the whiskey-drinking regulars every night, men who came to gamble and the women who followed them. Every sort converged at the Elks Club. The cattlemen who grazed their herds on the open range drank elbow to elbow with sheepherders, fishermen, loggers, hunters and backroom whores.

Protected in the tall trees, the tavern offered consolation to the busy and isolated colonists so dependent on this mountain for their existence. The Royal Villa of Santa Fe had been founded along the river below in 1604 because of these abundant forests that provided water, wood, game, and now the new illicit pleasures of the Elks Club. The huge mountain had always been Faustino's home. He knew every part of it, and this afternoon, stepping through the patchy snow still on the ground, he tugged at the burro's bridle, humming to himself.

As he walked, he thanked the Virgin for Her direction interspersed with instructional *dichos* to his burro, Olivia María: "*Tanto tienes, tanto vales. Nada tienes nada vales,*" he reminded the patient animal for the fifth time. "A man is worth only what he owns, and right now all I've got is you."

But this was soon to change. With Her holy promises ringing in his ears, he arrived at the tavern intentionally late, looking for Abran Ulibarri's regular Saturday card game. The men never managed to play on Sunday; their wives dragged them one by one into the cathedral for the *padre*'s long harangue against the very place they now haunted. Because of the Elks Club, the priests were kept busy and the collection baskets brimmed with fines from sinners' penances.

When Faustino arrived at the saloon, not even breathing hard, he tethered Olivia María at the hitching post and walked up the stairs through the welcoming open door. He picked his way through the smoke-filled room, searching for the *monte* game. This fortunate and auspicious Saturday, the women lining the long, wooden bar noticed Faustino's passing as they glanced up from their own reflections in the dusty mirror. La-Easy-Does-It--said to be a remarkably relaxed *puta*--watched him as he threaded through the tables to the center of the room to join the four men already at play. He passed close by and she ignored him, knowing him to be a proud and pious man with a weakness only for drink. He had never been a customer of hers. The other whores casually watched the game, knowing it would end only when all but one man were penniless and all were staggering drunk.

As Faustino approached the table, two men tipped their hats in greeting, one motioned a silent welcome with his mouth, and Abran pulled a chair over to make room for him. Hours later, some of the barstools were vacant, and La-Easy-Does-It was back from her patient ministrations to find Faustino sitting bolt upright while the other four men hunched forward on their elbows. By this time, the gamblers had played out their US currency, and the losers were working through valuable pieces of Mexican silver and other coins. When Abran Ulibarri scooped up his small pile and stood to leave, Faustino joined the other men to force him to stay. "*No, hombre*! Have some more whiskey."

Accepting the Taos Lightening, Abran sat back and proceeded to lose his winnings. By the end, he hesitated. After losing his belt buckle and a ring, having nothing left to stake, he slapped a folded, yellowed paper on the table. It was Tía Doña Catalina María Josefa Serafina de Montoya y Gomez's hand-drawn map to the lost treasure of the mad Empress Consort Carlota secreted out of Mexico days before the pitiable execution of her husband, the Emperor Maximilian, at the hands of Benito Juarez in 1867. Abran had boasted openly (and too often) that Doña Serafina had personally entrusted it to him years back on that very afternoon she died.

Faustino had accused Abran of lying. Serafina gave him nothing on her last day; he was not a part of her family. He would not have been allowed in during the vigil surrounding Doña Serafina's death--her own family crowded every room, all praying, all on their knees, weeping. Had Abran been noticed, he would have been asked to leave them alone to their grief. Faustino himself had found the heat in the viewing room suffocating and had been pressed against a wall while the pack made room for the Bishop and his Holy Oils. His sainted Aunt Serafina did not physically hand over the map to Abran on her last day. It would not have been possible. The map was always meant for Nicasia, Faustino's wife.

This missing map had been drawn on a folded sheet of heavy stationery; it was said to represent Doña Serafina's best guess as to where the treasure must be buried. She had certainly known where the gold was not, and with a nib dipped in black ink, she outlined connecting rooms. On the last, the smaller footprinted area—an addition similar to a closet or a storeroom—she penned a heavily emphasized *X*. In a corner of the opened note, she marked a rose-pinned cross, her seal. Before her death, she had dictated her wish that Faustino's wife, Nicasia, who was both Tía Serafina's great-niece and her goddaughter, be left an undivided portion of this great *hacienda*, one wall of which was said to contain the smoldering treasure. That prayed-over map, drawn by her own hand, had been intended only for Nicasia with a proviso that some of the gold be used for her sons' education. The rest was needed to redeem those lands lost to their family when the United States invalidated and then sold off their huge Mexican Land Grants. This map was due his wife and Faustino had now come for it.

"*Para todo mal, mescal...*" began the drunkest, pushing his glass forward. "Mescal cures every evil." Abran took a slug of it and finished the *dicho*. "*Para todo bien, también!*"

"*Tómelo.*" Faustino pushed the bottle at Abran again, grinning. Liquor was fixing him up real fine tonight. Just as Mother Mary had predicted.

The *monte* game wore on deep into the summer night, and Faustino's hands trembled as he continued betting and dealing, both losing and winning. No matter how much Taos Lightening he himself consumed, his brain (so full of intention and concentration) never clouded; the heady liquor merely seeped through his sinews and evaporated on his leathery skin. As the Virgin had hinted, the four other men leaning on the table were soundly inebriated; Faustino, unusually cordial, pushed another bottle at them. Totally alert, with little or no expression in his hooded eyes, skinny Faustino outstayed the heftier men now fighting to keep their liquored eyes open. Agile as a mongoose and still sober, Faustino collected his prize from Abran with a pair of aces. It had taken hours, but he had won it fair and square. The map was the start of his newly recovered life.

His heart beat wildly. The restoration of his lost legacy rested in his hands. He took a deep breath and tightened his grip on the folded paper, guarding it. This promise was Blessed Mother's reward for his fervent prayers; to prove his faith in Her, he had walked his burro up the mountain that July night, gratitude in each step. For She had sent him these clear instructions: "Go to the Elks Club; play *monte*." When he had confided the Virgin's whispers to his wife, Nicasia said he was as suggestible as a child. Her mistrust simply fueled the sweetness of his triumph.

Leaving the table, he gingerly opened the parchment to caress the old woman's trembling scrawl. The map, smaller than he had envisioned, had yellowed and was partially worn through along the centerfold. His eyes went directly to the X on the far right of the vague sketch, presumably indicating a layout of rooms. The riches, she seemed to indicate, were in the outside wall of the kitchen *dispenza*, behind the shelving of healing herbs that had accumulated over her forty years as a valued *curandera*. This map was as solid as a bank note or a government patent; it certainly designated where Serafina's second husband had yet to excavate in his tireless search for the cache of gold, Empress Carlota's jewelry and a leather pouch of uncut diamonds. Tía Serafina signed the map with her own signature, a drawn rose and an *X*, sometimes viewed as a skewed cross. She had not addressed it to Nicasia for she could not write.

Faustino let out a laugh of recognition. Yes, this was Tía Doña Serafina's signature as he remembered it. His heart ratcheted once more as he refolded the brittle, hand-scratched map and shoved it into his worn work pants' pocket. "*Es mío, por fin*! Mine." He was no longer a poor man born as an *hidalgo* but with no land to back his title.

Once outside the Elks Club door, he shouted the Spaniard's legendary battle cry: "*Dios y Santiago*!" Unhitching his mount, he threw a leg over Olivia María's back and gave her flank a sharp kick, urging her to carry him down the mountain in triumph. But the burro stood her ground. He took a resigned breath, got off, and set out on foot down the five-mile track in the moonlight, back to his two-room adobe where his wife and two young sons would be deep asleep. Buoyed with his prize, he seemed to float down the mountain with Olivia María clopping along at his side. He was a man vindicated and restored to his born station in life, an *hidalgo* now, an important man with the promise of restored lands.

His forebears had been granted titles and rewards by the kings of Spain, their names written on deeds to vast stretches of land grants and *encomiendas*, with serfs to pay them tribute. All was lost when in 1848, the once-royal colony became a territory of the United States of America and, through "due process," outright thievery and taxation, the titled Hispanic colonists were left absurdly poor and landless. As *Don Faustino*, he would ride tall on his horse, his pride intact, while his servant followed alongside on his burro. He gave Olivia María a loving scratch. His truest desire was as much to restore his title by owning land as it was to be able to range freely on this mountain, teaching his sons the old, valued ways. He wanted life unchanged—just as his people had known it for four hundred years in this remote Royal Colony, back again the way they all lived before the gringos arrived.

Now, with the map for a fortune in gold and diamonds in his pocket, Faustino had the means with which to return to the elegant, courtly old ways. He could teach his two sons to be *caballeros, hidalgos caballeros*—men who mattered—Spanish-speaking men on horses who were favored by the King and who commanded herds of sheep on large grants of land.

The Gloriously Independent Nation of Mexico had been forced to cede what is now the great Southwest to the United States after a trumped-up Mexican-American War over some boundary disputes in Texas. The *americano* Surveyor General was dispatched to tally the winnings and returned with a helpless shrug. He saw what Coronado had described as a vast land, "poor, sterile and worthless" and how protecting such a dry enormity from marauding Indians with a ragtag US Cavalry and an empty treasury was simply impossible. The population was Indian and Catholic and spoke no English. The solution was to break up the huge land grants and disperse the present inhabitants throughout the bleak land as homesteaders, asking them to personally protect their own livestock and women—while taxing them as well. The US courts contested the legality of the ancestral Spanish and Mexican land grants. Many of these grants were challenged because of their enormous sizes; the deeds were declared invalid. What remained in original hands was often sold on the courthouse steps to cover unpaid tax debts.

Bitter and stripped of their lands, the once-proud *hispano* descendants buried what valuables they managed to salvage, plastering them within the walls of their adobe homes for safekeeping from the tax collectors, their canny lawyers and even the Catholic Church. And men drew maps.

So much treasure had been hidden away for safekeeping that the Hispanic stories of lost gold bounced around the small mountain town like billiard balls, colliding through winter nights around the corner fireplaces. Children propped their chins with their small, clenched fists to listen again as their grandfathers related how Uncle Sam had swindled away first their vast land holdings and then their savings. Faustino and his generation were now charged with the enduring mission of recovering their legacy—their land, wealth and rightful honor.

And this very map was the start of his personal *reconquista*.

According to the map, his gold was inside a certain wall in Doña Tía Serafina's fourteen-room adobe house on Canyon Road. Already a large *hacienda* during the Mexican Independence, the house still stood like a brood mare a century later, having birthed generations of pious souls all in line to inherit their due portion of this property. Doña Tía Serafina was related to Faustino through his mother and more closely through his wife, Nicasia, baptized and named Nicasia Serafina Mária after her. When the somber tolling of the cathedral bells had broken through the silence of that winter night in 1915, announcing Serafina's death, the colony fell into loud mourning. Hastening to her side, the bishop had to press through the crowd to reach the great bed where La Doña Serafina María lay freshly dead, her mouth slightly open as though responding to her angelic guides.

The bishop's arrival with the Holy Oils abruptly silenced the wails of uninhibited grieving and noisy prayers. As the bishop bent over her, he found her already washed by her servants and prepared for burial in Franciscan robes, awaiting only his blessing. Her hands were crossed over her generous heart. For the last half of her life, she had been a *tercero*, an honored member of the Third Order of St. Francis, the highest position the church could award to laypersons who vowed to live a life of humility and spiritual poverty. She looked every bit the saint.

The women, draped in their *tápalos* (black, fringed shawls) had kept two all-night vigils, praying quietly among the whispers and food passing in the *gran sala*. They had been witness to Doña Tía Serafina's affirmation of her strong faith in the Miracle of the Cross, and they heard her whispered intention to pass this house on to all of her heirs. The hidden gold alone was reserved for her goddaughter, Nicasia, and her sons.

"Remember, *Hita*, you owe your children only three things: good food for strength, good shoes to walk through life and a good education to be of benefit to others. You owe children no more than that." And with those admonishments, she had verbally assigned the gold to Nicasia. "Leave the rest to the Lord."

All of this was said shortly before the clanging from the cathedral tower had announced her death, bringing the bishop. Nothing was due to Abran Ulibarri. Why would there be?

Doña María Serafina Montes y García had dictated a proper will, naming the Blessed Virgin as executrix, and thanks to the translations by her Anglo attorney, all was pronounced in immaculate order.

The door to his *casita* had no lock. Creaking it wider, Faustino slipped through, certain he would find his wife in the second room asleep with the boys. He tiptoed across the small front room and was surprised to find Nicasia in her cotton flannel nightgown, very awake, under a worn *colcha* in the same old rocking chair where she had nursed her sons. The *colcha* coverlet had been a wedding gift embroidered by her godmother, Doña Tía María Serafina, with that remarkable signature, red roses adorning crucifixes.

"Faustino?" Nicasia said softly. *"A dónde fuiste?"*

He moved to the side of her chair and, kneeling next to her, took one of her hands and placed it over his eyes. She felt the tears on his cool face. Men's tears are not like women's tears—in men, tears flow out of vengeance or, at rare times, because of triumph.

"I have Doña Tía Serafina's map."

Nicasia's gaze followed his hand as he pulled something from his back pocket. Without opening the paper, he handed it to her. "This is yours."

"It's for our sons," she said. He gazed on her beloved face and was again struck by that classic beauty she shared with the true Castilian Spanish. "We need land," he replied. If they owned land, they could use their family titles; they would have fresh honors.

"Mi querido," she said. Then she hesitated. "This is a gift with consequences: death and gold are interlocked. Always. Gold is charged with a mass of accidents: an ominous fall from a horse, a disease, perhaps the scourge of smallpox—or, say, gangrene from a hatchet wound, a

lightning strike, a bear bite. Behind these everyday disturbances lies gold, the poison of its clattering glint. You can hear the sound of women wailing on the path behind it. Always."

Faustino's voice interrupted her. "I have to get into Tía Serafina's hacienda. The map says that the gold is in the wall behind the shelves in the kitchen *dispenza*." He looked at his wife seriously. Kitchens were women's place and often kept locked--these *dispenzas* where men were forbidden.

"I need your help," he whispered. Doña Tía Serafina's *dispenza* had been a museum of moldering herbs, the pride of an esteemed *curandera*. "Please help me."

Nicasia pulled her hand back from his face, knowing the havoc he would wreak in his efforts to collect his scraps of gold. Heaven help us, she thought, glancing in the direction of the Blessed Virgin's shrine. The vigilant statue, Nicasia's revered heirloom, had been given to her by her doting father and centered by his own hand in the deep *nicho* next to the doorway. The *virgencita* had been carved by a master almost two hundred years ago and stood over a foot tall with luminous eyes, a beatific smile and articulated arms. Year after year, four generations of women had dressed her. Nicasia now made new blue satin robes to honor the feast day of her bodily Assumption into heaven the fifteenth of every August.

Her shrine in the thick adobe wall was now blackened by smoldering candles, votives that Nicasia lit to bless her home and honor the Blessed Virgin's image. Rising from her rocking chair, and with a brief, hesitant prayer, Nicasia placed the folded map under the statue's feet. She made the sign of the cross, and looking into the Virgin's luminous glass eyes, asked for clear instructions about the map.

The Virgin replied to Nicasia, "The gold is cursed."

Confused, Nicasia stood, made the sign of the cross again, and turned to go into the bedroom. Behind her, Faustino turned off the bulb hanging overhead, bowed his head to the statue standing on the map, and followed silently into their bedroom. Still in his work pants, he crawled into the warm bed, trying not to jostle their two sleeping sons. But even with his eyes closed, he was unable to sleep. He must have dozed off because in the morning he heard the percolator burp—the musical heart of the kitchen—halting his uneasy dreams of salvaging anything from his old aunt's house. In spite of the comforting scent of coffee, he was overwhelmed with the sheer hopelessness of even setting foot in the old *hacienda*. It was now owned by Anglos—not just Anglos, but Anglo Protestants, *luteranos*. These were hideous Anglo *extranjeros* and something worse...homosexuals, men who flaunted the natural law. One of them had been stricken with tuberculosis and should have learned respect because of it.

All the next day, glancing hourly at the statue, Faustino reminded the Virgin that he was her faithful subject and to stand guard over the map. He approached Her, begging Her to intercede. *Please get me inside the fourteen-room adobe.*

But She refused to answer him, though Faustino redoubled his pleas hour after hour, and he realized he needed to layer his requests with promises. By evening, he had intensified his bargaining, stopping just short of promising never to drink Taos Lightning again, ever. Even so, She still had not replied. He complained to his wife.

"What more does She want of me?"

"Faustino, *La Santa Madre* says the gold is cursed," Nicasia said in a whisper.

"*Qué?* She was the one who told me to go to the Elks Club last night. She told me to get it from Abran Ulibarri. She always answers my prayers!"

Nicasia shook her head and walked out of the kitchen, leaving him to come up with his own plans of attack, most of which guaranteed him severe dog bites or having his skinny ass peppered with buckshot. "Please," he begged the statue, "tell me how to get inside Tía Serafina's *hacienda*." The second night, he imagined that She sweetly answered, "I'm forming a plan. Trust me, my servant. Trust me."

Faustino was so dazzled trying to contain his secret that, against his will, it burst right out in front of his sons, whom he quickly swore to secrecy, threatening frightening penalties if they told anyone at all. And indeed they needed to keep this secret from the neighbors, the priest, the police, the government and, most of all, the owners of the fourteen-room house.

The one positive effect of the presence of the map that Nicasia noticed was Faustino's noticeably lightened mood, for he had been a man of few words until now. "Read, read!" he insisted, ignoring his sons' protests. "You will need to read Latin perfectly when you go to the Christian Brothers."

In spite of his sons' panic over this threat, Faustino continued to say that it was the very best school in the whole United States. And it was no more than a ten-minute walk from their house. But the boys had nightmares over the very thought of attending St. Michael's School under the strict control of the La Salle Christian Brothers. Their best tactic was to change the subject and get their father talking about their noble beginnings or buried treasure.

To the boys' horror, this possibility of properly educating her sons pleased Nicasia, who was grateful to her sainted aunt. Eight-year-old Franque and six-year-old Melicio had grown up ridiculing St. Michael's College and having to speak in Latin, and now, for the first time, they were made to understand that any discovered gold placed them in serious danger of being sent there.

"*Es la verdad*; it is not another tall tale—our patrimony has been returned!" Faustino declared, and as good as it sounded, Nicasia protested that they might be in grave danger if they didn't fear the devil's interest in the gold. The Virgin had issued a clear warning. "Have you forgotten that the Holy Mother's *santo* has been in my family since before my mother was born?"

"Have you lost your mind?" Faustino challenged his wife. "She wants me to have the gold."

"Then why did She tell me to beware of the gold?"

"She spoke to you, when?"

"The night you came back with it."

"I am sure you imagined it! You said She never speaks to you." Faustino's anger frightened the boys.

"Papa, could we have a *cuento* tonight, please?" Franque begged to end the row. "We'll go to sleep right away." Faustino took their bait; it calmed him to repeat old stories.

Often on dark nights like this, after red *chile* mutton stew, young children crowded the kitchen table begging for any *cuento* that began, "*Habia una vez.*" Favorites had always been the scary ones about *La Llorona*, the tormented woman who stole children to replace her own dead ones. But they loved any treasure story even more. The most thrilling were the many versions concerning the Empress Carlota's buried jewels, the same treasure as the *X* on the map. The Empress died in Austria while awaiting her shipment of jewels, sometimes thought to be hidden near San Vitorio Peak in the White Sands dunes. Every few years, another search party straggled back into Santa Fe, empty-handed, their investment spent. Yet treasure hunters continued to mount searches for it. Faustino smiled slyly when he heard these reports. He knew where it could be found.

Closer to home was the true and uneasy tale of Ulisis Martínez, a man who stole another man's gold. Martínez dug out a secret hoard buried in the walls of a low-slung shed by a bean field off Canyon Road; it was all solid history, and it began, "*Hace diez años*" or "no more than ten years ago..."

Faustino never passed up a chance to bring the *cuentos* home. "And what did Ulisis's greed do for him?" They knew the answer by rote: the Devil himself appeared to Ulisis and told him to safeguard his thieved fortune in the First National Bank on the Plaza, a treasure valued at eighty thousand US dollars. Just touching the money tainted him, and Ulisis became so consumed by avarice that he lost the respect of his *vecinos*. By the end, he had no friends and dogs barked when he passed.

Nicasia loved to growl at the end, "They went Ruff-Ruff," nodding as she rocked on her chair. "*Ay,*" she added, "Ulisis Martínez grabbed it all for himself." Reeking of sin and greed, he got his just due. Everyone in the small mountain town knew how Ulisis had been advised to trade the silver and gold coins he'd taken for hard cash and put it into the local American bank under an assumed name.

"*Cierto que sí,*" Nicasia said, "he wanted to hide it from everyone, even his wife, although she along with his neighboring family were the true and rightful owners." They all farmed along the Santa Fe River, sharing what they had, and knew that Ulisis's wife, Oralia, was a García first cousin. She had been, they all said, pathetically hypnotized by the riches and begged him to build her a brick house on Lower García Street, closer to the cathedral, closer to the Plaza. A European house, not a *vecinos'* adobe house surrounded by their relatives. Three thousand dollars out of this trove would set her up right and she claimed he promised it to her on his mother's grave. Just the night before he decamped.

Ulisis's promise about the grand, two-story brick house alienated all of Oralia's *vecinos*, so they nodded in satisfaction when the Devil persuaded him to stash it in the failing bank. By that time, he was soundly cursed by everyone and wisely fled for his life. Really fled, never to be seen again.

Oralia refused to request a death certificate because in her small, two-room adobe she hoped at least for her residual widow's mite when his body was found.

"Imagine! Why would anyone want a two-story house? Only people like lawyers and railroad bosses live in cold places like that," Nicasia said within her sons' hearing. "Who would the children play with?" And she waited a few moments before continuing with another warning: "Gold bears a curse. Ulisis lost all of his friends. That's what happens when you're greedy." *Oro es un aborto del Diablo*; the thought swam through her mind before she spoke again. "Gold is the Devil's abortion."

"*Ay*. American banks steal your money. Never trust a bank." Faustino bobbed his head up and down, wincing to indicate a painful truth. By 1929, all the local banks had gone under and everyone lost their money. This one had bellied up much earlier. So everyone, not just misers, but all cautious and wise men hacked small openings like *nichos* in their soft adobe walls and safeguarded their savings with a new plaster patch hidden behind a *retablo* of their favorite saint. Votive lights were placed before the hole so that while some worshipped virtue, others posted guard.

For four hundred years, houses had been built of adobe bricks, dirt baked dry—walls constructed for easy channeling of holes. A European brick house would have impenetrable walls, unless of course the hand slipped a brick out to leave a dark, secured cache. Still, adobe was more practical than either bricks or banks.

"*Papá*, just one more *cuento, por favor*."

Close to Faustino's heart was the story of the statue of gold from the Josephine Mine, still hidden on the Ute Reservation in a cave. The story told how the men were arguing as they divvied up the gold when Divine Intervention declared that one fifth of the gold belonged to the Crown, the royal *quinto*, and if their lives were to be spared, all the gold must be cast into a holy statue of the Christ Child and given up to the *padres* for the poor and their church. The hot-blooded men did as they were bid and because of that, their lives were spared when others were massacred in the hopeless Ute attack. The escaped men set out to find the trail back to Santa Fe, carrying the statue, but the gold Christ Child grew heavier daily. Fearing more Ute activity, the men hid their treasure in a cave and carefully drew a map. Many men have gone in search of it, but all accounts reveal that the statue has never been found.

But another true *cuento* about the *pinche rico* in Taos had a moral to teach his sons, so it was that story he repeated. *Habia muchos años*, there was a rich man in Taos who rented out his mother's adobe house to Mabel Dodge and her fancy artist friends from big cities in America and Europe. He was such a miserable miser that all the money and gold he'd gotten from rents was stashed in his own home underneath the bricks that lined the bottom of his fireplace. He never drew a map and never told a soul where his fortune could be found. Not even his wife. Of course his heart turned to hard stone and he died suddenly from a seizure. His resentful neighbors alerted the priest even before his scrawny wife discovered his lifeless body and within minutes the *padre* rushed over to console the new widow.

"And what were your husband's last wishes, María Regina?" The *padre* wished to claim a large percentage of the rumored wealth for Christ's hungry flock.

"*Ay, Padre, nada...*" She feigned ignorance, wanting it all for herself. Claiming grief, she purposely avoided her neighbors and the good priest as well. Left alone, she tore the house to pieces with a steel pick in her bare hands, bottom to top, and found nothing. As a memorial to her mean-spirited husband, she left the standing chimney set with a vase of artificial flowers as a token *descanso*. That was another famous story.

"And it is late now and time for all good children to go to bed," Faustino said.

"Why do they bury only gold, *Papá*?" Franque asked, stalling for time.

"Not always," he said slowly, and his mind went back in history to treasures of silver, ivory and diamonds. But, gold? Easily recognized yellow color, slow to tarnish, dense and compact for its importance and power. He considered the question.

"Everyone wants gold, everywhere in the world," he said and then paused in his thoughts again. "Without it, you are poor. You must work for everything you want."

True, life in the isolated colony was all work for barter. A sheep for your efforts, perhaps for your daughter—*Pero no*! Five sheep and a goat. I'll work in your field, and you work in mine. For four hundred years this frontier outpost of New Spain, and later Mexico—so distant a colony, so dangerously remote—had relied on every Hispanic soul's cooperation. Wisely, the fifty Spanish *Primero Fundadores*—those steadfast settlers and staunch souls who for one inconvenient reason or another ended up fifteen hundred miles north of Mexico City with no more than seeds, blankets and metal shovels—joined hands as *vecinos*. Laboring with bent backs, they farmed with what they had, and pitching in, they all worked to shape and stack not only their small, sun-dried mud homes and subsistence gardens but also the defensible Palace of the Governors. They joined together to build the churches and *acequias*; because the Crown had no need for schools, none were built. Few could read.

The pious settlers helped their *vecinos* for almost four hundred years of impoverished self-sufficiency. They trusted in God, and their king honored them with the royal title of *hidalgo* and gave them their *Mercedes Reales*, royal land grants, for their loyalty. In fact, the king dispensed land and titles, but he kept his treasury of gold to himself.

"Gold makes a man a king," Faustino said after a while; then he stood to shoo the boys off to bed.

Later that night, Faustino got a second wind. Thoughts of the awaiting fortune now revived him. It whispered to him from inside the wall of the *dispenza* in the fourteen-room adobe. Hundreds of solid gold coins from Old Mexico. Rumor told of doubloons and a leather pouch secured by rawhide strings holding more than a handful of uncut diamonds waited expectantly for Faustino's unearthing. In corners of the *hacienda*, Nicasia's step-great-uncle, Elodio, had hacked test holes searching for it; then, disappointed, he had plastered them over and moved on. These were small, silent tasks of an afternoon when no one was about. A perfect afternoon would be Good Friday, when the entire household left him alone wearing black rags, beating "*mea culpa*" into their breastbones, thump-thump, "*mea maxima culpa.*"

On such a day, the old man's last, being alone, he had interred his own ordinary, small savings in the very darkest walls of his dark adobe. This earnest man had worked quietly and quickly, taking time to smooth over his patched vault, concealing it and protecting it from the wrong hands. With the mud still under his fingernails, he fell in place and died. What brought on his sudden death? The next death swiftly followed when his widow, the elegant Doña Serafina, perished soon after from grief. Two unanticipated deaths.

What Elodio plastered over was not the fabulous treasure reserved for Doña Serafina's favorite niece. The map she had signed with her characteristic rose and a cross was for the historic, undiscovered cache. That map was kept in a sealed envelope tucked in Tia Serafina's daily missal.

Chances were that Tia Doña Serafina had removed the damp plaster over her husband's savings and had given them to the cathedral, asking for holy Masses and *novenas* for Elodio's eternal soul. So soon, the repose of her own soul was added to the active prayers for the dead.

One funeral right after the other. Half of Canyon Road, relatives all, attended Serafina's one-week Mass and rosary. Also present was A. Douglas Cleveland, her *americano* lawyer, holding what he announced to be her "signed" will in hand. And how did she sign it, this charming, illiterate Spanish *doña*? Did she draw the crucifix with a rose, the same she had embroidered on her *colchas*?

Dressed in a black suit and wearing a necktie, the lawyer read aloud the widow's dictated will, which he claimed to have scrupulously translated into English, to a gathered cluster of family. Shaking his head as though in disbelief at his sudden fortune, the lawyer gratefully announced that Serafina had left him her large house with its fields on Canyon Road in satisfaction for his excellent services. She also left him the property burdened with tax penalties. Every eye was on A. Douglas Cleveland. All of this was in English, which few of those present understood at the time.

This would have been the appropriate time for the lawyer to present the missing envelope to his benefactor's goddaughter, but Nicasia was collapsed with grief. "She left me everything," the astonished attorney said while the cherished, well-worn missal was stolen away from him by hands carrying Serafina's rosary, the mere touch of which was said to bring miracles. These things turned up a few years later, left on a pew in the cathedral with no explanation. And the map that fell to Faustino's winning aces had come deviously into Abran Ulibarri's pocket.

Now that The Virgin had overseen the restoration of justice, what remained for Faustino to resolve was the tricky matter of slipping inside the grand house to dig out his riches. He considered how the house sheltered heathens, offensive heathens. He would have relished facing down a pudgy lawyer such as A. Douglas Cleveland, who had sold the *hacienda* to these eccentric tuberculars rather than pay the accumulated tax liens he no doubt had voted for. The *hacienda* was now owned by "lungers," as the new owners were called, part of a throng who invaded the high desert seeking private cure from industrialized filth and contamination. And their disease was dangerously contagious.

Faustino despaired at the thought of entering the *hacienda*, even passing through a lungers den. He preferred to come stealthily as a thief in the night rather than be taken ill with TB as a trusted servant. There were huge pitfalls. Nevertheless, he courageously decided he'd humble himself to ask Nicasia's Uncle Procopio to recommend him for temporary work there. Procopio was for many years the groundskeeper there. And his wife, Telesflora, whom they called "Flora," was the housekeeper. It was from their astonishing stories that Faustino had learned everything he presently understood about the house, including the fact that the owners, two men, were *homosexuales*, a word Faustino preferred not to translate. Doubly repellent was the fact that they were white-haired, old enough to know better, and they had turned away from Christianity and the natural law. They were perverts, true enough, and as they were not Catholics, they were not among the blessed. That left them pagans.

Procopio said he understood that Faustino was scandalized, but by everything sacred, he pledged that these two men were *muy buena gente* and gave to the poor when asked. They were, he proclaimed, very God-fearing. Their generosity was, in fact, remarkably Christian.

The one way into the pagans' house was through Tío Procopio, and as Procopio, being a relative, had a valid claim to a share, Faustino could not reveal his Virgin-inspired purpose. "*Dios y Santiago*!" Faustino needed a miracle.

* * *

An Important Excursion into the Past

Fifty years before Don Juan de Oñate founded La Villa de Santa Fé in 1610, Francisco Vasquez de Coronado himself, the intrepid early explorer, had walked this continent with the same dazed hopes of finding not only riches in gold, silver and lead but also a passage to the Pacific, giving access to the rich spices of Cathay. Coronado returned to Mexico empty-handed and was immediately seized and arrested for attempting to defraud the Crown over the matter of riches in the North. He was jailed and tried before the courts in Mexico City for secreting the enormous wealth for himself. By the trial's end he was exonerated and finally released from prison. It is written that Coronado had found nothing: no splendid cities, no gold, and no silver. As he attested in 1549, he saw only vast lands that appeared poor, sterile and worthless. He was the first to have been deluded into taking such a venture.

Still, the legend of untold riches in the unexplored lands north of Mexico would not die. In 1596, Don Juan de Oñate, already an exceedingly rich man with silver mines in Zacatecas, set out with a huge retinue to prove Coronado wrong. He had in hand a royal directive to gain nuevoméjico for God and Philip the Second and for his successor-kings of Spain. Gold-hungry and self-assured, Don Juan de Oñate staked his own impressive fortune, bringing his eight-year-old son with him and the complete provisions for himself, his horses and his servants. Oñate's inventory included his private supply of olive oil and sugar plus medical supplies, arms and armor, livestock for the expedition and trade goods to offer as gifts to appease the aboriginal natives. These requirements were all loaded onto numerous wooden carretas ready to colonize the Tierra Adentro, that beckoning, forbidding land four hundred leagues remote from civilization.

Also in Oñate's retinue were four hundred soldiers who furnished their own supplies and provided protection for the accompanying Franciscan friars who came to bring the yet unseen populations into the Roman Catholic Church. For all who joined this risky venture, it was brutal work—a heroic gamble for manifold rewards. The Franciscans were lured by the promise of easy sainthood through piety and martyrdom; the others sought riches as great as those discovered in Mexico and Peru as well as a guarantee that each man would be granted the title of hidalgo—*a social honor elevating one as a person of substance.*

The great Oñate Expedition consisted of eighty-three oxcarts, eight priests and two lay brothers along with uncounted Mexican Indians as servants and laborers. There were also 130 wives with their children and the 400 soldiers, one of whom was the early Don Fructoso de García, Faustino's ancestor and one of the founding fathers of Santa Fe.

Having already crossed one desert in what is now the northern part of Mexico, they left El Paso del Norte *and forced themselves to continue north along the final three hundred miles of barren land peopled by Indians who lived by stalking their prey—man and animal—with bows and arrows.*

This lengthy caravan made its weary entrada to establish their New Colony half alive and covered with dust after the final waterless ninety bitter miles of La Jornada del Muerto. *They named it the Death March, or the Deadly Day-After-Day's Trail. Able to walk only fifteen miles per day, or five leagues and no more, foot after foot, they never outpaced their bullock carts and never moved faster than the slowest animal in their mobile commissary: the pigs.*

What Oñate and his conquistador *explorers saw on their three-month journey was worthless to both man and beast. Hope alone prodded them north seeking gold and the delusional access to the wealth of spices, gold and silks of the East. Yet they pressed on.*

The single-slice wheels of these overloaded carts groaned and creaked. The sounds complained of the men's thirst-wracked and aching bodies in high, shrill notes as the dry wood rubbed the cedar axles. What did they seem like to the unseen, shining, dark eyes watching them as they approached in a choking veil of dust and screeching noise? The sturdy, oxen-pulled carretas were like so many screaming beasts arriving to give notice that their conquerors had arrived.

The sun glinted off the ostentatious metal armor blinding the observers' eyes accustomed only to the glare on water. When the natives did venture closer, their shamans warned them off. The sight of the occasional friction of the wheels setting the carretas afire was taken as an omen. Much later these natives would face a devastating outbreak of smallpox.

The entire expedition should have been scuttled.

The Spanish set up the first military camp populated by the soldiers with their retinues plus many mestizos (mixed Mexican blood) protecting some thousand native Indians from other tribes and nomads. The Indians flocked into the camp fleeing the continual predatory raids that plundered their livestock, their women and—later and more alarming—their irreplaceable New World horses. In 1598, the land was hostile even to the natives, and the wise choice was to accept a Christian baptism in exchange for armed shelter. Clearly, no one flourished in these vast lands.

Oñate's expedition itself had proven bleak, the promises deadended; the fabled riches and spices of China were not across 'a sea of pearls' just over the next horizon; there was no silver, no gold. The quest was an idiot's vision. Even Oñate's own soldiers mutinied, wanting to disband the settlement, setting the date of June 30, 1608, for their anticipated abandonment.

But the Franciscans presented the Viceroy with growing lists of newly baptized Christian souls and petitioned the Crown for military guard and more supplies for the converts. Still the soldiers requested to pull out of this rump colony and return to Mexico City. The Franciscans held their ground at time when the power of the Spanish Inquisition was in full force, and they won out. By agreeing to protect the outpost, the Viceroy in Mexico City committed even more of the strained royal finances to supporting the missions' defense of the newly Christianized Indians from the ransacking heathen tribes.

Taking into account that by 1625, there were only fourteen zealous friars baptizing the natives in New Mexico, their influence was powerful, with notable successes. A year later, eleven more Franciscans arrived, bringing with them the holy statue of La Conquistadora, the new queen of a small, dingy colony, staked out in a vast landscape offering isolation, drought and hostile tribes. For the continued church-building efforts, goods such as metal shovels and pickaxes were dispatched to the friars from Mexico City.

Only fifty out of the original four hundred soldiers signed on to stay with their families for an additional ten years in exchange for certain concessions. Admitting that their gamble for riches had been a delusion, many had already deserted the post; two mutineers had been tracked down and executed, a few others beheaded.

Faustino's forebears arrived with Oñate and the earliest settlers. Also called the antiguos pobladores, they settled in the remote garrison a few years before it had even been granted the title of villa, a legal municipality. Don Fructoso de García had staked his youth, his hopes and his fortune on finding gold. Mounted proudly on his fine steed, Relámpago, Fructoso de García doggedly stayed to defend the colony. Ever stalwart and probably stubborn, he soon married Celestina María Flor Duran, the widow of a captain killed falling off his horse while on patrol. She came with a young daughter named Guadalupe María.

Much later, the García name was found on the tax rolls as a man raising sheep, and, posted with the other vecinos antiguos who stayed on, it was noted that he married. Relámpago was put to stud, and his excellent line of Spanish Barb horses flourished as well.

Because he had agreed to stay in the missionary province for ten years, Fructoso García became an hidalgo. The now titled Don Fructoso de García and his wife, Doña Celestina, were granted deeds to fields along the Santa Fe River as well as an estancia south of La Villa de Santa Fé. Along with the irrigated fifty-hectare estancia, Don Fructoso de García was given three pueblo encomiendas, native serfs who paid tribute with a portion of their harvest. These *royal grants further exempted them from paying taxes during their early years.*

As he then was titled Don Fructoso, he commanded respect—a fine figure of a man on his celebrated horse. He held his head high and enjoyed the friendship of the governor, the devotion of his wife and three children, and the fruits of his burgeoning estancia. *He was an excellent citizen, a true* vecino, *and when the first church in* La Villa de Santa Fé *collapsed, it was with their García hands that he, his wife and their small family joined the neighbors to rebuild the* parroquia, *as the church building was known.*

And so the García family prospered for fifty years, their loyalty loudly praised by the Franciscan friars even to the King. Celestina gave her husband two sons and another daughter. Their lives were manageable until the great drought of 1670. The fifty-hectare estancia, *now divided equally between Don Fructoso's sons, Don Juan Miguel and Don Fructoso Francisco de García, yielded no crops, and their own families nearly perished from starvation along with the natives. Most of the survivors were too weak to ward off the opportunistic Apaches and other nomadic tribes who further ravaged the lands, repeatedly carrying off their livestock.*

Ten years later, dissatisfied and disillusioned, the Pueblo Indians rose up and brutally slaughtered every Spaniard they were able to capture in the province. The Pueblo brutality to the Spanish mirrored the same vicious punishment the Spanish had inflicted on them, and any Hispanic fortunate enough to survive the butchery, priest or laity, fled south and then further south to El Paso, abandoning everything in the uprising. The García family managed to escape.

Fortunately, the first Caballero Hidalgo *Don Fructoso de García did not live to see the horror. Both of his sons perished in El Paso del Norte, the temporary encampment for the refugee colonists. One died of old age in his early fifties; the other was ravaged by the hard times.*

When the exiled Spanish returned to Santa Fe, twelve years after they had been run out, they titled their reentry the "Bloodless

Reconquest of 1692" (discounting the ninety dissident natives who were hanged in the reoccupied plaza). *Three surviving branches of the Fructoso de Garcías again tenanted the home with the irrigated fields on Canyon Road, partitioning the García house and adding onto the existing five rooms. The fields were planted and watered again, and this same house, once cleaned, expanded and whitewashed inside, welcomed them home again.*

All of Don Fructoso's lands outside of La Villa Real de la Santa Fé de San Francisco *had been lost in the uprising, and no* encomienda*s remained. Most of the missions and churches had been sacked and burned. Now lacking property, the men saw their* hidalgo *titles slowly fall into disuse, and they persevered as laboring, illiterate vecinos. All the same, they were good neighbors, devoted Catholics, virtuous with expectations of reward—earthbound or heavenly. Proud, as always, of their founding ancestors, they claimed to have unsullied Spanish blood.*

One hundred and thirty years later, Elodio García's family was awarded the Santa Ana del Valle Estancia—*their enormous ninety-seven-thousand-acre grant from the new Independent Mexican government as a reward for their usefulness and loyalty to the Church. Being landholders of a grant so vast and important restored part of the García family to positions of affluence, and they resumed using their titles. Their flocks of sheep surpassed eight thousand.*

CHAPTER TWO

Nicasia and Faustino were well suited to each other. She was steady and calm in the face of his emotional outbursts. The two boys, born a year and a half apart, were a comfortable blend of both parents, inheriting Nicasia's fine bone structure and love of music. From their father came their inborn horsemanship and love of the mountains as well as a new lack of caution—or better stated, audacity—because their lives were now no longer circumscribed by the historic dangers of hostile Indian raids, starvation and disease.

The boys and their generation took no great pride in being descended directly from the founders of the colony, the *antiguos vecinos*, who had been exacting Inquisition Spanish and characteristically old school. The García children aped the gringos; their English was as good as their Spanish.

Their father, Faustino, never relaxed the elegant and inflexible courtly code of his distant ancestors. Right was right and wrongs were righted. He openly scorned the *americanos* with their cheap morals and corrupt politicians. Even the mention of their lawyers caused the dutiful father and devoted husband to rage violently. Any reference to or mention of these legal criminals set Faustino off. The family called a truce during mealtimes because when he was provoked, his temperature rose close to 100 degrees; his face would blanch and then redden and this was followed by a fit of shouting and table banging. Franque and

Melo held their breath during these rages, hoping for a quick end to the frenzy. Nicasia typically took a steadying inhalation, closed her eyes and rose silently from her chair to leave the table. Without allowing him the satisfaction of even a flicker of response, she turned her back on him and faced the basin to begin washing and rewashing the dishes.

"String them up!" Faustino would say. "*Lo mande todos al diablo*!" Faustino was adamant that the deceitful bankers and lawyers be made to honor the old rules. "The law of decency under the One True God and his Merciful Mother!" These gringo usurpers fouled his Royal Villa and her noble subjects.

When these tantrums first exploded, Nicasia, newly married, fled home to her mother and brothers, thinking her marriage ended. Her father returned her to her new home, assuring her that Faustino mirrored his own sentiments—the US government was corrupt and imposed a new arbitrary legal system on the people's own royal courts. They all felt the same, possibly less violently. Otherwise, Faustino was a hardworking provider, a father proudly involved with his two sons and a husband very much in love with his beguiling wife.

Now a state since 1912, New Mexico was sparsely populated but with conflicting allegiances and two languages. To Faustino, the past that flowed from the Kings of Spain was all important and should be reestablished for the good of all. Nicasia certainly agreed, but her practical attitude made her bend. She knew of Indian women who had been kidnapped, courageously enduring brutality and grievous wrongs for the sake of their children. They had saved themselves by adapting. There were times when these women even quietly developed into leaders by learning the languages of their captors. In this way, they were able to cope with their need for safety while the men continued fighting to the death for their old causes.

Certainly Faustino fostered both the past and his strict code of behavior by giving his boys sweeping descriptions of their ancestors and elaborating on the exciting beginnings in King Philip the Second's Royal Colony. "By 1610, when my *padres* arrived here, the Spanish empire was the most important empire under the sun. And the ceremonies! They were grand, colorful and rich. We had splendid regalia and innumerable ancient languages with traditions all to enhance the splendor of our most glorious kings of Spain." Faustino would pause while his imagination ignited his thoughts, and then he'd lapse into his diatribe against the gringo occupation and the invasion of the Protestants, with their flat language. Their thievery.

"You have to speak *inglés* to get a job around here." His fist hit the tabletop, his sons winced, and his wife turned to face the stove. "We have been raped and held captive during these last eighteen years of statehood." Faustino claimed that their souls and their faith as well as their lives had been woefully debased since 1848, when Uncle Sam was stopped just short of annexing the whole of Independent Mexico to the United States. Even the Treaty of Guadalupe Hidalgo was written in that unpronounceable language, English, and not accompanied by signed translations as was promised by treaty.

Worst of all, this foreign *idioma* and these enemies of religion caused deep sorrow for their Most Compassionate Virgin Mother.

And for himself.

He claimed his own blood was pure Spanish, as clean as any past *hidalgo*. At birth, he had been baptized *Don Juan Faustino de García y Montoya*, a descendent of the *primeros fundadores*. He refused to speak anything but his native Castilian tongue. His two sons, however, had been obliged to speak and write English in school, although Nicasia spoke Spanish to them at home.

The radio spoke to them in both languages and sang to them in their mother tongue. They'd heard this over and over a thousand times.

Faustino refolded the map pointing to the wall of the *dispenza*, the pantry, in the grand house on Canyon Road and replaced it under the Virgin's foot, genuflecting before Her, appealing for Her intercession in retrieving the gold. Her glass eyes were shaded; he could learn nothing. Then he set out to call on Flora, who with Procopio worked for the *patrones* of the fourteen-room adobe. Crossing the river to the north side where she and Procopio lived was a matter of using the stepping stones where the river fanned out into a wide boulder field. When he reached the far side, he found Flora hanging sheets on the line to dry. When she saw him, her smile pleated wrinkles across her soft features.

Pulling the clothespins out of her mouth, she called "*Venga, venga!*" Faustino followed her into the cool, dark kitchen where she poured him a cup of American coffee. He took a sip of the warm brew and launched into a tale about having a pounding headache and needing some miraculous herbs found only in the *dispenza* of the deceased *doña*.

"Please, Flora, can you let me search through her shelves in the *dispenza*?"

"The *dispenza*?" she replied, confused.

"Tables, shelves, drawers and cabinets," she listed. "I don't ever remember the pantry."

"But Tía Serafina kept herbs and medicines. She kept everything in her *dispenza*." He had studied the folded map well and knew that the *dispenza* was just off the kitchen. "How can you forget?"

"*Pero hace muchos años*; so long ago!" Flora nodded. She was beginning to recall that Doña Serafina had been a *curandera*.

"Don't you remember how she prayed as she entered the *dispenza* to select her remedies for hundreds of illnesses, sometimes running her hand over her bags of herbs, her eyes closed?" Faustino still held *La Doña* Serafina in awe. She never even needed her twigs and leaves; her touch alone put a colicky baby contentedly asleep—the power was in her hands. And no one was surprised when she was accepted into the Third Order of Saint Francis, the highest honor granted to a laywoman for a life of service and spiritual poverty. She had earned full rights to be buried as a Franciscan, in Franciscan robes, rather than in her finery. But then even venal women favored this burial fashion for open-casket send-offs at that time.

"The *dispenza* was just off the kitchen."

"Richard and Michael cleared out the old pantry to enlarge their new *cocina*," Flora said.

Faustino blew on his coffee to cover his shock and then scooped in an extra spoonful of white sugar. "You're telling me that these *patrnes* destroyed the kitchen?"

"*Ay*, not destroyed at all! We've been with them eight years now, *pues*."

"They destroyed Tía Serafina's celebrated *dispenza*?"

"*De ninguna manera*! It is beautiful now. *Una hacienda sensorial*— like in the movies," she said, her wide eyes contemplating the extraordinary changes in the old adobe house.

"Herbs and medicines belonged only to Doña Serafina, not these *patrones*," Faustino insisted. "Who has them?"

"I have no idea."

"Destroying the *dispenza* is an abomination."

"But it is wonderful now! I'll show you. Meet me there."

Faustino sat back. Flora had offered to take him into the kitchen but all the while he had to submit himself to more propaganda about these wicked *mariposones*. Flora was so protective of these homosexuals that he concluded both she and Procopio had been brainwashed. He took a deep breath.

Next he learned that these infidels had a dismaying army of Anglo friends who wrote poetry, painted and traveled everywhere, often to Europe. Both men and women. Faustino shuddered. Language, religion, race, morality—mannish women drinking alcohol. Everything. All of this put him on edge.

"*Ay*, Flora, how can you stand being with these freaks?"

"We're all family now," the woman said. "Normally, I go three times a week to clean."

"And at night?" Skin prickling, Faustino imagined the two men— in the dark, by candlelight.

She laughed to herself, and her eyes twinkled as she insisted on regaling him with descriptions of the parties they gave. "You should see how the men and women smoke and drink alcohol! Whiskey and bourbon," she added. Faustino drank of course. Men drank, but it was rare that decent Hispanic women drank alcohol.

"I need to ask Procopio to help me get a job there," he said, and Flora's eager eyes lit up happily. "*Qué bien*!" she exclaimed and continued to praise the two men and how enjoyable working for them was. Just being in Serafina's gracious *hacienda* was reward enough.

Slowly, Flora coached Faustino in the different courtesies he should follow when addressing these two men. He would be considered a ruffian and rude, not to mention intrusive, if he simply knocked on the *zaguan* door, expecting a welcome without first telephoning.

"*Claro que sí*," he agreed, but he did not have a telephone.

"I will tell Procopio to expect you tomorrow, then." Flora had settled the matter with one cup of coffee and a hundred warm smiles.

Faustino had now betrayed his own principles by accepting an invitation to cavort with these sinners. "Nicasia would be happy to do the laundry as well," he added. "And everyone loves her tamales."

CHAPTER THREE

A *zaguan* gate may well appear to be the *hacienda*'s front door, but it leads only to another open area with more closed doors. So Faustino, of necessity, had to bang on the solid wood urgently enough to be heard from somewhere inside the ample *placita* beyond. His insistent pounding made a hollow drumming as the sound thudded off distant inner walls, returning to him as a deep, unanswerable echo.

"*Vengo, vengo*!" Nicasia's old uncle, Procopio, was annoyed. His voice came from deep within the *placita* where he had been sweeping. He took his time and when he greeted Faustino, who was also his distant cousin, it was with warmth; he was pleased to usher him through the gated entry. Faustino stared past his uncle, forgetting the customary *abrazo* as he was unprepared for the extraordinary beauty inside the open court. He had not come to Tía Serafina's fine old house since her funeral, more than a decade ago, and he was drawn, stunned by the transformation, slowly into the *placita* that no longer served as a raked pen for chickens and dogs. This open space was not used to line dry white sheets and work shirts. There was no catchall for tools or room for herb-filled clay pots; there were no stands of chile and corn back against the far wall where the ancient apple and apricot trees spread.

Now, replacing the several *communes*, those in use and two abandoned outhouses, this old family *placita* was filled with flowers and scents more astounding than those of the cathedral gardens. Sixty years ago, homesick for his native France, Archbishop Lamy built his Frankish cathedral; he surrounded it with lilacs, roses, asters and flowers of all hues. Rhizomes, too, and bulbs, all of which he had personally hand carried from France in boxes of sand; he brought seed stock to beautify his high desert town. Since the late 1880s, the shoots and cuttings from his cultivated stands in his orchards still thrived in Serafina's old place; some now burst out with bride-white blossoms on the apple trees while others exploded white on the plums and apricots. Each time Serafina's admirer, the pious Archbishop, sent over peaches and pears, he repeatedly reminded her to either plant the seeds or pass them back to him. Pruned, gnarled and abundant, many trees survived in back and were still thriving.

Faustino spun slowly to breathe in the scents of red and blue flowers, his mouth filled with the flavor of the French and Persian lilacs captured in the air. Tulips in bold swatches of color danced under a passing breeze, and taking a few steps further into the *placita*, Faustino was dumbstruck by the color and balance of this flower-filled court. The sudden garden filled him, a small man, with so much pleasure that he asked God's great hand to hold a vision of this rapture as a gift for Nicasia.

"*Qué pasa?*" Procopio nudged Faustino, who was still frozen and standing mute. Procopio repeated his question and received no answer; Faustino was transfixed by the splashing music of the three-tiered fountain rising up from the classic riot of the raised flower beds. Breathing deeply, tasting the overlays of fragrances and colors, Faustino heard his own hungry breath, louder than the water and the distant bird chatter. This garden was the gift and spiritual legacy of Archbishop Lamy's devotion to the watery cathedral gardens that thrived as a botanical wildness grown in spite of the wind and high desert sun.

"So beautiful..." Faustino uttered reverently. "A blessing as much as sunlight."

Historic roots and luminous seeds had been imported like exotic creatures to the far-off town a generation ago to console the lonely Frenchman, to remind him of his lost, beloved home. It was said that without even placing a conch shell to your ear, you could easily hear the Mediterranean Sea and feel her cooling the air. Because of Archbishop Lamy, these cherished flowers still bloomed in unexpected gardens.

Procopio broke into Faustino's reverie, recalling others who had been similarly overcome. *"Fausto, en qué piensas?"*

"Oh, Procopio!" said Faustino, shocked into the present, remembering that this *placita* was where Tía Serafina and her husband gathered eggs for *flan* and butchered the pig for Sunday dinners. He had forgotten the treasure, forgotten everything that did not concern this wonderful *placita*. He was slow to return his *primo's abrazo*, but when he did, his greeting held a new, warm gratitude. Breaking the manly embrace and standing back, still weakened by the abundance, he said, "I thought everyone grew *chile*, like me."

"I follow directions," Procopio said, glancing at the timid rose beds leafing out in a shiny, deep green. "The *caballeros* are very serious about flowers."

It was late May; the rosebushes had not begun to bud, but the flowering fruit trees, lilacs, red poppies, bulbs and flax surged to announce the coming summer. "Is there something you need from me, since you are here?" Procopio broke into Faustino's trance, knowing his cousin had come asking for a favor.

Faustino wished for several favors; he wished never to leave this lush courtyard, whose beauty made him bold. "I am desperate," he said. "I must work here, *primo*. I am asking you to help me—not just me, but Nicasia, your *sobrina*—she needs work, too."

"Nicasia asked me to speak to *Señor* Richard yesterday when I saw him..."

"Y qué dijo?"

"He said he'll try to think of something. He is a kind man."

"I'm going to bring some of Nicasia's *tamales* for the *muy estimado señor*. Some for you as well." Just then one of the gringos came into the patio, a cup of coffee in one hand and a copy of *The Santa Fe New Mexican* in the other. He was thin, very thin, dressed in gabardine trousers and an open-neck shirt. So thin that he looked starved.

"Please, ask him just one more time." And Faustino flourished a reverent bow for the strange *patrón*. *"Mis saludos,"* he said, not knowing if this man was the "husband" or the "wife." Surely he was a wife who did not have to cook, or perhaps he was the rich one who almost died from tuberculosis.

"*Señor Miguel*." Procopio extended his palm upward in his *patrón*'s direction to introduce Faustino. "*Mi primo*, Faustino de García."

"*Mucho gusto*," mumbled Faustino, bowing low while looking up to notice that Michael, who nodded a dismissive response, had eerie, washed-out blue eyes lost inside a brief smile.

Michael seemed too distracted to return the bow and continued along his path through the courtyard toward what Faustino would later learn was his studio. Michael, he was told, was a serious artist, as though this excused him from manly principles.

After this futile performance, Faustino sensed the interview had come to an end and he was being encouraged to leave. But he stalled, remembering to memorize the lay of the place, to know the placement of every brick and the feel of the very wall with the buried treasure. And he did not want to tear himself away from the garden.

The original farmhouse from the 1600s had been added to and extended each time another relative married. One room and then another was added until the house was four times the original size. Each attached new room contributed to sheltering and enclosing the *placita*. The gringos' final addition was a back wall that buttressed their *plazuela* from the wind, leaving the *zaguan* doorway as the only entry, wide and high enough to admit a man leading his horse. All the interior doors opened into the courtyard. The outside windows were laced with wrought-iron grilles to protect the many servants and family clustered and living in what had become the fourteen-room adobe.

Parts of this fine mass of dirt blocks had been birthing rooms to generations overseen by the neighborhood women and then finally by Tía Serafina herself. Countless of Nicasia's elders, many of Faustino's as well, had been born in this house, all claiming the robust genes of the founding four hundred, with their fine bone structure and narrow Castilian noses. Pretenders to this bloodline were caught out in a lie. If you had *hidalgo* blood, you looked like you had *hidalgo* blood. Faustino insisted his García stock was pure; they all had elegant Castilian profiles.

A hundred years ago, this adobe, then a house of eight rooms, had been passed down to four sisters equally and the house cut into quarters, not by separating rooms but by dividing the number of pine ceiling beams, the *vigas*. The will had been written thus: "To my daughters I hereby bequeath sixteen *vigas* each, it being my desire that you live together in harmony preserving our Holy Faith and good name."

Each pine beam was spaced the width of two hands, and interior walls were put up. Unfortunately, two sisters loved the same man, and any intended harmony was impossible. Later on, the house then passed in divided parts to children of one sister and her husband, who then added more rooms. Another part was set aside for an unmarried, somewhat demented nephew, and two parts were joined to be passed on to Doña Serafina, Nicasia's godmother and great aunt. By this time, the house had the full fourteen rooms and had become *una propia hacienda* growing with time all under the control of the one *dueña*, *La Doña* Serafina and her second husband, Elodio.

For ten years following Serafina's death, the house was vacant. The grasping lawyer, A. Douglas Cleveland, did nothing with the tax-burdened estate. The potted herbs desiccated, the chickens were dispatched and the *chile milpas* were left to weed. The doors on the outhouses rotted from their hinges, and the outhouse closets slumped and fell while the US taxes continued to accumulate with penalties. The *hacienda* became its own shadow, and no music played on Sundays evenings in the *sala*. Only the trees managed to hold on.

Having discovered each other and filled with the ecstasy of romantic love heightened by dreams of elegance, the two present gringo owners paid the back taxes ("not as much as we had been led to expect!") and worked together to restore this prominent property on Canyon Road. And music started up again. What remained was no one's family home now since the cherished *hacienda* with its important history had fallen to these queer Anglos and their unmannerly social friends. In his daze, Faustino condemned these new *patrones* for not respecting the soul of the old community and for ruining a *curandera*'s treasure-laden *dispenza*.

"*Con permiso*," Procopio said, needing to return to his sweeping and hoping that Faustino understood that his visit had come to a definite end.

He moved to give his cousin Faustino an *abrazo fuerte*, assuring him that he intended to help him find work there. And Faustino, accepting that he had been caught stalling, shot a last, lingering look at the magnificent gardens.

"*Hasta pronto*," he said dragging his feet. Soon, yes, soon. Once outside, Faustino shook his head and examined the street-side window grilles. Even a lean fellow such as himself would not be able to squeeze through. As he walked the perimeter of the double-thick walls, he tried to recall everything he had heard over the past few years about these two alien gringos. The skinny Richard had been lodged at Sunmount Sanatorium up on Telephone Road, a mile or so from this present house. He had been a disappointment to his family, having no ambition to take his father's seat on the New York Stock Exchange. When he was diagnosed, a large portion of Standard Oil of Ohio preferred stock was transferred into his account and he was sent west to die, with faint hope of a cure from tuberculosis. Faustino muttered to himself that this seemed to be the general story—people all came from the East, and they came to die but didn't. They were paper rich, and once they'd made friends among themselves, they refused to return to their families.

Soon afterward, Richard experienced another miraculous recovery. He discovered that he had a talent for painting mountains and fell into an unholy new life with Michael, his former painting instructor—pale as well. And Faustino was frankly disgusted with how Procopio and Flora glossed over the horrible sins these men were committing. Daily. Nightly!

How was it that everyone made light of their homosexuality?

Yet the Virgin had commanded him to get into that very house. It was She who gave him the map. Surely it must be a test of his devotion to Her.

"Michael is a famous artist," Procopio boasted. "Really famous."

"You'll catch TB from them." Faustino was highly troubled over this.

"Michael never had it. He came here to become an artist when his rich uncle left him a fortune. You are thinking of Richard, and he's cured—100 percent free of tuberculosis, cured." Procopio insisted that Richard was no longer contagious, that they were both vigorous and healthy. In fact, Richard, in particular, looked forward to a long life ahead, his bank making regular contributions that he used redoing everything in the house. "Top to bottom—starting with the entire dirt roof, running electricity through the old house, adding four indoor bathrooms, hot and cold water plumbing—every modern convenience."

"Four bathrooms?" Faustino exclaimed. This old family house had spawned thriving García offspring without those absurd running-water additions. So Faustino scowled and silently placed his hands on his heart, defeated. Filled with longing and regret, he remembered the old house and its *comunes*, the several outhouses. This noble old house had been home to the *tías*, *tíos*, *primas* and *primos* of the Garcías' abundant generations.

All that was in the past, when the small *población* had thrived in the Villa Real de Santa Fe, marrying and baptizing children, all related by language, heritage, devotion to the Church and adherence to the Golden Rule—and their own hard-won code to help each other. In those days, they farmed along the river, kept goats and chickens and dispensed herbs, nourished by the mountain and her river filling the Acequia Madre, one of the oldest irrigation ditches on the huge, empty continent. They had needed so very little else, being accustomed to even less.

Faustino was too distressed to speak, even while the garden reminded him of Eden. These unneeded luxuries, paraded so blatantly before him, mocked the colonists' self-sufficiency and brutal work.

* * *

A Discussion of the Selling of Santa Fe

The Great Depression walked the land; Santa Fe was dead. By 1930, the villa *was isolated in her unique poverty, a mountain town walled off by its own culture, located at the end of miles of dusty, jaw-jarring roads. It had a limited economy based on barter, subsistence farming and making homes from the very dirt underfoot. If there was indeed work, salaries were twenty-five cents per day, and able-bodied men, including the young men of the town, swung onto trains bound for the sheep camps up north or took Route 66 to the orange groves of California for better pay. Salaries on the coast ad crawled up to a dollar a day.*

The mayordomo *of the* Acequia Madre *lamented that* Los García *was short on men for the spring ditch clearing on their own section of the ditch. The* parciantes, *those householders with rights to the water, were obligated to clean the* acequia *each spring. A few years back, he could count on a line of more than fifty men, shovels in hand, standing in the dry ditch, ready to dig out sediment washed in from the snowmelt. They could clean the ditch, pull out those tenacious weeds and remove the fledgling green sprouts, too new to be named, that longed to steal some of the water soon coming for a short day of a few hours' flood. Today, he counted some twenty men and knew the work would drag. Along the sides of the ditch, birds still pecked remnant seeds from the waiting earth, flitting up when the workers approached.*

Somewhere lies the black and white WPA photograph of this sacar la acequia *ritual showing the men in warped hats, dungarees and faded shirts, chronicling the state of New Mexico and this particular region. The women in their everyday clothes, their skirts and aprons muted, stare seriously at the lens. They wear hats and sturdy boots for walking their cooking to the tables that hold veteran, smoke-worn, covered* cazuelas, *clay casseroles and speckled metal pots with handles. Yet, workday as their dress is, the air and mood are full of happy expectations and the dream of spring. A confident bird has flown to the table and is settled on one end. Square in the center of this frozen history would be the tables stacked with bowls, cups and piles of spoons; the women lined behind their preparations for the meal smile just as they are told to do.*

There are fading shots of the long gang moving down the trench, calling out as they bend to their work. They appear to be singing, regaling each other with stories and gossip. Another captures the women loading the plank tables with chile-flavored meats and beans. A keg of beer warms in the sharp sunlight; pitchers of water and lemonade flash under the sun.

Faustino was a young man at this time, returned from roving the limitless mountainside of Upper San Benicia to work alongside his father, who was fuming as he held back from joining the men. His protests lay not with the hard work ahead, for he was used to that, and certainly not with the poverty because that, too, he never questioned. It was the missing gaps in the line of parciantes, *the beneficial owners of the irrigating water in this very old* acequia. *What work he left his family for he postponed to fulfill this duty and to maintain his derechos, his water rights. His father waited with the rest of his family in* Los García *to turn up for roll call on the day the* mayordomo *selected for this work. After completing his duty, he, too, would leave to tend and shear another man's sheep. Many had already left. The food for* la cena *was abundant because the women now outnumbered the men two to one.*

When the mayordomo *called the noon break, the thirsty men crowded the burdened tables and said grace before turning to their bowls. After the meal, the* mayordomo *laid out his instructions for the completion of this section of the* acequia.

In casual conversation around the several tables, it was reported that the gringos were upset and restless. Their large country had come to a standstill. Remittances from the East were drying up, banks imploded, luxury hotels were shuttered. Travel was more difficult. Paintings were not selling.

"Give them shovels," Faustino answered.

The Santa Fe New Mexican *disagreed. It was the gringo-biased daily newspaper, now published in English. Pitching in with the banks and chamber of commerce, the paper backed a campaign to boost the economy of Santa Fe by bringing increased business to* La Villa. *The college-boy land speculators and Anglo investors had cried disaster. The dustbowl coupled with the depression had interfered with profits, land sales were a catastrophe, cattle and sheep were dying and tourism was lifeless. People no longer arrived to pile into tin lizzies and ride off under the clear skies and warm sun, waving good-byes, their scarves trailing. What was left for the disfavored town to market? A solution was necessary, said the pape and jumped on an easy solution: sell those skies and the sunshine to the highest-paying tuberculars, and take in the miners with black lung disease only if necessary.*

This promotion took fire. The invasion of diseased gringos was the prayed-for, sought-after infusion the failing mountain town needed to obtain new life and sustain the economy. Politicians gloated.

Did they think the hispanos *were fools? The overwhelming success of this invasion, desecrating an historic culture, was welcomed with gringo applause. Doctors set up shop, and the nuns at St. Vincent's welcomed the poor and suffering. Many were Italian Catholics and several were Protestants.*

The dying ricos, *the rich patients, flocked to the expensive Sunmount Sanatorium up on Telephone Road. TB was a fashionable disease and the gringo upper crust had been seeking cures in Swiss hotels. Capitalizing on a failing economy, Santa Fe's salubrious climate, remote as it was, could be reached from Chicago overnight by train. Now the swanky patients arrived at Dr. Mera's elite Sunmount Sanatorium in response to professionally worded advertisements disseminated in daily papers throughout the large industrial cities. And they came in droves to live in cabins reminding them of their summer camps. At its height, the small town's population grew by 10 percent, all infested with tuberculosis.*

The campaign was a success, and The Santa Fe New Mexican *crowed, featuring front-page interviews of doctors who attested that this frightening influx was not contagious. When one of the doctors died of TB, the newspaper printed his obituary, saying he died of natural causes, continuing to trumpet the new industry, pleased to state that because of these infected* ricos, *(and the less fortunate* miners), *the tax base made city-wide improvements possible.*

Faustino blamed The Santa Fe New Mexican *for turning Santa Fe into a pesthouse. The paper not only promoted tuberculars as sought-after transients but also invited the invalids to stay on, buy land, pay taxes, and even consider running for government offices. Faustino had been scandalized by a demeaning advertisement geared for the East Coast published by the paper. The offensive and insulting advertisement boasted the following:*

The buoyant-looking stranger on the streets of Santa Fe is a lunger at Sunmount, while if a visitor asks about some haggard, careworn-looking individual, he is told, "Oh. That's only a native; there's nothing the matter with him."

A flurry of angry Spanish letters to the editor demanded immediate apologies. This disrespect weighed on the town's long memory, irking everyone from the padres *at the cathedral to the* alcalde, *the mayor. It drew a dividing line in the sand between the* ancianos fundadores *and the newcomers, alienating Anglos and the* hispanos *from each other. More than a thousand* extranjeros *had flocked to this sweet piñon-scented town carrying their industrial-caused infestation with them and the Hispanics disapproved.*

There were so many tuberculars that some slept in tents before they were moved into cabins. And once settled, they stayed on and cluttered the town by buying the vacant land around Sun Mountain and having houses built so they could romantically ride their horses to the Sanatorium for additional treatments. They bought the neighboring properties, turning the old ruins and small adobes into gringo copies of the twelfth-century Taos Pueblo. Some homes were

41

much larger than Tia Serafina's fourteen-room adobe on Canyon Road. A building-boom ensued. Supplies were shipped by rail and although men like FAustino had work, more patients arrived.

With the addition of more cabins, the fancy sanatorium expanded and continued, always filled to capacity, calling for additional doctors and nurses. Sunmount Sanatorium built even more cabins on the contaminated grounds, creating entertainments, lectures, and diversions to sustain the bug-ridden spirits of the slowly recovering lungers.

Poets and artists conducted classes; cars arrived to take the patients on excursions to the nearby Indian pueblos. Professors and anthropologists lectured to full rooms on the ancient traditions of the indigenous people, some dating back eight centuries or more. These professors and teachers marketed the theory that uneducated, illiterate Indians knew more of God and His Truth than the Roman Catholic Church and its two thousand years of God-inspired wisdom. The Pueblo Indians, their adobe villages, and their idolatrous ceremonials were called pure, too, as well as romantic and untouched. There was a movement afoot to "unbaptize" these Christianized natives, to return them to paganism.

Faustino's ire rose at learning too how these famous archaeologists and anthropologists gave no importance to the local Spanish, whom they considered dependent and dispossessed. Servants. With the lungers, everything now had to be Indian—pottery, dancing, jewelry and weaving—and they cherished what they called their authenticity, the new antidote to the industrial world from which these coughing Anglos now fled. The newcommers showed no interest or curiosity about the Hispanics' noble, four-hundred-year culture that civilized this New World and gave so many their hope of redemption and the love of Jesus Christ.

These fancy Indian lovers happily abandoned their former foggy lives for the brilliant light of New Mexico, forming a small, moneyed culture of their own,. Their families were no doubt happy to be relieved of these sick and useless children, some singled out as their dumber sons.

Faustino felt quarantined, both from the luterano *Protestants and from the pagan Indians. To the Spanish, all Protestants were Lutherans, and they were not going to heaven.*

The Indians were an entirely different matter.

CHAPTER FOUR

Faustino's head was filled with the vibrant colors of Michael and Richard's *placita*, yet he mulishly refused to link them to the Archbishop's cathedral gardens, which were spoken of as a living prayer. To distract himself, he paced the outside length of Tía Serafina's fancied-up adobe, muttering to himself. By seriously studying the thick outer walls both stretching along the river on the north and fronting Canyon Road on the south, he hoped to shake off his remembrance of the *patrones* overindulgence. But the memory of the tulips, purple, red, yellow, white, smooth and fringed, had overwhelmed him. He was relieved the roses were not yet blooming, their scents dormant.

By the time he turned the corner of the walls fronting Canyon Road, he reminded himself that the road once had been a path winding uphill, leading the woodcutters to the now fenced-off forest. His recurring resentment welled up over the gringos' deviant modernizations so that he stumbled, almost falling. The dirt road still twisted the ankles of the unmindful, pitted as it was with cart-jarring potholes and animal droppings. Once he caught himself and stood steady again, he found that he was alone on the street facing the solid, windowless, double-adobe wall of the kitchen and what had been the cherished *dispenza*. He shook his head. As much as he was incapable of shaking off the seduction of the refashioned *placita*, he was viscerally certain that the alterations and additions had obliterated the connection to Doña Serafina and her family's importance and even the memory of how indispensable she had been in the community. She, of all godly women, might rise bodily to support his holy mission when he took a pickaxe to it; it was no longer her home.

If anything, it was now a *posada*, a place for itinerant strangers. And leaning back against the sun-warmed walls, Faustino stretched out his arms, crucified with regret that this house, which had housed dozens of pious souls, was now silent. Empty, home to nothing more than two immoral men. The *sala* went unused until a piano player arrived and chairs were lined up; several sleeping rooms had been gutted for an art studio. Where were the birthing rooms and laundries? Did guests come for weeks at a time just to buy Indian pottery and leave TB germs behind as notes of their enjoyments?

According to Procopio, who boasted he had been their *mayordomo* for the past eight years, the enlarged *sala* was now used only for the fanciest and most important social gatherings. Faustino was wholly bewildered when Procopio called these get-togethers cocktail parties and said they were like *tertulias*; Faustino spluttered his objection, saying that to call them *tertulias* was to dignify what actually went on. A *tertulia* was an invitation to enjoy singing and good food in the worthy company of family and special guests. But now in the evenings, as many as 60 to 150 guests arrived to listen to piano playing. They were expected to make conversation only when they were standing, holding cocktails and smoking. When the music started, the audience remained silent and continued drinking. Some dozed off, of course. All of this Faustino had learned, word for word from Procopio, claiming himself honored to serve at such evenings, to mingle with their friends addressing them by name.

"They listen to the music. They do not sing," Procopio had informed him with some pomp.

"No guitar, no singing?" Faustino found his uncle's airs annoying. He made it sound like church. Who ever heard of a single person, much less a woman, playing a lone piano to silent chairs after snuffing out her cigarette?

"No, no singing until they have had too much whiskey." Procopio seemed to have drifted off into some sort of a reverie. When his memory returned, he added, "They serve imported whiskeys and everyone smokes. The *señoras* cough as much as the men."

Faustino had shaken his head in disbelief. "Women drinking whiskey while someone plays a piano?"

"And they all smoke," Procopio repeated, "even in the movie theaters here."

"Of course," Faustino said. He still called them "talkies" as his mind churned up *Nanook of the North*. He'd smoked tamale husks and mullein leaves back then. The memory made him smile even as Procopio drummed on.

"Not just *las putas*," Procopio had said before, presenting this as a fresh revelation. "Now, the *ricas* all drink whiskey."

Certainly, the Virgin is offended, muttered Faustino. Then, he blurted out, "Have they no rules?" It was likely, he thought, that these *americanos* were so rich that they followed only their own blaspheming rules. Procopio stared at him without responding, trying to formulate a rebuttal.

"Your Tía Flora loves the *patrones* too." Procopio was quick to explain that his wife relished being their housekeeper. "We stay late when they are having a party."

Faustino closed his eyes and lowered his voice to a faint whisper, "But maybe the *gringos* give you *una copa*? Whiskey?"

"No, *primo,* sometimes I take a beer or two, but not their whiskey. Flora can smell it from here to there." With an open palm, he gestured from his house on the Santa Fe River all the way to the crest of the Sangre de Cristo range standing proud over the small town.

"And so, you have seen the *hombres* kissing good night?" he asked in a small choked voice.

Procopio wanted to put an end to Faustino's perverse preoccupation on how the two men fucked each other. "*Basta*! They are kind and educated. More than you or me. No more. *Basta*! I mean it."

Then he threw in, "*De veras que* nobody's ever going to fuck you, you skinny old dog." And Faustino had to laugh for sheer relief. But when he convulsed choking and coughing, he realized that he had stopped breathing.

"*Bueno*," he said to himself, "just get me into that house, *pues*." The sight of the gardens and their abundance blinded him to familiar things and the more he dwelt upon the desecration of his aunt's old house, the greater grew his misery. He rubbed this heart's bruise until the pain was unbearable and left the *gingos* to their own wrongdoings.

Now, stalking the perimeters of the house in an effort to assess his attack on the outer wall of the *dispenza*, Faustino was again confounded and distressed. The *dispenza* had been destroyed and stories of the solitary piano player and the rich ladies drinking imported whiskey made him gag. He had witnessed these Anglo women moving about town since before the Sunmount Sanatorium opened and a few were unsettling as they strode across the Plaza wearing men's dungarees and *vaquero* hats or promenaded their little dogs on leashes. When they first arrived, they had worn skirts. He easily mistook them for mannish schoolteachers or the tittering tourists who stayed at La Fonda before riding off in Harvey touring cars with a happy wave, headed off to mingle with their precious Pueblo Indian potters. No one would ever have mistaken any of them for Hispanic ladies.

"Whores drink whiskey," he said softly to himself, glancing around to see if he had been overheard. In the distance, lower down on Canyon Road, he noticed a playful cluster of children returning from school; he was alone and overcome with a feeling of abandonment. No one was close enough to greet him politely with an *abrazo* and a soft kiss on each cheek; he felt forsaken, stripped of any personal grace or beauty. He missed Olivia María's sympathetic bray—he should have brought her with him for consolation and to warn her to beware of the invaders who struck at the core of the old values.

They spat on the royal kings and queens of Spain.

Later, he took a shortcut through Paco Gurulé's apple orchard, seeking reassurance and some human warmth. On a bench, he saw ragtag Paco slumped against the crumbling south wall of his cracked adobe, snoring, surrounded by his *perrada*, his pack of dogs. Paco was napping, as he did on pleasant afternoons, his felt hat shading his eyes from the sharp sun. Since his wife had run off to California years back, he slept more. But he bathed less.

Faustino's sudden appearance set Paco's growling pack of generic yellow dogs to barking, each braver than the next. Paco gave a jolt and called out, *"Quién es?"* He did not listen for a quick answer as even a passing bird could rouse them. *"Quién va p'acá?"* he repeated. *"Hay gente?"*

"Ay, solo yo. Faustino." Paco looked, as always, disappointed at the reply.

"No one ever comes but you!" he complained, and slowly standing, Paco threaded his way to meet Faustino through the gnarled trees that famously bore such small apples. They gave each other an *abrazo*, a man's greeting—the hearty clinch, belly to belly, cheek to cheek, rhythmically slapping each other's backs with a type of acknowledgment for a person too seldom seen, which was not the case. And Faustino felt welcome, if even just by Paco, who was bald as a melon and crazy *como un idioto*. A nutcase.

"Ay, cómo te vas?" Paco said. *"Me dormía..."*

Faustino nodded, shrugging. He was pleased that the two-timed fellow had few concerns other than his pack of matted-haired dogs that were cleaned only when the river ran high. Nicasia doubted Paco could ever find another woman, even in this town that counted more women than the men who had left to find work where the pay was better. He was too raw an *hombre*. But the *viejito* appeared to be fairly comfortable, relying on Nicasia and his sister to bring him a *cazuela* of beans twice a week, both women arriving with their dishes held high above the excited dogs. Not even Paco knew the exact count of his dogs.

"Ay, Fausto, I got me a quarter elk." Paco's old singsong voice rose above the strident animals. "You come for some?"

"Qué bien!" Faustino cheered, hungering for elk simmered in red *chile*. The best elk was found in his wife's *empanadas* and *tamales*, the same he intended to present to the *patrones* for letting him worm his way into the fourteen-room adobe. The hideous house where gold called his name in a sweet duet with the whiskey-laden shelves.

"Bring back the bones for the dogs," Paco reminded him.

"*Cómo no*!" Faustino said, grinning. Sharing was the way of the *vecino*, the old way of generosity and survival. When Channy, who was like a brother to him, got an elk, they all had a haunch, and the bones were tossed to Paco's dogs. Together they thrived; together they starved. It was the way of the land. And elk was the secret ingredient for all Nicasia's famous *empanadas*, *tamales* and red *chile* stew.

Paco disappeared into his house and returned with a slab of newspaper-wrapped meat in his right hand. With his left, he flung scraps of gristle and small bones to his dogs that fought in a snarling, dust-clouded knot. Faustino carried his few kilos of elk home feeling consoled and as good as rich for a moment or two. But by the time he stumbled home, he was again awake to the fact that he was just a man whose gold had been taken from him. His gold, his land, his titles, his self-respect, his dignity and the dignity of the *vecinos*.

Approaching his two-room adobe, he thought about the huge differences between his warm and comfortable home, the home of an honest man, and the fourteen-room house once alive with a large community of cousins, aunts, uncles, their children and sets of grandmothers and grandfathers. To the Anglo outsiders, his small, two-room house went unnoticed. It was too inconsequential to alert the gringos to the fact that it was indeed the household of a proud, seventeenth-generation *hidalgo*, now too humble and God-fearing to strut his lineage before the common-born Anglos. Don Juan Faustino de García y Montoya felt lowly and called himself simply Faustino García. A man with a burro, not a *caballero hidalgo* on Relámpago, the famous Spanish Barb stud.

Given the gold, however, Faustino García might indeed resurrect his own hereditary title. Don Juan Faustino de García. As he imagined himself in this way, he was struck by how his own arrogance raised up a frightening vision of the overwhelming Seven Cardinal Sins. Rounding the back of his small property, he tried to picture himself as God did, a humble soul worth redeeming, confronted with this slippery tunnel that ran directly into hell itself—his own arrogance. And it occurred to him that he was more Devil-fearing than God-loving, more concerned with hell's fire. Perhaps, he considered, most men were the Devil's prey, and he approached his empty house needing to be welcomed.

As he entered, he gave a quick nod to the wooden Virgin guarding the map underfoot with the rose and the cross. He was certain She (so pure and unblemished) had never tasted whiskey.

On the other hand, imagining what the two gringos did to each other was repulsive. Which one played the sheep?

Seated at the kitchen table, elbows planted, he held his head in his hands, preoccupied with the conflicting enticements presented to him by the map. He was the man, the husband, the *pater familias*, and by reason and rule, he was required to set a clear example. Greater men than he had fallen. He argued with himself: all the *ancianos vecinos* knew the value and importance of the García family name and needed no reminding of its heritage. But these Indian-loving Anglo lungers treated him like a *peón*, a dayworker, and had no interest in hearing about his *hidalgo* families' tributes and the awards from the Gloriously Independent Mexican government for their loyal services: the eleven-square-league *merced* in Santa Ana del Valle County. A *merced* was a gift, and his ancestor, Don Elodio, profitably ran a model sheep operation on this huge acknowledgment of the García worth in their community. That *patrón* had married Doña Serafina and was Faustino's late great-uncle, the one who had buried his own savings while excavating for the grand treasure of the Empress Carlota.

* * *

The Details of the Lost Land Grant

Don Elodio de García's eleven-square-league merced *was ninety-seven thousand acres in the plains stretching toward Kansas, land under a dome of flat, blue sky and swirling winds. He was the last great* patrón *of this vast stretch with no minerals, no year-round streams. Over his enormous lands, he ran eight thousand sheep, prospering until barbed-wire fencing ruined the open range. Strung by the mindless* americanos *for their cattle, barbed wire stretched straight as far as the eye could see, disappearing into the horizon. It confined him to funnel his thousands of sheep along the US survey-crew staked roads, the only clear paths to the railroad tracks, his sheep choking the thoroughfare as he progressed. The sparse traffic was made to slow to the sheep's pace.*

Soon after, the fence posts bore the following notice: no sheep on the road. Don Elodio raged. Delivering a herd of sheep was now impossible. And recently, the lush grasses of the high Western plains had been browning out. No rain. In the lead, the Mexican peónes *stayed in front of the dust when the sheep were moved on those section roads by night. Don Elodio rode behind for the stragglers.*

A few more years, and dead coyotes clotted the route. Elodio swore the stench was heavy with poison. "Vaqueros." The cattle farmers were closing in on him, on them, he said to himself. This land was never home to cows. Basta con los gringos. *Why cattle? Because people in Kansas and the big meat-packers in Chicago called for beef, not mutton. Don Elodio knew the land would support only sheep, so he persevered in selling his wool, driving the sheep on the gravel highway to the railroad line. At last, he bought a secondhand truck like the ones used by the US government survey crews.* Así es la vida. *Life had its ups and downs, and the noble Spanish spirit was honed sharper through hardship.*

"No me importa nada," Don Elodio the patrón *announced. Without his paying attention his drought-touched* merced *began to*

lose value. Uncle Sam's taxes went unpaid, with penalties escalating above the land's market value. Typewritten letters came hand delivered to Don Elodio from the Internal Revenue Service. Once the agents' dust plumes faded, Don Elodio fed the blue enamel ranch cookstove any letter written in English. Here was a man proud and titled and he disdained the English language. In fact, Faustino was never certain this accomplished man was even literate.

Time passed, the drought increased and the huge ranch was no longer worth the paper the deed to the land grant had been written on. Whatever gold remained for his descendants was thanks to Don Elodio de García's craftily driving his remaining sheep to Mexico. He sold fast and cheap, carefully wrapping the proceeds in leather coin pouches.

After the tax men came to board over the windows, nail the doors shut and load the few remaining sheep in huge trucks, this huge estancia was sold on the courthouse steps to cover delinquent taxes. The grass had died and the winds were so dry that the electricity in the air leaped from hand to shaking hand, and no longer did men give each other abrazos because of the static jolt. The children coughed and the animals died, a few more each day.

The winds came up after 1912 when Nuevo Méjico had become the forty-seventh state in the Union. The cattle and taxes began the noble García family's fall from grace. And the huge grant was sold to portly businessmen, with their slick land agents. None of them had run head on such a high and dry expanse. Don Elodio, who loved his land, had warned the new owners that this climate was not suited to cattle and singing cowboys. It was a home to sheep.

The new owners kept him on as a piece of the inventory, appurtenant to the land as much as the head of cattle. He was kept on as the foreman... Although the heavy men in vests and ties were grateful to pay him to run their operation, they gave him no ear when he insisted that cattle degraded the grasses, bringing on the dust bowl. He pointed out that the land was dying. Any man whose padres rode with the first adventurers to settle the huge, dry miles of *sage and burning sun could talk sheep. These* americanos *refused to hear what the* anciano *was telling them.*

Soon, the small, eight-month river flowed but for a week or more. The moisture was sucked down through the dry sands, settling deep in a fissure twenty feet below. Then the river ran no more and the wind crackled with static electricity. The grasses dried up and the air was heavy with flying dirt.

"Cattle!" The americanos *refused to relent. Don Elodio told the young, impressionable Faustino that he would have stayed working sheep for the new people, but they called him stubborn and intractable, with no understanding of cattle. He was ridiculed for refusing to ride a mare, for requiring a stallion with huevos. With their pale eyes, they saw no difference between Don Elodio de García,* anciano fundador, *and their* peónes, *the crusted Mexican migrants. They fired men for speaking Spanish, claiming they were plotting against them. To them, Mexicans, Indians and the native* nuevomexicanos—*the last full-fledged but reluctant citizens now of the United States and guaranteed the same full rights—all looked alike. So they paid him in cash and called him a Mexican. A* méjicano! *Elodio an immigrant?*

The huge Santa Ana del Valle *grant was only one of the great blocks taken and sold for unpaid taxes. The most noble subjects of the imperial kings were now impoverished.*

Faustino's wedding promise to Nicasia was to restore what he could of their lost honor and family gold. His weapon was not a raised steel blade with the battle cry "Dios y Santiago." He was forced to rely instead on his own native wits and a platter of Nicasia's elk-filled empanadas *to regain what had been lost.*

CHAPTER FIVE

As a gift for their wedding, Nicasia and Faustino were given Tía Julia's two-room adobe in Los García Compound off their dirt street. Widowed and growing old, Julia moved nearby to be cared for by her daughter, leaving a worn and loved home for a new generation. Small, it had everything a family might need. A black wire had been strung between houses, bringing electricity—one ceiling light centered in each room—and the water came from the public water utility. Each month an offensive bill arrived for any usage at all, even a glass of water, and if they shut off the tap, they received a bill for nonusage. This water for pay had been a scandal from the start.

Before the wedding, Tía Julia's house was made ready. Faustino channeled the walls, bringing the electricity in for a radio. He plastered over the wires while Nicasia's aunts worked with her mother, buzzing around, delighted over new curtains. Her father re-tiled the kitchen sink. The outhouse was refreshed, and all that remained after the days of celebration was to visit the married couple in their new home and to have it blessed.

"That's my job. I will arrange for the blessing," Nicasia's father, Nando Larrañaga, insisted. "Blessings are men's concern." Nicasia shot him a questioning look—this made no sense because Tía Serafina was still alive and all ceremonies, be they blessings or healings, traditionally fell to this great saint of a woman. Still, her father insisted on stepping in, while the women were primed to bake all manner of sweets and put coffee out for everyone. Any house blessing was reason for another family gathering and gifts as well. Both the Larrañaga family and the Garcías were looking forward to this, so when her father stopped by, Nicasia asked him what the priest had said.

"Just not this month," Papa said. She waved *adios* from the doorway while he coasted away in his truck down García Street to the filling station on the corner of College Street, saving, he claimed, enough gas money to buy her a new house, which she no longer needed. He was her papa and she trusted him, figuring he had some delightful surprise up his sleeve.

She had not moved far from where she had grown up. The Fernando Larrañaga house was within a mile of this new house down a tiny, unnamed dirt lane. It was a large house surrounded by summer's fields of corn. An old willow tree shaded the yards and everyone knew where they lived, including the postman, who knew them by name. The García Compound was another matter, filled with no less than thirty García families on land that once fronted the river before the Works Progress Administration and the Civilian Conservation Corps channeled it away.

As more Garcías and their families built their adobes, their plots were again divided, and what was left to Faustino was a small plot. Having suffered years of neglect, the hard-baked earth was unworkable. Faustino, however, was determined to farm what he was given and he opened an old channel off the *acequia* to guide the river water to soften a marked-off corner. A flowering apricot tree would be his first gesture as a *vecino* in the García family *puesto*. As he bent to the work, Nicasia, young and laughing, in love with her capable husband, fingered the apricot pits in her apron pocket.

As the water flowed into the newly hacked channels, Nicasia was full of pride. In a few years, the tree from the saved pits would cool that corner of their yard, creating shade for her many children to come. In the fall, the small apricots would provide *confitura* for the winter. Every house needed apricot trees. Most indeed had them.

At first, the water trickled down Faustino's channel and disappeared, sucked into the thirsty earth, making a mud nest to give life to the seed. Faustino, as agile as an antelope, darted over to close the *acequia* gate. His land had been allotted the rights to use the flow on Tuesday for two hours, too much water for their needs.

Once he had worked the flat metal plate open, he sprinted back to his yard, kissed the tanned cheek of his bride and took a hoe to the dirt. In the turned dirt, he found large bone fragments from butchered forest game intermingled with bones from chickens, rabbits, sheep and goats. Years past, the blood had pooled and hardened this same soil, making it more fertile, waiting to be softened by the slow, seeping water. Faustino first worked the corner for the apricot tree. When he had mud deep enough for young roots, Nicasia, holding her skirts up with one hand, tossed her pits in and blessed them aloud.

Her father drove up, spraying gravel as he wrenched out the parking brake on his pickup truck.

"*Hola, querida*!" Leaning out his open window, Nando Larrañaga called out to his only daughter: "*Qué hacen?*"

"*Papá!*" Nicasia ran to greet him.

He was always delighted to see her, and he smiled as he stepped down, holding the carved statue of the Blessed Virgin that Nicasia had grown up with. "I bring one of your house blessings! Every home needs a *santo*." The Virgin was dressed in gold-crusted lace, her long skirts covering two stiff legs, her articulated arms bent up to receive the holy words that told her she would bring the Savior into the world.

"Your mother wants you to have this," Fernando said, adding nothing. To him, this statue had no real spiritual weight. He forced himself to stand back, waiting to see that his only daughter did indeed cherish it. No one knew who had made it. Some said it was carved by an angel in the 1700s, but to him this idol was not what the women claimed it to be.

"Get ready for Father Gabriel's blessing next Sunday after Mass."

"But *Papá*," she protested, "the statue belongs back home. It's been there for generations!"

There was much he was tempted to say. "Your mother agreed that you must have it. You do love it, don't you?"

She reached for the image of her cherished *santo*, the Blessed Virgin, cradling it. "But what did *Mamá* say?"

"She knows you love this *santo* the most." Love, he had been told, could change matter itself, wheat into gold. But to Nando, it remained what it was when he first saw it, an early statue of the Venerable *María de Jesús de la Concepción*, the cloistered Spanish nun, and not the Blessed Virgin. No matter that Tia Serafina had laid her hands on it and rebaptized the carving as the Virgin Herself. His opinion was that the statue had not been "fixed," that it had never achieved being the Mother of Jesus.

"I do; I truly do!" She shook her head in happy disbelief, holding the Immaculate Conception up to the sky.

"You know that Tía Serafina blessed this *santo*," Nando began; then he smiled, saying no more. Perhaps, he mused, another blessing from Father Gabriel would fix its power.

"Tía Serafina assured me it had special power and when I pray to her,"—Nicasia stroked the smooth, golden head with her hand—"she never fails."

"I remember when the goats were let out..." he conceded, unwilling to say more. The goats had returned of their own accord, true enough. And out overnight, none had been taken by coyotes. Not one was lost.

"And I prayed that Faustino would be the one," she said, wiping two glistening tears from the corners of her eyes. "He is!"

Nando put his arms around this lovely daughter. He could only wish her the same happiness she had brought him, and part of his joy was in believing that her world was as beautiful and honest as she held it to be. When he saw her smile, he believed that her loveliness would never fade.

"Then you must have her." Taking the statue from her, he went inside to place it in the *nicho* to the left of the kitchen door for her. He even straightened the Virgin's silken dress, hoping Serafina had been able to empower this *santo* just as she had claimed. He was not a skeptic. He did not disbelieve in *María de Jesus*, the century Franciscan nun. Remaining always in her convent in Spain, she had bi-located to bring the Word of God to the aborigine *Jumanos*, a tribe wiped out now save for a few who lived in Texas. Bi-location was what they always called it and he knew that Sor María's apparitions were entirely possible, but he found Texas hopeless. She had appeared some eighty miles down the Rio Grande in New Mexico requesting that priests be dispatched to Texas. Texas was perennially lacking something, he thought to himself. The *Jumanos* had been begging for baptism, so because of Sor María's intervention, or bi-location, these priests had been called. They were to journey to San Angelo in West Texas, where the Jumanos welcomed them with a symbolic cross decked with *Rosas de Castilla* that had never grown there. A miraculous sign indeed. The weary priests baptized two hundred adamant *Jumanos*. In one day.

The *santo*, originally carved as the Venerable María de Jesus, had worn a gray sackcloth habit, tied by a cord, with a blue veil. This is how Nando's father had first seen it as a boy. The blue veil, legend said, left a trail of radiant fragrance in its path, and indeed bluebonnets five feet tall grew up where the veil had passed, covering the hills around San Angelo. The *Jumanos* called her The Lady in Blue, for she appeared to them over five hundred times during the 1600s, teaching them the way of Christ and his Church, preparing them for baptism.

Bueno, why not? For Nando, it boiled down to believing that the nun remained The Venerable and not The Blessed. She had not been canonized as a saint, this Sor María de Jesús. Even though Serafina had fixed the statue and reported that she had been transformed into the actual Mother of Jesus, the Holy Protectoress and Queen of Humankind, Nando claimed that all Serafina did was change her vestments.

And Nando was no fool; he certainly was no fan of San Angelo, Texas. He'd never seen a bluebonnet, the Texas state flower, that grew more than about twenty inches high. Not five feet tall.

Since the Virgin of Guadalupe also appeared in Mexico around the same time in the 1600s, the several attempts to promote La Venerable Sor María de Jesús to sainthood lacked even papal confidence. Yet Tía Serafina burned herbs and blew smoke on her. Placing both hands on the small, wooden head, she blessed her and rebaptized her to represent the great and powerful Mother Mary. The carving of Sor María was ceremoniously dressed in courtly silks and placed in the family shrine to celebrate the birth of Nicasia, the only girl.

When the statue had been placed in her own home, Nicasia asked Father Gabriel to bless this beautiful lady again along with her home and all future dwellers therein. For his own empty shrine, Nando went into the cathedral shop and bought a small plaster-of-paris Santo Niño de Atocha, who for him was a real person.

About a week later, Nando returned to inspect the muddy patch in the otherwise hard yard. "Oh, *Papá*," said Nicasia, "I planted the apricot seeds I saved for the tree. See?"

He shook his head. Nothing grew there that he could see. The moist dirt refused to swell. *"Ay, Mija!"* he said, giving her an *abrazo*. He kissed her warm, round cheek and turned to drive home to the lively Larrañaga house where she had been born. The house she had left was a house of abundance—people, shade, sheep, goats, corn, peaches, pears and apricots from the shade-giving trees. Every home needed an apricot tree and the richness of leggy *Rosas de Castilla* climbing over walls and fences along the ditch banks. Nicasia had grown up with that very rose originally carried here by the *conquistadores* to remind them of their beloved Spain, and now her new home needed apricot trees for fruit and shade. "Wait. I'll bring you a proper apricot cutting," he said, and Nicasia agreed.

"Oh, *Papá*, how wonderful to have both the tree and the Blessed Virgin!"

"The Virgin," he wanted to agree. "Yes."

When he returned, he had several saplings from his own trees, sprouts taken from an ancient, overgrown apricot behind his house. His own tree was taller than his adobe and no longer lush, providing the goats now with their spotty shade. "But this tree wants to live forever!" he said, presenting the cuttings with root-like hairs holding pebbles and old dirt from her family home.

And this was the beginning of the tree Nicasia and Faustino planted, pruned and fertilized; later it was prized for its trunk of great girth. The tree had been watered by the *acequia* from the beginning of their married life; its roots reached down into the water table. Irrigating it was no longer necessary. And when the tree had grown for just five years, Olivia María, the patient and long-lived burro that Nicasia so disdained, was tethered there, resting on only three legs, her tail swishing back and forth.

In those early years, Faustino raised Olivia María, his barely weaned burro, as his beautiful wife nursed her babies in a rocking chair. For Faustino, the burro was heartbreakingly adorable and he found his own sons the same. His heart was full. With manly pride, he brought wood from the mountain, sang to his sons, and formed the adobes to build the shed for his burro, with another locker off to the side for hanging meat. And his words were in a refined, sixteenth-century Spanish, his voice the deep tone of an *hidalgo* who dreamed of restoring the monarchy of Spain to the far-off state of New Mexico. Always when he spoke to Franque, his elder son; to Melo, the younger by a year and a half; and to Olivia María, his burro, he spoke elegantly. And always to his wife.

CHAPTER SIX

While his father was away working in sheep camps, Faustino had stayed with his grandparents, Elenita Montoya de Mendez and her husband, Eloy, on the far side of the mountain. An eight-year-old, he was cramped in town with four younger sisters, so he begged to live in Upper San Benicia, the small village high on the huge three-hundred-and-fifty-thousand-acre San Benicia Spanish land grant. His grandparents were overjoyed to have him there, and his grandfather, Abuelito Eloy, taught him the time-honored skills: woodcutting, rough building, animal husbandry, butchering and farming during the short growing season, too short to plant tomatoes. Faustino showed the same inventive resourcefulness his *padres* had relied on for survival early on. And he thrived on the vast mountainside.

The villagers of Upper San Benicia lived traditionally as they had lived for three centuries. When the state of New Mexico's compulsory school system mandated that the thirteen students in their small mountain school speak English, the protests were intense. Faustino's *maestra* herself disliked the new, imposed language, but eventually the children managed to read in both languages. The old villagers spoke antique, colloquial Spanish that was a hearty dialect of the 1600s without a Castilian lisp. *La Profesora* Carmelina found Faustino the most appealing of her students, with his intelligent face and lively eyes, and she melted when he greeted her. His grandmother was captivated by him, too, all the while knowing that when the young man's sap rose, he would leave. By the time Faustino chose to return to *La Villa*, she would see to it that he would be self-sufficient, dutiful and accomplished in men's work. He was already fiercely loyal, with the noble convictions of an *hidalgo*. His grandfather Eloy kept him busy mending tools and caring for the goats, two burros and his donkey, and it was from Eloy's own gentleness that the boy learned the unique form of kindness that belonged to men.

His grandmother Elenita said, "*Muchito*, I'm going to Mass *es'e mes* when Padre Juanito comes just to thank *el Buen Dios pa'a ti*." Once a month Padre Juanito was driven up the rutted mountain track in a sputtering old truck from Lower San Benicia to say Mass and hear confessions. The town always roundly welcomed Padre Juanito with a hearty after-Mass meal, so they hoped he'd arrive on time. They had, after all, been fasting since midnight to receive Holy Communion, and when his truck was first heard laboring up the rough road, they flocked into the small chapel, clanging every bell. Their chapel had been built by the hands of the entire village in the early 1800s. The adobes had been made by the same men who cut the beams; the women carried buckets of water and stacked mud bricks for the walls. When the walls were finished, the women whitewashed them.

The road connecting Lower San Benicia to Upper San Benicia was not always passable. It wound from the Pecos River through the pine and scrub oak up to the village. A small plaza faced the chapel where the road, a track only, broadened and then passed on, veering steeply toward the thickest pine forest, where it stopped. There had never been a mine on this part of the old Spanish land grant, so hunters and woodsmen were the sole traffic, unable to come in winter because of the snow cover. Then nothing broke the silence of the forest except the priest's arrival in a crescendo of pistons and pothole rattles.

Not even the dust and excitement of the Santa Fe Trail that brought outsiders, trade goods, and the harsh sounds of English impinged on the sweet air and patterns of the villagers' slow, traditional lives. Elenita and *Abuelito* Eloy thanked God and His saints for their meager gifts, telling Faustino *cuentos*, stories of bravery and cunning from long ago. In the late spring, when the winter roads were clear, Faustino's father borrowed

Uncle Enrique's truck, arriving with his mother and silly sisters—like the good *padre*, heralded by grinding noises. Faustino hovered close, listening to his father's stories and admiring him but never knowing him well. By spring, Faustino's father would leave again for the sheep camps in Montana, staying until after the shearing in the fall.

Of the 150 inhabitants spread up and down the shoulders of the mountain, Faustino had two friends his age, Channy and Justo. They were *cuates*, best friends, mates, bonded by the mountains. They sat together in school, built their hut under the trees where they camped, slept with their mongrel dogs, and watched their family goats. Every skill taught to Faustino by Abuelito Eloy was taught to the others as they put up fences and cut wood for their fort. Self-sufficient by the time they were eleven and twelve, they were fully able to forage and erect shelters. Everyone in the small village called them the *pegados*, boys so bonded that they were glued to each other, ready for a life together on their mountain.

In the summer of 1918, a remarkable thing happened. The remote, high village was invaded by some sixty people, *gente* from *La Villa de Santa Fé* thirty miles away, to celebrate Sofilia and Bobo's wedding. It was a Thursday in June. The three thirteen-year-old *cuates* stood *pegado*, chaffing, nudging each other on the dirt plaza, offering a taut greeting to knots of relatives, and leery of strangers. Everyone rushed from their homes applauding the visitors as they staggered in, group after group, with their trucks and wagons. Out of breath but still cocky, boys swung off their ponies on unsteady legs after riding up from Santa Fe at dawn. Faustino and Channy hung back. Justo started forward to take their reins, but he was pulled back by his shy *cuates*. Other villagers pressed in to help the riders.

The preparations for the wedding had been in the making for weeks, and the agreeable Padre Juanito jiggered his routine for the Saturday wedding Mass. Pretty Sofilia Ana was securely pregnant and Antonio Luis (Bobo) Baca (who should have gone by Louie) stood ready to take his manly place in the tender community.

"Sofilia y Bobo will be married at Upper San Benicia on Saturday. *Qué vengan todos*! Everybody is welcome." Weddings were on Saturdays,

Mass on Sundays and funerals on Mondays. The ladies wrapped themselves in shawls, *tápalos*, for all three events, and today for the wedding they brought homemade gifts as well as food.

Guests arrived in wooden wagons, and two in a cloud of dust in Ford Model A's. The most fortunate had sturdy pickup trucks. All brought shouts and greetings and excitement, much of it coming from the villagers themselves. Abuela Elenita had talked of nothing but all the things she would be cooking until at last the day had arrived. The youngest goats had been butchered for *cabrito*, the highlight of any *matanza*. The Friday supper overflowed with mutton stew, tamales, enchiladas, beans, *posole*—every household heady with the scent of simmering *chile*, garlic, onions and meat. Weddings were vital to the very existence of the village, where boys grew into robust young men armed against the shrinking threat of raiding Indians. The dependable Bobo, seventeen, had a steady eye and a strong arm: he was given to picturing himself as a knighted warrior, a sauntering hero in the mountain town. But Faustino saw only that Bobo Baca's real worth was in being a cousin to a most astounding girl, Nicasia Baca Larrañaga, who came to the wedding with her parents.

Faustino's bed had been made up for his mother, while his four sisters, identically dressed from the same bolt of blue and white checkered fabric, were to be split up and parceled out to other relatives. *El Tío* Enrique, driving them in his pickup truck, had been delayed, stopping time and again to rearrange who rode in the cab and who stayed in the back, each girl fussing for attention. Somewhat after noon, Enrique's pickup arrived coughing dust and scattering pebbles. Faustino respectfully greeted his mother, kissing her hands. She gazed at him with tears cutting through the dust on her cheeks. "*Mijo*," she said, smiling and crying at the same time. "*Mi hijo*." Strong but still thin, the thirteen-year-old boy shied away from her, hating to be so carefully examined. Backing away, he retreated to the safety of his pack, standing behind the two *cuates*.

Even the color of sunlight shifted when Nando Larrañaga's old carriage came up to the Plaza and stopped. The sight of his daughter, Nicasia, in her dusty rebozo over a yellow dress in that rattletrap carriage halted the boys' antics as they wrestled in the dust trying to attract attention. They turned suddenly meek when she shot off past them, her skirts in one hand, racing up to her *tía*'s house. Without even a squint, she ignored Faustino, who was dazed, too shy to remember to hold her father's horses; he was panicked.

The three *pegados* stuck to each other stood watching. Strangely, an extraordinary silence muted the eager salutes of happy welcoming; their lips moved, but no words were heard. That same sudden vacuum had snuffed out all sounds: crickets stopped, birds froze, and even the pines sweetened their scent. The mountain rumbled from an earthquake miles deep, and far off in Mexico a volcano erupted. Something profound moved.

Faustino stopped dead. "Freeze!" he yelled to the *cuates*. And Channy and Justo turned rigid, holding their heads at stiff angles. Halfway up the hill, Nicasia threw a confused look behind her as the three *varones* fixed their unblinking stares on her. Steady stares, frozen long after she had turned a corner.

"Melt!" Faustino called out, and the *cuates*' dusty scramble resumed, now less boyish, more driven. Soon the festive throng flooded the small plaza to set up plank tables on the compacted dirt, followed by women parading plates and trays of food and beer-filled men making ready to cook the meats. A man struck up a tune on his guitar, inviting others to join, and a squeeze-box pulsed out folk tunes, causing the three *cuates* to hunch and bob, ignored for the most part. Their game was now focused on the prize of a chance sighting of the pretty girl from town. Once, crouching, they caught a glimpse of her through moving skirts and a forest of pant legs. Then she vanished.

Faustino was struck dumb by something he'd never seen before—a pretty city girl who looked like she could climb tall trees. The three boys agreed that she rode bareback and could make a mule clear ten bales of hay in one lunge. Plus, she must be as strong as they. Two of the girls in their small school split cedar for the cookstoves, but they'd never scale ponderosas. Sofilia, the pregnant bride, had been good company in the past, but now she was as tedious as all the rest, chattering like an old woman about keeping house and having kids. And Faustino's harebrained sisters were too babyish to count.

Nicasia was clearly head and shoulders over any of the others. The three elaborated on her imagined abilities and yearned to make friends with her, but when she did notice them, she just threw a quick look and shook her head. The thunderstruck boys pulled at their chins and elbowed each other in the ribs.

Faustino said gravely, "Watch, it's like magic and she appears! Every two hours, exactly every two hours." He pointed to the clock on the church. "Right here, *aquí está*," he said, pointing and then checking the clock. It was ten past ten. Then again at twelve ten, they saw her standing in the line holding a plate. Even in her yellow dress, to them she looked like she was born with a shotgun in her cradle. She showed supreme confidence. Faustino knew she was born to live on the mountain.

Channy seemed fixated on her as well. "Let's take her to our fort." It was their small hut hidden in the trees where their dogs were brought to chase off coyotes and wolves. Faustino said he'd seen that she was a cunning animal tracker by the way she moved, but his voice quivered. He backed off asking her to the hideout. Justo was as timid as the other two.

For two full days they gazed at her. At the end of the wedding, with the *despedida* breakfast being broken down, the three stood glued as always, *pegado*, nodding and smiling derisively as the *gente de la villa* hugged and embraced, singing out their good-byes and "*gracias*" with repeated invitations, pressing all the villagers to come to Santa Fe as soon as they could. Nicasia looked squarely at the three boys without blinking and then turned her head away while her parents called out blanket invitations, never singling out the three inseparables, the slack-jawed *pegados*.

Faustino felt heat rising to his scalp and turned to make himself appear masterful by lifting a heavy table plank to carry up the road. The other two disappeared as quickly, chairs in hand, as her carriage rumbled away.

"*Vengan, vengan!*" was a threat to boys who despised going to Santa Fe. Town was dead—there was nothing to do, nothing interesting. Without his father at home telling his vivid tales of the thousands of sheep they had grazed on the eleven square leagues in the north or how another uncle, Fructoso Hernán de García, ran off Comanche warriors, life in town was women cooking, women sewing colchas, church and more church. Now that the *americano* Protestants had moved into *La Villa*, it was worse, with baseball games and fraternal lodge meetings, often with potlucks on Memorial Day and Rotary Club picnics. Sundays meant mostly women walking in some solemn procession honoring a saint. No boy would willingly leave trapping small animals in Upper San Benicia for the tedium of town.

Yet from the middle of summer onward, Abuelito Eloy insisted that Faustino accompany him to town to vend his cut wood. These monotonous, long days began with an endless, predawn trip by mule-drawn wagon down the bone-jarring mountain to join the worn Santa Fe Trail. Hours later, the wagon passed the springs men used to clean up, rounding to the first view.

Abuelito Eloy allotted four interminable hours to circle the mountain. Once the promise of a shortcut from Pecos over the crest waved in the wind, but nothing came of it. That was the famous Prisoner's Road, another bungled project from Uncle Sam.

In town, *Abuelito* Eloy stood by the *vagonada*, one eye watching the boys unload and stack his excellent, dried firewood, the other eye searching the Plaza for his old men friends. He would barter the wood for twenty-pound sacks of flour and jars of lamp oil and by the end of the day, the spoils would be heaped and tied onto the bed of the rickety wagon to weather the return trip. This outing gave Eloy immense pleasure. He nattered and gabbed, told jokes, slapped his leg and laughed until he snorted, trading stories all day. "Don't take any wooden nickels," he said. On the return trip, he repeated all the stories for Faustino with brown-toothed delight.

But the hard truth was that Faustino and the *cuates* were outsiders in town and they looked "poor." The two vicious gangs that controlled Santa Fe bullied the mountain boys, menacing them even more than they did the Anglo kids who scared easily. After his third encounter with them, Faustino pulled his grandfather's sleeve. "Please, *abuelito*, please let's just go home."

Abuelito Eloy ignored Faustino's protests about the thugs, saying only, "Indians got it worse than you do." Finally, in his own time, he would glance up, stop gabbing, give *abrazos* all around, and call for a hasty departure. Faustino would jump into the wagon as the whip was cracked over the mule's back and the wagon gave a jerk in a race against the fall of night. The pattern never changed. *Abuelito* lived for these interminable days.

Faustino felt suffocated and corralled in town. Bad people and not enough trees for shade. The rock-bed river wasn't a real river; it was no more than a wide rocky drainage, staked out by the gangs. The Banana Hill Gang dammed the *rio* closer to town by stacking rocks in it, while the Chinatown boys rocked off their own territory. Faustino, Justo and Channy all agreed that being chased by the gang members still beat the stultifying hours on the Plaza with *Abuelito* Eloy gabbing on and on, repeating his tired joke about the wooden nickels. The gangs had it in for everyone and even Anglos stayed away. So with no horses to ride or chickens to throttle, there was nothing a fourteen-year-old boy could do to kill the dreary hours *Abuelito* ate up bending ears on the Plaza. All *Abuelito* Eloy ever said was, "If you are bored, it's your fault." Seems it wasn't ever the old man's fault. So Faustino hatched a plan and begged a dime from his *abuelo*. As plans went, it wasn't a great plan, but it might kill an hour.

That summer, times were strained. Crops were scarce even before a giant hailstorm destroyed the squash crop for the year. Justo had managed to wiggle out of coming into town, claiming he had to protect the goats from what he said was a pack of coyotes. That left Channy and Faustino to work out their scientific experiment. There were several steps in this plan; the dime was key. With it, the two boys strode up to a truck with a bed filled with produce parked near the cathedral. The dry land gringo farmer from beyond Galisteo Village was selling what he had, conniving to gouge. When the sun scattered the shade from the truck, Faustino held out his hand with the dime as Channy stood back, watching. They had picked out two large watermelons.

"Two watermelons—only a nickel each?" the gringo with the straw hat croaked, shaking his head. The boys looked poor, and their timing was perfect—the gringo was parched, ready to turn in for a beer. Channy and Faustino bowed their heads in the hot sun. "*Dos para cinco centavos,*" they said. The old farmer gave in; he was tired and the mountain boys looked penniless. Pleased, the boys grabbed two heavy watermelons and trotted off to La Fonda Hotel, catty-corner from where the truck was parked. On the last trip to town, they had cased out the place; it had two entrances. They entered the one farthest from the cathedral, out of sight of the truck.

Inside, the hotel was cool, dark and welcoming. A place for *ricachones*...Leather chairs and couches were filled with wealthy strangers. The country boys eyeballed the ladies' getups and stared at the hatless men and those who kept their cowboy hats on. Some of the *gentes elegantes* wore gloves; some did not. Some had hair piled up; some had hair cut short and sharp. It was such a mix that Faustino could not determine who there was famous, but the girls in their starched blouses and pretty skirts looked the best. They were the ones working in the restaurant. He thought they looked like movie stars. Faustino immediately pictured Nicasia there seated at a white cloth–covered table, eating white cake after a morning spent skinning squirrels. He knew she'd have refined sugar in her *manzanilla* tea. He dreamed she'd share her cake with him. A small bite on the end of a silver fork.

The clock behind the reception desk said 12:45. "*Uno menos quince*," Faustino gravely noted. Holding their watermelons in both hands, he and Channy turned to walk quietly down a long hallway leading to the staircase deep in the cool building. The watermelons were unwieldy as the boys struggled down the passage along the glass doors of the open patio, where fancy visitors were seated at tables set with flowers. Faustino was set to return in exactly twenty-five minutes, at 1:10, just to see if the magic still held wherein Nicasia would suddenly appear, seated. It would be 1:10 on the mark. In his mind, he saw her smile. He imagined the white cake placed squarely before her, one small bite taken from it. The silver fork lay across the plate.

"*Ándale*," he said, tearing himself away from staring at the lavish patio, supposing Padre Juanito might be there as he was the most important person they knew. Not finding anyone they recognized and turning to continue, they were stopped by a man in a uniform and cap carrying several valises who put down his load and looked over the rough-dressed *muchachos* with a cold eye.

"*Qué pasa?*" he asked. "*Qué están haciendos?*" A demand. Channy replied that they had been asked to bring watermelons to the cook. The nasty man exhaled sharply and then pointed in the opposite direction. "*La cocina está pa'a allá.*" Both boys looked as servile as possible and equally appreciative. They waited for the porter to turn the corner before they spun around and sped toward the stairway leading to the tower on the roof. Three flights up, they threw themselves against a swollen, weathered, wooden door opening to the hotel tower, the empty tower missing a bell.

Catching their breath, they were surprised at how narrow it was. Above even the main flat roof of the three-story hotel, they looked down to see Abuelito Eloy telling one of his stories to two men with burros, waving his hands enthusiastically. It was one o'clock and Faustino estimated they must hurry down in time to check the restaurant for Nicasia and her white cake.

Across to the east, they saw a cloud of pigeons circling the cathedral bell tower.

"See those?" Channy said, taking in the view. "Pigeons around the big bell?"

"*Son sabrosos,*" Faustino agreed. They were boney but would taste better than stringy old guinea roosters. He made a note to bag them on the next plodding day in town. That excursion would be called hunting and gathering, while today's was pure science. Or gaping and staring at the sights.

They moved to the west side of the tower, and from it they saw the meandering Santa Fe River fanning out in a flat, rock-strewn bed, a dribble easily crossed even by women stepping on the stones. Not much good could be said about such a town with a dried-up river and a gang of mean-faced bullies. A few blocks over, they saw the railroad bridge where one day, they'd catch the two o'clock train to Taos. Montana was farther still, the trip Faustino's father made each spring. Three different trains served Santa Fe, but at 1:07, none was in sight.

When they looked to the south, they saw the bell tower of the *Misión San Miguel* on College Street leading south past the large Christian Brothers School. The stories about the school were chilling. It wasn't just English; it was Latin, too! *Dios mío*! No one had money for the tuition they charged. Faustino whispered, "Poverty"—and felt rich.

Ándale!" Poising their watermelons on the ledge of the tower, they regarded one another seriously. This was science. They began counting, *Uno, dos, tres* and at *diez*—coincidentally 1:10 on the dot—they heaved both watermelons from the rooftop onto the narrow street below. The green-striped bombs smashed onto the brick street below at the same precise second, confirming gravity's evenhandedness.

The large fruits exploded to freckle the shop window glass. They splatted the pedestrians, sprayed the few automobiles, and frightened one passing burro. The bellows of protests grew loud. Threats echoed. God was called down.

Leaning over the parapet, Faustino gave a shiver. She was there below them, not where he had thought she'd be. Just as Channy ducked down, Nicasia's eyes shot up for a clear fix on Faustino. He waved like an imbecile. There was no mistaking it; she had seen him clearly. He waved again.

Grinning like a lion, now slightly ahead of Channy, Faustino flew through the half-closed door, down the steep steps to the small hatch door of the laundry chute on the second floor. He lifted the latch and they both slid down to the ground floor inside the galvanized laundry chute. By the time they clattered down to the basement laundry, they heard men's boots overhead running in heavy pursuit up stairs and down halls. As the laughing boys tumbled into the huge laundry bin, loud and frantic shouts in both languages echoed overhead. Their only regret was that Justo had missed this great shake-up. Even the Banana Hill boys would be impressed.

Faustino lay on his back on a large pile of soiled, white sheets and damp towels, listening to the thundering pulse in his skull, his heart smiling. She had seen him. And he had held her gaze. He was thrilled.

The next trip could not come soon enough; Faustino resolved to bag a dozen pigeons and save the whitest for her, certain she kept pigeons. Their heads together, Channy, Justo and Faustino laid plans for the pigeon hunt. They had never been inside the huge cathedral and none had any notion where to find the climb up to the cathedral bell tower. Faustino insisted if they failed this time, there would be more opportunities.

Two weeks later, *Abuelito* Eloy suppressed a wry smile when the three *pegados* fairly flew onto his wagon for the ride into town. He took their prompt helpfulness loading a cord of oak as a sign of the boys' maturing, smiling again as they swung onto the wagon ready for the day in town. More than four hours later, dusty from the wagon ride, they left Eloy to his hobnobbing, wished him well, and headed in the direction of the cathedral, burlap bags rolled under their arms.

Inside the cathedral, they looked sharply about them and took the last pew, stuffing the bags under the seats. As Channy had advised, they fell to their knees with their hands clasped in prayer, trying to be inconspicuous as they searched for a passage to the bell tower, pointing to likely corners.

With a bang, the gate to a confessional swung open and a priest came out, strolling in their direction. They held their breath as he came near and stopped behind them, resting a gentle hand on Justo's shoulder. Justo started and blanched. The priest smiled; his black cassock appeared new. Bending over Justo, he asked, "Have you come for confession?"

Faustino stood to answer for his dumbstruck *cuate*. "No, *Padre*. *Gracias*." Facing the priest, he extended his hand. "We live on the San Benicia Grant."

"Padre Juanito, yes?"

All three nodded. The young priest smiled again and asked their names. Faustino wanted to tell him that they had nothing to confess, that they lived on the mountain. Abuelito Eloy said boys could do no wrong if they lived in the pure air of God's forest. He strained to remember what temptations he'd heard about in Lower San Benicia, where two-year-olds might succumb to deeds too horrendous to report. But the *cuates* did not sin, said *Abuelito* Eloy. Could not, in fact.

"I am Father Sebastiano. It looks as though you have ridden the whole way on a dusty wagon." The three nodded, trying to appear scrubbed.

"May we look around?" Channy remembered and tacked on, "Father?"

"Come with me, I'll show you around this cathedral. It was designed and built by Bishop Lamy forty years ago, may God rest his soul."

"Can we ring the bells?" Faustino asked. "Please." To their astonishment, Father Sebastiano led them to a small door off the sacristy revealing the narrow staircase. "You can ring the bells only at five o'clock, but you can help me chase the pesky pigeons out of the bell tower."

Faustino was incredulous. His heart racing, he hesitated and then burst out, "Can we take some of them?" The priest paused, pressed his lips together, and shrugged his shoulders. The boys might need food, as poorly dressed as they were.

"We have three bags."

"You might do better with a stick as well." He went to a closet and took out a polished brass rod used to snuff tall candles. "Hit them on the head with this."

Later, when the *cuates* heaved two limp burlap bags onto the bed of *Abuelito*'s wagon, they crowed with triumph, vowing never to reveal how they had been given the birds. To their shame, they had neither hunted like men nor stolen the birds. A third bag shuddered with the life of the whitest pigeon.

"Free *pichones*?" *Abuelito* Eloy shook his head, amazed. "Free? Not a gift?" Gifts had to be repaid; theft might pass unsettled. The Navajos stole sheep and horses and never thanked the settlers. Gifts, though, had to be repaid, and this made Eloy uneasy.

Faustino handed the pigeons over to be served at Sofilia and Bobo's baby's baptism feast on the weekend. The entire Baca-Larrañaga family would attend. He caged the one pigeon still alive for Nicasia. Faustino was even more obsessed with her now. His heart raced as he remembered her upturned face.

"*Cretino! Imbécil!*" she had howled up at him, brushing the pulp off her skirt. Had Faustino not been totally love struck, he would have ducked his head. But he could not. He smiled, and actually waved to her twice, until Channy yanked at his arm. Still he had grinned and held on for another few seconds.

"Nicasia!" he said aloud, electrified by the music of her name.

"*Monstro*!" she screamed up at him, the idiot boy from San Benicia.

Again in the mountain village for the baptism of the baby girl, Nicasia saw him moving through the crowd, popping up here and there, silently watching her. Sofilia, holding her precious baby girl in her arms, said everyone knew that Faustino was very smart and handsome—as everyone could see, he was *guapísimo*. Yes, he was handsome.

Nicasia thought not. Faustino might have the blood of noble *fundadores* coursing through him, but he was still just a mannerless mountain boy. But knowing him best, his grandmother said Faustino was surely going to go far. He had *posibilidades*. He was a great provider. Any woman would be fortunate to be his.

Sofilia and Bobo's baby girl was layered in the same thinning antique laces that generations had worn when the holy water scoured off the child's original sin. The *padre* raised his right arm above the child, pronouncing each echoing word, "*Yo te bautizo Nicasia Sofilia Catarina Montoya y Baca en el nombre del Padre, y el Hijo, y el Espíritu Santo.*"

"You named her after me!" Nicasia burst out. She was too young to be a *madrina*—the church said godparents had to be at least sixteen years old. Even in the backwoods.

"Yes. We want her to be just like you," Bobo said quietly. Nicasia hugged him, tears brimming. When she looked up, she again saw the fourteen-year-old boy's eyes boring into her. He made her tears itch. She brushed the sides of her face, staring back.

"*Basta*, Faustino," she mouthed and then looked down at the baby again. "*Bruto!*"

The following year, he began to spend his weekends in town, joining the parade of young men in the evening's walk around the Plaza. The young girls walked in the opposite direction, making sly comments among themselves. Sometimes bringing Channy or Justo, often by himself, he set his gaze for Nicasia, and every so often he managed to find her. She, on the other hand, watched all the boys with a broad sweep, glancing cagily at Faustino, shaking her head and smiling in spite of herself.

Faustino's parents were torn at sending Faustino to Sweeney High School knowing that Bishop Lamy had proclaimed that it was a mortal sin for Catholic children to attend the public schools. In spite of this, when he turned sixteen, his parents could not afford St. Michael's College. In addition, Faustino could never pass the entrance exams without any Latin, and Father Sebastiano, young then, allowed that as their intentions were pure, no sin would be assigned. "Remember to send me your grandchildren—but only the boys," the priest had said. Faustino was then brought back to town and enrolled in the public high school the following day, where he was often held back for obstinately refusing to turn in his English essays. Missing the mountain, he slouched, daydreaming alternately of the mountain and of swaggering around the Plaza, searching out Nicasia.

He knew his place was in the mountains, and throughout his life, she would be the only woman for him. There was no one else.

* * *

An Excursion into the Spanish and Mexican Land Grants

From the time of Santa Fe's founding until Mexican Independence from Spain, the land grants were called mercedes, *and they were indeed royal gifts deeded through the king, from his superior, God Almighty. In the* Tierra Adentro's *broad, dry lands these prizes were necessarily huge, with sparse vegetation to support both sheep and men. The San Benicia Grant was over three hundred and fifty thousand acres, with grasslands and mountain forests. With their two villages, one on the Pecos River, the smaller one on the side of the mountain, the land grant holders built their homes, farmed and tended their growing herds of sheep, armed and protecting their broad lands against very real Indian incursions.*

Lower San Benicia, quiet and pious, lay on the edge of the five-hundred-square-mile plain. The earliest settlers had built the church, the plaza and fortified village according to the plan the viceroy of New Spain had set out for all such royal communities, and each grant owner had been assigned ten acres for his family to farm— which could be bequeathed or sold. The vast open balance was held in common by the grant holders. Outside the clustered village, the mounted vecinos *fanned out on their full-horizon grass, herding to sustain themselves and their families. Each man was armed, and in the main, colonial life was slow and measured, protected from any outside influence. Trade was confined within the Spanish Empire. Any commerce from Santa Fe in the northern part of Mexico moved south along the thousand-two-hundred-mile* Camino Real *to other royal cities, with exchanges of woven goods, tanned hides, leather jackets, buffalo hides and salt for silver pesos and other goods. China, silks and spices came to Santa Fe shipped on Spanish galleons to Mexican ports and brought up the* Camino Real. *It was a slow process and kept Santa Fe isolated.*

In 1821, Mexico declared itself independent of Spain. No longer a Spanish colony, Santa Fe became the upper, remote part of

Mexico, and Spain's long-enduring trade embargo was shattered. A burgeoning free commerce was now centered at the meeting of this new Santa Fe Trail, which ran from Independence, Missouri, meeting the well-worn Camino Real leading south to Mexico City. Unheralded riches were now possible, and foreigners exploded into the isolated communities bringing everything from machine-milled fabrics and manufactured tools to silver, luxury items and the first printing press.

Nuevomejicanos had always been paid in Mexican silver pesos for wool and meat on the hoof. And this was the currency outsiders sought. What remained unsold from the Santa Fe Trail continued south to Old Mexico, doubling in price again. The profits were monumental, causing a hesitant American trade to increase exponentially for forty years, continuing well after the Spanish-American War.

The caravans were heartily welcomed in Lower San Benicia, arriving exhausted, triumphant and dusty after a six-week or more drive. A brothel sprang up, a blacksmith, a cantina -—and baths. Each loaded wagon passing through Santa Fe was assessed the equivalent of five hundred dollars in duties, giving rise to Lower San Benicia's prosperity as a caravan stop to redistribute the loads, doubling the packs on each wagon to avoid extra tariffs. The village's spacious plaza fronting the church, once quiet, now bustled with clamor, dust, voracious men, animals and wagons gearing up for their exultant and noisy entry into Santa Fe.

By 1870, the traffic on the 780-mile-long Santa Fe Trail from Independence, Missouri, brought thousands of wagonloads, millions of dollars in inventory and a steady tax revenue. Every village strung along the trail boomed. Strangers of all stripes poured into Lower San Benicia; with the men came women, children, non-Catholics and shiftless vagrants. Now, even the sheepherders and fishermen earned pesos from the outsiders moving north and south along the river.

Abuelita Elenita would have been able to attend daily Mass had she endured the constant turmoil in Lower San Benicia, but

trading her peace and tranquility (even for a higher place in heaven)
would have been too harrowing, so she settled for a once-a-month
Mass in peaceful Upper San Benicia to thank El Señor *for her*
hands-on life. Wisely, it appeared, for the instant the first Atchison
Topeka and Santa Fe trains roared past Lower San Benicia, the
flourishing village fell deserted. Holy Mass was cut back to twice a
week. Overnight, all commerce moved to the rails, and the new train
bypassed the merced *at a steady speed. The buildings and brothels*
that had been so quickly built lay abandoned; communities along the
way crumbled. The Santa Fe Trail had made men rich and richer for
sixty or more years when, overnight, the grand moments ended; the
towns were left desolated. Up to two thousand wagons per year had
stopped to water in Lower San Benicia.

During the boom years, Upper San Benicia was defensive and
untouched. Eventually the younger generations were lured away, and
the northern lands were now governed by a second new government,
the United States of America. Nuevoméjico, *the most northern*
Mexican state, had been tragically sheared off and thrown to the
United States as booty from the trumped-up Spanish-American
War in 1848. The Surveyor General, who could not read Spanish,
examined the maps and deeds of this new acquisition and announced
that the United States had been burdened with a vast, arid land
surrounded by rapacious Apaches and Navajos with their taste for
horses, sheep and sometimes women. As he left his post, he requested
that the standing army be dispatched to protect the new citizens, but
the treasury had no funds to do so.

Washington's solution was to arm the available villagers and
spread them across the territory as a form of unpaid militia. The
huge land grants were broken up to disperse the people into small,
privately owned fenced lands and farms of 160 acres. These confined
homesteads were remote from the villages, the communities and the
church. What made sense on paper was devastating to the Hispanic
villagers with their tight culture and roaming herds of sheep.

The Court of Private Land Grants, an arm of the new US
Territory, allowed that Mexican claims before Americanization

in 1848 need not be honored. Even the antique Spanish land titles were questioned. The Supreme Court backed adjudicating the open lands in The United States v. Marques et al., 1897. Legal theft ensued, and one US surveyor general asked Congress to intervene. But Congress, having dealt with land grants in Florida no larger than eight hundred acres, balked at the enormity of these hundred-thousand-acre spreads. Between this form of usurpation and the derelict towns bypassed by the railroad, the land grabbers smelled a wealth of vacant property and vast stretches of wide-open lands for the taking.

A highly placed politician leaned in to help himself, and the San Benicia merced *was lightened by three hundred thousand acres. The villagers ended up grazing five thousand acres and were urged to homestead portions of the remainder of their lands deeded them through the royal grant, the King's gift.*

The new government began to set corners and auction off the measureless lands to outside homesteaders, aiming to populate every lonely square mile of the plains. Landless families swung off the moving trains to stake their claims. They put up fences and killed the buffalo. They broke the ground cover with their steel plows and tragically threw the desiccated earth to the windstorms of that new century. All protests were lost in the escalating winds ripping across the grasslands.

CHAPTER SEVEN

Elena and Eloy Montoya de Mendez disapproved of the lively commerce in Lower San Benicia, calling it greed. What amounted to a simple rivalry between two land grant villages ended in 1887 when Uncle Sam broke up the lands. As much as the concept of homesteading had been explained, none of the traditional settlers and grant holders understood this wreckage of both their land and culture. The citizens of Lower San Benicia grasped the takeover first but too slowly; they could not translate legal English into everyday Spanish.

Padre Juanito, young then too, put aside the Gospel, interrupting Mass in that very small, hand-built chapel and turned to the thirty-five faithful facing him. His dramatic silence and some insistent throat clearing startled them out of their prayers into attention.

"The old lands are being stolen by the *luteranos*," he announced. When he called Protestants Lutherans, he meant infidels. "The Surveyor General wants the *gente* to break up the village and spread out all over this land to protect it against the Indian raids." He paused, needing to steady himself before continuing. "The *americanos* continue to take the land from the Indians. Your land, too; they are giving away your land."

The government had sent a land man who spoke halting Spanish to explain to the land grant holders what changes to expect. "There are still thirty-three hostile tribes out there," the land man had said to those gathered at the time. Spreading his papers out, he pressed the landholders to sign up and "homestead." In this way, they could regain at least a partial title to their land in the fertile plains. To the villagers, the idea of anyone's owning their common land was incomprehensible from the start.

They did not grasp what he was saying. "We must ask the *padre*. He knows what a homestead is." The *vecinos* clamored for an explanation.

"It's the cheapest way out of this mess," the American had said in honest sympathy with the problem.

Padre Juanito held his head in his hands; he finally understood what the land man had been trying to explain. And now, it was too late. Nothing could reverse this tragedy.

"Each man is to mark off 160 acres for himself." Padre Juanito waved his hands toward the wall. "Out there." And the faithful, seated on their familiar benches in the small chapel, followed his hands with their eyes. "You will live on your own private *merced*, build a home and put up fences."

"Fences?" one of the sheepherders asked. Their flocks numbered in the tens of thousands.

"Fences for goats. No fences for sheep." And all nodded in agreement. However, if they were to relocate and singlehandedly defend their 160 acres (no more than that?) the village would fall to ruin, the church was sure to crumble, the language would die. First, the roofs of the small churches would leak and collapse, and later, the adobe houses would begin to melt with the spring thaw followed by the summer's deluges. And as the woodcutters of Pecos grew stooped and old, they had nothing to leave but widows. The village life would be lost.

The cherished old ways were to fall to inevitable dust.

Because his mother and sisters lived in Santa Fe, when Faustino turned sixteen, he moved into town, leaving his aging grandparents to fend for themselves. This story was repeated in every home.

In town, electricity had recently snapped into use, creating a furor. Families hoarded and reburied gold in the walls of their homes to the broadcast tunes of New York and Chicago. Foreign names and magic music overrode the burros braying, the dogs barking. Mothers called their children to dinner against a crackle background of the dance bands. Charles Lindberg had landed at Harkle Airport and the Fiesta Queen revealed that she had learned the new dance craze; she, too, could lindy hop.

Once Faustino had thrown himself into the water of progress, the new excitement was irresistible. The world looked brand new to him and he was young. He took a job driving wagon-loads of cement for the government's grand designs. For this, he had change in his pocket. At the same time, his friends Justo and Channy were lured out of their rich mountain life by wild dreams and unlimited promises—things easily bought with paper money.

In the early years, Faustino was swayed and distracted by the *americanos'* innovations. His strong body swayed to the music on the radio, and he listened to the world news, transfixed, dreaming of spellbinding Nicasia with all he had learned of the world. As a child, he had found the capitol dreary, but now the boredom had ended: electricity sizzled with sounds, words and worlds. Anglo babble, some in Spanish. He heard short wave static from Chihuahua coming through, broadcasting *ranchero* music. *Mariachi* with trumpets and guitars played loud and louder. Any time of the day.

Abuelito Eloy said it was likely that electricity came from the Devil. These wires could kill; Baby Jesus was no longer safe in his manger. But it brightened the dark cathedral, fired hot plates for the tortillas, and ironed men's shirts. When the mesmerizing electric fire serpent hissed, many villagers threw down their axes and flooded the town. The population doubled, crowding the dusty streets.

Then came the telephone.

Gas-fired furnaces to heat the old adobes caught on, and Faustino was a good *vecino*, digging out dirt floors to sink furnaces into dark basements under newly rigged suspended wooden floors. These floors were expensive because even the woodcutters had moved to town. The Santa Fe canyon had been foraged and stripped of trees these past four hundred years, and rumors grew louder that soon their mountain would be closed, locked against her own people. The secret trysts on the Prisoner's Road were over. The clear water from the river was no longer free for the taking. Even the gringo Boy Scouts had left their tents and now mustered inside lamp-lit buildings under ceilings with glowing bulbs.

Seventeen-year-old Faustino was seduced by the haunting melodies from the radio, fascinated by modern things while they remained new. A few years later, his fascination wearied, and he yearned to return to the mountains and clear air of Upper San Benicia. He knew what they all knew: The old ways led men to God.

And the bulk of the citizens did persist in their old ways, neighbor helping neighbor, covered dishes sent from house to house to feed the sick and the old. Children were born at home. Men and women married young; families grew large in number. Men made adobes and added rooms to the small houses, new outhouses were dug, and nothing was thrown away. They continued to hunt in the fall, the venison and elk butchered and shared. But the onslaught of progress could not be ignored; even though the town's *vecinos* resisted, slowly, eventually, the traditional ways were challenged. Half spoke only English by the time Faustino married Nicasia.

The house Tía Julia gave to Faustino and Nicasia was modest at best, a two-room adobe surrounded by Los García, who once had enjoyed vast reaches of the territory. What Faustino brought to the marriage was his fortitude and his mountain wholeness. As his material prospects were gone, he had no more than this to offer Nicasia, to whom he would have given everything. Even his father grieved, regretting that he had so little to give the young couple—fifty dollars saved over years. Her father was able to bring no more than the family *santo*, the few hundred dollars he'd saved from selling his woven blankets, two sets of scissors, and six blue and white cups. Nando brooded over what his daughter might have expected in better times. And what Faustino rightly should have inherited. They all knew the *cuentos* of their historic losses.

The quest to find the buried gold was the first step toward Faustino's regaining the lost lands and, more importantly, his honor. He took this as his mission, while his two *pegados* set out looking for work by speaking English.

Channy had hired on with the US Forest Service "to protect" the already denuded river canyon from everyone, including himself. He could not stay off the land and continued to hunt and bring those sixteen-inch trout home through the padlocked gates. A true *vecino*, he could buy a beer with government pay and then in the same breath swap a fish for a smoke and throw in an elk haunch or venison. Channy lived in town, close to the chained-off canyon, and courted Ana María de Ortega, a charming sixteen-year-old who sang to his guitar.

Justo, the third *pegado*, was lured into town but chose to ride the trains north to Chicago, where he'd heard the pay was high. But the excitement of the huge industrial city wore thin. He could not escape the incessant, cold wind off Lake Michigan blowing the stench of the stockyards to the crowded streets where he had a room. Each month, after working cattle in the stockyards and picking up his stack of money, he would put some money aside for a truck. By month's end, every bit of it had been spent for a place to sleep, clothes and food to eat. Still, he heard the siren call and saw himself racing that new truck, suntanned left arm out the open window and a rifle on the rear rack. Smiling at the *chicas*, he took a deep drag and blew Chesterfield smoke out his nostril until it wrapped around his hat. He came close to big-city style even though he didn't last a second year. When he came home empty-handed, Faustino took him in.

Nicasia introduced him to Maribel, whose only wish was to be married and have a home busy with dutiful children. One, she insisted, would become a priest to pray for their souls. And when she first saw him, Maribel, thinking she held the cure to his wanderlust, listened to tales of his travels, the train ride north and Chicago's German food. Nicasia insisted that he marry this adoring, very pregnant creature, as the child might be the very priest to excommunicate him should he not do right by Maribel.

At their wedding, Faustino was the best man and Channy supplied the elk to accompany the *biscochitos, posole and tamales*. But the day after the wedding, Justo made his way from Maribel's family house to the train station on Guadalupe Street, set for Colorado. "Cowboy," he said, blowing a smoke ring at Faustino.

"For a dollar a day? Who'll plant your fields?" Faustino wanted Justo to live traditionally. He said his *pegado* should stay home and sing the old songs. Justo was swayed, but he wanted to know how he was going to pay for the smokes, the beer and the priest's robes for the yet unborn boy.

"There's ways without money," he was assured. Everything settled down for a year, but Justo weakened a second time, leaving his baby boy, another on the way. And still dreaming of his truck, he rode north to herd sheep in Colorado and Montana. It paid less than in the mines above Taos, less than the stockyards in Chicago. Everyone said Justo did not think straight. He made the wrong choices. His spirit had been destroyed.

CHAPTER EIGHT

Through his own resourcefulness, Fernando "Nando" Larrañaga was able to remain with his family in Santa Fe and not be forced to seek work outside the state. To support his family, he grew what they ate and sold sheep on the hoof to traders headed south across the border, and later when it was cheap enough to send huge bundles of wool on the train, he packed off as much as he could to the mills in Kansas. He managed to swap part of his abundant flock of goats and sheep for a pickup truck. Also, he had sold and bartered skins on the Plaza in Santa Fe in exchange for useful household tools before he took up dealing in blankets. Having a good eye for fine blankets, he began by trading an excellent Saltillo *serape* with golden tan chevrons to a *méjicano rico* from Parral for six blue china cups and saucers and two sets of scissors along with a few hundred silver pesos. Eventually, he bought his own large loom, dyeing his wools himself. Hispanic men took pride in their weaving; the Navajo called it women's work.

Nicasia watched her father work in his weaving shed while she and her two brothers cared for the chickens, the goats, the burro, a horse and a pen of sheep—chores that Nando oversaw like a nervous schoolmaster. Lázaro, the elder boy, stayed back on the three Larrañaga acres to help his father while Nicasia and her brother Carlito took the goats up the mountain to graze. By summer, Nicasia, now fifteen, went alone, taking their yellow dog and five goats to graze in a secluded meadow where a spring bubbled into the rock-scattered Santa Fe River. Faustino had seen her pass, the goats' bells tinkling as she followed them up the dirt path. Her walk was supple, moving with that same intriguing ease Faustino had noticed when he first laid eyes on her. He was even more obsessed with her by now, believing that the small goat bells called his name. But she continually ignored his presence.

He managed to befriend her brother Carlito and took every opportunity to appear at her home, *Los Larañaga*, to hang over the fence around the goat pen, casually looking past Carlito's shoulder for his sister. The week before, he had offered to help Lázaro plow their small *milpa* for corn and *chile*, insisting that the time was right. With the mule, he and Lázaro cut perfect rows while he strained to hear the tinkling of the returning goats.

"Hey, Lázaro, *compa*, if the wind comes up, these rows are going to fly away! Let's give them water now."

"We can wait," Lázaro said. Late spring brought heavy rains. "Maybe the rain will beat them down."

"I hate the wind," Faustino said. In Albuquerque, even on the best days, the sagebrush blew across the two-lane dirt road, crunching into cars, spikes poking out their car grilles. The wind blew all spring.

"If it snows, the winds don't blow," Lázaro said, giving Faustino an *abrazo*. "Thanks. I owe you one."

The Saturday after Easter, the wind blew in sixty-mile-per-hour gusts. It came out of the west across the flat desert plain and gathered speed until it pulled loose soil from any tilled field, lifting a cloud of dirt, throwing it between houses and across roadways. The severe gusts sanded paint from automobiles and downed ancient cottonwood limbs. Faustino bent his head and scurried down Canyon Road toward the rutted road to the Larrañaga house, shielding his eyes. As he came to the short, unnamed lane he saw a new sign marking it grandly as Camino Sin Nombre.

Seeking shelter from the wind there, he ducked into the goat shed to be greeted by wobbling bleats. A saddle blanket had been pushed against the side of a nanny goat, blown in from off the fence rungs. He took it off the animal and held it up, shaking down the dust and straw. The blanket was bright yellow, sunflower bright, cheerful—a girl's saddle blanket, one of Nando's weavings. He rolled it and hunched through the blowing dirt to knock on the backdoor, hoping to be heard over the rattling windows and the banging screen door.

Nicasia's mother called out, "*Entran!*"

He knocked again, "*Pásale,*" she said even louder. Faustino struggled against the wooden door, and stumbling into the kitchen, he dropped the rolled saddle blanket. He found Nando sitting at the kitchen table holding a cup of coffee and talking with Lázaro. Neither Carlito nor his sister was there, causing Faustino great apprehension in such a wind as this. But he kept his tongue. Instead, he said, "It blew into the shed," and held up the blanket. "It is beautiful."

Nando looked up from the table and smiled at him. "Not a good one," he said. "Aniline dyes. Cheap, from the Indian traders. But Nicasia says yellow is lucky, so I spent a few days on it." Lázaro laughed and shook his head while his father continued. "Men don't pick colors for luck."

Faustino nodded, pulling at the sides of his eyes hoping tears could ease the grit out.

"Men make their luck," Faustino offered. Lázaro pointed to a chair.

"*Siéntate,*" Nicasia's mother insisted, plunking down a sugar-sweetened cup of coffee in front of him.

"Your field is messed up," Faustino said, taking a seat, glancing at Lázaro. "I'll give you a hand with the hoe when this wind stops." He hoped his eagerness was not too apparent.

"If you do that, I figure with three of us, we'll get it ready in half a day," Nando said. "We could risk planting the seeds. Deep," he mused. "Then wait for the *acequia* water when it comes."

"It'll still snow!" Faustino jumped in too quickly.

"*Claro,*" the old man agreed. "That happens." And Faustino gulped his coffee and got up to leave before they had time to change their minds.

"I'll be back when the wind dies," he called at the door. Facing the field, he wanted to kiss the wind. And because he wished it, the next day, the wind subsided, leaving only a breeze. The clouds were sailing as slowly as Manila galleons crossing a coral sea when Faustino returned early to *Los Larrañaga*, bathed and carefully dressed. He brought along a leather halter he'd braided out of cowhide. "It's soft enough now," he said to Carlito, who was busy opening a feed sack. After twisting the halter in his hands for a few minutes, Faustino handed it over. "This is for your sister."

"Give it to her yourself; she's just a girl." Carlito turned his head to see his father and older brother coming out of the toolshed, hoes in hand.

"Ay, *Mano*!" Lázaro yelled out to Faustino, "*Venga aqui*. And make the brat come too."

Carlito winced, bending down to hide. "If they even see me, they pile it on," he told Faustino.

"Hey, *déjalo*. I'll do it; it's easy," Faustino called out manfully and turned to grab a hoe to tackle the field that the wind had rearranged. He worked like a whirlwind reforming the troughs, anything to impress Lázaro and Nando.

"I am a human *remolino*," he said aloud, twice. "I'm a dust devil!"

"Gracias, *Señor Remolino*," Nando called when they had finished their work for the day. As he was leaving, Faustino glanced again at the kitchen window in time to catch Nicasia pull the curtain back.

"Come back anytime!" Nando said, and Faustino seized on it. He reappeared again the next day, saying he'd come to see Carlito. He was happy to do anything at all. Anything to see Nicasia pass. To have Nicasia hear that he was *El Gran Señor Remolino*. The cyclone.

"Hey, *Remolino*!" Carlito came around the corner of the house bellowing. "Thanks for nothin', *hombre*! I hate garden work, and now they want me to plant the damn seeds just because you said it was okay."

"No, no, no!" Faustino protested. "I'll do it. Take your goats to the movies. Go to the Plaza. When you come back, I'll have it finished." And almost falling, he twirled around like a dust devil, glancing back at the kitchen window, anxious for the curtain to move again.

"I'll plant the seeds deep like the Indians do."

"'*Mano, Señor Remolino*, you really know your shit!" Carlito said, and Faustino grinned. His youth spent in the mountain village had done him well.

That day, Nicasia opened the kitchen window and waved. When she came down the two steps from the kitchen, she looked straight at

Faustino and said, "I have goats, but thank you." The halter dangled from her hand, and she made him take it. This time she smiled.

"But you do like it, don't you?" he said, accepting the halter in his left hand. "I made it for you."

"I can't use it."

"What about putting it on your burro?"

"I don't have a burro. *Papá* does. And I hate the thing. If you ask, he'll give it to you."

"What is so great about goats?"

"They're really smart." She laughed and whistled. An old goat looked up, then put his head down and aimed straight for her, but she stepped aside, beckoning for the goat to plow into Faustino. He was knocked to the ground and out of breath with a goat's beard in his face. He was overcome with shame.

"I said they're smart," she said, looking down at him and beginning to laugh. "So, *Señor Remolino*, do you want to see more goat tricks?" Her laughter faded.

"These goats ever butt Lázaro to the ground?" His feelings were hurt; he might even be angry. And as he began to get up, he kept one eye on the old billy goat and the other on her. She bit her lower lip, watching him.

"Only once," she admitted. "Lázaro is smart enough to stay away, and now the goats answer only to me and Carlito."

"I've seen you going up the path to the mountain with them," he muttered, slowly dusting the straw and dirt from his shirt. He was growing angry. "You never wave. Never say hello."

After a while, she said, "Sorry. *Lo siento.*"

He watched her.

"You are a nice person," she said, her voice low as she searched his face. "Everyone says so." He said nothing as he brushed the back of his pants. His rib was sore and he winced. To his mind, the goats smelled of shit and sour milk.

"I really am sorry," she said.

"Show me where you take them."

"I won't do it again to you."

"Please," he said. "Show me where."

"Maybe."

"I know you like yellow." He'd been watching her for years. She had been wearing a yellow dress when she had come to the village for Sofilia and Bobo's wedding. Years ago, it seemed. And he knew he deserved better than she gave. Eventually she motioned to the woodpile of *sabina* for the cookstove next to her house and gestured that he might sit with her there.

"I'll make it up to you."

They sat, trying to get comfortable on the unstable cuttings. Barely breathing, he took her hand. Miraculously, she did not resist at first, but after a minute she bolted up, no doubt believing he had accepted her apology. Standing, she brushed the bark splinters from her skirts and turned away from him. As he tried to sit, small logs rolled out from underneath. He winced again and held his rib.

"Are you hurt?"

"No, I'm all right."

Then she laughed, so he laughed.

Cocking her head, she bent down squarely at him with her hands on her knees and announced, "No one knows where I take my goats. Not Carlito, even."

"On the mountain, of course. I know every inch of it."

"Keep a secret?"

He placed both hands on his heart; he could always be trusted. That part of him must be obvious, and she broke into a smile.

"I know. I'm sorry. You wouldn't have done that to me."

He rose, and shaking his head slowly, he watched her for a moment and then said, *"Andemos entonces?"* He slapped his thigh. And from the pile of pelts and blankets hung over the goat pen fence posts, he picked out her yellow saddle blanket. "You need this?" he asked.

She nodded and then, not glancing back for him, started steadily out the gate with the five goats. She agreed that he was very handsome, *guapísimo*, as they said. But she had ridiculed him, and she knew better. Hispanic men were proud.

Walking up the canyon, they brushed against each other. First he, then she. Behind the next likely tree, he took her in his arms, breathing in everything about her, and then touched her smiling lips. His heart raced, pounding in his ears. She stood on her tiptoes, nuzzling for his mouth. No more was said. He knew what he had always known. She was the one. And in her mind, her likely future with Faustino began to play out—this was how married life began, the start of life as her mother knew it and her grandmother before that.

The silent trees shifted; the breezes lifted the aspen leaves. A coyote wailed in the distance, and somewhere not too near they heard the goats and their small bells. The river's only sound was the shifting of a few small rocks. The clattering town below was too far off for Nicasia and Faustino to be aware of barking dogs, truck rumbles, car horns and children's games. It was nearing sunset. A lone mule brayed that night was descending on the mountain. The lovers raced back down the path only to return again the following afternoon, leaving the goats behind. In an abandoned *ramada*, they made love for the first time on the yellow weaving. Two wild hares zigzagged, bolting off to hide.

"Do you prefer white sugar?" he whispered afterward.

"I like honey," she answered. "Why?"

"Ahh." He could raise bees or trade for honey. Anything she wanted; he'd find a way. "I'll bring you everything you ever want." She studied his face and was not surprised; she knew that about him from years of seeing him and from Carlito who admired him. Slowly, she was falling in love with love.

"It's late; run!" She stood and pulled him up. "Hurry! *Apúrate!*" By then, the dark was on them.

Nando sat comfortably in the corner of the large kitchen carding wool as Zenobia Larrañaga wiped her hands on her apron, frantically pacing the floor of the kitchen; Nicasia had not been seen for several hours. The goats were in their shed. "Nando, when did you see her last?"

"I don't remember," he said.

"*Querido*, it is bad for a young girl to be out by herself." She stopped short when Carlito came in. "*Hijo*, where is your sister?" He stood facing his mother and scratched his head.

"The last I saw, she had Faustino lying in the dirt, and the billy goat was butting him. But that was yesterday."

Upset at this, Zenobia inadvertently wiped her hands on her blouse. Then, looking down, she dusted the flour from her breast and touched her cheeks.

"*Dios mío*!" Her cheeks were white with floured handprints on them when, breathless from running, Nicasia and Faustino fell through the doorway. "*Hita*!" Zenobia called out. "*A dónde*?" she demanded, looking distressed, her elbows flung out. Carlito had neglected to report seeing the two slink off without any goats.

"Married, *Mamá*." Nicasia said, gasping for breath. She took Faustino's hand in hers and brought him forward. "We are going to be married." Then she burst into tears.

"*Con su permiso*?" Faustino asked, too nervous to look the frantic woman in the eyes. And he continued with an apology, saying how he should have done things properly; he should have waited for his family to make a formal visit. Marrying Nicasia was, he explained, all he had ever wanted in his life.

Zenobia sank into a chair and looked at Faustino, a boy from a family as old as her own. Nicasia could only think to say, "You have flour on your face, *Mamá*."

Zenobia brushed her face, and Faustino glanced away. Custom had it that a squash left on the boy's doorstep meant, no, the marriage offer was rejected. Three squashes meant three times no. He knew this and looked up to find Nicasia huddled in a corner sobbing with pent-up relief and finality. She saw herself blessed with the same full life that flowed from all the generations in her small community. She would now have a house of her own, children of her own. And a capable husband.

Nando nodded his assent and gave his blessing with a broad smile. Zenobia, still seated, had begun to sob as well. Everyone knew how decent the boy was. They agreed to have the families meet to set the plans.

The next afternoon, both houses were put to work preparing for the betrothment dinner. The kitchens were hectic, and the clay pots bubbled with purpose. Azálea María and the rest of Faustino's family were thankful about the engagement, as Faustino had been mooning over Nicasia for years, but the boy seemed agitated. He was distressed that something might go wrong. Pacing, he was desperate, knowing that his wedding had to be delayed until his father returned from the Montana sheep camps. It would be late fall. So to hasten this, Faustino excitedly wrote to his father about his restlessness: "Please come home as soon as you can."

Tía Serafina smiled when she was told of the wedding and, nodding her delight, offered to dress the bride in her own "lucky" wedding skirt for the nuptial Mass. Nicasia's mother cooked *quelites*, wild spinach gathered along the side of the paths, adding onions from the garden, *piñones* gathered last October, store-bought raisins and her own hen's eggs. She cooked *rueditos*, rounds of squash that had been dried on strings hung from the *vigas*, and added pumpkin and then *chicos*, last summer's dried corn. Faustino anticipated his traditional male responsibility, tabulating that only the raisins required pesos. The rest he would grow.

Azálea María, his mother, brought her red *chile* pork stew in a *cazuela* along with an heirloom gold cross on a fourteen-carat chain, a gift for the *novia*, the bride. Tía Serafina stood, raised her glass of Elodio's "sacristy wine" with her eyes closed and imparted an involved blessing with a few wise admonitions. Nicasia made the *sopa* herself, and before the bread pudding could be served, more toasts were given. Nando stood to announce that, like her exceptional mother, Nicasia would be an excellent *alma*, keeper of the hearth. He then welcomed Faustino into his family, saying how they all expected great things from him. The women were sentimental, his sisters giddy, the men drinking too much. And the *novia* was so beautiful.

The excitement of his engagement electrified Faustino, and the loud beating of his heart awoke him in the night during his dreams of her. Barely a week later, however, his self-doubts and hesitations slapped him down. He was not the man Nicasia deserved, and his marriage to her was wrong. Only in her presence was he reassured. The following week, he was relieved to find his grandmother Elenita in town and alone in his mother's kitchen shelling peas while his jabbering sisters were out. He sank down on a wooden chair looking miserable. She smiled at him without speaking, and the only sound was the small pop of each pea as it fell into the old metal pot.

"*Qué hay*?" she finally asked.

"Nando is giving me his daughter, giving her to me as a gift, like a thing," he said, solemn. "I know he wants to keep her, though."

"Why are you surprised?" his grandmother asked him. "That's what marriage is. The father gives his daughter away—and I'm warning you, you'd better take good care of her."

"He doesn't have to give her to me. She's not a 'thing' like a burro."

"You are not giving yourself to her? She's the only one being passed along?"

"I would care for Nicasia anyway, forever—we don't have to be married," he said.

"That's love, *hito*," the mountain woman said. "Look at Eloy and me now, still together like a three-legged race. But your mother had to leave me. I left my mother and father."

Faustino considered her words. "Didn't you ever want her back?"

Elenita sat back on her wooden chair and nodded. "*Cómo no*. I wanted Azálea Mariá back! When she moved to town, I was lonely and didn't have anyone to help me. I missed the easy way we women laugh together." Her memories placed the past before her. "So long ago..."

"Did she ever try to come back to you?'

"No, more like I moved in with her to help her when you were born. We both fell in love with you and"—she paused, her eyes smarting—"when you were old enough, she sent you to me up in the village to pitch in because she could not come to help us herself."

"I loved living with you and *Abuelito* Eloy."

"You were the gift. You were always the gift." She shelled another pea and then blinked off a tear. "Nando has always wanted Nicasia to have everything she ever wanted. I'm glad that one of those things happens to be you."

Faustino put his arms around her shoulders and kissed her silver hair. "I don't think I'll make it waiting all these weeks for Papa to get home."

"You'll survive," she said and reached back with a moist hand and patted his arm. "He never gets back before late September at the earliest." She shot him a stern look. "So you'd better get over to *Los Larrañaga* and make yourself useful, or your *suegro* might really take her back."

"She says she'd run away with me."

"Nando knows that, or he wouldn't give her to you in the first place. Now, go on over there and learn to weave or something." After her grandson left, she wept for the sweet years past, longing to have her seven-year-old boy child with his angelic skin returned. She remembered the delight on his face, listening to Eloy telling stories of the early days, the fire blazing and red *chile* stew simmering on the cookstove. Such a pretty boy then. On the mountain, in the village home.

He was handsome now, and soon he'd marry to become the man he needed to be. Soon. She knew how men needed marriage to mature.

Shortly after this conversation, Faustino strode beside his queen leading the pack of five goats up the river to graze. In his mind, she radiated such loveliness and wonder that her presence was wrapped in sunshine sparkling as thick as *La Guadalupe*'s aura. Standing tall, he noticed how much taller he was than she, and in fact, it had never occurred to him that she was not taller, greater proportioned and more important than he in every way. He floated alongside as she cajoled the goats, "*Vengan, amorcitos, vengan!*"

"I'm worried about my father never getting here. If the trains derail, if he gets sick…"

"*No, querido, no*. Don't worry. Everything will be fine, and your father will be here in time. I know it for sure." Then she turned back to the goats: "*Anden chivos!* Come on, or we'll never get to the grass." Three goats quickened their pace, coming alongside Nicasia, butting against her with their boney heads for a scratch. Faustino dropped back to force two laggards forward, stomping his feet and yelling. When they arrived at the lower meadow, the goats bent to the grasses as the lovers sat on the ground, holding each other under the secluding trees.

Faustino's kiss lingered on her lips as she rolled into him, wrapping her leg over his. "Not yet," he whispered, pulling back.

"It's okay, Faustino. We're going to be married. It's okay now," Nicasia coaxed. Close by he heard the melody of rushing water and goat bell tinkle. "Really, it's okay," she said.

"It's not right," he said, holding her face in his hands, kissing her hair. "We'll both have to receive communion at our Mass. We'll have to stand in front of everyone and take communion together."

She pushed against him, shaking her head. "Silly, all we have to do is confess before the Mass. I've already confessed about us." She took his earlobe between her teeth. "Please," she said.

"We must be strong. We need to save ourselves for our wedding day," he said, slowly rolling away. "We have to wait..." More than chastity, he had a dread of Nicasia's discovering how ham-fisted he was. Their first time had been breathless and stolen, but now he needed to call down the blessings of the Sacrament to transform him from a nineteen-year-old into her perfect mate, wondering what desires might be in a girl so at ease in her own splendor. He needed the power of the Sacrament in his soul before he fell down before her, humble, overcome and uncertain.

"You really mean this?"

"I do," he whispered. Nothing could change his mind. He first needed the security of her promise before God and their *vecinos* never to leave him. Her first pregnancy would be a blessing of their faith, all in the order of time. "Please," he asked, "please respect this. Your father expects me to wait." Faustino was not far off track regarding Nando's expectations of him.

She cocked her head, took a deep breath, and shook her head. "Sofilia, Bobo...none of them held back. You really think this is a mortal sin?"

"It's always a mortal sin." And he made her promise not to tempt him beyond his resistance "as a moral duty."

Zenobia, her mother, agreed that Faustino was demonstrating his deep respect for her and that he was admirable. "It's not every day that you see such strength and goodness in a man. You must wait until your wedding."

That wedding day refused to come. His father wrote that shearing would be later than early October and that the market for wool was not good. Times were difficult there, too.

"It's the will of the Lord," Zenobia consoled Faustino when he returned with Nicasia from taking the goats to the high pastures. "As long as we announce the banns now and the *padre* is at the cathedral, we can wait for your father."

Nicasia said, "October 20 is the latest because the weather gets cold after that."

"He won't miss it. He'll get here in time for our wedding." Faustino wanted to believe it himself, and for the rest of July, he spent his days making himself useful at the Larrañagas, rewiring fence posts, weeding the gardens. Any invitation from Nando caused him elation; he was allowed to ride shotgun in the cab of Nando's pickup truck going up into the forest to cut wood. He brought more feed for the goats. He replanted the garden rows when the squashes had been harvested, which distracted his anxieties over the wedding's ever happening. But the days dragged. And Faustino's self-confidence went hot and cold. Nicasia eyed him but held to her promise.

October 16, just in time, Faustino's father swung off the boxcar before the train came to a complete stop in the station on Guadalupe Street. His duffel slung over his back carried cash and his old clothes. He was lean, weathered and muscular. For the wedding, he wore a white shirt, an *hidalgo*'s black bolero and a ribbon tie. His son, the groom, had a dark suit, new. This suit would serve him for a lifetime, both for weddings and as a pallbearer at the many funerals to come. The weather was dry and crisp; the breeze shook the autumn leaves, their vibrant color turning the sky bluer.

Faustino was close to collapse as he stood with his father by the cathedral altar waiting for Nando to bring him his gift. Looking down the long aisle, he took a steadying breath and saw Nicasia at last materializing on the arm of her father, dressed by Tía Serafina in the lucky wedding skirts. The organ played a long chord, and everyone stood to applaud the bride. Approaching him, she began to hurry, almost dancing, urging her father along with an enormous smile, nodding to everyone, and finally settling her smile on Faustino alone. Nando passed her to him and stood back, joining his father to the side of the altar.

She took his sweating hand, and in the presence of God and the assembled guests, she promised to stay by his side until death. He fought tears and breathed in every blessing the priest could give.

Faustino and Nicasia were paraded out of the cathedral to more applause and *abrazos*. Serafina had insisted on a pair of pale horses to carry the bride and groom to *Los Larrañaga*, where even the goats wore flowered collars. In the flat dirt yard, long tables had been set with white cloths for the wedding feast and Faustino's four sisters pelted the couple with wildflowers.

Toward the end of the feast, Faustino silenced the guitars, and standing, he turned to Nicasia first and then to his father. Acknowledging the hundred or more guests, he gave his second wedding vow: *he would restore what had been lost.*

"Our nobility and self-respect have been stolen. Uncle Sam has taxed us. Breaking his treaty to honor our titles, he sold our homes, *mercedes* and *estancias* to cronies. I do not want to work far away in the mines or sheep camps for money to pay taxes to the *americanos*. We are now landless. I do not want our children to leave home seeking jobs." Raising a glass from Elodio and Serafina's Prohibition reserve, he vowed to restore their legacy, and vows for Faustino were sacred. "We will take back the land that was given to us by the Kings of Spain."

The guests, one after the other, gave *abrazos* to the *novios*, looking to young men such as Faustino to set things right, to return the colony to the old ways.

Nando stood to toast the newlyweds and to praise his new son-in-law with mounting respect. Everyone stood. "*A Nicasia y Faustino: viva!*"

"And now, let the dancing begin!" Nando's face glistened with tears.

That night, the newlyweds fell on each other, and Faustino at last buried himself in his bride.

CHAPTER NINE

Faustino flamed his loathing for everything *americano*. It took almost nothing to set him off. He was right, but his battle was unworkable; nonetheless, to most of the men in Nicasia's family, conceding in any dispute would be unmanly.

On a beautiful summer day, well past June's great heat, Nicasia sat counting her ripening apricots on the spreading tree. The deep breath of air she took tasted of freedom. In earlier times, the colonists had stayed out of sight from the raiding Kiowa and Apaches, terrified of being captured along with their horses and sheep. Since 1912 with statehood, the instances of nomadic attacks had dwindled. Nicasia and her children were poorer but safer under the protections of the US government. Now she could stand out in plain view and contentedly watch her two sons wrestle in the sandy dirt, feeling physically safe. Yet she almost preferred Indian attacks to the unease caused by the gold and the mortal sin of greed it brought. The Madonna had warned her, and she took a deep breath. Greed tempted her with property where she'd be the *alma* of a thriving *hacienda* surrounded by unending lands as before.

Just then Faustino's voice called out, "*Hola, chicos.*"

Nicasia jumped, and the boys looked up to see their father leading Olivia María through the wooden gate, loaded with two panniers of bottled beer. "Good times are coming. *Tiempos muy felices,*" Faustino said, plucking a fresh bottle from the pannier and raising it toward Nicasia with a small wink. "Procopio told me the *hotos ricachones* pay good." Suddenly he clapped his hand over his mouth, shocked that he called the *patrones* "rich queers" in front of his sons.

Nicasia turned away to hang damp towels on the fencing to dry, ignoring his comment. The *patrónes* paid a stunning twenty-five cents an hour, which he left unsaid in the presence of his sons. *Dos reales* was what the finest doctors charged for a visit. A quarter.

"We don't need pesos if all you buy is beer," Nicasia said. "Pesos are not worth it when you can trade."

Faustino gave her a smile and lifted the panniers from Olivia María, who brayed after him as he went to the shed with them. Daily, Faustino tabulated the (homosexual) mortal sins Michael and Richard were committing. He was obsessed with the men, the fourteen-room adobe and now the flower gardens. Prowling about the place, he had discovered an out-of-the-way, tin-roofed shed where lately he envisioned himself stabling burros. A good part of him had moved into that house where he would naturally be well dressed and righteous, his long hair in a braid, with the present owners penitent and dressed in rags, repentant when Faustino patiently explained to them how much the severity of their wrongs displeased the Almighty. He considered how, in an act of true remorse, they might award him the fourteen-room adobe—throwing in their personal fortunes as alms.

"Please, take it all. Just take it." His hand could feel the metal keys as the pitiful infidels pressed them in his palm, backing away barefoot to leave on a pilgrimage. Faustino considered immodestly allowing himself to show the greatness of his own soul by immediately and emotionally forgiving them for being the contemptible Freethinkers they were. After all, he'd have to concede that Procopio's continual insistence on just this kind of understanding and clemency might have some Christian basis— that even supercilious Procopio might have valuable wisdom to impart. In his last conversation with Procopio, Faustino, who had been drinking beer and belaboring his mania, protested that if he were to work for the *patrones*, he'd work for nothing. "The twenty-five cents an hour is tainted money," he said.

"The two *caballeros* are *ricos*. They pay a little more to show their gratitude because they have been granted a fortune," Procopio repeated.

"Do they have some new God, then?" Faustino wanted to know to whom this gratitude was due. Procopio held up his hand for silence while he stressed that his (high-standard) *patrones* followed God's law of kindness; they performed almost all the corporeal works of mercy, and they were gentle. He claimed they were Christ's true *caballeros*.

Faustino said it was a lie and interrupted Procopio's musings. "I say, they insult everything we stand for—especially our Church." It was true that he was bitter, having lost Tia Serafina's *hacienda*, so he discounted every attempt Procopio made to defend the new *dueños*. Still, he needed his uncle's help to get into the house to search for his fortune.

Procopio was patient, slowly laying out the facts of the Great Depression. Men were now starving, and families had lost their homes. Even though the suffering was slight here, with so few jobs to lose and a staple diet of beans, the *patrones* were charitable men. So with these added facts eddying in his head, Faustino led Olivia María home to García Street. He realized that to an outsider with an appetite for charity, the checkerboard lineup of small García houses might appear poverty-stricken. *Habia una vez*, there had been only one comfortable *hacienda* on this land, surrounded by ample irrigated fields to feed the growing family and their Indian servants, with a stable of Spanish Barb horses and plow mules. That was the *hacienda* he aimed to enter.

Faustino was no longer an *hidalgo caballero*. His only mount was Olivia María, the obdurate beast Nicasia refused to touch. "Do you understand that without burros, there would have been no Oñate Expedition, no *conquistadores* and no colony?" he asked her. "The pagan Indians would never have known Jesus Christ's redeeming powers without the *bicho* that proved more tenacious than a horse."

"No more burros..." Nicasia felt her choler rising and steadied herself against the door frame. "Rich people have their tin lizzies. Everybody else crowding into this town rides buses. No one rides burros anymore." She set her jaw and clenched her teeth, angry now. She refused to pay homage to the simple burro.

"*Mamá*, please..." Franque repeated a story from Father Sebastiano's catechism class. "Baby Jesus rode on a burro when María and Joseph fled to save him from Herod, who killed every baby boy."

"That was an ass—much better." Nicasia called it an *asno*. When her voice pitched upward like this, he knew she was at a breaking point. "The newcomers here never bring smelly burros." And this reminded her of another peeve. "Too many people now. They are moving here from the villages because of radios." As she beat her skirts to shake the dust, she ended with: "*Albóndigas*! That stupid, smelly burro is going to end up in a bowl of soup! I'll chop her up into little bitty meatballs!" She was fed up, too, with Faustino's continual talk of gold and homosexuals.

"Burros are able to find water in the desert," Faustino said.

"We have water enough and one burro too many!" she retorted and turned toward the single door. "*Basta*, enough." She did admit that travelers dying of thirst and lost in the dessert could cut the tips of burros' oversize ears and survive by drinking the blood, but her heart remained with goats, their milk and their playfulness and charm—though their yard was too small to hold a pen, and the mountain was now fenced off.

Franque followed her into the shade-darkened house spiced by the bean pot simmering on the wood stove and stayed quiet, almost hypnotized by the shadows from the burning piñon that flickered on the rough plastered walls of the kitchen.

Faustino ignored his wife's tetchiness, assuming it was really about burros and not his dangerous obsessions caused by the map. Or even her disbeliefs over his frequent visitations from the Blessed Mother. He sat waiting for dinner at the kitchen table, nodding, smiling and admiring his two sun-browned sons. Nicasia silently placed four bowls of beans flavored with *curitos*—those small bracelets of pork rinds—on the table and sat. Hunched over his dinner, Faustino ate with a spoon, his elbows on the table. He wiped his mouth with a cotton neckerchief, and the boys ate without speaking as well.

Later, still in the silence, Faustino sat back waiting to talk to his wife after the boys were tucked into their one bed. When she returned from the bedroom, Nicasia went straight to the sink and began washing the dinner dishes. Rising, Faustino removed the folded map from under the Virgin's foot and spread it out. He asked for his wife's full attention as he laid out his plans for the future.

"Talk. I'm listening," she said, her back to him. She knew where this conversation was headed. And he knew to ignore her convictions regarding greed.

"You know the *cuento* of the Emperor Maximilian and Carlota's lost treasure?" He could only see her dark hair shifting as she nodded to the sink; then she managed a quarter turn and continued to towel dry their four bowls. Afterward, she began to scrub out the bean pot for a second time.

The story of Maximilian and Carlota's lost treasure had been passed on for a hundred years without anyone's admitting to having found it. He looked at her, testing her on the significant details. *"Dígame qué fue?"*

She repeated the story from memory, word for word, singsongish like her son Franque, the catechist. "Three thousand pounds of gold bullion with a chest of diamonds on a cart with gold-wrapped wheel spokes were accompanied by soldiers and guides. They were all killed in an Apache raid."

The 1869 Apache raid was rock-hard history. This bloodbath was certainly led by Vitorio himself, the most feared Apache warrior of all. She knew, too, how the soldiers had kept the treasure from Vitorio by burying it in the soft mud of a roadside *ciénega*. They were crafty and lit a bonfire directly on top of the hole, which fired the mud slip into a kiln-baked cover. Hearing the Apaches' war screams, they fled for their lives leaving the fires still burning

Nicasia sighed. It had to be true. For her, this story was really about the homespun ingenuity of her gifted Spanish bloodline. The soldiers were of their same stock, intelligent and sturdy. They were clever. Lighting the fire was inspired.

Faustino urged her to continue.

"But Vitorio chased them down, massacred them all in a sickening, bloody fight," she intoned, taking a breath before tacking on the ending. "One small boy escaped, only one."

"Correcto," Faustino said, nodding for her to continue. He smiled up at her and paused while she dried her hands on her apron. She fetched

two blue china cups and poured their coffee. Now sitting in silence, the couple listened to the sound of the spoons stirring the honey in their coffee. She found the exaggerated sound of his sipping irritating and took a deep, silent breath, waiting for him to pick up the story to force his point. "And two years had passed when the boy led the padre and his mother along with a string of burros to bear the gold home. With the boy's help, they found parts of the abandoned cart with gold-wrapped wheels." It was important for oral tradition that with each telling, the story remain exactly the same, nothing new, no interpretations. The wheels were always "wrapped in gold."

Faustino pressed on: "A tree had taken root near the abandoned ox wagon." His voice grew louder. He took a sip of coffee and nodded, giving her time to step in to continue the story, but she gestured that he should continue.

"But they found nothing; the frail woman and the old priest, they abandoned their search. Afterward, men with iron shovels, picks and axes arrived and began to dig." He drained his cup and placed it on the saucer. It was her turn to speak.

"You never see the true moral of this, Faustino," she said. "The Devil haunts treasure troves. The priest died suddenly, yes? He was buried by the widow, yes? Not the other way around."

"Don't change the story!" he said. "The Devil has nothing to do with the Empress Carlota's treasure!"

"Of course he has! Since the widow could not give the priest the last rites, his soul never got to Heaven. Can't you see it?" Faustino's eyes searched her face; he did not know how to respond. She poured him another cup of coffee and stood over him. "He could not give himself the holy oils. Now, his soul is trapped, wandering forever."

"That doesn't even make sense," he said. "He was baptized. He gets to heaven one way or another."

"No, he was greedy. All he wanted was the gold. His soul is in hell, or wandering."

"Just one minute, Nicasia. The point is that someone actually found the treasure and secretly brought it here. It's in Santa Fe." He stopped for air. "Everyone knows it's reburied here. So just where is it?"

"You think it's in Tía Serafina's house?" A statement more than a question.

Faustino nodded yes. Variations of this story formed the background music for many family homes.

Nicasia shifted on her wooden chair, saying, "You don't know what the Devil has done to the ones who found it! The family could have met a bloody end, or the house might have been stolen...by a legal trick. That's exactly the sort of thing the Devil does."

"Ask *La Santa María*," he insisted. "Just ask her." Nicasia gave a long look at the statue in the *nicho*. Faustino attributed whole conversations to her, and through the two generations this pretty carving had been in her own family, Nicasia had heard the Virgin speak only once while Faustino basked in Her daily presence and guidance.

"She will not talk to me like She does to you."

"Well, you don't pray to Her like I do." Faustino smiled at her and then bent to his map on the table. He left a finger on the map as he rocked the chair back. "She says the gold is right there."

"What if it's another trick of the Devil?"

"It's not." Later, his heart softening with the compassion he imagined himself to possess, he said, "I'll try again to get work at the *mariposones'* house." He looked awkwardly at the packed dirt floor; he'd have to humble himself if he wanted to retrieve his prize. Procopio continued to insist that these men were good men and that they would try to hire him, but no one had come by offering him work. And each time he'd heard a branch brush the side of the house or a strong wind, he ran to the door thinking they had sent someone with a need for him.

"Faustino, you are a capable man, *muy capaz*," Nicasia said. "Just go there."

The next day, Procopio opened the *zaguan* door to find Faustino standing there. "I am a good carpenter," Faustino said. "I'm like you, tío. I can do anything."

Procopio looked down at the ground; he shook his head. "They are using Narciso Rodrigues as a carpenter. He makes their furniture."

"But, they are always building more. You even said it." Faustino was pleading. Just then Procopio straightened as Michael came into the patio looking for him.

"Ahh, there you are."

"*Su servicio, Señor.*" Procopio responded automatically.

"And this is your *primo,* is he not?"

"*Si, señor.*" Both men looked deferentially at the pale-eyed artist. Some had said blue eyes brought bad luck. Every Evil Eye was sky blue.

"I do need some help for a big party next weekend."

"Faustino is offering to be a carpenter."

"What else can you do?" Michael asked, smiling. His light eyes were eerie. "Do you play the guitar?"

"*Lechón, cabrito.* I can cook both pig and goat. I can do *enchiladas,* and my wife makes the finest *sopa* in *la villa.* She makes *empanadas* with tongue and currants. *Arroz con leche...*"

"But do you sing?"

Faustino was utterly thrown by this question. Michael saw that he was handsome enough to sing. Didn't they all sing?

"*No muy bien.* But my wife..."

Michael smiled, and his black pupils enlarged slightly, eating away at the blue. He and Richard had agreed to be generous to the poor but in a personal way. One-on-one. He took a deep breath and began again.

"Ask your wife to make something people can hold in their hand to eat"—and he held his fingers apart to show how little. "And bring me some to taste. If they are good, we'll order several dozen, and you, can you be the bartender?"

Faustino's head reeled. This was a triumph. He saw himself with a bucket of ice, handing out bottled beer to the Anglo guests. "*Cómo no, Patrón!*" he said, standing straight, military style.

As he explained it later to Nicasia, both he and she would be together in the large kitchen, exploring the big house. And with time, as trusted employees, they'd tap all the walls searching for a hollow sound.

"*Bueno,*" is all Nicasia said, a gesture of acceptance but not agreement.

"Ahh!" All he wanted was her help. "Be realistic, *querida*; this is our big chance." Faustino touched the folded map, genuflected before the statue, and crossed himself. "I'll ask Paco for some elk."

The following morning at 6:00, Paco Gurulé banged at the unlocked kitchen door and called out "*Hola*," just loud enough to alert Olivia María in her shed. When she began to bray, Faustino jerked awake, and in his daze, he believed his *burro* was being stolen. Nicasia then stirred and returned to her deep dreams with her boys next to her. Pulling on his pants, he stumped out of the *dormitorio* through the kitchen, grunting at Paco as he passed. The outhouse was next to Olivia María's shed, and before returning to the house, he would toss her some grains. Paco Gurulé had a way of coming at the wrong time. "Eh, Paco. What stupidity are you up to now? *Qué tontería?*"

"Couldn't get no elk, so I brought you this venison, see. This is the side she slept on; this is the tender side." He shoved a carelessly wrapped slab of meat closer to the center of the kitchen table. He called it an *anta*, a female deer, out of season and poached.

"You climb over the fences?" Faustino pointed east, to the closed-off mountain. Paco tapped his forehead with his knuckle, shaking his head. "No, *hombre*—I'm smart—I go where the fences are already down."

"Where are they down?"

"Same place as last time." Since the US *Floresta* had closed, fenced and protected the mountain with well-posted, easy-to-read Department of Agriculture warnings, freshly cut, rutted tracks led back in and hunting continued. Poaching was an English word.

"You haul this *bicho* out yourself?" Faustino assessed that Paco could barely lift one of his mangy dogs these days, much less a full-size *anta*.

"*Como no!*" Paco crowed. "*Claro qué sí.*" Both men smiled. Paco tapped his forehead again—"You gotta use your head." Paco liked to bore Faustino telling him how to manage everything.

"You see *mi pegado*, Channy?"

And Paco nodded wildly. "I tol' *El Floresto* you sent me. I always tell him that."

"So Channy quartered it for you?"

Paco's response was to purse his lips, helpless to suppress a grin. He nodded wildly to show that he had also enlisted Channy to load the doe onto the US Forest Service pickup for him. Channy would never refuse when Paco had asked him to be a *vecino*.

"*Bueno*," Faustino said, taking this as another sign; the Virgin was staring straight at him from her *nicho*. Everything was a sign for him—the sounds of the wind in the pines, how the morning doves cooed at dawn. He decoded raindrops and enlisted Nature herself to play a significant role in his quest for the treasure. Poached goods were yet another heavenly sign from *La Guadalupe*. She soothed him, confirming that as much had been taken away, so much would be returned to him. If anyone deserved God's small favors, it was Faustino, and to him this poached deer promised that his gold was still beckoning.

Paco shifted and shuffled. He placed his hand on the back of a chair, angling to sit down for a cup of coffee. "I got a good one for you," he began, stalling for an invitation. "How do you make holy water?"

"*No se*," he responded, baiting Paco, who was already laughing at his own joke and was now wedged halfway between sitting and standing.

"You boil the hell out of it!" he replied in English. The maniacal guffaws were Paco's most vexing trait, and they woke Nicasia. Faustino ignored him and cracked the bedroom door, signaling to Nicasia that he was coming right back to bed and had some fancy ideas. Paco caught the gesture and dropped his grip on the back of the chair, winking and chuckling to himself, rocking with small bursts of sly humor as he wobbled toward the front step, trying to think up another *chiste*. None came, so he announced loudly, "Hey, *Mano*, I was hoping you could come over to my place and help me push some coyote fence posts back up?"

Paco bungled everything: he laughed at his own jokes; he came too early for coffee, and he cut fences—*americanos* got real mad when you cut their fences. The fact was that *hispanos* had no use for barbed-wire fences.

"*Luego, luegecito*. Not now," Faustino assured him. Of course, he'd be over there; they were *vecinos*—scratching each other's backs. Not necessarily friends. And as Paco lumbered back out the kitchen door, lighter now without his slippery ten pounds of meat, Melo and Franque burst out of the bedroom, whispering and giggling. Faustino opened his arms to receive his sons.

Hearing their tight, high voices, Nicasia rose to feed them, wearing only her white nightgown. Her hair was loose as she came into the kitchen to start the coffee with her sons crowding around. She smiled, feeling that happy completeness she enjoyed being with them in her small home surrounded by generous neighbors. She should never leave this home; it was another sign to destroy the map.

Faustino considered a new universal truth: "Every fence has its hole." He was stirred to make himself valuable to the *mariposas*. Nicasia put out their beans, bread and coffee, and the small family took their usual places around the square table. Faustino ate silently and then carried his bowl to the sink as the boys interrupted each other, exaggerating everything their older cousins were allowed to do. "Can we go back? Can we go back?"

Kissing both sons and his wife, Faustino left the house. He squinted as he stepped from the door, expecting harsh sunlight, but to his surprise, the sun was behind a cloud and the light was soft. Paco Gurulé was waiting comfortably under a scrubby apple tree, enjoying how his hungry dogs snarled as they tugged at the severed head of the poached deer, raising dust. No dogs looked up or barked when Faustino ambled over. By midafternoon, the skinned carcass head would be so wrecked—and the eye sockets only bloody holes—that Paco would haul it up the shaky ladder himself and leave it on his flat roof next to the other skulls for the turkey vultures to scour clean. From the high branches of the ailing apple trees, the vultures were already gathering as they eyed the dogs snarling over the skull.

"I got a job over at the gringos', bartender."

Paco lit up; he was fascinated with the light-eyed gringos, the same who avoided him for looking so scruffy. Faustino told him that Michael's face was as pale as a peeled aspen branch and his eyes were washed-out blue. Paco was hungry to know more: "So, what does the sky look like if you have eyes like that? Ask him, okay? Is it white?"

Faustino had never spent much thought on their faded eyes, which he found ugly. But Paco could not hold back. "Or do you think they can see through your skin with eyes like that? Like an X-ray?"

"You ask really stupid questions." Faustino took a deep breath, his patience strained. But Paco lived alone and needed to talk, so he waited while the dogs snapped at an antler and let Paco continue.

"So what about Nicasia? She tol' me she's goin' to cook for the gringos." Paco stopped short of an answer to listen to the distant thunder on the mountain.

Lightening chased the other poachers out of the water shed, and the temperature had dropped ten degrees, making Faustino feel energized. "Rain," he said.

"Nicasia taking their money?"

"That's what she says," Faustino answered, still captivated by the thunderheads clouding the sky, the distant lightening and the smell of electricity in the air. After a while, he said, "She says money is not the way of her people, *la gente*. Before pesos, *la gente* helped each other."

"So she's not going to take the gringo money?" Paco needed to know.

"No, probably not," Faustino said, watching for rain. "She'd give it to the poor, maybe..."

Paco shook his head and kicked himself for being *tonto* again. "I should'a sold the *anta* to the gringos and pocketed the *reales*. You woulda come help me anyway even if I didn't give you the meat." Faustino and his *vecinos* would always come over; they always had. He was such a *tonto*; it was a missed opportunity. If he still had a wife, she'd help him, and he'd get pesos to buy...what, beer? "Since Nicasia makes the *empanadas*," Paco mumbled, "she keeps her pesos."

"*Basta*, Paco," Faustino snapped back, still staring at the clouds. "Cut it out!" Thunder growled closer. The raindrops were larger, heavier and slow. He wished he could have told Paco about the map but the missing gold was a close-kept secret.

"Eh, *compadre*, don't get so hot in the head. I got only enough pesos for gas but no more. When I bag me some food, I get food for you, too. Now it's called poaching. Ten years ago, it was all ours."

Both men nodded sadly and aimed for the bench leaning against the south side of the house, where they could rest while the first drops of rain exploded the dirt. They would not get to steady the fence too soon, though, if it was a gully washer. And they watched the heavy, gray sky bend the trees, seeing a light break through a hole and illuminate a rainbow to the east. The turkey vultures continued to watch the dogs, occasionally lifting up off the branches, changing position, their eyes resolute. Thunder close by.

"So I went to the lumberyard to buy those boards you see over there," Paco began loudly, breaking Faustino's strange look of reverence. "And I told old Buck there that I wanted six two-by-fours, and he said..."

Faustino turned and tried to follow him. Paco had no idea how annoying he was.

"He said, how long d' ya want 'em? You want to know what I tol' him?"

"*Ándale*," Faustino said, prickliness creeping in as he kept both the condors and the double rainbow in view.

"I said, oh maybe I'd like 'em for ten years, maybe more." And he roared with laughter. "That joke don't work in Spanish."

A sudden cluster of thunderclaps called the dogs' attention away from the meat.

"Loosen up," he told Faustino, who simply stared at him, too enervated to make himself agreeable.

Faustino dropped his cloud watching slowly. "Your last one about the holy water didn't translate either."

That night, resigned to following Faustino's mad obsession with the buried gold, Nicasia obediently dipped into her sack of flour and rolled out dough to make samples of her sweet *empanadas*.

"Ten dozen," Richard ordered after tasting one.

Michael agreed. "They are marvelous."

Faustino bowed with a pinched smile, not quite covering his nervousness.

"*No me digas nada*," Faustino cautioned Nicasia back at home. "*Son gente buena*," he mimicked her uncle Procopio word for word. Forget it, he thought to himself. Overlook the obvious: two men married like man and wife, while the Bible...Say nothing; let it go.

"My idea is to tell the *muchitos* these men are Latin teachers," he suggested. "They'll hide."

According to gringo-loving Procopio, these strangers desired nothing more than to abandon the great eastern cities and live simply with *nativos*, which meant Indians, not the native colonists, the sons of the *conquistadores*. And all they dreamed about were utopias, not popes or kings. These bizarre *tipos* were poles apart from the *gabacho* ranchers who stole their land grant titles and ran the Spanish *caballeros* off their ancestral land, taking their sheep. Gentlemen such as Michael and Richard walked softly and spoke only of beauty. According to Procopio.

"It's because they are so rich?"

Procopio stood taller and more erect. His dignity was increased because he worked for these American "princes." He acted as though he'd received an imperial appointment, being their *mayordomo*. "They are rich, yes. Also educated, courteous and generous."

At home, Faustino tried to repeat everything clearly and without judgment to Nicasia as she stuffed her pastries with the sweet filling. He explained that it was a costume party.

Nicasia nodded, delighted to be able to get into her tia's *hacienda*. She was intrigued by the gringos, curious about their ways.

CHAPTER TEN

The next day, Faustino was apprehensive. Why had he vowed to get the gold? The Virgin was the one who spoke of vows; it was all her idea. Vows were serious matters. God listened to vows—marriage vows, vows of charity, Lenten vows of fasting, and yes, vows of revenge. He recalled how at his wedding, raising a glass of sacristy wine, he'd stood to attach a second vow, like a wagging tail, to his marriage "until death" vow. All hundred relatives and many of their friends had been the earthly witnesses.

Nicasia argued that it was a *promise* and not a vow. And that her *madrina*, Tía Serafina, had left her the gold with these serious and inviolable instructions, which she counted on her three extended fingers: one, shoes to walk through life, two, food to be strong through life, and the most important third, her sons' education to benefit their community. Restoring titles, lost pride, or buying up land was not Tía Serafina's mandate. And privately, she considered that her husband was overcome not by the true Virgin but by a false Virgin or possibly by whispers of greed from the Devil. Meanwhile the truth was simply that the gold had rendered Faustino powerless.

Between the Devil and his gold, her husband's excellent soul was caught in a hopeless conflict.

Ten days later, Procopio came by the García adobe to collect two very large platters of the small, warm *empanadas* Nicasia had made for the large and elaborate costume party coming up that night. She worked with Flora and her neighbors to fulfill the large order, and at dawn, cookstoves in four kitchens were fired up for the baking. The food was ready just in time when Procopio arrived to collect it for the exciting event. The *tamales*, though, were still being steamed.

"I can't wait for you to see what the *patrones* ...!" he said as he pressed the silver starter button; the rest of his sentence was swallowed by the roar of the engine and the backfiring tailpipe. Having placed the order of *empanadas* on the driver's seat, Nicasia wiped her hands on her apron and turned back into her house, grimacing at the spent gasoline from the disappearing truck.

The group effort to make the dozens of *empanadas* brought two of Faustino's sisters and Nicasia together. After Melo and Franque had ground the meats, Nicasia mixed the filling and seasoned it, while Dora Elena and her sister stuffed the bite-sized delicacies. As they sat around the table working, the women did not talk about their husbands, children, or school. Nor did they discuss gardens and recipes, but they had immense curiosity about the *dueños* in Tía Serafina's house. "So, tell me, what's it like now?" Dora Elena had to know everything.

Nicasia said, "Flora says it's more gringo now. Right, Flora?" Everything she knew about them came from Tia Flora, all the small intriguing details. Tio Procopio only praised them, which told her little.

"What's that? Gringo house?" In the movies, fancy houses had heavy draperies, martini shakers and mirrors in the *sala*.

"For one thing..." Nicasia began and then paused to collect her thoughts. She wanted to speak kindly of the eccentric *patrones* who knew nothing of Faustino's sworn intent to bring down complete walls of their house.

"For one thing," she began again, "they took all the *comunes* out of the *plazuela* and built the *inodoros*, the indoor water closets."

"*Pues?*" Dora Elena said. "That's nothing new. Mine is in my bedroom." This was true; her own toilet was under a window close enough to her small bed to serve as a night table. She got water from a green garden hose attached next door to her sister's spigot. The hose snaked over the windowsill directly into the back of the tank. All she had to do was call out, and if the water in the hose was not frozen, someone would open the spigot to fill the tank. The indoor toilet flushed back down to her sister's cesspool because everyone agreed that she was too old now to trudge to the outhouse in the dead of winter.

Nicasia, who still had an outdoor *común* next to Olivia María's shed, tried to interest them in another detail. "It's not fourteen rooms anymore. They used four rooms to make one *gran sala* for big *tertulias*." That interested the women as much as it confused them as they continued stuffing *empanadas*.

"Why would anyone do that?" they demanded to know. But this to Nicasia was not the most interesting of what Tia Flora passed on. What she truly relished were the wacky stories about Mary Austin, whom she called God's Mother-in-law, and all the Anglo *chisme*, the gossip. She wanted to know more of how insanely jealous of each other they could be. And how these Anglos hung on each other, telephoning, writing, when, at the same time, they turned to backbite, saying the very worst things, only to patch it all up with French wine and kisses. It seemed they were bonded to each other because their families all lived in distant New York or London, but most of them insisted that they hoped never to live with their families again. None of it made complete sense, but Nicasia was dazzled.

It was as Procopio had said: "We're not the same." The Catholic Church made the crucial difference; the *vecinos hispanos* were souls fused by the Catholic Church, all fearing the same God. These *americanos* merely sampled—yes, sampled!—passing gods. Another thing about the gringos was how they were all besotted with the local Pueblo Indians and their *kachinas*. What began as a charming curiosity had risen to an imbecilic passion, entirely based on a misreading of the heathens' world. They claimed the Indians represented all things pure in God's creation. They believed anything the native Indians said.

That part was upsetting, but on the other hand there were great stories about the gringos' shenanigans, which involved much expense and imagination. There was one whole prank involving left-handed burritos. Whenever she thought of it, she was forced to laugh.

"The right-handed burritos had been filled and were set out 180 degrees different from the left-handed burritos. Of course they ran out of those in the first hour." Procopio had to repeat this one twice before they all giggled. "So Will Schuster had to cut the left-handed ones over and put them on a different platter before people would touch 'em!"

"Did I tell you how long it took us to clean up after they pitched soft-boiled eggs into the electric fan?" Flora had said, shaking her head.

But Flora's all-time favorite story was that of the chicken soup shower. Witter Bynner, the poet, stuffed chicken bouillon cubes in his shower head and screwed it back into place so that his partner, Spud, came out all sticky. Flora snorted with delight each time she repeated this one. "He had those little specks of parsley all over him!" She howled.

Nicasia was still laughing when Faustino shot her a look. "Only a few of them are *mariposones*; only a few," Procopio had explained. "And not every one of them is an atheist freethinker.

Procopio continued by saying that, being atheists, the gringos were not depressed about "not believing in God." On the contrary, they claimed to be quite at peace with the extra time gained by not going to Mass and not doing penance. Instead of God, he claimed, they were devoted to each other, a human *caritas* bound up inside a working love/hate bond. Some of them he described as God-fearing Protestants—those were the *luteranos*. A few were even Catholics in good standing. Procopio was their salesman, praising their devotion to the Golden Rule, each competing as a good *vecino*. Several, he said, were adamant do-gooders, even though they were heavy-handed when they thought things needed to change, and they used their newspaper to complain. More organized each year, the tight gringo cocoon yearned to be helpful, to be completely free of the industrialized world and presumably free of their families. Free to live in very large houses. Nicasia thought they were all comedians, and she liked that they cherished Tía Doña Serafina's old home.

So it was with escalating anticipation that Nicasia and Faustino set out in the late afternoon in their Sunday best to work at the large *reunión*. As they walked, Nicasia turned to him. "Just one last time, please promise me that you will not drink any of their whiskies."

Faustino said he would not.

117

"Promise again?"

"I promise not to drink anything."

When they arrived, all the lights were on at the old *hacienda*. Nicasia high-stepped through the open backdoor, confident and ready. They found themselves in a blue and white tiled kitchen, blessedly alone. Her *empanadas* had been stacked on serving platters and covered with starched linen napkins. Everything was immaculate and neatly in place.

Faustino stiffened, seeing Nicasia walk directly ahead of him and open the door to a marble-faced powder room. Refusing to enter it, she firmly closed the door, announcing, "There is evil in that room. Stay out." Looking fiercely into Faustino's eyes, she crossed herself from her forehead down.

"No. No. Just let me tap on the walls in there..." Suddenly the outside door was pushed open, cutting his protest short. *"Quién va?"* Faustino challenged.

Procopio, dressed in a bright red vest, was swathed in his general aura of overbearing tenure. Seeing Flora's apron, Nicasia realized they intended to stay.

"Aha! We surprised you, didn't we?" Flora embraced her niece with such enormous warmth that both Faustino and Nicasia felt their resentment dull for a moment. "This is their biggest *fiesta* ever! Wait until you see!"

Faustino took a step back. "We can manage by ourselves. I know how to make drinks."

"We know you'll be in over your heads, so we're here to help." Procopio misread Faustino and Nicasia's unhappiness and began to fill the kitchen with his jovial good humor.

The scheme for this evening's party was so elaborate that a landscape designer had been called in from his estate in Nambe to design the setting. Richard and Michael had wanted to leave the whole execution to the professional, but knowing the stout pride of their caretaker, they felt obliged to have Procopio working on it. True to form, and with only a few arguments, he had pulled it off. Everything was perfect, ready. Against all odds.

Flora, too, smiled on her shining kitchen. "I scrubbed and cleaned this kitchen top to bottom."

"Tía Flora, *qué bonita*!" Nicasia said aloud, trying to distract from Faustino's sullenness. She could see that he was still smarting from his uncle's continual interference.

"*Mira*!" Flora took Nicasia's hand and pulled her into the *sala*. "Ahh, but now, you will not believe your eyes. Come Faustino!" Flora called over her shoulder.

The *gran sala* was filled with trees.

"*Todas a mí*," Procopio said, taking credit for creating a Central American rain forest indoors.

The day before, sixty large palm trees and as many shrubs had been delivered by two trucks from Albuquerque. Four short years ago, the only road between the two cities held a treacherous one-and-a-half-mile section of twenty-three hairpin turns. Engines overheated before the top. This decorating scheme would have been ludicrous when cars negotiated the steepest climb in reverse because of their gravity-flow gas tanks, the fuel sloshing back-to-front. The new road cut opened entire new possibilities—like delivering two loads of living trees and shrubs intact for the amusement of just one evening.

Now, the trip took four hours, and after their roadside lunch, the drivers and their helpers climbed into the beds to trim away the branches damaged during the first half of their potholed journey. They watered and resecured their cargo before continuing on, arriving smartly only an hour late, hoping to stage a very professional show for Procopio's picky inspection.

It was late afternoon by the time the men had unloaded the trees, pushing for a return to Albuquerque by nightfall. Procopio had ordered them to slow down while he deliberated the placement of each burlap-balled tree into the ready drums, creating a green tropical forest with cozy nesting spots and a clearing for the bar.

This extravaganza was to be a birthday fantasy for the men's clever lady friend, Amelia White, who would be paraded *en masse* down Canyon Road to the First Annual Jungle Ball at La Fonda. It was to be a surprise "delirium," Amelia's favorite term.

Procopio fussed over Faustino's canopied bar sheltered in a clump of palm trees. Wearing a vest, Faustino was to stand behind the broad table with the crisp damask tablecloth, passing out punch from a pyramid of small, brown cups, not crystal glasses. Several silver buckets and pitchers of rum punch stood next to a punch bowl large enough to bathe a child. Blocks of ice were ready to be chipped. A *barretero*, a pickaxe, lay alongside for shaving the ice.

Procopio pulled Faustino over to admire the jungle bar created especially for him. Searching his face for approval, Procopio said, "*Qué bonita, no?*" Nicasia, who had trailed along, saw Faustino freeze when he caught a fleeting glimpse of the two *es* in Franciscan robes.

"*Qué digas?*" Procopio asked, banking on Faustino's wild approval and congratulatory *abrazo*. But Faustino was speechless, disgusted with the entire fantasy, which he read as blatant sacrilege. He gagged. Between the *patrones* dressed as Franciscans and the bar set up like an altar, their creation was a chapel in ruins. Here nature was overtaking civilization, Indians were encouraged to undo their hard-won Christian conversions, and the hosts in Franciscan robes trebled the blasphemy. Feeling beaten and vulnerable, having sworn three times not to drink, he wanted to scream, "Stop destroying this house!"

Sensing his upset, Nicasia put a calming arm around her husband, trying to talk him out of his dismay with her delight. "*Qué bonita, no?*" She was indeed impressed and flashed a smile.

"This is like a huge *fandango*!" Procopio explained, looking to be thanked for his efforts. But everything Procopio said scandalized Faustino now.

Nicasia led her husband back to the kitchen, carefully watching his expression. "Let's go; we have work to do."

Not paying attention to her, Faustino leaned back against a blue tile counter, slowly rubbing his head. He spoke directly to Flora. "I have a headache. *Hay hierbas?*" He concentrated on the far wall. "Something from the *dispenza* now?"

"The *dispenza*?" Flora stopped filling water pitchers. "They tore out the *dispenza* before they even moved in. I told you this. Remember? Years ago! All the shelves were rotten." With broad smiles, she tried to jolly Faustino out of his misery.

He refused to succumb. The house had been altered, damaged and he could not overcome the present obstacles: the missing *dispenza* and Procopio's incessant hovering.

Nicasia patted her hair, retied her apron, and avoided her husband's eyes. His disappointment was unbearable. She nervously eyed the patio through a many-paned window and saw musicians gathering outside around Michael, one of the hosts costumed as a plump Franciscan in his brown robes. Procopio threw in another irritating detail. "The marble for the walls was imported from Italy."

"Gravestones," Faustino said. Turning his back, he shuddered. Marble was death. Suddenly his mutterings were interrupted by a blast from a trumpet, announcing the start of a courtly march. The first guests had arrived. Procopio held out a black bolero vest with a satin back and a worked wool front. "Here, *'Mano*, put this on."

Grudgingly, Faustino slipped it on; it was baggy on him. He straightened the vest across his starched, white shirt and ducked into the powder room to examine himself in the gold mirror. Standing erect, looking in the glass, he arched his back and saw nothing. Nothing?

He stared. He squinted. He had no image; he was not there. No one looked back at him. No left/right reversed self. Leaning closer, as though looking through reverse binoculars, he could not find even his miniature.

Nose-to-nose with the glass, his breath left no fog.

The powder room was dead.

The wall behind the gold mirror was covered by a glass so clear that it was blind to his image—to any image. He was petrified, dazed. He stopped breathing, hoping for a figure to take shape. There was a pounding on the door. He began to choke; he grew more aware of music from the *placita* filling the closed room. More knocking, but he was too faint to respond.

The banging grew insistent. This startled him; he was late for something. He was late for the bar. He was late pasting on his smile. He took deep breaths and bolted out of the powder room, expecting more than an empty kitchen. In slow motion, he steadied himself. He needed to regain his strength and took a nearby chair to collect himself.

Finally entering the crush and uproar of the party, he squeezed between guests in animal costumes—apes, monkeys, bears, cats. Inside, the musical fanfare reverberated from the lively *grupo* outside in the *placita*. As Faustino took up his position behind the punch bowl, the musicians pranced the guests around the *placita* in a true *entrada*, strutting them like crowd favorites. A bell rang from the gate, and the music countered with a trumpet flourish. The next swarm of charmed guests radiated delight as they, too, were waltzed into the *placita* from Canyon Road. The *patrones* had effusive greetings for everyone.

Faustino was still unbalanced. He tried to put on a more convincing smile. Three irresistible *mariachi*, borrowed from La Fonda's celebrated *El Grupo Mariachi,* charged the evening air. They were dressed as a Brazilian samba team in tight, red trousers, yellow blouses and sky blue, satin sashes. Faustino stood hidden in a knot of potted palm trees, slowly being prodded off his religious objections and disappointments by the two guitars and the trumpet exuberantly greeting the guests, dancing them straight from the hosts through the dense jungle to him as he mothered his punch bowl. "Not drinking," he muttered to himself aloud.

Nicasia darted between trees, charmed with the indoor forest, charmed with everything. She found her husband in the *sala* and was happy to see him at the huge punch bowl, his mood improving. Like a nymph, she danced for him, waving tantalizing fingers and faded into the trees. When Faustino looked up, she had vanished, and he was shocked to confront Michael nose to nose, fingering the brown cups.

"I hope these look like small coconut shells; it's the best we could do," his *patrón* mumbled.

Faustino knew enough to move his gaze away from the borrowed Franciscan robes.

"The White sisters like to make an entrance. I hope they won't come too late."

"*Si, Señor Patrón.*" The two sisters would be the last to arrive for the last cocktail party. Faustino knew them as true ladies.

"After they've all had drinks here, at seven-thirty we are forming a hysterical parade to La Fonda. They will be talking about this for absolutely years to come."

Faustino took a deep breath. "*Muy bien, Patrón.*"

Richard strode up, another defrocked monk, and Faustino gave a stiff bow. More rain forest animals and frisky apes piled through the *zaguan* door, spreading out under the trees. When the musicians surrounding him ignited into a samba, Richard applauded and dropped his reserve. Eyes shining and hips swaying, he lewdly lifted his robes and shimmied—one-two-three, pause. One-two-three, pause.

Discovering who was under the costumes caused wild delight. The gaiety was intensified by the compelling tropical rumbas and carefree kisses. Faustino managed an elegantly remote stance as he handed out punch cups to the ever-more-lively guests. Encouraged by the hosts, the guests gave out whooping jungle calls. Leaping about, they started to knock over tables. Richard and Michael beamed. This party was a success from the first trumpet blast.

No sooner had the hosts welcomed one rush of guests than the musicians paraded in with more, returning repeatedly from the gate with a new troop of prancing Anglos. After the welcoming embraces of the glad hosts, they stormed Faustino's tropical hut. A little steadier now, he stood ready to pass out punch, making hesitant eye contact.

The guests were wound to a pitch by the music, avid to be there and heaving at each other; they embraced, talking all the while: "Oh, my dear, marvelous to see you!" Michael and Richard darted like forgiving confessors between the knots, kissing most faces and shaking only a few hands, blessing all with a "*Dios bandido.*"

Men in grass skirts pushed in, waving peacock feathers. Hot on their trail was a flock of giggling women archaeologists carrying binoculars, poking and pinching their ticklish quarry. Faustino singled one woman out who avidly pursued Spud, the small man with the big glasses—the man everyone adored—tweaking and tickling him until he cried, "Uncle!"

He loved it; they all loved it!

This *reunión* was more splendid than other gatherings, and even though some guests occasionally addressed him, Faustino stayed elegantly remote, superior in fact, frighteningly sober. A slight bow, a small smile tightening his eyes. No more than that.

The music continued without a break.

"Such fun!" a small, round woman with penetrating eyes called out as she entered the fray. "Aren't you the clever ones!" She was robed as a white African queen, accompanied by a heavyset Taos Indian in his traditional blanket. The Indian winced at the chaos and called for an immediate whiskey. Faustino was taken aback. He shot a prayer up to the Virgin. Honest white men refused to serve Indians whiskey.

Avoiding the Indian, Faustino turned to the lady. "Will the *señora* have a drink?"

He could sense this woman's power. Was it because people gave her slightly more passage when she moved through the room? Faustino was certain she had houses in very rich cities, and those houses were larger than this on Canyon Road. He thought of her as *La Gorda*; others called her Mabel.

"A drink? Oh my God, yes!" Her voice was beautiful. She stepped up to the bar. "And a whiskey for Tony."

Waiting for divine help, Faustino saw the Indian anxious for his whiskey and managed to serve him last and silently. Throughout the hours that the flourishing jungle party whooped and cawed, he followed that silken voice weaving in and out among the others with the power of command. Once, it soared maddeningly above, as *La Gorda* delivered a statement: "Ray Otis says no one gives a damn what you do here in Santa Fe just as long as they hear about it the next day."

"Not true!" Faustino wanted to bellow. The opposite was true. His people cared what was done. Cared utterly.

Suddenly the music paused, picking up with a special fanfare for two new guests, the guests of honor, escorted by an elegant man in European clothes carrying an elaborately covered gift in his arms. The two unmarried White sisters, dressed as Cuban dancers with flounces and banana-heavy bonnets, surveyed the gathering with delight.

"Awwk!" said their gift.

"We brought you a little nothing."

Richard indicated that the cage should be handed to Procopio, and the man turned smartly on his heel to leave. The ladies called to Procopio in unison, "Do take care; it's quite heavy."

The cage lurched in Procopio's arms and spoke: "Bring me a drink! Bring me a drink!"

"He's a young parrot," Amelia said. "Very quick."

"Oh, you're so divine," the hosts enthused. Kissing the sisters with lavish flattery, they waved for Faustino to come forward with the punch. The samba music launched into a hip-grinding "Happy Birthday."

"Terrible of us to be so late! Shoving that naughty little parrot back into his cage took absolutely ages!" the shorter sister said, laughing. "Fabulous what you've done here."

"Then we ran out of enough paper to wrap this gift," Amelia, her taller sister, said. "What a glorious party!"

"Happy Birthday, dear Amelia! Happy..." the walls reverberated.

The sisters smiled graciously as they were lathered with praise and carried off to dance by the other guests. The laughter rose again; the conversation and animal roars picked up. "That was their butler," Procopio whispered, passing the bar. "You remember that they have their own theater?" It was true; Procopio had described the theater and the stage at their big property, El Delirio. Every March and April, those months of dust storms and high winds, they staged riotous productions to keep spirits up as had been done in the old days at Sunmount Sanitarium. No one dared miss a performance, and in fact, everyone jostled to star. "For a small town," Amelia White claimed, "we have a lot of talent. In fact, it is *all* talent!"

"They're always like this. *Son así, todos.*" Procopio danced through the great *sala*, in and out of the greenery between clutches of costumes, nodding to each guest, recognizing most by name when their masks slipped. Faustino fretted that Nicasia liked these startling Anglos almost as much as Procopio did. And Procopio clearly loved them.

Faustino had drifted off, daydreaming about the ladies, when Procopio called urgently, "Hey, 'Mano! Refreshments?" Procopio's patience snapped; Faustino was too slow. "Refreshments!" Procopio repeated. "Drinks!" Frustrated, he grabbed a tray with jungle punch and rushed to present it to the White sisters, usurping the bar duties. Faustino was left stuck behind the damask-covered table idly chipping ice. Practicing how he would dig with his *barretero*.

Faustino nearly missed the grand entry of God's Mother-in-law, heavily laden with Indian silver and dressed as a Pueblo maiden, complete with white leggings. Her hair hung free; she did not smile as she moved her sideways glance across the roiling crowd. He did hear Michael bellow out, "Darling! You are too kind to come!" as both disappeared into the palms to reappear at the bar.

"None of your evil punch, Michael monk!"

"You are too queenly for this jungle, my darling Mary." He turned to Faustino and said quietly, "There is a special little treat tucked down under the cloth."

Faustino was glad he had not known it was there as he poured the Scotch over ice, offering it with a slow bow. "*Señora*," he said. She received it slowly, and looking him in the eye, she nodded her head slightly. After she had left, he pondered this exchange, and because he found her so principled, he took this small gesture as a greeting between equals and that she had honored his presence in return. Faustino smiled and, without luck, scanned for his wife among the trees. Over and over, refilling cups, he returned to his *quejas*, his complaints.

"*Son muy buena gente.*" He parroted Procopio's endorsement, testing it to see how it sounded from his lips. Procopio was as great an obstacle to finding his treasure as the marble-surfaced walls. Ever present, Procopio popped into view and whispered in Faustino's ear that the short lady dressed as the African queen got syphilis from her husband, the Indian. "Big trouble up in Taos with syphilis," he whispered. "Over two hundred in the Pueblo."

After that Faustino felt sideswiped. He was shocked, fascinated and vindicated. Indians were his founding colony's traditional enemy. Feared for centuries, and now this new contagion! They were throwing back diseases on the white man, reinfecting even the *ricachones*. Defending the gringos now, he muttered, "*Son muy buena gente.*"

Carrying his tray of jungle cups, he tripped. Cups fell and broke—the guests pulled back. Relieved that he was sober, Faustino knelt to gather the broken crockery. Glancing up, he was amazed to see the Virgin herself parting the branches over his very head. She looked down to remind him of his vow to persevere. Still on his knees, he crossed himself and implored the Virgin to act quickly. She was witness to how Procopio and Flora hovered and could easily send them home. Crossing himself again, he begged Her to help him break up what remained of the *dispenza*, the wall She had revealed to him, the wall behind the gold mirror. It was truly *She*! She was shepherding him. Faustino, Her humble servant, bowed as he worked. Praying to be saved from *la sífilis* as well. *Sífilis, tuberculosis...*

Another twenty minutes passed, and the *mariachi* players broke into a medley of bright Brazilian songs, indicating that the cavalcade was to begin. The guests drained their cups and began to gather up their things. The apes replaced their masks, straightened their costumes and slowly lined up behind the *mariachi* players ready for the jungle parade. Procopio, with Faustino behind him, moved in and out of the groups, collecting cups. At the sound of a deep gong, the trumpet called for the menagerie to advance, and the merrymakers fell in line, hooting and calling out, impatient to begin their dancing, whooping procession.

Procopio retreated to the kitchen, dropping his tray piled high with cups and overflowing ashtrays at the sink. Nicasia turned to smile at her uncle. Faustino, looking wretched, came in with his own heavily laden tray. The hosts ducked in to dismiss the help and to grab the parrot's cage before they escaped to join their friends.

"Get me a drink!" the young parrot screamed when his cage was jostled.

"*Señor* Michael," a sober Faustino said to the *patrón*, "Nicasia and I would be pleased to stay late and wash the dishes."

"It's not necessary at all!" He was handed ten pesos and given both a Papal blessing and a broad smile. "Procopio and Flora have everything under control."

Then the hosts and guests all streamed out to parade down Canyon Road, past the cathedral and on to La Fonda, the pulsing Brazilian music and hullabaloo of jungle calls announcing their progress.

The music faded; the songs and laughter died in the distance.

"Lock this door when you leave," Procopio said, indicating the button on the inside door plaque. "We'll do the rest," he said, throwing a smile to Nicasia and holding his hand up in silent relief that Faustino had not taken a drink. "I have already locked the *zaguan*." He left to bring more flowing ashtrays from the *gran sala*.

As soon as Procopio left the kitchen, Faustino bolted to the powder room.

"You two can go now. We can finish up." Flora placed her arms on her niece's shoulders. "You both did beautifully."

Nicasia folded her dishtowels, intending to walk home. "Faustino!" she called to the closed powder room door. "*A casa!*"

He did not reply—he was concentrating.

Tap tap tap.

He was listening for a hollow response.

He crossed himself three times. *Tap.*

Tap, She answered.

CHAPTER ELEVEN

The last hard freeze was expected in early May, when the fruit trees had already set their blossoms. The fields had been prepared, the planting held off until the beginning of the second week in May, so this Saturday morning, Melo and Franque were free. Taking Olivia María by her lead, the two boys set out for the Plaza to meet up with friends. Earlier in April, the boys had helped their father clean out the *acequia*, making it ready for the rush of mountain water that would bubble between the troughs of the planted rows.

"*Luegecito, Mamá,*" they called from the yard. Slowly the house grew silent as the boyish jibes faded downriver. Faustino's eyes softened as he followed his wife's movements. After kissing her sons at the door, she had turned toward him, standing in the shaft of light on the hard earth floor. To him, she had that serene beauty of a generous woman, which in the Blessed Virgin was called *gracia*—one step beyond natural human grace, but attainable.

His smile radiated over her, and she nodded a silent gratitude as she returned to the kitchen table. Nicasia put down her blue cup, and he heard the hollow clatter of china on china. "I really do like those high-tone *amigonas* of the *dueños*."

"Those rich matrons?" he responded. Her statement shook him.

"*Son divertidas.*" She got up from the kitchen table, untying her apron. "I like them."

Amusing? Faustino thought not. "The richest got *sífilis* sleeping with Indians." He, the *pater familias*, was scandalized. As a man, he was guardian of the family's morals. *El hombre.*

Ten years earlier, these outsiders had arrived dying of tuberculosis. They had overrun the entire community of Santa Fe with their sickness, sin and perversion. What they did was mocking God's Law—call it what you like. "Their diseases are contagious!" He shuddered at having been forced to serve whiskey to a blanket Indian, to touch his glass.

"Procopio and Flora say that the *señores* Ricardo and Miguel are healthy and their hearts are full of charity and goodness, that they are *personas lo mas buenas*," Nicasia said. "They are fine humans, like us, and they believe in nature, not religion."

"What?" Faustino said too quickly, too loud.

"They say nature is mysterious and that the Indians know how to utilize her powers." When she said it, this sounded innocent, not heretical, and Faustino was quiet awhile. Still, it gnawed at him.

"Do human beings fight over a little man like Spud?" Faustino's many disappointments had come to a head, the marble on the *dispenza* wall being the agent of his immediate frustration.

"Spud is my favorite." She stood hands on hips.

Their bickering had begun late the night before when Faustino had pulled out the map for the gold, and she began to deeply regret having allowed it to stay under the wooden foot of the Virgin. She connected the Blessed Mother to Faustino's strange moods of remoteness and depression, his bouts of drinking that began with the map. And she blamed herself. Once a girl so certain, so defined, she now backed down, doubting her own mind, and left decisions to Faustino, the head of the family. Time and again she acted like a typical Spanish wife, giving in to Faustino's questionable authority.

Now they argued about the little publisher. "Spud is secretary to Mabel Dodge in Taos, but he's also friends with *La Señora* Austen. The two women are jealous of each other," Nicasia explained quietly, trying to calm him. "Both ladies are famous for writing, and Spud prints what they write."

"He sleeps with two fat, old women?" Faustino spat back.

"No, Spud's lover is a poet, a man," she said flatly. She walked out of the room, leaving Faustino to pace. In exasperation, he stomped out of the snug house and was shocked by the dazzling sunlight. He cut through Paco's orchard, rousing the dogs, aiming for the chopped-up, fourteen-room *hacienda*, his mind filled with pickaxes.

A brisk wind blew from the west, dropping loose dirt and turning the sky silver. Standing in the *plazuela*, Procopio was pruning roses sheltered by century-old courtyard walls from these continual late spring winds that incited man's fury and woman's snappishness. He stood back to examine the first bush he had been working on. The courtyard was the genius of colonial homes, a space of calm contentment, an outdoor room sheltered from the dust and the overwhelming sight of the thousand-mile vastness that spread from the edge of the small mountainside *villa* with its ten thousand Christian souls. Procopio took in the warm sun, pleased that the garden had begun to reach out with new life. And what a garden! His satisfaction with it had spiritual ingredients.

He held whetstone-sharpened clippers in his hand, admiring the basket of cuttings from the bush he was pruning, but his calm pleasure was broken by a loud banging on the *zaguan* door. Still holding the pruning clippers, he moved to open the small window cut into the heavy door to find Faustino still pounding the door in a mounting rage.

"*Qué quieres?*" Procopio said, reluctantly allowing his *primo* to ruin the beauty of this May morning. He let him in and closed the door with an echoing thump. Abruptly, he returned to his pruning. Faustino followed, ready to harangue the windless calm.

"Well, now what is it?" Procopio demanded over his shoulder, bending to the basket of cuttings.

Faustino fumed. This was too small a question for what was on his mind.

"What are *they*, not what is *it*." Plural best suited his list of burning complaints and protests. "*Primero*," Faustino said, "these newcomers are infidels. They are wrong, they are diseased..."

"*Cálmate.*" Procopio shook his head and refused to look at Faustino. "You were the one who asked to work here. I'm happy to have Nicasia come here anytime. But you?"

"She forgives those people; I cannot," Faustino growled.

"Many are *muy buena gente*. Besides we have all seen that when you drink their whiskey, you become more reasonable."

"They have destroyed Tía Doña Serafina's house. They have destroyed her *dispenza*, where she kept her herbs and cures."

"*Correcto*." Procopio severed whole rose stalks in their sheltered beds. "If I cut these right, they will bloom twice."

"Why destroy Tía Serafina's *dispenza*?" Faustino's voice resounded off the window panes, moving the reflected sunlight ever so slightly.

Procopio's response was to give the spiky roses a whack.

Faustino paced, taking the brutal pruning as argument.

After a while, Procopio said, "The *dispenza* is now a magnificent powder room. Why are you so disturbed? It's not your house." Receiving no response, he resumed his task. "Actually, this house was never yours except for some small hope that your wife's family held out for a portion of a few *vigas*."

Faustino glared at him. "Why is it called a powder room when it looks like an *onodoro*, a toilet?"

A sudden nervous tic pinched Procopio's face as *Patrón* Michael strode toward him. He appeared in the *placita* to oversee the pruning of his prized roses, and he was not pleased to discover Faustino there. Procopio smiled and Faustino tried to cover his discomfort as he bowed to his *patrón*. "*Buenas tardes, Señor Miguel*."

"Oh, there you are, Faustino. Still not able to *hablar inglés* at all?" Michael managed to make himself sound like the judge at a trial, which upset even Procopio's professional equanimity. Faustino winced, reminding himself that Richard was the one who spoke passable Spanish, definitely not Michael, who this past weekend had actually greeted his guests with "*Dios bandito*," idiotically calling God a bandit instead of extending His blessing.

"*Sí, pero prefiero mi lengua norteña*," Faustino replied in his concise Spanish, smoldering while he considered what might have brought on this rebuke. Michael might be out of sorts over something that had nothing to do with him or Procopio. Either he was sick again or in a jealous fit over someone, maybe even little Spud? Faustino swallowed hard.

"You'd better learn to speak English," the art teacher said, looking squarely into Faustino's eyes. "English is the way of the future. You owe it to your people." Michael was standing too close and didn't notice that the sunlight picked up the few drops of his spittle now planted across Faustino's face. "They will need to write and speak a passable English if they are to get anywhere in life."

To Faustino, these words were daggers. *"No me importa, Señor Patrón Miguel."* Faustino tried to sound respectful while an ancient fierceness rose to color his face. Now darkening with a flush of blood, he was more tan, more burnt, with more fire in his dark gaze. How could he explain to this newcomer that the only purpose for English was to read the packaging on the box of Saltines, the label on Jergens lotion? All trivialities. At school, English had been tedious and boring, filled with useless rules. What was important was God's Holy Will and the Virginity of His Mother and Eden, the garden where Adam and Eve lived and had committed mankind's Original Sin. English was not important.

Procopio sent frantic signs to Faustino—"Please leave now!"—and behind his *patrón*'s back, he indicated that Michael had been drinking. "Go!" he mouthed as Michael moved in close.

"Mark my words," Michael said. Faustino, stiffly nodding a polite assent, saw again how Anglos had no respect for the *fundadores vecinos*, those first citizens who paved the way for the lungers to move right into a stable community with running water and subdued, servile Indians.

"Can you even read?" Michael pressed.

Procopio shot Faustino a nervous smile, warning him for a second time to leave, but Faustino was feeding his *patrón*'s fury by staring straight into the faded eyes of the fleshy artist while his own complexion turned from clay to dusky.

"Leo unicamente la biblia—en Castellano." Faustino swallowed, trying to keep his emotions in check. He knew he should back away from this unfortunate exchange if he wanted to remain their bartender. He closed his eyes and bowed in a courtly manner.

"The *biblia*?" A trigger apparently fired in Michael's head, causing him to throw his arms up in a frustrated rage. "Oh, not those stupid stories again." Michael was using his hands to punctuate his pidgin

Spanish. "*Mucho no me importante*," he said. "How can you stupid Spanish Catholics still believe in fairy tales?" But he did not stop there. "Evolution is a fact."

Faustino lowered his gaze and nodded that he heard what the *patrón* was saying, respectfully bearing up under the slander. He had been cautioned to allow this *mariposona* to rant, to defame God's Truth and massacre his own lovely language. Procopio insisted that he appear servile, to show respect to the *dueño* through silence, bowing, forbearing his spit. Faustino took deep breaths. No worthy prince would speak to the *fundadores vecinos* with such disdain. Michael was absurd with his prize roses, his ant-laden peonies. His rich and famous friends were inconsequential.

Faustino took more deep breaths and moved his eye up the man's distended body, thinking that his stomach resembled an ape's. He was, in fact, ugly. And he was red-faced, sweating, with his hands apart and trembling while he continued his rant, spitting. When Faustino glanced higher, now staring into Michael's bloodshot eyes, he saw truth. He saw how it shone slick and dropped close to the ground, and as his eyes focused on Truth, it whipped across the mud, leaving a viper track. The image of Original Sin, the First Lie. This sloppy desecration of the Bible meant one thing only: Faustino was face-to-face with the Antichrist. His blood raced.

God spoke, had spoken: "People will rise and play the harlot with...the foreigners of the land...and they will forsake Me." Before the Lord's Second Coming, false prophets would appear and then the Antichrist. Faustino scanned his brain for the known characteristics of the Antichrist. Some mark, some bestial mark. Was it the washed-out, pale eyes?

If Michael and Richard did not fear God, it must be because they had succumbed to the Antichrist, the one who looked like all others on the outside but cast no shadow, corrupted man's very soul. Adrenalin now coursed through his body, his heart ratcheting, and his ribs drummed excitement. He faced the enemy alone now, the embodiment of evil, the long-awaited Antichrist who exalted science and books, who denied the Garden of Eden and that Adam and Eve had ever lived. They who were parents to all men, white, tan, yellow, red and black. Everything began with Adam and Eve and the serpent. This man he faced *was the serpent!*

Michael grew agitated, hands flying, trying to explain to a simpleton what had been brought to light by the newest painstaking archaeology, stuff he'd gleaned from the courts and the Scopes Trial.

The blood surged to Faustino's head. His ears rang. The American scientists had killed off Adam and Eve, said they did not exist, that they were apes, corpulent monkeys with hair on their faces and hideous, hanging arms. They said they were like those imbeciles at the drunken Jungle Ball. Faustino's heart wept for these crimes of scientific insolence. He tried to obliterate the lies about Adam and Eve, about himself.

"Science!" Michael faced Faustino. His breath was sick with whiskey. He took up some long-handled shears and began to thrash his roses, ranting about the ignorance of the illiterate.

Faustino was not illiterate—he could read. They all knew how to read. There was a difference between the beauty in the Bible and the gossip in popular magazines. "Adam and Eve were not apes," he said in clear English.

"Then who did Cain marry?" Michael stood taller to punctuate his argument. "You people live in the Dark Ages!" He picked up a thorny stalk and beat it against the kitchen wall. A thorn pierced his hand, and Procopio rushed over to him.

Faustino's heart was crucified. He bowed. Trying to make himself small, he crouched, backing his way out of the *plazuela*. Then he stood to full height, turned his back on the *patrón*, and walked toward the door. Beaten but proud.

"I mean it," Michael called after him. *"Dígame, como mariachi Caen?"*

What kind of stupid Spanish was that? Faustino did not care who Cain/Caen married. Everyone knew God made women out of ribs. So what if He just made another one?

"Only Adam and Eve *y* Cain." Michael waved his arms in the air. *"No señoritas.* None."

Faustino was fed up. All human life began with *Adan y Eva*. He turned to flee the vicious heretic. The drunken swine.

"*Muerto Abel*," called Michael. "Dead, I tell you." Faustino was overcome by a furious headache and stomped out into the dirt street, slamming the *zaguan* door behind him.

He wept as he walked home. Richard and Michael's ilk destroyed everything that was important: God, truth, the *dispenza*.

He wished them dead. He wished for the easy justice of the Inquisition.

"I am never going back there again," he told Nicasia when he barged into the kitchen. "Never."

"Never, ever going back there?" Nicasia asked. "*Jamás?*"

He shook his head.

She said nothing.

"I hate them," he said. And gave himself over to an elaborate bitterness.

CHAPTER TWELVE

It was dusk. Faustino shouldered a bloodstained burlap bag containing goat scraps as, one-handed, he pulled himself rung by rung up the ladder to the roof of his small adobe. His flat roof, divided in two parts defining the rooms below, was littered with whitened animal bones picked clean by vultures. Each wall of the house formed a foot-high parapet above the roof, high enough for a man to sit for a clear view of the western Jemez range and the mountains beyond. Faustino had tended his own roof assiduously, repairing it and building up the compacted dirt and newspapers overlaying the large, supporting pine *vigas* of the ceiling below. Depending on the depth of the packing layers, the roofs were claimed to withstand one or more days of continual rain and melting snow.

Faustino's was a three-day roof. Sloped for drainage, it sagged and had its own seasons. In the spring, fed by the melting snow, clumps of grass grew up green and fresh around the discarded carcass scraps, and in the winter, the frozen tufts, yellowed and stiff, reminded Faustino of midsummer's dried grasses when the earth on the sun-heated roof hardened to baked clay. Until, of course, the rains came and this three-day roof absorbed the water before it was shed through the wooden downspouts called *canales*. But with vigilant care, this small house would remain hardened in place for another hundred years.

Down below and in the distance, he heard the boys playing king of the mountain, calling out, "Come get me!" Olivia María brayed, and the hens' deep staccato filled the background chorus to the rhythms of the village evening. A far-off radio played a *ranchero* tune.

Sitting on the parapet, Faustino steadied himself from the climb and let his sack of goat scraps rest at his feet. Sunset was setting up across the sky. The light played off the clouds, bringing a rosy tinge that enlivened even his clay-colored complexion. To the north floated huge thunderheads, blue-gray, flashing lightning inside, but this vitalizing charge did not lift his low mood. Slowly, he moved his gaze to the burlap sack. He had climbed to his roof with the rotten meat and severed bones from last week's *matanza* to leave the putrefying flesh for the buzzards. Taking a step toward the roof's uneven center, he kicked the old scattering of desiccated goat and sheep bones into a pile. Turkey vultures gathered overhead. These bone-littered roofs served as trays of rotting meats for them; the neighboring roofs were littered with skulls, upturned rib cages and the smaller white bones the crows had scavenged clean. What was not torn to bits by the ravens and vultures was gathered and thrown back down to be spaded into the garden, proving up larger apricots and apples.

Faustino glanced over to Paco's roof nearby; it had weathered poorly. His foundation walls had been critically weakened the afternoon Paco dozed off, forgetting to close the *acequia* gate, which flooded more than his orchard. Once his water-wicked walls had dried, Faustino had arrived with neighbors and their shovels, set to replaster and buttress the crumbling house, but Paco had refused the *vecinos'* help then. Dispirited and mourning his runaway wife, he said his life was over, so he would let his *casita* crumble. Faustino estimated that without help, the house would return to a pile of dirt and rubble within a decade; sooner with the next sleepy flooding. Houses needed care.

Paco had not been up on his roof for years. It was weedy, windblown, peeling. Any bones he'd had were given to his pack of mongrels that growled off the predatory crows and fought among themselves for scraps.

An alert flock of turkey vultures lifted from Paco's ailing trees to close in on Faustino's rancid, burlap-wrapped meat. They crowded

Faustino, flying close. He waved them away with an angry fist. "*Más tarde*!"

They cawed their response. He counted seven turkey vultures spiraling above his head. "*Suéltame*!"

Hearing his own voice surprised him. The elongated shadow he cast concerned him even more. It was true: he was a man but a cowardly, lowly man. His spirit had been splintered. He had not stood his ground; he had fled, routed at the God slaughter. He had not confronted Michael's despicable logic, and he had humiliated himself by allowing the *americano* freethinker to spit in the face of God. He had allowed this through his pandering to the gringos. He was actually guilty of blasphemy; greed as well because he would have traded truth for gold.

Slumped now on the parapet facing west, Faustino held his head between his dry hands and grieved for his lost, holy fierceness.

"Who did Cain marry?" An echo of jumbled science taunted him.

He had *not* passed a sharp blade across their vile necks.

He had *not* called the holy battle cry of God's own soldiers—"*Dios y Santiago*!"—consigning them to Satan and certain defeat.

He had *not* held up the image of the Astounding Crucified Christ before their false eyes.

Above all, he had not called, "*Dios y Santiago*!"

The blue sky weakened above him, hot with orange and red, staining the far-off Sangre de Cristo Mountains with the same ruby splash that had caused Don Juan de Oñate to bow his head, his great hat over his heart. His royal pennants fluttering, Oñate finally received the very sign he had sought. It was a sign from the heavens for the Franciscans as well, on their knees beside him, whose prayers were lifted on those rose-colored waves—the robes, they said, of the risen Christ. The colors shot past the clouds to embroider their pious faces with the red of the very Blood of Christ, the *Sangre de Cristo*. With this, God's approbation and grace, the *entrada* named for Philip II could finally rest. The royal colony could be founded by men of courage and conviction—Oñate's blameless men.

The same violent sunset assaulted Faustino with a vision of his own slaughtered integrity. For ten seconds, he stopped breathing. When he again gasped, his breath had the color and taste of sunset. "Let this be my redemption," he said, his feet motionless, fixed to his rooftop, to the land, to the shattering memory of that other sunset, which to him was the sign of the Risen Christ. The gift of God's visible sustenance had been passed down to him through his Catholic kings. It was the sign that his pleas could be heard. And he vowed to make another prayer for strength each summer night as the living clouds careened across the vastness, vapor bellies swollen with life-relishing rain.

And the mornings! Since Oñate, when his men's rested eyes had opened to be greeted by the peach dawn, they were reborn, feeling new, clean. Faustino prayed that he might awake again invigorated, vowing to defeat the blaspheming *ricachones*, monsters who now held his birthright with their fake deeds and who entangled him in their unnaturalness. The might of God would set things right. Faustino had only to pray and to offer more penance.

But he lacked hope.

Turning his thoughts just so, Faustino became alive in the past. He contemplated the heavens with the same awe that brought the first García to his knees when dismounting Relámpago on Christmas Eve of 1598. He inhabited the very skin of Don Fructoso de García, that young and able founder of Oñate's troubled colony where their settlement had first begun. He felt the purity of intention with which the good Don Fructoso de García had joined the expedition, setting out to herd hostile tribes into Christ's embrace. How he had staked his fortune and his honor to bring the unbaptized into the Light! And when the king awarded Don Fructoso his abundant *merced real* and the *encomienda*, Faustino was certain his forebear had accepted the riches with humility and purity of heart.

His own heart stung from the loss of both his noble past and the lands, and this loss had now become his dragon. Scorching, it breathed fire and must be killed. Shamed, Faustino mourned the ways of the *caballero*. He sought the return of his own soul and his true parents, Adam and Eve. He craved the death of the dragon.

The sky's drama played out a historic blunder. He knew, they all knew, that if President Polk in his mad ambition had demanded all of Mexico, not just California and New Mexico, for his ten million dollars, wrongs could have been set right. Then, with the embezzled deeds to all of Mexico in hand, a multitude of seething warriors would have risen against Manifest Destiny. There would have been blood. But the sons of the conquistadors sought blood; they lived by it. Only by blood could they regain their lands.

Faustino breathed in the clouds' colors and wept for Independent Mexico's stupidity in trying to outsmart the double-talking negotiator by throwing away her poorest cousin, her unpopulated north with Santa Fe, as a scrap—much the way Faustino was now tantalizing the vultures with his goat parts on the rooftop. Mexico was crippled, trying to save her heartland by severing the very limbs best ready and able to defend her. The brazen *americanos* and their Manifest Destiny claimed another conquest and overwhelmed the land once protected by God and the kingdom of Spain, devastating her *antiguos vecinos*. Four hundred years of the *villa* at the end of the Santa Fe Trail were wiped away. The landowners fell to penury, the land grants were shredded, and English hid the beauty and lilt of Castilian Spanish. In the waste, a traders' pidgin mixture sprang up. Only nineteen of the several hundred Indian pueblos survived.

Faustino's heart ached. He knew things could not be more wretched. Emptying his sack, he consigned the goat flesh to be picked clean, to join the dead. The turkey vultures fell to their feast. Faustino added his battered soul to the banquet, and before he descended the ladder, he made the sign of the cross.

Once down, he planted his feet in flat dirt on the shadow side of his house. In the distance, Olivia María brayed, and he could hear his sons call out to each other in high, tremulous voices. These homey sounds increased his wretchedness. Anglos, lawyers, Freethinkers, artists and perverts hooted through Faustino's thoughts. With more despair, he pinpointed money as the direct agent of the ruination.

Money: no one had needed money in Upper San Benicia's forest where Faustino had grown up with his grandparents. Treasure was not buried or maps hidden. Their land was the gold, the land lived and breathed. Money was the locust plague.

In town, *la villa*, his mother and four sisters needed money—cash for doctors, shoes, and sacks of flour. *Reales*, now *dólares*. It was a trick to tax printed money. For this, his father sweated in the Montana sheep camps. Each October, at the end of the season, seventeen train cars of piñon nuts were shipped north to gringo markets. The boxcars returned empty; fathers and brothers rode hobo back to their families, with money earned to pay debts. But first, taxes. Soon, an armed gringo militia was conscripted to collect these taxes.

Faustino pulled his pole ladder down and moved it to the far side of his house, where he carefully laid it on its side. To relieve his pain, he sat on the rigid side of the twelve-foot ladder and leaned back against the shaded wall.

Of course the Mexicans and the Spanish Crown had reasonably taxed the fruits of their lavish gifts, the land grants. Faustino would not begrudge reverting a portion of the surplus to the crown. And there had been a surplus when Elodio ran eight thousand sheep.

Faustino closed his tired eyes. The true darkness was the false god, greed. Money was her weapon. An invading army of merchants with pretty cloth, gleaming tools and milled sugar rang hypnotic bells at the opening of the Santa Fe Trail. They came like a silent disease and managed to make vast trading fortunes out of the dry frontier.

These men were as rapacious as their language, helping themselves to any spoken words they fancied, babbling in twice the words with less music. The language was not the same on both sides of the table. Faustino hated them and reviled their watering down of true religion. He called for another Great Inquisition to stand greed on trial and to unify the crusaders of the king.

He thought again of the crimes committed against his uncle Elodio, the last *patrón* of an ancient land grant who understood the land. The *americanos* ruined a man who spoke rooster, sheep and goat. He could gentle a wild horse, shear, butcher, cook and set a broken arm. He came from a race abounding with native intelligence who revered the values of the earth herself and the blessings of a Catholic God.

By the end, Elodio, the venerable last *patrón* of the ninety-seven-thousand-acre *merced real* was surrounded by the stench of starved animals, dust and written demands for taxes. He was among the last *patrones* to weaken and buckle. Elodio was capable against his natural enemy, the horse-riding, sheep-stealing Plains Indians, but against this unnatural enemy he was halted, dismembered.

Defeated, Elodio forfeited his vast *merced* to the tax collectors. The lost land was dead. It lay like the bones on Faustino's roof, loose, neglected and it was there for the taking. Through stupidity and misuse, the land had been broken and eroded. Vultures circled.

Faustino understood Elodio's isolation. His *antepasados* and brawny *padres* had walked the twelve hundred miles north with their holy faith and muscle. They had tamed a hostile desert in the name of the Crown. And generations down the line, Elodio had still been taming the raw land when those Anglo bastards ended up with the tax deed to the García grant. The last *patrón* was now a squatter.

Elodio then decamped for the Montana sheep ranches seeking pay, joined by his younger brother, Faustino's father, but they both crawled home drunk and penniless, their ranching hearts broken. Elodio sold his dust-covered 1923 truck and, carrying what he owned on his horse, headed for town, a refugee in his own country. *La Viuda* Tía Doña Serafina took him in, a woman who restored the luckless with her medicines and food. He married the ample widow, and she wove him blankets and cloth, sewed for him and healed him.

Later, when Elodio began to prosper from a boot-leg still west of the Plaza in Agua Fria Village, he gave what he had to Tía Serafina for safekeeping. At the same time, the *gente* of Santa Fe came to the *dispenza* for help, and La Doña Serafina was initiated as a *tercero*, a member of the Third Order of St. Francis. Elodio lived out his years in the great house, strengthened and saved by Serafina's warm gaze and comfort while the rest of the García family was dirt poor.

Unable to drop his bitterness, Elodio ached to restore his usurped legacy to his descendants. He began his determined search for the fabled treasure, worth more than enough to regain what impoverished lands of his were yet unsold. He knew Carlota's wealth was within his reach. With his search half proven, his heart seized, and he died in the very *dispenza* known and celebrated for restoring health to the weak. Nicasia called it an omen.

The blur of backyard sounds had lulled Faustino deep into his dark sorrow when Paco's shadow passed over him in the failing light of that spring day. He flinched, but he refused to open his eyes. Paco stood to the side, examining Faustino's face, seeing how it had been frozen with his perpetual dark memories. As he walked past, his shadow crossed Faustino's closed eyes a second time, startling him into the present. And when a hand touched his shoulder, Faustino bolted.

"*Todavía así?*" Paco demanded, standing over him with his hands on his sides, shading Faustino's face. "You got yourself two sons, a beautiful wife. She cooks and does everything, and here you are, all *triste* over nothing. Me, I got nobody."

Faustino said nothing and stared at the pack of yellow dogs pressing on Paco's legs.

"I should be depressed, not you!" Paco added when he received no response.

"You got those goddamn dogs..." Faustino stood up, stiff from having been slumped against the cool wall. The dogs crept forward.

"You act like it's the end of the world," Paco said, and Faustino waved him away with the back of his hand because he was wrong again. Always wrong.

"The end of the world has already happened." Faustino dusted his work pants in quick slapping motions.

"I must'a missed it."

"Your dogs barked like crazy when it happened, but you didn't wake up. Dogs—they know."

"And can you tell me what happened at this End of the World of yours?" Paco took a deep breath.

"Uncle Sam."

"Uncle Sam what?"

"Stole everything. Took our language, our money, our land and our religion, and then he took God."

"God?" Paco was unprepared for this last allegation.

"Yeah, God. Seen Him around here lately?"

"No. But I think I seen His Mother." Paco's irritation with Faustino began to take its usual form of exasperation.

"His Mother? How?"

"Nicasia, *cabrón*. Nicasia reminds me of *La Santa María*." Paco pulled back so that the last of the sun again troubled Faustino's eyes. "You are not grateful to *El Señor* for the good that He gives you." He paused for a short breath and then continued. "You never have been."

CHAPTER THIRTEEN

Faustino dropped deeper into his splintered being, obsessing with having walked out on the most significant test of his life. He had denied his one true church and the unassailable Bible, exposed them to mockery. He had been struck dumb; he had been a pillar of salt. He had let stand what no *conquistador* could permit. And he bitterly vowed to never again enter the fourteen-room adobe while Michael and Richard were squatters there.

Michael, drunk Michael, had called him ignorant, superstitious and stupid, words foreign to the sons of the *hidalgos*. Let his weighty treasure suffocate in the *dispenza* walls. *Además,* if either of these pagans approached him on their knees, he would repel them with an upheld crucifix, loudly yelling, *"Dios y Santiago."* He would see them defeated.

"Please, Faustino," he heard them cry out. "We beg you to forgive us!"

"Never, *jamás! Nunca!*" The only acceptable apology would be a formal recantation and a public request for baptism. On the gallows steps.

More and more often in the early hours, Faustino ranted, talking aloud to himself, waking Nicasia and leaving her helpless against his surging anger. Truth was beyond all debate; any inference to the contrary caused Faustino to feel orphaned and indeed abandoned. How could anyone not believe in Adam and Eve, first man and first woman? That man's forebears might be apes and not that young, pale and graceful couple? When the night was darkest in the small adobe, Faustino became a caged brute, a subhuman fitfully waking his wife and sleeping sons. In daylight he was calmer, but lack of sleep caused him to drift and lose hope. He found no rest.

"*Querido*, the *muchitos* are upset when they see you sitting like this," Nicasia said, trying to shake him to attention. Indeed, he sat miserably at the small kitchen table, his arms limp and heavy. He claimed to be infested with rashes and phantom fleas. He pulled at his chest, scratching himself, inflamed.

"It would do you good to get some fresh air, to take a walk."

"No."

"*Papi*, you'll feel better if you come and feed Olivia María with us," Franque said, pulling at his father.

"No."

The García *vecinos* were all aware of the distress Faustino was causing Nicasia and the children. They had never witnessed such a descent—and in the one man they had deemed fit and reliable. Faustino had always been reliable. He was known as the courageous embodiment of manliness. He had been a churchgoer and a true neighbor, inventive, strong, dutiful and capable. Not until his mind seemed fractured and strangled did they understand just what a fine man they had lost. The collapse of his vitality was enormous and baffling.

"He is wallowing in self-pity," Paco said.

"Not at all," Nicasia said, looking him straight in the face. "He grieves because the gringos believe they are smarter than the Bible." Nicasia tried to reason with Faustino, relieve his anguish. He was suffering his own Armageddon—men sleeping with men, women with women. All mocking God.

"He told my husband it was about desecrating Adam and Eve," Escamila López said when Nicasia ran into her at the Cash and Carry on Palace Avenue.

"*Correcto*. They told Faustino that man came from apes." Nicasia was not bothered by incidental arguments such as this. She shrugged this one off as another stupidity. "The Pueblo *nativos* believe that the first man came from a deep chasm in the earth."

"I hope his name was Adam," Escamila said. Nicasia nodded and walked home almost laughing.

"Faustino, please forget what Michael says when he has been drinking." Nicasia approached him quietly, counting on dinner soothing his temper.

Faustino had a ready response. "He attacked the foundations of civilization and insulted the Bible." He nodded to his sons, alerting them. The boys stood stalk still, prepared for their father's bombast. "Listen to me, *hitos*; this is important."

Nicasia cut in, "Why do you care, if it's a lie and he is a fool?"

"Because I was asked to stand up to them as a Christian, and I failed." There was nothing left to say.

"Faustino, just pray for these men," a neighbor urged, wiping her hands on her apron. "That's all you have to do."

"That story about the apes—it's a stupid lie, not a personal insult," Paco said, loud enough to be overheard. Nicasia sighed, knowing that Faustino's pride had dropped like the curtain of death over any dialogue on the matter. The Freethinkers were tainted, their words poison, and the one Christian who might have saved them had failed. She, on the other hand, found their bold thoughts risky; short of deathbed repentance, they might well be condemned to the everlasting fires. Even so, Nicasia found the gringos amusing and often astonishing, and now as a last resort, she fancied she might need their help to save her collapsed husband.

Were Michael and Richard even aware of Faustino's crack-up? Probably not.

By this time, Nicasia, too, was showing signs of severe strain and dragged through the day, depressed. Dishes were left in the sink. The house was dark, and these days neither she nor Faustino said anything when they caught the boys sitting on the front steps engrossed in their traded American comic books. Now, Nicasia was tortured by the rising panic that she might never be able to save her husband's soul from the ever-present Devil. As a consequence, her boys might be lost as well. This real terror crept from house to house. An exorcism was in order, but Faustino refused, though others saw it, and the very pious could actually visualize it. The *vecinos* were at a loss, and endless quiet conferences in the García Compound led to a plan to rescue Faustino from the clutches of the Prince of Darkness.

Concerned after a long stretch of silent weeks, Nicasia felt that she might risk looking for the gold as a last gasp to bring Faustino back to life. She asked Procopio whether they had hired other bartenders for their gatherings, and he reported that the *patrónes* were preparing for a trip to Europe and had been dining out most nights. Their *hacienda* was unexciting—no music, no gatherings. They were, he said, preoccupied with plans to join Mary Austin, Spud and a party of others for a European tour of art and antiquities.

Nicasia sucked on her lower lip. "Have they turned their backs on Faustino?"

He assured her that they were completely sidetracked with packing for their coming trip. Valises were brought out. Fancy suits were taken out of mothballs for airing and starched shirts were counted as the two men prepared for their grand tour and the formal dinners aboard the Cunard Line's *MV Franconia*. Only Procopio and Flora went in and out these days.

Should she believe this? Procopio insisted that the *dueños* had given no thought at all to his ill-tempered relatives, and he turned from her, dropping the subject. "Why should they bother themselves?" Procopio asked.

"But the huge fight over the Bible?" Nicasia persisted.

"A fight?" Procopio seemed genuinely puzzled.

Nicasia was shocked. Could Michael simply be careless and inconsiderate? "The big blowup between Michael and Faustino. The Bible? Learning English and not speaking Spanish?" Nicasia asked, bewildered; she felt helpless and turned to Procopio, who shook his head, dismissing her concerns.

Later Flora insisted, "Michael gets dramatic at times. He runs hot and cold. It means nothing." This battle that had so upset her household, her husband, and even Paco and the *vecinos* was now being blamed on Faustino's boiling brain. Procopio, she knew, would defend his *patrones* to the death, even against witnessed history and the Natural Law. He had been bought. Nicasia had no doubt that Michael had indeed offended her husband's set values, triggering his self-righteousness, that self-defeating arrogance. He had set out defending the Word of God, making vows of vengeance and refusing now to ever again enter Tía Serafina's *hacienda* or accept the *patrónes* money or their imported whiskey.

She saw how futile this visit was, so she doubled her praying, and midweek, with her father driving his pickup, she made her second pilgrimage to Chímayo, determined to plead for a swift end to this misery. In his present condition, Faustino was a burden. She, with the neighbors, tiptoed around him and then fled, hiding behind domesticity and more prayer.

The Santuario at Chímayo, some thirty miles north of La Villa, was adorned with (now) useless crutches and worn shoes of children once crippled. The sacred healing earth of the high desert performed the same miracles as the rich waters of Lourdes and Fatima. The tiny room built to house the pit of holy dirt lay off of the main altar at the old church. To reach it, Nicasia genuflected and opened a gate in the communion rail, and bowing her head, she walked directly in front of Christ in his tabernacle, the red lamp of Christ's presence flickering.

Her father accused Faustino of malingering, and she was too discouraged to mount a good defense. They knelt before the Virgin to repeat the Act of Contrition, then the Apostles Creed and finally, moving to the rim of the deep earthen pit, the Lord's Prayer. She stated her intention aloud: "Please, Dear Lord God, make Faustino strong again." She pictured him healed in her mind, not depressed and spiritually sapped. Then she bent into the pit and took the dirt in her hand to place it in a jelly jar.

When Nicasia arrived home, she dusted her husband's chair with the sandy dirt. At night, she spooned a small amount into his boots, wishing Tía Serafina had been available to end his madness with her herbs, teas and poultices. Days passed, and still Faustino remained drained, his color going cadaver gray. Was it a coincidence that his silent gold also lay entombed?

Entering the third month of her husband's misery, Nicasia decided the only thing left was to use the gold as bait. Near the breaking point, she was at her wits' end and resolved give Faustino one moret week before she gave up hope. At first, she had relied on new remedies and prayer. These had proven powerless and regardless of how much she invoked the spirit of Tía Serafina, no improvement was forthcoming. Even the most concerned relatives were growing indifferent to him. Finally, Paco persevered in his own simple way by repeatedly insisting that a simple solution like a little fresh air might be more beneficial than sprinkling Faustino with holy water or dusting him with sacred dirt that did not faze him. "Make him come with me into the *floresta*."

One afternoon Faustino put on a clean shirt and laced his boots, suddenly making ready to leave the small house. Going outside into the sunlight, he secured the panniers on his burro. Convinced that Chímayo's sacred dirt had finally begun its medicine, Nicasia smiled as she watched her stoop-shouldered husband move off past the metal gate, heading east toward the hills. She shook her head until her hair came loose around her shoulders and felt mercifully unburdened. Once he neared a branch in the road, she waved to him as he and the hateful burro moved slowly away, growing smaller—as small as Faustino claimed he felt. Then she took deep breaths of clean, summer air that tasted of her secret mountain meadow, goats' bell sounds in the shadows of ponderosa pines. She, skipping ahead, called back to the goats, "Follow!"

She must have lingered in the doorway a long while, aching for their sun-filled, early years. When she turned her glance toward the *acequia*, she was elated to make out the figure of Procopio walking purposefully along the ditch bank. She called and beckoned to him with a broad smile, curious to know what chore had brought her uncle, still in his work clothes, close to Los García.

"*Vente, Tío!*" She beckoned to him, realizing that his loyalty to his *patrónes* was as strong as hers to her husband.

He acknowledged her wave, quickening his stride without shifting his gaze from hers. He smiled, glad for the sunlight shining on her strong, dark hair.

"Ah, *buena, buena, buena!*" she greeted him, running to him as he came to the metal gate. "*Tío querido, entre.*"

He gave his *favorita* a huge *abrazo*. "Faustino's still sitting in the dark?"

"No, no! He left this morning. The first time in more than a month."

"That's a hopeful sign." He stood back to look at his niece and putting his hands on her shoulders, he turned her around. "You must take more care with your dressing," he said, smiling. "Old clothes like this make you look unlucky." He chose his words carefully because to him she looked "unloved" more than merely unlucky. He, on the other hand, wore his *mayordomo*'s khaki shirt and pants with military pride. His work pants held Flora's careful, knife-edge crease.

Once inside, Procopio sank into the nearest chair at the kitchen table. He had come to voice his deep concern about Faustino's unreasonable misery and how he was neglecting his young family. A quick cup of coffee appeared in his hand, and Nicasia motioned to the can of evaporated milk, the top punched three times with an ice pick. Helping himself to a stream of the milk, he saw the imprints of other cups in the oilcloth and made a game of keeping his cup in the deepest indentation. He presumed it had been left by Faustino. Nicasia took a cup for herself and sat solidly down, smiling hopefully at her uncle.

"If anyone can help, *Tío*, it is you. Please tell me again what Faustino did that started this mess."

"*Nada. Hizo nada*," Procopio said, recalling that spring day when he was pruning the rose stalks. "Faustino came by to ask for some favor, and Michael seemed surprised to see him. Suddenly he insisted that Faustino learn English. 'It's the way of the future,' he said. Faustino grew stubborn and stomped out. Michael was just drunk; he didn't mean what he said. Tempest in a teapot."

"The *muchitos* speak English. Everyone does now."

Procopio reluctantly pulled the words out. "Michael was drinking whiskey. Sometimes he gets crazy and starts drinking." Nicasia nodded, not smiling, realizing how criticizing either of them caused Procopio to feel intensely disloyal. "He stopped for a while. Before they left."

"You've never, ever, complained about them before."

"Michael is a great artist. He's entitled to be dramatic."

"Of course!" Nicasia had always listened to her old *tío*; he was the first to notice how promising the adolescent Faustino had been as a youth.

And he could see her present misery, and how she wantedto walk out and go back home. She sat back and closed her eyes, trying not to weep. "He is breaking our hearts."

"He's a strong man. He'll come around, eventually."

"This will sound very strange, but I suspect that the Virgin over there is talking to Faustino late at night."

"That statue there?"

"All the time. He is the only one who hears Her. I sleep through it."

Procopio threw up his hands. "So Michael didn't really start all of this?"

"The Virgin, Jesus, the Heavenly Father—all of them counted on Faustino's being strong." Nicasia paused. "Adam and Eve. They all expected him to correct Michael's thinking."

"That would have made everything far worse. But now his guilt and blame are unbearable—for you and for everyone here."

Nicasia brought more coffee. "This is the first time he has left the house. I can breathe again."

"*Hija*, even the Mother Church stops Lenten penance after forty days. Faustino has gone on too long. It is terrible and wasteful." When he looked up, he saw tears streaming down her cheeks, and she gave in to sobbing.

"I can't cry in front of him."

He moved to her and held her, rocking; it seemed like a moment and a long time all at once. "What does your father think you should do?"

"He wants to"—and she stopped to wipe her tears—"give the Virgin to someone else. I grew up with Her, so I asked him to let Her stay. What harm can She do?"

As Procopio sat down again, he stared at the statue's glass eyes. Her gaze was vacant. "Didn't he give you the statue? I remember it from long ago, before you were born. It was Sor María de Jesús then before your mother said she's the Madonna."

She nodded yes. "I'm more worried that Faustino believes that the Devil has your *patrónes'* souls, and not his."

Procopio looked at her, saying nothing.

"I know they are good men," she said, and paused to wipe her eyes again. "You really love them."

"They would pay you good money for that Sor María statue," he said, calculating their delight with this treasure in the back of his mind. "They are collectors."

Nicasia's eyes pooled, her mouth would not close. Thoughts collided: Tía Serafina had sanctified her as The Blessed Virgin, The Queen of Heaven, and not the cloistered Sor María with her packs of devoted Indians. The men were not Catholics, and they were homosexuals; what good was money? She, the Mother of God, belonged in the family. The *hacienda* belonged in the family. Uncle Procopio betrayed his Hispanic heritage over and over and over. And now, again! Sell the Virgin Mary?

"You dare not think of asking for my *bulto*. She was given to me."

"Just don't let your father hand Her off. My *patrónes* will revere Her if only for the history of this lovely carving. If you like, I can bring you a fine Guadalupe statue for your shrine. One that does not talk to your husband all night."

Nicasia shook her head and squeezed her eyes shut. There were some things she could not, would not, do. After watching her husband and her family life disintegrate, trying to hold herself steady, not breaking down, she half stood, facing her uncle and yelled, "No!"

"*Corazón*," Procopio said, standing to reach out for her again. "Darling girl, I only want to make your life better."

"You believe homosexuals are in the state of mortal sin?" She whispered this into his shirt.

"I can't judge..." He smiled down at her.

"That's just what everyone says. No one will say yes or no." Her voice was harsh. "Except Faustino and Father Sebastiano." The good *padre* who offered the Sunday Mass in the *Misión San Miguel* was a legendary old windbag.

Procopio shook his head and held her tighter. "That withered Christian brother? Every Sunday, he rails against everything and everyone."

"The *muchitos* had nightmares about being thrown alive into hell's fires," she said without apology. "Faustino still goes to Mass."

"I know you and the boys stay home on Sundays." Procopio pictured Brother Sebastiano surrounding himself with images of the martyred Saint Sebastian, whose name he took. In the bloody, holy paintings, a handsome youth was bound naked to a stake or to an overhanging tree. A hundred arrows pierced his body as, eyes toward heaven, San Sebastian died blessing his tormentors. "Father Sebastiano is so old that he probably dreamed of being shot through with Apache arrows himself. Not a far-off fantasy at the time."

She wiped the sides of her face with a small smile.

"I was memorizing the catechism with Brother Sebastiano years before Faustino was climbing trees in Upper San Benicia," the smiling uncle reminisced. "Faustino appears to be the last to remember what we've all forgotten." He made her laugh, and she pulled away as he continued: "God loves all His children."

Standing behind him now, she leaned over his shoulder and said in a low voice, "Do you think there are any homosexuals in heaven? Have any died yet?"

"We don't know who is there. Serafina is, and I hope Elodio."

"Are your homosexuals even baptized?" Nicasia paused. "I'm not letting them have my statue; you know that."

Procopio smiled at her and shrugged, sorry that he had suggested selling the Mother of Jesus. "My *patrónes* are both kind and generous men," he insisted. "They will be back soon from studying art in the great museums of France." He finished his coffee and looked into his niece's eyes with such intensity that she dared not pull away.

"I believe," he began, "that artists who do beautiful paintings do them as their prayer. Beauty comes from God. Michael's paintings are filled with beautiful color. I don't understand them, but I know it's a prayer."

"I believe my boys, my Melo and Franque, are a prayer..." She said this slowly, considering her uncle's words. As she contemplated this possibility, her world grew larger. Huge, in fact.

"Studying art is a prayer for them..."

"Then they are lucky," she said. "I pray only for Faustino now."

Procopio looked at her suddenly and slapped the table. "You almost made me forget why I've come to see you." He shook his head. "It's the gringos; they're coming back from their ocean voyage."

"Faustino hoped they'd never come back." And she shook her head with a wry smile.

"No, they'll be back soon. Richard and Michael wrote me to tell you they will need you to help with a big celebration."

Nicasia looked conflicted. "I can't. Going there is bad for Faustino."

"I have an idea for Faustino," he began.

She nodded. "Well, outside of prayer, nothing else works. Everyone here prays—they are prayer warriors, these Garcías. They all keep praying for Faustino and for me."

Her uncle stood. "I can get Faustino work outside the *hacienda*, not inside."

Nicasia thanked her uncle. "Oh, try, please..." When she walked her uncle to the door, she saw Faustino coming home in the distance, leading his burro stacked high with wood for the cookstove.

Three weeks later, Procopio filled the doorway to give Nicasia a high sign, thumbs up. Faustino merely shrugged as he glanced up from his bowl of simmered beans. Procopio brushed past him with a tentative smile and sank into an empty chair. Faustino barely acknowledged his presence until Nicasia brought Procopio the ready cup of coffee and prodded him into talking.

"Go on," she said. "*Díme!*"

"We are going to mud the entire house. The *patrónes* have asked me to gather *trabajadores* to plaster their *hacienda*. I have five men for the team, and I need one more." He pointed his lips at Faustino. "*Tú.*"

Nicasia shot a look at her husband, knowing this plan had been hatched mainly to help her. Faustino's mind was elsewhere.

"Hey, *Primo*, they need some help. It will do you good to go out with your *cuates*. If you go, Nicasia will make the enchiladas with the other *mujercitas*." Procopio smiled invitingly.

"Never. Going. Back. There," Faustino said, separating the words. Never again. Procopio cast his glance down to the blue and white coffee cup and waited. Nicasia flashed a grateful smile, and later when she walked him to the door, she thanked him, hoping Faustino would come around.

Procopio had convinced Richard and Michael to provide the money and have the Tesuque Pueblo deliver their choice dirt. The companionship alone would help Faustino.

After another fitful sleep, Faustino relented. "I will refuse their money," he said as he left to find Procopio and join the brigade.

Nicasia knew there were two ways to tunnel into a wall. And one was from the outside.

CHAPTER FOURTEEN

"Faustino, my faithful servant, take heart. I am with you in your misery." These words floated into Faustino's dream; he recognized the feminine music in Her Castilian lisp.

"My Lady?" He answered. In the darkness, the sound of his own voice awakened him.

Faustino slipped out of bed, tiptoeing to the shrine. He did not want Nicasia to intercept his prayed-for tryst with the Queen of Heaven. He was Her lover, Her sworn knight. Kneeling on the cool floor at Her feet, looking up, he could not see Her approving eyes.

He stood to bring the statue forward in the *nicho*, the better to adore Her. Returning to his knees, he caressed Her small head with his eyes, his heart pleading for Her whispers.

But Her silence hung in the air.

"Gracious Madonna, please do not leave me like this. Speak to me, please!" Still She waited, and Faustino's knees were wicking cold off the floor. He shivered. "Please Most Blessed Virgin, I am your servant-champion."

"In the library, you will find a chaste woman; seek her out. Do not be afraid for I will be with you."

"My Lady." Faustino bowed lower before her. He knew that library books were guarded like newborn chicks under pinch-faced mams, certainly all unsullied.

"As You wish, my Queen." Overcome with heaviness, he submitted, and then he returned to a sleep drugged with menace. He implored morning to spare him, yet he arose and pulled on his best work pants. *"Como Usted me manda,"* the humble servant had said and began to plod his way to the public library. Olivia María brayed to come with him.

Faustino showed signs of breaking out of his madness soon after his prescribed convocation. It was a warm August weekday with the monsoon clouds building over the Sangres when, as usual, Paco slept leaning against the shady side of his house under his spindly limbed apple trees. Faustino dozed next door in the kitchen rocking chair, a spiral notebook having fallen from his hand. Most of the houses were silent, and the afternoon atmosphere grew thick with promised rain.

Procopio stopped on the dirt street outside the García adobe and set the brake on his truck. He cut the engine and honked a tinny bleat at the same time. The door to Faustino's house was wide open, but looking inside he could only discern the deep hollow of the front room, dark as a gullet. Behind Faustino's home, seven similar García adobes appeared sound asleep. Above the flat roofs, a lowering, gray thunderhead would soon end the siestas by routing the sleepers with a sharp clap of lightning followed by the approving resonance of deep thunder. After a gust of wind, cold drops of rain would turn the bare dirt yards to mud, sending the ruffled chickens squawking for shelter. Faustino, jolted awake, might hurry to lead his burro to the shed as surely as Nicasia would jump to close the open windows and shut the front door.

Meanwhile, Procopio hit his horn a second time, arousing no one. The cloud's shadow crossed over the hood of his truck as he took an impatient breath. Olivia María stood under the apricot tree, shaking her furry head and periscoping her ears as if to greet him. She scratched her hindquarters on the hard edge of a nearby broken wagon that had baked in place over several years, a plaything for the boys when they were younger. Most yards hoarded parts of once useful things. Nothing was ever discarded; even the profane dirt was mounded for making clay for the roofs and floors and for firing bean pots, while the small fistfuls of sacred dirt were carefully shelved in jars.

"*Venga*, Faustino, *eh hombre?*" he called out the open window of the cab and gave a quick, tinny honk. Olivia María brayed her annoyance, predictably drawing Nicasia's quick step to the open doorway to scold the miserable beast. "*Cállate!*"

When she saw her gracious, old uncle climbing out of his pickup truck, she beamed at him.

"Elk for you," he said, moving his chin toward the bed of his truck.

She was delighted to spot a bulk wrapped in burlap. "*A ver?*" she sang back. Following him, she stepped to the pickup bed to inspect.

"Hindquarter of an elk." Procopio shouldered the sack, heaving it over the side rails of his truck. His shirt bore a bright red stain and a watery streak. His wife would certainly ask him to take more care; the fresh blood had to be soaked off.

"*Qué bien, Tío!*" she cooed. Elk was perfect. "*Los Señores* Miguel y Ricardo will come back on the *tren* from Chicago tomorrow." Nicasia bounced to the house, stepping aside to allow him into the front room, smiling broadly. He set the heavy sack on the compacted dirt floor; a new bloodstain would seep unnoticed into the dirt hardened with the blood of slaughtered pigs over the fifty years past.

"Faustino!" she called. His best sleep was during the day and hardly at all at night these past few months.

"*Qué?*" he called out, startled. The house was not on fire and the storm had not yet broken, so he settled back with his mouth open, his eyes closed. Inadvertently, his left hand reached to search for his pocket. Not finding what he sought, he snapped alert with a snort of alarm.

Neither Procopio nor Nicasia spoke as they stood silhouetted in the doorway, the glaring sunlight behind them, gravely observing him in his confusion. Faustino was unable at first to distinguish either his wife or Procopio; once his eyes adjusted to them, he shook his head and returned to his search for whatever he was missing.

"Ahh!" he said, discovering a spiral notebook on the floor.

"For a moment, *Primo*, you had us worried again," Procopio said. Informed that Faustino's depression might be weakening, the old uncle took most of the credit, convinced that his plastering idea had done the trick. Nicasia gave him a feeble smile because she gave credit to the sacred dirt and her own (and the entire García compound's) constant prayers.

"I told all of you to stop worrying about me. I mean it."

"*Querido*," his wife began, "*Tío* Procopio brought this meat for us; can you please take it to the shed?"

"We still have plenty to eat here. Shoes for the *hitos*." Faustino had maintained that his misery had caused his family no deprivation. Whether he worked or not, everything continued the same; the *vecinos* or Nicasia's large family would bring over what was needed. In fact, everyone owed him for his generosity as a *vecino* over many years. He was owed, he claimed.

Nicasia turned in surprise. Procopio cocked his head to stare.

Faustino began with a stunning announcement: "I found the day in history when God created our world and Adam and Eve." He produced his notebook and smiled victoriously. "I found this historic date in the library downtown."

Nicasia shot Procopio a dumbfounded look, but with Faustino there was much she did not know or understand. Surprised he'd gone to the library, she had no idea what he was talking about.

"Please be clear," Procopio said. "I remember that you and Michael fought over Adam and Eve but I don't remember anything about dates... dates for what?"

"God created the world on October 23, 4004 BC, at 9:00 in the morning. The librarian said she read somewhere in a book that a famous bishop in London, England, had written this date in his Bible."

Nicasia and Procopio both stared at Faustino, trying to make out what he meant. When they did, a shiver ran through them. It felt like another invitation to pass through the gate to the altar. God moved closer, present in the room in fact. Or at least nearby.

"Add five days for *Adan y Eva*," he said, patting the notebook in his breast pocket. "Not gorillas." Nicasia was weak with relief; the war was ended and the Church had been saved.

Procopio found a chair to drop onto. "When?"

Faustino repeated the date for him and withdrew the hard facts from his pocket. "Bishop..."—he leafed through to the worn page—

"James Ussher. *Inglés, famoso.*" His voice grew insistent. "He wrote it three hundred years ago. It is history."

Nicasia swallowed this sweet fact slowly until it became hers, flowing with her blood. She, too, pulled a wooden chair to her and sat. "*Dónde están los muchitos?*" She needed to pass on this exhumed truth, to fasten it to her sons. Their home had been saved; education saved her husband. Truth was written in black and white.

Faustino moved toward the open door. Skirting the sack of elk, he called outside for the boys, who had been spending the days by the river stacking rocks, making their own swimming hole. "*Franque! Ven acá! Vengan, Melo y Franque.*" The boys had heard him; already they were scampering past Paco, awakening him. In the near distance, Faustino heard Paco's dogs growing louder, marking the boys' passage until the pack had barked themselves into a frenzy. By the time they ran breathless into the yard, Faustino had taken up the moist sack. They stared after their father as he strode toward the shed, shouldering the meat. He looked taller, and his gait was determined. He was smiling.

Once inside, the boys were asked to sit quietly. "We are waiting for your father to come back."

As they waited, both Procopio and Nicasia repeated the date to themselves: "October 23, 4004 BC, at 9:00 a.m."

When Faustino reentered the house, he went to the sink to wash his hands while the boys stared. With his mouth, Faustino motioned for the boys to take chairs on the far side of the table. Eyeing each other askance, they did as they were told. He gave the much-handled notebook to Franque, the elder. "We will take this to Padre Sebastiano. He has known me since I was your age, when he showed me the secret stairs to the bell tower." Franque looked at the small page and then quickly up to his father's face, questioning. He glanced at Procopio with misgivings.

Nicasia placed both hands on her heart, a sign that something God-driven had come over Faustino, had saved him, had saved all of them. "Your father has Biblical proof that Adam and Eve did live in the Garden of Eden, that they were created by God and looked just like God." She squeezed her eyes shut to prevent tears from flowing. "They lived!" she said. "They were real and they were beautiful."

Franque, the open notebook still in his hand, understood that this news had the power to heal their father of his anguish. Mother Mary Herself had answered their perplexed and desperate pleas. Tears furrowed his dusty cheeks.

Nicasia held out her hand. "Wash up and change your clothes," she said. "I'll hold the paper."

Procopio took a deep, restorative breath, stood to leave, and headed out to his *troque* on the street. Waving good-bye to him from the door, Nicasia was relieved knowing that the Bible was historical fact, that her husband's combat had value. She turned back into the kitchen and called, "Don't forget to change your shoes..." Once the boys were in their Sunday clothes, she pronounced them ready to march their father's prize to the Christian Brothers School for verification from the renowned *padre*.

"He can read Latin," Melo said as Faustino dusted off his own pants and turned to follow his sons for the ten-minute stroll to College Street with revelation in hand. "Everyone there can." Faustino assured them that it wouldn't be necessary to know Latin to talk to the *padre*.

Surrounded by playing fields and trees watered by the Santa Fe River, the school was a large, two-story building, silent now for summer vacation. Next to it in Barrio Analco, the old worker's settlement, the Misión San Miguel doors were closed to the street. Entering the *colegio*, they encountered a drowsy woman behind the admittance desk. She looked up as the father and his two sons entered. "We are bringing something of immense value to Padre Sebastiano. He knows me," Faustino announced in an overloud voice. The boys, filled with scorn for any mention of St. Michael's College, hung back in their father's shadow, hoping to go unnoticed.

"Second floor, room...ah, room. I don't know. Just go up and you'll find him," she said. "He's the only one up there."

The stern padre was seated behind a wooden desk in his spare office when the three Garcías came down the hallway, trying to muffle the echo from their steps. Indeed, there was no one in any room except one. The door was open; they knocked on the doorpost. The glum man of God looked up from his breviary and gave a shivering smile. Behind his desk was a life-sized painting of his arrow-shot patron saint. Both boys held their breath, thankful not to have been sent to this school.

"I hate it here," Melo whispered to Franque.

"*Permiso*, Padre Sebastiano?" Faustino said, looking at the skeleton of a priest. The *padre* put aside his breviary and grimaced. He was met with an unkempt peasant in soiled clothes, who in his rush had not combed his own hair although the two young boys were dressed for Sunday Mass.

"Our classes are quite full. Sorry. You might apply for next year," he told them firmly, showing no memory of their father as a boy or that he had prepared both sons for their First Communions.

"No, no! We've come with a wonderful discovery." Faustino placed his hands on his sons' heads. "We have found written proof of the day on which God created our world!" The *padre* leaned across his desk, straining to hear. His eyebrows raised in interest. Franque and Melo leaned toward their old catechist.

"*De veras*! I mean it," said Faustino. "I have the date, *la mera fecha*." He pounded the desk with his fist to awaken this priest.

The severe *sacerdote* shook his head and continued to stare at Faustino, his mouth slack. It was a vacant stare. "I don't understand," he said.

"You don't understand what?" Faustino demanded, setting his book on the desk within reach of the priest. The *padre* was as deaf to the truth as the hell-fated Freethinkers. "What do you not understand when I tell you that I have the date, the exact date when God created the Earth?" He realized slowly now that the old priest was senile. This scientific information must be beyond his understanding, beyond his caring. Or, Faustino considered, had he been so isolated that he had not perceived the horrendous threat the invasion of the gringos posed to the Holy Catholic Church?

"Nine o'clock in the morning, on October 23, four thousand and four years *antes de Jesucristo*!" Faustino spoke slowly and clearly, each word louder.

The old man gave a flash of interest and then closed down again.

Faustino stood and prepared to leave. The emaciated priest stretched out a hand for the slip of paper. Faustino debated whether to risk parting from it. To him, it was evidence of the first parents' existence, as valuable and worn as the treasure map. In the end, the *padre*, rheumy eyed, took it in his hands to examine it. He placed it on the bare desktop.

"It is wrong," he said. "The world was created years earlier. At least four thousand years earlier. This date is too late. It is wrong."

"Thank you, Father," was all Faustino could manage. He snatched back the notebook. The three Garcías turned to leave the old man to his daily office. They walked down the waxed hallway, down the stairs, and out into the coming storm with its rush of wind that chased leaves and loose papers into corners. The lightning struck before they had reached the corner and the sharp rain began to pound them. Melo stuck out his tongue to taste the same rain that must have fallen on Eden on the third day, two days before Adam's birthday. To Faustino's satisfaction, Padre Sebastiano had validated his discovery, with the small alteration of the year. When he arrived home, soaking, he put the rain-wet paper under the Virgin's foot, on top of the map.

To celebrate Faustino's epiphany, his inspired recovery, the following Sunday after Holy Mass, the García families held a *recepción* in the front yard. A large keg of beer sat on a tabletop balanced on two sawhorses shaded by the apricot tree. Nicasia smiled with such gratitude, giving full credit for her husband's miraculous cure to the thousands of prayers they had all said for him. She came out the front door bearing a tray filled high with her exceptional elk-stuffed empanadas. The boys' washed hair shone satin-black in the sunlight.

A *lechón* lay buried under the hot rocks in the cooking pit, and a larger part of Procopio's elk had been sent over for the feast. Neighbors brought *chicos, enchiladas tamales* and several dishes featuring the ever-abundant green and yellow squashes. In a sense, it was both a type of graduation celebration and possibly a feast to reward the *vecino* well-wishers.

Toward dark, Nicasia readied a platter of ninety small pork and chicken *tamales*, which Faustino bore proudly over his head, welcoming more neighbors. "'Do you have books on Adam and Eve?' I asked the lady at the library," Faustino said, explaining his miraculous turnaround as best he could to the men gathered at the keg. "She claimed the Bible had the best story about it but that this old Bible scholar in England knew just when it all happened."

"'So, why don't the Freethinkers know this?' I demanded. But she, too, was dumbfounded; it has been in print for three hundred long years!"

Paco squinted his eyes and nodded his head. "It was written in English, right?"

"The bishop lived in London, England," Faustino said. "Unless he wrote in Latin."

Paco bobbed his head.

"It's not like he wrote it in Chinese." Faustino turned to Procopio. "Take this historical information to your *patrónes* and tell me they don't believe in the Bible now!"

Nicasia, standing by the plank table, proclaimed to the women that her husband had received a vision and from that moment had figuratively taken up his cane and walked. "It's like he had never read the Bible before." She held them rapt as she added, "He said he lost his taste for alcohol. He'll never have another whiskey."

"When a man gets a visitation from Mary, the Mother of God, this can happen!"

Nicasia took this explanation into consideration; it was entirely possible. "I hadn't thought of that, but of course! Faustino said that his vision was like a conversion."

He had said: "I saw the firmament coming into being. I saw the waters, the colors, and the glorious garden with a gem-like, feathered serpent that, too, lost his footing at the Fall." Nicasia repeated his words for they were like poetry: "I saw the handsomeness of a God-mirrored man and his beguiling, weak wife. I know their names, their birthdays, their choices and the strength they required to sustain themselves, similar to all of us here on the land—like the *primeros fundadores*."

"Faustino, all of us, we are sons of Adam, made in the likeness of God." Nicasia thrilled in his Virgin-inspired revelation. "Apes live in zoos."

Faustino had been healed by this vision. He spoke of things they all believed with a new clarity, a warrior's faith. *"Por Dios y Santiago!"*

CHAPTER FIFTEEN

Leading his burro, Faustino followed Paco up the mountain to carry out a poached deer, Paco's mutts parading alongside. They trailed outside the fence of the protected watershed to where the *floresta* met the steep winding prisoners' road. The overgrazed mountain had been closed off since 1932, and the undergrowth flourished. Paco worried that he'd not be able to relocate his kill. As they trailed uphill, Faustino was silently hatching his newest scheme to hack out the gold from a house he had vowed never to enter. A runaway truck might well break a hole in the kitchen wall of Tía Serafina's house facing the street by hitting it dead-on. "Tell your brother Panky to sell me his truck. We coulda' got all this meat out last night."

"A truck would be a help. For sure, we can't get the whole *anta* out on one lousy burro," Paco said. "Panky wants to sell it, so he don't want me drivin' his precious *troque*." It was cool in the trees, and being in the watershed was illegal, so just being on the mountain made their hearts drum. "So I end up with you and your stupid burro."

"We better get there fast; what the coyotes leave, we can take out in our back pockets," Faustino said, as they followed the fence line searching for the wires Paco had cut to mark where the doe had fallen. "I don't see any vultures circling." Faustino thought it was a waste of time walking up the mountain with only a burro and a pack of dogs. "Might be nothing but bones left now."

"I'd let the vultures have some pickings if I get enough for you and me," Paco said, huffing from exertion. "And the tongue, especially the tongue."

"Channy'll come. He always does," Faustino continued. "Wouldn't need to bother him if I had a truck." They walked softly, leading Olivia María slowly through the fallen debris and needles, past scrub oak and stray alfalfa holding over from years past. As they walked, they listened so intently for coyotes that their breathing seemed too loud. "Tell Panky I'll pay him later. In gold."

Panky, Pancracio Luis Carlos Gurulé, owned an exceptionally sturdy truck. He was the youngest cousin in Paco's large family, and although he was a genius, times now were brutal and he was broke.

"What'd you need a truck for?" Paco asked Faustino.

"Work. I got big work to do. You too. I'll get you on a job mudding Tía Serafina's house?"

Paco lit up. "And you need Panky's truck?" Paco said. "Those Anglos still got whiskey?"

"A peso a day. No hooch."

Paco shrugged and gestured his hand back and forth until his thumb shot up: "Count me in!"

Faustino hid his smile, and after a half hour more of walking uphill through the dense forest, they heard the sound of pistons throbbing as a vehicle approached. Chances were good that Channy had brought the Forest Service pickup to pack out their meat for them. The barking dogs stopped their noise and sniffed the air; Olivia María bellowed.

"*Cállate*! Shut up!" Faustino grabbed his stubborn burro, commanding her like a dog, and she turned her ears to him giving a misleading impression of intelligence. Then she brayed again, answering the metal clatter of the truck.

"Tell Panky I'm as good as gold." Faustino grinned, watching the government truck pull up on the other side of the fence. It was Channy, right when they needed him. If they'd had a telephone, a call would have spoiled it. With a phone call, he might be early or late, but never as welcome as when he astoundingly appeared out of nowhere.

And from the driver's open window, Channy's grin confirmed what Paco knew: if you've got *vecinos*, you got all you need. Channy was Faustino's *pegado*, still glued together as close as humanly possible.

"*Ay*, Channy!" The men, the dogs and the burro came out in plain sight. Faustino waved his arms. "Channy! You found us!"

Channy cut his engine and got out of the Department of Agriculture truck dressed in his Forest Service uniform. "You knew I'd get here," he said, taking his clippers from the truck to cut the fence. "Saw a mess of buzzards up yonder," he said with a grin, stepping through the fence and coming over to them. "I figured it was your kill."

"Hey, *hombre*, good to see you." Their heads bobbed happily.

"I heard coyotes howlin' too." Channy gave both men *abrazos*, thumping their backs. He then turned to give Faustino a second long *abrazo* on their private mountain.

"Anybody follow you?" Faustino asked. He pressed his lips together, hatching a plan. "If I get me a truck and bring it up here, is there some jerk doing night patrol up here?"

"Nope," Channy said, climbing back into the big pickup. "No night patrol."

"Good," Faustino said. The forest was as safe a place to bring the treasure as any.

"I need a hand packing your deer out," Channy said to Paco in all seriousness. The three men laughed. Paco was useless. Even the burro wouldn't follow him back down into town; that's what he had Faustino for.

"But before we go up there"—Channy handed Paco the pliers—"I'm gonna show you how to put the fence back up. How to fix your own damned cuts..."

"He's slow to learn," Faustino said. Just seeing Channy made him genuinely happy. "I'll get back down before you do." He patted Olivia María, and a cloud of dust rose off her. Then he whistled to the dogs and turned downhill. "I'll be waiting for you to bring that deer down."

Channy swung into the cab and shifted into first, motioning for Paco to hop in next to him. The rattling and engine poundings lingered in the kicked up dust as they pushed off into the forest to find the meat. Paco asked, "Think there's anything left of my kill?"

"Hopin' so for your sake," Channy said. "What's new with you?"

"I'm gonna get paid one peso each day to bring 'em beer and haul water while Procopio and them plaster mud on Tía Serafina's old house." His grin stretched wide enough that Channy could count the missing molars.

"That's great," Channy said. "Where do you figure that deer is anyway?"

"Keep going." Paco pointed into the trees. "Sure am grateful to you."

"There's this thing about fences," Faustino told Nicasia later that night, waving his spoon in the air. "Only the folks who put 'em up care. Others pay no mind to fences unless somebody's got a gun."

He sat at the table propped on his elbows, hovering over a cup of coffee. Nicasia had been standing near the stove, patting out tortillas before tossing them on the *comal*. She dropped the one in her hand on the heated plate and turned to look at Faustino. He was starting to come around after the big Adam and Eve scrap, but he wasn't completely back like before. He had aged, but at least he slept quietly now, not talking to himself and tossing.

"Channy come get you today?"

"Right on time. Paco knew Channy'd catch on when he saw the vultures. Sometimes he acts smarter than he is. Channy was right there to haul it out. Easy, in the Forest Service truck."

"What if some other ranger had found you? Some Anglo?" She continued patting out tortillas. "They make up new laws every week, and they don't write them down with disappearing ink."

"But we're too smart," Faustino said, tapping his temple, and he meant it. "Anglo *locos* remind me of their fences. But they don't realize if we see a fence, we know there's something we need inside." He paused awhile and then added, "Fences actually sing out loud to us."

Nicasia snatched a burning tortilla from the *comal* as the smoke filled the kitchen, rising to lick the ceiling. She sensed he was dreaming of the treasure again. Thoughts traveled like smoke, wrapping around each person, floating out the window. They could even creep into anyone who walked by. When Faustino thought about the gold, Nicasia caught a picture of gold in her brain that nudged out other thoughts. Dreams, too, moved from pillow to pillow. Now the daydream of gold floated across the room and tickled her neck, growing in size and color—and, of course, she saw the curse grow, too. Distracted, she burned three more tortillas.

Meeting the familiar waft of toasted *masa*, Channy, still in his khaki uniform, did not bother to call out at the open door. In his hand he held two bottles of beer that were quickly warming, so he counted on Nicasia's having some ice in that icebox of hers. Adjusting his eyes, he came into the smoky kitchen calling out, "*Buenas!*"

Faustino looked up and grinned. "*Hola, amigo!*" He bolted from the table to give Channy one of his own long, strong *abrazos*. Channy could be trusted. If Faustino ever needed help, Channy was his first pick.

"I brought what was left of the *anta* in the back of the truck. Less than half is better than nothing."

"*Gracias,*" Faustino said, putting his arm over Channy's shoulder with a brotherly shove. Standing back, he smiled, noting that Channy was getting fat ever since he and Ana Lisa had gotten married. He was still strong, though.

"I'm just a skinny old dog still, but you are *muy guapo, muy hombre,*" Faustino said.

"Getting fat," Channy said, offering Faustino one of the large beer bottles. "*Y los hijos?*" he asked. Nicasia had been watching the two old friends with a reminiscent smile. At the mention of her boys, she snapped back to the present.

"*Bien. Bien.*" She bragged that both boys were getting high marks. They would go very far in this new world with reading so many books and being excellent at long division. Franque, especially, could become governor one day because he had such a nice way of talking to people, even switching languages midsentence, midthought.

Channy nodded back to her. Childless still, his sweet, trusting Ana Lisa worked as a sales clerk on the Plaza, selling silver buckles and necklaces to the Fred Harvey tourists. Lately there had been an influx of famous people riding the trains into town to stay at the Harvey House, completely turning the poor girl's head. She came home with exciting gossip about the movie stars she met, and now she was used to being the center of attention. They all agreed that the sooner Ana Lisa got pregnant and left that shop, the better. She was dressing like a gringo covered in Indian jewelry, wearing the broomstick skirts that the movie stars all wanted now. The last famous movie star nearly bought out the shop, and the boss gave Ana Lisa a bonus.

"*Qué pasa*?" Nicasia asked Channy with a straight, meaningful look. "Not pregnant yet?"

"She hasn't said nothing." Channy shrugged his shoulders, and Faustino slapped him on the back. He understood Channy had been laying track every night, but still no *hijos*.

Nicasia stayed at her woodstove, grilling more tortillas while the two men sat at the kitchen table, elbows on the oilcloth, beers in hand. "Next time you shoot a *bicho*," Channy started in, "you better tell me when you are coming up so nobody finds out and starts to haul your asses in!"

"Oh man, this government is Anglo crazy!" Faustino said. "Everything around here is scary crazy..." And as though he could not stop himself, he proceeded to tell Channy about the marble bathroom in the *dispenza* and what was in the walls. "I'd say chances are fifty-fifty those *hotos* have taken my gold and made it into a frame for the mirror."

"How much gold do you think there is?" Channy asked, surprised. He had been completely in the dark.

"Enough for you and me to buy back the *floresta*."

"Who hid it there to begin with?"

"The guy who found the treasure buried next to the wagon with the gold-wrapped wheels. Carlota's jewels, the ones Apache Chief Vitorio tried to get."

"You don't know who hid it, actually?"

"No, nobody knows, and nobody knows where it is. Elodio tried to find it and couldn't, but it's there. I've got the map.

"When we get our hands on it, I'm quittin' this job of locking all my buddies out of the forest every night. Got a plan?"

"Yeah, this has to work." Faustino explained how he and Paco were going to work on the outside walls. "First, we get the walls all wet, and then we smash into the kitchen wall with the truck. Once we get it really wet."

"Crazy! You can't bash through a double-adobe wall and just walk away."

"So what if I drill holes through the adobe wall to weaken it?" Faustino flexed the fingers on both of his calloused hands. He could feel the cool mud plaster between his fingers; as with what was left of the deer, half of the gold was better than nothing. He needed the help of the one person he'd always shared with.

Channy mulled the plan over. "You gotta do it from the inside of the house, I'm telling you."

"I can't. You can, maybe. I made a vow I'd never go inside that place again. The only work I got now is outside, plastering. Monday, we start." Faustino knew pretty much where to chip, but he refused to go inside. That was where the truck came into the picture.

"You scare me. You know the crazy Great Society of Whitemen's gonna skin you alive. That's before they hang you up real high."

"No, I've thought it through! First, I get this truck and my foot slips, see...I roll out, and the truck goes through the wall. Looks like another dumb accident."

"Driving through the wall in a truck will get you dead, and they'll make me bring you home wrapped in burlap."

"The truck I got my eye on already looks like it's been through some walls."

"It won't work..."

"Don't worry about me," Faustino said, crossing himself to guarantee the Blessed Mother's support. "I'll be okay. Don't tell anyone. Only you and me and Nicasia. Nobody else. Swear? Not even Ana Lisa." Faustino made Channy agree.

"Especially not Paco."

Channy polished off the beer. "The only way is to get inside the house."

"No can do," Faustino said, and Nicasia turned from the stove, letting another tortilla burn. "I'm getting Panky's *troque* and bashing down the wall."

"You're gonna kill yourself."

"The Virgin here says it'll work," Faustino said. The two men shouted a whooping war cry and clinked their warm bottles, toasting the Virgin. Aware of the Marian statue's steady stare, they again raised a toast to Her in Her shrine. "A la Madre Purísima!"

"*Dios y Santiago*! All we gotta do is pick the gold coins out of the mess," Channy said. "The sky's the limit, then."

"The *patrones'*ll even pay us to haul the rubble out." Faustino no longer felt alone and in secret. They'd drive the mud up to the watershed and pan out the gold by the Santa Fe river at night with the headlights on. "You sure there are no night guards up there?"

"I'll be with you the whole time. Nothing to worry about."

Early evening the following day, the ponderous thunderheads weighed on the peaks of the Sangre de Cristos. A curtain of rain moved south across the broad valley, bisecting the Rio Grande's rift. More clouds stacked twenty thousand feet into the sky, sending strips and ribbons of rain slanted by the wind. *Somas* evaporated before touching the ground. Standing on the roofs, the *santefesinos* counted as many as seven storms crossing the expanse, all bringing rain. They scanned the sky above the faraway colony, so vast and beautiful.

A platter of venison tongue *empanadas* in her hands, Nicasia walked sedately with Faustino from their two-room house to Paco's yard, rousing the dogs and waking Paco himself.

"Ooof!" said Paco, trying to sit up. His feet had fallen asleep. "*Dame unos, por favor,*" he said when he spotted the warm pastries.

"Call your dogs off," Nicasia said as one of the Taos yellows jumped at her skirts to get at the platter. Paco yelled at them and stood up to grab some *empanadas* for himself. Still crowding around, the dogs paid him no mind, so he kicked them away. They were filled with poached meat, a small gift from Uncle Sam—before Sam, it had been free for the taking. Meat had always been God's gift.

"*Sabrosas*!" he announced, having swallowed two at the same time. Some crumbs fell from his mouth, and three dogs lunged for them.

"We got work coming up," Faustino said. "So, I don't know how, but you gotta get me Panky's truck. That thing's all steel, and it's big enough."

"How you payin' for it?" Paco asked.

"I told you I'll give ten *reales* down, and the rest real fast. Then I get you a *real* each day for work," he said, adding "*Ojalá*!" which meant, *si Dios quiere*, or *God willing*, and so forth.

Paco's eyebrows shot up and he nodded happily. "I already told you yes, on the mountain, yes?" Men were known to work for less. Faustino took Paco by the shoulder and said, "No *troque*, no work."

The following morning, Paco arrived at the García gate in a dented Ford truck, leaning on the old horn that had the same pitch as the burro's infuriating braying. Nicasia, inside, had been listening to her crackling radio, hips moving to the music as she ironed her boys' shirts. Irritated by the truck outside, she slammed the iron down on the collar of Melo's white Sunday shirt. The kitchen reeked of toasted starch. The horn grated on her and reminded her how much she hated Olivia María. Closing the door would not help.

"Faustino, *compa*, *venga*!" Paco yelled outside the house, his engine gunning, pistons still firing loudly. Nicasia slid the iron back and forth and then shunted it over to the wood cookstove. She turned the music louder to cover the frantic engine outside and placed the iron on a cool corner of the stove.

She called out the door, "*Faustino no está*." The engine continued to ratchet. Olivia María had not stopped her burro screech, and the pebble rattles in the coughing pistons grew even louder. Three yellow dogs circled in the back of the truck barking joyfully, and her own disgruntled chickens protested in their pen while Olivia María never stopped pitching in. A new baby was sleeping three doors down, and this truck stirred the uproar into a full-scale battle assault!

"Quiet!" She rushed out of the house. "What's this commotion all about? *Qué pasa*?"

"My *hermancito* said he's gotta sell it," Paco announced regarding the truck. "It's almost empty and needs oil. Takes four pesos to fill it up, and he says it's not worth it anymore."

Nicasia knew all about this youngest of the eleven Gurulé children, the "genius" of the family. Now his truck was there stinking up the dirt street, back pipes belching smoke.

"Faustino needs it. It's almost new. Fifty pesos and it's his," Paco said, cutting the engine. As the engine died in slow fits, the sun exaggerated the shadows of the dents. The color had faded from bright red to pink.

"How does Faustino think he's going to pay for this *troque*? If Pancracio is so smart, he'll sell it to someone else."

"It's a long story. You got some coffee?" Paco headed into the house aiming for an empty chair around the table. As Nicasia reheated the pot, Paco, lonely for anyone who would listen to him, launched into his story that Nicasia knew only too well. It began as always with the bad luck of the dust bowl and a bloodless invasion of gringos, their cows and their illegal tax sales. She knew it all, short of the last part, the part about why the truck was parked outside her gate.

Paco put six spoonfuls of sugar in his cup of coffee and settled back into the story of Panky's faded, red truck. "Elodio's boy, Junior, had a son, Pancracio, who rode only stallions with *huevos*. I already told you that?"

"*Sí.*"

"And how he bought the red Chevy truck because he said it, too, had *huevos*? I told you that too?" She shook her head no and wet her lower lip with her tongue, suspecting that Pancracio had jumped camp in a stolen truck. Still, there was a justice in that; he'd been owed—they were all owed. She sat wanting to know where Panky was living, if he was too old for a wife. Important facts she needed to know.

"Did Panky teach you how to drive?" she asked Paco flatly, considering in the back of her mind that she'd be happy to replace Olivia María with anything, even a noisy contraption.

"Driving is easy. The *trocón*, lots bigger than a stupid *troque*, speaks Spanish. *Primero, segundo, y tercero adelante, y número quatro atrás.*" One, two, three forward, one reverse. "So simple that children can drive. I'll show you."

Paco got up, left the house, climbed into the cab, pushed the starter, leaned out the window, and continued to talk, barely audible through the mechanical clatter. He waved as he spun the truck onto the dirt, kicking up pebbles. With her right hand, Nicasia pointed downhill to her husband walking home with the two boys. Spotting the truck, they broke into a run.

When he wasn't waving his spoon for emphasis, Faustino's conversation had always been restrained. Now, however, he was invigorated just describing their future with a truck and earning money with it, dotted with a few references to paying for it by finding the lost treasure. Nicasia tried to avoid taking a stand by changing the subject when mention of either the treasure or the truck surfaced. Regarding the gold, hadn't Serafina insisted that it was earmarked to pay for her sons' Christian Brothers education? Not for a truck. So she listened and changed the subject.

"I could deliver more than wood to people," Faustino chirped between mouthfuls of *frijoles*. To which Nicasia replied, "Do you want the boys to be altar boys this year?"

He'd say: "If I go all the way up to the top of Rowe Mesa, I can cut cedar posts to sell."

She'd say: "Your father's been dead three months now, and your mama's birthday is next week."

But, when he'd say: "Did you feed Olivia María?"

She'd say: "No."

CHAPTER SIXTEEN

Habia una vez. In better times, the *vecinos* went house to house to plaster the outer walls with a fresh coat of mud on warm days well after the last winter freeze. The entire community pitched in, the women singing, gossiping, flirting and telling jokes while the men oversaw the mud. Mudding was in Procopio's blood; he was born to the feel of it. With the authority of a chef, he would approve the mixture before throwing in that last handful of straw to shine in the blue moonlight. His *ancianos* knew the mix: which dirt was best and how much water. Young men stripped to the waist and carried the slurry in rope-handled buckets to the men on ladders, who pushed the mud onto the walls with trowels, letting it sun bake. This fresh coat built up and stabilized the eroding walls but allowed the adobes to breathe.

Tiempos pasados, a huge trough was used. Pigs joined the goats and children in stomping in the mud, mixing it with sticks and feet. And the mudders moved from house to house, plastering—a celebration of the true end of winter.

Monday morning, all five men conscripted by Procopio were asked to meet outside the *patrones' hacienda* at 8:00 a.m.; most arrived early with thermoses of coffee to jovially greet each other. Mudding had been a manly *vecino* ritual for the past four hundred years. Crisp mornings and honey-warm afternoons signaled the proper autumn temperature to bake and cure the mud used to seal the adobe walls. A trough had been placed alongside the north wall, and the hose had been extended far enough to reach a ready pyramid of sifted dirt. Up toward the road, a wooden table on sawhorses had been set up to feed three times the number of workers; the benches were borrowed, and red gingham kerchiefs covered the standing pitchers of drinking water. The midday break would be a feast, and, adding a tone of importance, the *patrones* were scheduled to make the gesture of a formal appearance at the meal.

After Mass, two of Nicasia's cousins and one of Faustino's sisters had come to help Nicasia cook for the mudding, all talking, laughing, agreeing and disagreeing as they sliced onions and grated cheese.

"Anyone need a fine burro?" Nicasia asked the three of them.

"Who would buy that bag of bones?" Elena María said "bones" too loudly. For the first time, Nicasia was roused to defend the animal.

"She can carry a load of six full kilos of *leña*. She's not a bag of bones..."

"She brays all night. *Qué plaga.* Give her to somebody across the river."

"Yes! Tie her up at Procopio's. Or you could poison her."

"The *muchitos* love her like boys love dogs. She's a fine pet!" The burro was antique in more ways than one, and Nicasia was slowly running out of ammunition for a sale. The boys had outgrown furry-eared burros in favor of fast horses. "Faustino wants to trade her for Panky's *troque*."

"They're both in sad shape. It's a fair trade," Elena María muttered. "Nobody's gonna hitch a ride on either one of 'em."

Nicasia backed off and returned to her simmering beans and the huge pot of *menudo*. The household next door had taken charge of the *tamales*.

The next day at noon, the women arrived with their heavy *cazuelas*, smiling and happy. *Habia una vez*, they used to feed the workers in the fields, when long fields stretched down to the river. Four hundred years of partitioning the fields from father to son had left only a small patchwork of kitchen gardens. *Milpas*, they were called. Since times were easier now, mudding houses and *piñon* gatherings in the close hills were all the more festive.

The first morning was spent setting up the scaffolding. Then a cry sang out, "*Á comer!*" Procopio was the first to lead the other five men to a table already crowded with chatty cooks advance-sampling their dishes. "Come to eat!"

After the school down the street let out, Franque and Melo, running the fastest, steamed up to the site. Melo peeled down to his underwear and jumped, screaming and hollering, into the trough of mud. The young boys could be counted on to squish the mud with their feet like grapes, pushing each other down and laughing. They were teased by the men working on ladders with trowels. "Weaklings! Who's afraid of a little mud?"

Franque stood off, watching his younger brother wallow in the goo. Thirteen- year-old boys were shy of stripping in public. Hosed off at the end of the first day, the grinning younger boys called out, "*Hasta mañana*." They grabbed *biscochitos* and apricots left over from lunch, heading home.

By the fifth day, the men had circumnavigated the house and were set to trowel the heavy mud onto the last standing wall, the thick, double-adobe wall outside the old *dispenza*. Faustino arrived oddly animated; he had been nervous and prickly the days leading up to this final, windowless wall. Now, revitalized at the end, he bent his shoulder to the scaffolding, climbing and double-checking it for solid connections and steadiness.

"Looks good to me," he called down.

"Yeah, man, we need you to get down so we can get a move on here!"

"I just want it done right," Faustino said, picking up his own hoses and mops ready to wet the high wall. For authority, he glanced over to Paco standing by, nodding.

"We know how to do this, you know," he was warned as he began forcefully flinging water to prepare the wall for the fresh mud. Only one man stood on the top of the scaffold, sponging water where he intended to begin plastering.

"Look, I've been doing this my whole life," Faustino said. "Here's more water!" He climbed to the top of the scaffold against the parapet and set a bucket on it. "The wall needs much more water than you're giving it."

"Back off, Faustino. The other sides did fine without being saturated."

"Yeah, but this wall's different. Full sun here. Weathered." Faustino sloshed water from his bucket and pulled out a knife to test the mortar between the adobes. "See?" he crowed. But the blade did not pull away desiccated mortar, nor did it penetrate the standing bricks. It was rock solid, and he took a deep breath. This was not what he'd expected to find.

"You telling me you think we're plastering a rotten wall?"

"Well, now, it is in pretty good shape, considering," Faustino answered, plunging his knife into another spot.

"I could've told you—the other walls held up fine. I didn't see you hopping around checking 'em."

"Some of it's from before the revolt, before 1680." Faustino had counted on time's weakening the old blocks, eroding the adobes from the inside out, like crazy old men. He thought of the plaster skin as scabs hiding the bones.

"I worked on this place when the Anglos redid it. They had stuff done that didn't even need it. Always paid on time, too, so back off," the guy yelled at him. "Get off of this scaffold."

"Yeah, Procopio says they're *muy buena gente*," Faustino muttered and climbed down to meet Paco, who was holding another bucket of water. "More men coming today?"

"Yeah."

Faustino flung his wet mop, making a rooster tail of water, missing the one worker at the high corner. When two more *vecinos* piled out of Procopio's truck, he called out orders, insisting that the huge wall be continually wetted and rewetted, slowing the progress for the day. High on their ladders, the men plastered across the parapet, with Faustino mopping water like a maniac. When the others broke for lunch, he continued wetting the wall, trying to soften it. That night he planned to break through the wall from the outside. He expected to find his treasure shining in the ruins.

"Water was adobe's only natural enemy," he said as he sloshed more buckets at it. Then he added softly to himself, "Never break a vow. Never going inside, staying outside."

"What's with Faustino?" Procopio was asked as the men gave him a wide berth, looking askance.

"He has his moods. Thank God today's the last day. Tomorrow we take down the scaffolds, clean up."

After quitting time, Faustino pulled his pockets inside out. Ten *reales* fell to the dirt. Then he insisted on climbing into Panky's *troque*, grabbing the steering wheel, and he made Paco sit next to him on the seat while he started it up. "I know all about trucks," Faustino said with an edge to his voice as the truck started to roll. "I'll show you!"

Paco held onto the door for safety, yelling back, "Shift!" The truck lurched to a stop, the engine cut out and died. "I told you to shove the clutch in more!"

Faustino barely controlled his irritation. He had to slam on the foot brake and pull out the emergency brake to stop coasting downhill toward his house. Nicasia stood in the doorway, surprised to see him behind the wheel but happy to have a halt to the noise.

"*Hola, querida!*" He called out. Olivia María brayed her long contempt as the truck was restarted and banged past.

Nicasia waved, and Melo and his brother tumbled out of the house to watch as the truck turned the corner, rasping, out of sight. Dust hung in the twilight air and the boys agreed that the clamor from Panky's engine gave the truck its enormous importance. Faustino dumped Paco out at his place and rolled off solo to practice more clutch maneuvers. He sat high and square on the bench seat headed for the quarry. He needed to load enough weight on the truck to damage the wet wall when he bashed into it with full force.

"Glad you're still here. Load her up," he told the quarryman who was still on his loader. "Give me all she can take."

"What size, *Señor*?"

"Whatever's lying around. I'll pay tomorrow." So the worker scraped up midsize rubble and dumped it into Panky's truck. Faustino beamed his huge satisfaction.

"*Mañana*," he announced, waving his arm to the worker, laughing. "Who'd steal rocks?" And stripping gears, he drove back to Canyon Road in a high mood.

"See me? I'm pretty damned good at this," he called to friends on the street. Driving the truck was the way to learn. He circled the Plaza. "Want a ride?"

Then gunning the engine, he shot downhill with his heavy rock load. To navigate the slight uphill grade of Canyon Road, he shoved the truck into low gear. As he gained speed, the bald tires skidded, spewing loose gravel on the dirt until he arrived at the fourteen-room house, his heart beating like hoofbeats.

Faustino grinned and shouted, "*Dios y Santiago*," and accelerating, he aimed for the wall, ramming into it with a chaos of metal and rock. The impact sounded like a cannon blast. The truck's metal went mere inches into the wetted mud wall. Paint chipped off the truck, the fender moved an inch closer to the engine, and the wall had no more than one interesting gash. Some moist plaster sheeted off.

Sitting in their patio, Michael and Richard dropped their wine glasses and raced in a panic toward the kitchen. Outside on Canyon Road, dust rose, but the truck looked appreciably the same as before.

Faustino leaped out of the cab and surveyed the damage. He was disappointed. His next attack would have to be when the owners were not in residence. As it was, the two *patrones* crowded each other pushing out the kitchen door, only to find some of the day's work ruined and Faustino standing next to Panky's beat-up truck.

"My foot slipped," he said.

The two men stared into his eyes without speaking Then they looked at each other, then at the truck, then at their wall.

"*Oh, Señores, discúlpame.*" Faustino tried to explain. "It is an accident."

"What kind of idiot are you?" Richard's voice pitched. "If it's not one thing, it's another."

"*Sí,*" Faustino admitted. "*Un idiota.*" He bowed and put his hand over his heart. "I promise to restore any damage."

"Come on, Richard, be nice. The man must be injured," Michael said. With this, the gringos began touching him, lifting his shirt, examining him for broken bones. Before Faustino could back away, they checked his breath.

"I assure you, *muy estimados Señores Patrones*, I am sober." He put his hand over his heart again and bowed his head.

"Just take care of yourself," Michael said very calmly.

Faustino raised his supplicating eyes directly at Michael, suddenly as courtly and graceful as any Castilian gentleman. "No, no! I insist. It's all my fault!" And he turned quickly to grab a rake to clear what plaster he had managed to break down.

"*Mi amigo*," said Richard, putting his hand on the wiry man, "do not worry. There is so little damage...It can all wait until morning. It's getting dark."

Faustino nodded. The slight damage was a severe disappointment; the wall still stood firm. Hanging his head was supposed to communicate his regret as he rethought how to better manage his next assault. Raking the last of the debris, Faustino closed his eyes and visualized the treasure calling out his name. He could sense the weight of the gold coins and the soft leather pouches with those rough-cut diamonds buried in the solid wall, whispering, "Faustino, look over here!"

He needed a better plan. In the meantime he cleared away his pathetic damage, piling it onto the back of the truck. The kitchen door had been locked against him, a chain no doubt drawn. Discouraged, he placed a dry, calloused hand over his heart. "*No me importa*," he muttered. "My word is undying; I never break a vow. I can never enter this house."

When he had finished clearing the mess, he gunned the engine to back his truck of rubble away. "Holy Mother María!" Nicasia exclaimed when she saw her husband come through the door. "You are a sight! Are you all right?"

"My foot slipped," Faustino said.

Later that night, he offered his dismay to his Madonna statue pushed back in her *nicho*. He was desperate for Her to soothe him.

"My child, trust that I will never forsake you," She replied.

That night, his dreams sifted through the heap of sweepings, finding nothing. The treasure remained sealed in the standing wall.

By the next day, the mudding was over, the scaffolding broken down and the men paid. Faustino refused the money as he refused also to abandon the site. Each morning, he parked his beat-up truck outside the kitchen wall, hovering, creating chores for himself outside the house. First light on Sunday morning found him sweeping the bare dirt.

"What the hell are you doing?" Michael said, stumbling out from the kitchen door, newspaper in his hand rolled for a weapon. "No more, *mi amigo*. Scram!" In a rage, he slapped his thigh with the rolled-up paper.

Faustino dropped his broom and threw his hands up.

"No. Just go home. It's over, finished. Get the hell out of here!" Michael said.

"*Pero, estimados patrónes...*" Faustino begged.

"Out, goddammit!"

He was thrown off the property and completely at a loss as to how to hatch a new plan. He needed someone to talk to.

The noise of his battered pickup announced Faustino's arrival at Procopio's four- room adobe across the river. However, seeing Procopio stomp out of his door, rolling up his white shirtsleeves, he knew coming here had been a poor choice.

Procopio was angry as he stepped directly up to the driver's door. Pinned in his truck, Faustino leaned out from the driver's window, insisting he was only trying to be useful to the two *dueños*. "Like a *vecino*."

"Leave them alone," Procopio said. "They think you are creepy."

"I was just doing a little cleanup out on the street. Not for pay."

"Come inside; we need to talk." Faustino cut the engine and followed.

He left his truck blocking Procopio's driveway as he followed inside, where he was told to sit at the kitchen table. From where he sat, he faced two telling things: a shiny church calendar and a small *nicho* shrine with a plaster of paris Virgin of Guadalupe lit by flickering candles. Everything here, including the residents, was orderly.

"Faustino, *basta*," Procopio began. "This business of Serafina and The Empress Carlota's gold is, first, no secret and, second, a hoax, *un engaño*."

Faustino was shocked; he felt faint. "Who told you?" He choked. "How?" Faustino could not understand how Procopio could have found out. Who had betrayed his sacred quest? He wanted to kick the dog, but there was no dog.

"Everyone knows," Procopio told him with a wide sweep of his arms. "We all know about it. Are you so *tonto* that you never knew there was more than one map?"

Faustino's ears rang; he refused to believe what he had heard. "Did she sign with her rose and the cross?" His voice faltered and he was unable to finish.

Procopio greeted this question with disdain. "You know she knew her lawyer was a crook. They were all crooks. I knew her far better than you did, and she trusted me." Procopio delivered this with a sickening flourish. "She made maps to throw them off."

"*Cómo?*" Faustino's ears began to ring louder, the volume increasing. He saw Procopio's mouth open but heard no words over the ringing, which grew into a whine. He felt faint.

"Faustino?"

"Eh?" He sat in silence.

"You knew she refused to pay taxes on the house," Procopio continued. "She knew she'd never be able to save it for all of us, so she told me where Elodio had hidden his savings. She drew a picture."

After a while, Faustino asked, "She gave you a map to the ancient treasure Vitorio intercepted?"

"That old wives' tale? I grew up believing that a young boy knew where to find it." Procopio shrugged and waved his palm. "One of the maps to the gold Elodio hid..."

"Elodio?" He was unable to finish.

"Yes, the map to Elodio's money that he'd plastered into the wall. I dug it out when the *patrones* moved in. Used it to buy my truck," he added.

"But..." Faustino did not know whether to stop before he began or to demand to see Procopio's map; he was afraid.

"Tia Serafina and I were very close, as I told you."

"You still have that map?"

"With my wedding photographs," he said, smiling. Faustino's head spun. If his life had any meaning and value, he chose to believe that Serafina had fooled Procopio and kept the grand treasure safely buried. If the Virgin's word had power, Serafina had tossed Procopio a mere trinket to appease him, and Faustino's priceless map was still to remain a secret only for himself, the Blessed Mother of God, and Carlota, the Austrian Empress. Over the clattering in his head, he insisted on the magnificent fact that his own map would lead his people home to their lost nobility. And that his ancestors deserved more than a Ford truck.

Procopio shook him from his ruminations. "I'm going over to tell the *patrones* that you have promised never to come to their house again."

"*Qué?*" Faustino needed him to repeat what he had said. Procopio did not reply to this question; instead he rolled his sleeves down and prepared to stomp, not walk, over to the fourteen-room adobe because his driveway was blocked. To emphasize his disappointment with Faustino, he refused a ride, and Faustino watched his back growing smaller in the distance.

Back in the truck, Faustino banged his head against the steering wheel, admitting that his mission had always contained mysteries, questions that remained unanswered. The gold and the map were a legendary promise; it was the lone hope of a symbolic *merced* to bring the Garcías closer to their God.

Meanwhile, Adam and Eve were historical fact; they were true.

For the present, Serafina in her splendid heaven must know that he had been thrown off her property. She must have asked him to be humble and to accept his impoverished life. Had she allowed him to be repudiated by the *dueños* so that he would give thanks for his home and family? Yes, he had Nicasia, Franque and Melo—as much love and respect as any man was granted in one lifetime. There were also Justo and Channy, his *cuates*, plus his married sisters, nieces and nephews as well as his worthy ancestors pointing to and guiding him along the one true path. Did she want him to understand that they—and she—would never abandon him? He wept, feeling treacherously abused.

Still sitting in the cab of the pickup, he was humiliated by his bollixed attempts to recover the treasure and vowed the Virgin would be the first to hear that Serafina hinted that he dedicate himself in gratitude to God and relinquish his quest for the gold. His real mission, he now accepted, would be to become a warrior and fight for his Spanish kings with their Wondrous God. Yes, out of the cinders, Faustino would be reborn into a modern conquistador, a man of the highest integrity. A warrior. This, he decided, was the bequest of the Great Tía Doña Catalina María Josefa Serafina de Montoya y Gomez.

During the night, when Faustino's heartbeat had quieted to match the comfortable rhythm of his wife's and sons' breathing, the Virgin appeared to Faustino in full size, floating above the rag rug. "Faustino, my own obedient servant, know that all warriors for the Spanish kings were awarded gold medallions." His breathing quickened as he gazed at the Holy Mother, not knowing whether his eyes were opened or closed.

"The warriors," She repeated, "have pledged their fealty first to me as their Heavenly Queen, and only after me, to the kings in their worldly empire." She was dazzling, trailing swirls of light as She moved, and She smelled of roses.

"I can't get the gold."

"Yes, my child, you can."

"I vowed never to enter the house. You know, My Queen, how I tried to take the wall down."

"It's there. Waiting." Her voice floated. She was a vapor in the night air.

"There are several maps."

"There have always existed false maps, my warrior child."

"I want to give up. To stop. I am tired."

"A man is arriving soon to help. He will lead you to it."

"But I can't enter the house. I've been thrown out. I made an unbreakable vow." He heard his own voice; it was strong. "My Lady, let me rest."

"My child, I am sending you an angel." She was clear.

"Please, Blessed Mother, I am too tired." He asked the vision to spare him. She would not stop.

"You will know him when he says to you, "An easy way." Listen for those words. *An easy way.*

Swooning over The Immaculate Conception's alabaster skin, he fell into a deep sleep until the knocking at the door pulled him to his feet.

"Channy!" Faustino greeted him.

"Sorry it's so early. I been thinkin' about the gold." Faustino laid a hand on his friend's shoulder to steady himself, hoping it was the sign from the Blessed Mother when Channy said, "I got an easy way to get it."

"Channy!" Faustino gave an *abrazo* to his *pegado*, his trusted *cuate*, his buddy. "An easy way?"

"Water. We'll use water."

"You'd better sit," Faustino said. "We got big problems. Procopio says there were maps all over town, each one different. Nicasia doesn't know about this."

"No, no. It's not true! He's wrong; the right map is the one you have." Channy's disbelief was identical to Faustino's. "Procopio's an idiot. Anyway, if he ever got his hands on Carlota's treasure, we'd never hear the end of it. Your map is different. I can prove it to you. I'll get it out. Easy."

"He said everyone knows about the gold."

"I know you got the real one, the real map," Channy insisted. "You do, too."

Nicasia came into the kitchen, "*Bueno*, Channy! Coffee?"

Faustino bolted to his feet. "Channy, you gotta see the truck. I bought Panky's pickup." He jerked his chin toward the door. "Come on, I'll show you where I hit the wall with the bumper. Almost had to use a tire iron to pull it off the wheels. We gotta talk."

As Channy followed Faustino out to the yard, Nicasia shot him a warm smile. "When you come back in, coffee'll be ready."

Standing by the bashed-in truck, Faustino took Channy's arm. He kicked the front bumper with his shoe. "Here's where I tried to bring the outside wall down. Didn't work. Now they don't want me on the property."

"This door still open?" Channy gave it a tug and it creaked as it swung on its metal hinges. The two men climbed into the truck. "I'm giving up. I mean it," Faustino insisted. I made another vow never to go inside that damned house. I'm quitting."

"Hell, you're not! I know an easy way."

Even though Faustino heard Channy's same words from the Virgin, he shook his head no. "Nicasia says the gold is cursed."

"But my idea is water." Channy was serious about this. He said, "Disconnect the float in the back of the toilet to flood the room. I'll do it. You don't even have to go inside the house, ever!"

"What if Nicasia's right? What if the gold brings bad luck? Say, my burro dies?"

"I'll get the gold and bring it right to you. You don't have to do shit," Channy said. "I don't even have to borrow your truck here. I mean it; I'm getting the gold out for you, and you don't even have to split it with me."

"The gringos ran me out."

"Fine, it doesn't matter. I'll get in there and wreck the pipes, too. There'll be a bigger flood." Channy was too excited to stop talking. "Come on, Faustino. Be reasonable!"

"It'd melt the walls?" Faustino pondered that. That was one thing about adobe; if it got wet, it went back to being mud. With standing water, the base of the wall would disintegrate. It would be undermined. "A flood can collapse a house overnight. A really good flood." Faustino was beginning to grasp Channy's science.

"The marble tiles will buckle off before the wall comes down," Channy continued, using his fingers to count out the steps. "That's where the gold is."

"You are a goddamn genius." Faustino nodded. Channy, like his founding forebears, was very practical. The plan was perfect.

"It'll work." Channy was reassuring. "I guarantee it! We're just gonna do what a heavy rain could if the roof fell in."

"I can't show my face anywhere close to the *dueños'* place now."

"You don't have to. Just tell me how to get into that powder room so I can jimmy toilet, or pop the water pipe. Think of something."

"Take some elk to Procopio. Then say you gotta take a piss."

"*Perfecto!*" Channy exclaimed.

"*Dios y Santiago!*" Faustino replied, his voice was hushed.

Mid-afternoon two days later, using the Forest Service telephone, Channy called Procopio purposely close to his quitting time at the hacienda.

"*Diga?*" Procopio answered, taking a stab at a military guard's voice.

"Faustino says he feels real bad about what he did to the wall and he asked me to bring the *dueños* the tender side of a venison and some trout. Just to say he's sorry, nothing more. He's not comin' around anymore."

"Tell Faustino it's off-limits here."

"I know, I know. That's why I gotta deliver it for him. You there now?" Procopio said that he was just about to leave for the day. "Wait for me, okay?"

"Come to the back. Not the main door."

A slow hour later, Channy set the meat on the steps while he rapped on the door.

"I been waiting for you, Channy," Flora said. "Procopio had to go. It's past quitting time."

"*Hola*, Flora!" He bent to give her an *abrazo*. "I brought this game for the *dueños*. You can freeze it. It's Faustino's way of sayin' he's sorry for causing any trouble." And he put it on the blue and white tile counter for her. "Okay if I take back the burlap wrapping with me?"

"Of course, *querido*." Channy was like another son to her. "Let me get some wax paper."

Later he told Faustino how easy it was. "I said I needed to wash up. Showed her the blood on my hands. '*Bueno*,' she said and pointed to the powder room. I was flabbergasted. Never in my whole life have I seen anything like that."

"I told you..."

"It looked like a church in there. Gold and that marble. So where was the powder?"

"That's just for the *señoras*; they bring their own."

Channy could not stop talking about the wash closet. "Did you see that mirror?"

And nodding that he knew everything there was to know about the gold mirror, Faustino realized he was actually jealous of Channy for getting into that ridiculous, stupendous bathroom.

"You remembered to put the seat back down, didn't you?"

"That's not all I did!"

CHAPTER SEVENTEEN

"Bloody hell, what in God's name was that," Richard yelled, shaken from sleep by a sound like a burst grenade on the far side of the sprawling house.

Michael awoke with a start, frightened. "Bleeding Jesus," he whispered. "Are they armed?"

"Something crashed, something fell. Sloppy work for burglars..." Michael lowered his voice, alarmed now, threatened. Both men fell silent. Frozen. "Doors slamming," Richard whispered when they heard more concussions.

"Not that idiot Faustino and his truck again?" Michael spoke in a normal voice, a lowered, normal voice. "Goddamn him!" Coursing with anger, he marched with heavy steps to the wardrobe, searching for a bludgeon, a baseball bat.

"I am going to maim that imbecile if I die trying!" He had no baseball bat, so he grabbed a man's wooden suit hanger. Holding it above his head, he ran into the hallway headed for the grand sala, screaming, "I'm going to get you, mule head! Goddamned Faustino! Come here so I can crush your blubbering, pea-sized brain!"

Richard realized that Michael was mad enough to attack anything that moved, so he threw off the sheet and shoved his feet into his slippers. Zigzagging behind Michael, he turned on the lights as he went. It had to be Procopio's maddening relative, that scrawny man they had hoped never to see again. God knows why they'd been forced into hiring him— time and time again!

"It's all over, Faustino. We know it's you!" Michael stalked toward the kitchen, the blazing lights casting long circus shadows in his path. "Come out and show your damned face!" he yelled just as another crash resounded, nearer in the powder room.

"Goddamn to hell," he yelled. Richard ran to him, sure it was Faustino bashing into that wall again. But when they opened the bathroom door, they were sprayed in the face and found the broken sink lying on the floor, layered with the ooze of mud seeping from the adobe wall. The toilet stood fixed in place, the base half buried by the residue from the crumbling wall. The seat was down. "Must be a broken pipe," said Michael looked solemnly at his older partner, shaking his head in horror. "This is a godforsaken mess!"

"Get the bloody water off," Richard yelled. "This time, call a real plumber, not Procopio for this." Michael tried to find the turnoff.

The marble tiles held the wall back by forming a skin holding the disintegrating interior adobes, now softening into heavy, viscous goo. Below the thin shell at the base of the wall, a mud outpouring puddled onto the floor. The rug was clearly destroyed.

"Do you know how to turn off the water main?" Richard asked him. "We must save what we can. You grab the mirror."

Michael was able to stanch the flow for the last hours of that night. While they lay in their bed, half of the marble tiles pitched off the damp wall and crashed like thrown crockery, one by one, onto the inundated floor with duller and duller thuds.

At dawn the next morning, Michael telephoned Procopio. "The back of the goddamned house is coming down!" He knew enough not to blame Procopio directly. Humiliating him would exacerbate the problem, but it was clear he and his incessant watering had brought this about. Most likely he had neglected to close the floodgates and left the *acequia* flowing all night. "Not the whole house, just the back wall behind the kitchen where you keep your wheelbarrow." Michael paused to consider that the back of the house faced Canyon Road and not the irrigated gardens.

"*Me voy.* I'm on my way," Procopio said. He buttoned his trousers and bolted out the door. "Shoes..." he remembered, turning back into the house. For a second time, he ran out his opened door, pulling on his shirt, frightened now. He cranked up his truck, and by the time he arrived at the adobe, the deepening mud from the disintegrating adobes had crept inches into the kitchen. As he stepped through the gummy mess, his boots were pulled loose. In the powder room, the collapsed wall was calving chunks. He felt guilty and blamed. The priceless gold-framed mirror rested safely away from the disaster, set on the floor against a dining room chair.

Procopio's pain was visible. He could see that a leak in the powder room had undermined the base of the wall supporting the fixtures. The marble tiles had concealed the water damage inside the double-adobe walls up to the point where the weighty sink fell from its supports with the crash the *dueños* had heard.

"It was fine yesterday," Procopio said, beginning to cry. "Flora was with me, and everything seemed fine. We did not check everything, but when I locked the garden gate, the leaves were raked, and I'd cut the hollyhock stems back. Everything was in order. Please forgive me!"

Richard said, "We are not blaming you."

"I am the *mayordomo*; it is my fault." He would have fallen to his knees.

The two *patrones* had retreated into the kitchen to make something for breakfast when they remembered that the water was turned off. Settling on some toast, they tried to ignore the last clatters as the tiles continued to fall.

The moment the plumber's truck pulled up, the last marble tile crashed to the floor, making a fainter sound as it landed on the wet earth of the double-thick wall. Leaning on the shaft of his hoe, Procopio rested in the doorway. He had finished pulling the mud away from the wall to allow the plumber to work.

"*Nunca en mi vida...*" The plumber was dumbfounded; he remembered soldering the pipes himself to create the bathroom. Yes, he always guaranteed his work, but now it appeared that he was responsible to replace the outside wall.

"The damage is huge. Certainly the sink, the tiles, the counter, the plaster, the lighting fixtures, the electrical connections. Nothing is worth saving." Procopio attributed this damage to the plumber. "The mirror, of course, has been saved." He gave the impression that these things were his own.

"The water supply to the house is turned off," Michael said.

"Nothing like this has ever happened to my work before." The plumber was contrite and apologized over and over to the *dueños*. "I will find men to replace the *adoves*. Of course, I'll redo the pipes." He shrugged hopelessly. What more could he say? All his other piping installations had held well. This was the one disastrous exception.

"At least get us some water to the rest of the house," Richard prodded, thinking the necessity should be obvious to this moron. The plumber nodded and left to fetch shovels and wheelbarrows and to bring two of his sons. Michael and Richard escaped to La Fonda, where they reported this tragedy to the regulars as they ordered an early lunch.

"Everyone was appalled," they reported back to Procopio. "Aghast!" By evening, the water was restored to the rest of the house.

After she saw the extent of the damage, Flora was convinced that someone had given the plumber the evil eye; someone was out to get him. It looked like the spiteful work of vengeful ghosts. A thought worth considering. "We must call the priest," she said. "We will ask for an exorcism."

Slowly and quietly just after dawn, Channy drove past the *hacienda* on his way to the national forest. Four hours later Faustino passed by, casually leading Olivia María with a load of *sabina* on her back, and as he surveyed the scene, the blood drained from his windburned face. Seeing the plumber's truck parked at a sloppy angle raised some small smile of satisfaction. No one was around, but of the three wheelbarrows, two were filled with glistening mud and broken adobes. After a few minutes, Procopio came out of the house yelling that the outer wall of the *dispenza* was on the verge of collapse. Faustino stood looking baleful. He stayed well off the property.

"My God, Faustino," said Procopio, exhausted. "Inside the house is a tragedy! The entire house could have gone if my *patrones* had not discovered the leak."

"But, *asi es la vida*; things just happen. Looks like a bad accident." Faustino winced, struggling to get the words out. He took a few steps back, farther away into the road.

"Flora thinks someone cast an evil spell on my *patrones*. Typical thinking for a woman, don't you think? There must be some very reasonable explanation for this." Procopio's mouth trembled as he spoke. "Flora says maybe it's the house that is cursed. Look at this mess!"

"*Duendes...*" Faustino suggested. "Vengeful spirits? Ghosts? I've seen them do worse around this town. Might be something about damaging the old *dispenza*?" His voice was weak by the end.

"You have a thing about that *dispenza*!" Procopio pulled at his shirt, nervous. "Right now, we need good adobe workers."

Faustino patted his work pants' pockets. "I can to do the whole job myself." He then dropped Olivia María's lead and casually bent to rummage between the piles of mud and rock. "I don't need pay."

His burro dug into the hard dirt with her hoof, waiting in the morning shadow. Faustino took up a shovel, intending to sift through the dirt in the wheelbarrows. But Procopio shook his head. "I promised the *patrones* that they'd never have to see your face here again."

"And I meant it when I said I'd never come here, ever. But as a *vecino*, I'll help." Faustino bent to pick up a shovel, holding it like a sword.

"They think you are clumsy and maybe a little demented."

"Don't worry! I will never step inside the house, ever." Then he stretched his back and moved his shoulders. He was an artisan ready to perform. "I honor my vows."

"Why can't you just go away, like they ask?"

"*Vecinos* never walk away from disasters; you know that!" Faustino squinted and said, "I will clean this up and disappear. No one will know who to thank."

"The *patrones* are inside; they'll think it's me out here. I wish you'd just go away! How long will it take you to clean this up?"

"With the *troque*, I can shovel it out in three hours at the most." Faustino stood erect, ready for a challenge. "Haul it away with the truck, yes? No one will know which *vecino* came to help."

"The next time I come out here, I don't want to see you, and I don't want to see the mess. Good?" Procopio would not have capitulated had he not felt responsible for this unexplainable calamity.

Faustino nodded.

"Good," Procopio said and went inside.

Faustino called to him, "If they ask, tell them it's the work of six *vecinos*, and don't tell them it's me. You know I can do the work of any six men."

"*Bueno*," said Procopio, closing the door behind him. He felt like an old man.

Faustino returned with Panky's truck and got to work, trying to be quietly careful as he shoveled. What neither he nor Channy had figured in was the budding audience as each passerby stopped to join the crowd on Canyon Road. "How much gold?" newcomers asked, watching Faustino shovel the dirt into his truck bed. If Faustino had let them, most would have pitched in to sift through the mess for the shiny, yellow coins, and by noon, the crowd, standing in full sun, had grown so large that children were selling lemonade.

Short of the three-hour time limit, Procopio appeared out on the street, prepared to upbraid Faustino for being there when he saw the gathering crowd.

"I'm almost finished," Faustino claimed.

"Who are these people?" Procopio asked, realizing as he took in the faces that he knew all of them. They, too, were *vecinos*, his *vecinos*. People he'd grown up with.

"Find the gold yet?" The crowd leaned forward. "*Qué tal*, Procopio?"

"Gold?" Procopio repeated, confused and surprised. "No gold here." He tried to remember what he had heard about Doña Serafina's maps. "Why are all these people waiting to see the gold?"

Rooting through the rubble, Faustino pointed his lips to the restless audience across the street. "None here. Procopio's already carried off whatever had been here."

"Which one of the maps says more treasure is here?" Procopio demanded. "The *patrones* are going to be really angry. First you here, then more gold?"

"There's no gold here!" Faustino repeated. It seemed that Procopio, who claimed to know about the maps, actually knew nothing. Faustino was relieved and continued to shovel broken adobes and mud into the back of his truck while Procopio wandered across the street to talk to the bystanders. "I'll be finished in a couple of minutes!"

When Procopio returned with a lemonade in hand, he said, "Tell me what you know, goddammit."

"The mirror," Faustino replied, testing him. He kept his head down as he shoveled. "I think the *patrones* had a frame made out of the gold they found..."

"One of the ladies who writes poetry gave them the mirror," Procopio said. "She said it was too fancy for her adobe house."

Faustino smiled; his legacy, then, was still in this house, hidden from the lawyer who stole the house—his gold.

"Are you thinking about Carlota's phony treasure...?" Procopio stared at Faustino with his mouth open, breathing in and out until he coughed. Bits of rumor he'd gathered over the years gathered in his head. "Vitorio's cache?"

Faustino looked him straight in the eye. "The gold is mine. *Si lo queda*—if there is any." He turned away, appearing purposeful and busy.

After a second's pause, Procopio began to run after him, shouting, "Get out of here. Get the hell out!" Faustino threw his shovel to the ground and marched over to his truck with his fist raised, glaring at Procopio. With a mighty force, he slammed the driver's door to punctuate his resentment and drove off with what dirt he had managed to shovel. Later, he would take it into the forest for sifting.

That night under a full moon and in the path of Panky's truck headlights, Channy and Faustino threw the dirt against a screen, sifting for gold. A mound of mud was left to the side.

"Just pebbles," Channy said, coughing. "Old stucco."

"Not there yet." Faustino's voice rasped with the dust. "They don't want me back."

"I'll think of something," Channy said. "So what do you think about us buying the *floresta* when we get the gold? Give it back to *la gente* like old times. Free water again."

"I was thinking of running sheep on the San Benicia Grant. Say ten thousand hectares?"

"No, better to get the mountain back."

"No reason why not."

Procopio found the *patrones* sullen. They sat on the *portale* without reading their papers or speaking to each other, both facing the garden as golden leaves slowly rocked down from the ash tree shading the far side of the *plazuela*. Ash trees that leafed out first in the spring were the first to turn when the nights grew colder.

"*Señores*," Procopio began. "*Permiso?*" They looked up at him. "I am sorry to have to tell you this."

"Not more water damage!" Michael was fit to be tied.

"No."

"Well, then, what on God's green earth is it now?" He searched Procopio's face for another calamity. "I can't take much more of this."

"There is a map that claims that part of the wealth of Mexico is hidden in the walls of this house."

"So?" The men glanced at him but allowed him to continue out of courtesy.

"The Apache chief, Vitorio, was said to have captured and hidden the Empress Carlota's jewels in the southern part of the state. Faustino says he's got a map that says the treasure was saved and hidden here in your house."

"Here?" they asked in unison. "Hogwash."

"Do you want to see his map?"

"Why here? What next?" Richard had the short temper now.

"The former owners knew about it and never found it." Procopio chose not to elaborate about the savings he'd unearthed years back.

"Of course not!"

"Faustino is sure the gold is in the wall. The one that is waterlogged."

"Faustino again? That impossible cousin of yours? Tell him to jump off a cliff."

"He's not my cousin. He is married to my niece." Procopio was uneasy about having to discuss his relation to Faustino.

"Well, then, thank God for small blessings." Richard stood to place a hand on his *mayordomo's* shoulder. "If he wants us to find his goddamned treasure, tell him from me: N-o s-o-a-p. No soap! There, I hope I'm clear."

"Yes, sir, *muy bien.*" Procopio was overcome with relief, and this relief would be complete when he saw Faustino face-to-face and pointed to a nearby cliff for him to jump off.

"Faustino is a damned pain in the goddamn butt!" Procopio told himself in his rearview mirror, uncomfortably jealous of the fact that more gold might be found in the walls. When he pulled into the yard, he found only Nicasia.

"*Nena*, where is Faustino?" he asked, not seeing the beat-up truck littering the yard.

"He's been gone all day," Nicasia replied. Seeing her uncle disappointed, she added, "Why?"

"Basically, I wanted the satisfaction of personally delivering a message from my *patrones*, but since he's not here, I'll tell you." He avoided her eyes as he spoke. "Tell Faustino to stay strictly away from tia Serafina's *hacienda*. Tell him that the *dueños* do not want to see him or his map anywhere near the house. Never!"

"What is this all about? What map?" Her face registered nothing, not even curiosity.

"The one that says the gold is in the old *dispenza*. Tell him to stay away."

Later, as Nicasia passed on these few words to her husband, she watched his face. The words were harsh and with each, he visibly shriveled. Having his wife tell him these things was unbearable.

"Stay even farther away than you have," she said.

That night, he sat rigidly in a wooden chair and refused to move. He was still sitting the next morning when she arose to get the boys ready for school.

"*Papi?*" They tried to engage their father.

"*Querido?*" She nudged him. "*Café?*"

Nicasia witnessed her husband slipping back into the dark mine of his past depressions, dropping by easy rungs into his former despair. In the matrimonial bed, she reached out her hand to touch a cold sheet where, for the past twelve years, she had found his warmth. Wiser, having lived through her husband's last breakdown, she decided to speak with the *patrones* herself.

The next day, she took the map to the *patrones,*, needing to tell them that the treasure had been stolen from the true owner and wanted returning. When she knocked on the kitchen door, she clutched the map, regretting she had not brought *empanadas.*

Procopio seemed pleased to see her when he pulled the door open. "*Nena*! Come in. The *patrones* have just finished their lunch. Have you eaten? Flora is here in the kitchen."

"No, no. Thank you, but no. I hope the *patrones* will let me speak with them for just a few minutes. Two minutes, that's all." She was led through the *plazuela* to Michael's studio, where the two men sat on stools facing a painted canvas, gesticulating with their hands, holding cigarettes. Their conversation halted at Procopio's tapping on the closed door.

"*Señores Patrones,* Nicasia, my niece, has asked if she might speak with you for two minutes."

"Is this important?" Richard flashed a smile at Nicasia. He was cordial but not endearing. Michael took a drag and turned from his canvas to face her. She saw that he had painted many bright colors, making squares and shapes desperately wanting to be trees, with the sunlight kissing odd leaves.

"Please," she said. "I need your help. It won't take much time. I know you are busy."

"Procopio, could you bring your daughter a chair?"

"Niece," he muttered as he dragged over a wooden paint-splattered chair and placed it square to the canvas. She stared at the working canvas, thinking it must be a map, or maybe it was the outline of something and they were debating whether to continue with it. She sat and sent a prayer to angels, asking them to make Michael's paintbrush carry nature's beauty to his picture.

"I see you are staring at it. What do you think?"

"It will be trees?" she asked Michael.

"Well, now! Procopio, your girl here knows the forest from the trees. Very good!" Nicasia blushed and decoded that she was correct about the painting. It turned out to be trees after all. Procopio's hand on her shoulder gave her a reassuring squeeze, warning her off the quicksand of modern art.

"*Nena*, please tell the *patrones* why you are here." She liked it when he called her *nena*, his girl, his daughter-niece-cousin-pet. It meant he'd take care of her; she was his. So she smiled tentatively at him and pulled the map closer to herself.

Procopio's hand pushed on her shoulder when she tried to stand, so she stayed seated on the chair, feeling small as she looked up at the two men on high stools. She saw only the gringos' faces and not her uncle's behind her. "My husband hears the Virgin Mary speaking to him," she began. "I do not. But I have the map here in my hand."

The gringos shot glances at each other. "That gold thing again?" Richard said.

"I thought we'd thrown that out yesterday," Michael said. "You said you didn't want to hear another word about this fruitcake fantasy. You, too, Procopio. You know how we feel about this idiocy."

"I have reason to believe that there had been some gold in the walls at one time." Procopio carefully chose his words. "But it was no longer there when you modernized the house."

Nicasia felt her uncle's fingers dig into her shoulder. "*Qué?*" she questioned, looking up.

He shook his head. She was to remain quiet. She made an effort to stand, but Procopio kept his hand on her shoulder, keeping her seated. He seemed to want her to let him speak for her, but she was on edge.

"Well, then, what else are you here for?" Richard said.

"Please," she began. It was wrong to be sitting when she wanted to throw herself at their pale-eyed mercy. "Please look at this map. It belongs with your house. It concerns this house."

Procopio lifted his hand from her shoulder to take up the map, but Michael touched it first. Now she was able to stand, and as he opened the map, she pointed with her finger, touching the X.

"The hoard of gold is here in this wall."

"In a wooden chest," Procopio said, pushing in to examine the map for the first time. "I've heard about it for years."

"Listen, missy, you really believe this fairy story?"

"Yes."

"Everyone in town knows about it," Procopio butted in. He stood taller—he was the *mayordomo*, after all. "Tía Doña Catalina María Josefa Serafina de Montoya y Gomez was my esteemed forebear as well."

Richard choked on a laugh halfway through the recitation of her names. He'd seen it on the abstract of title and declared that they were buying the faded palace of Philip the Second's lost daughter.

"So she was your cousin, too?"

"Yes," Procopio said. "And the godmother of Nicasia here." The two men looked at Nicasia in a kindly manner, polite. The house they had bought was historic, and they liked it for that fact. There had been others available in better condition, but this old elephant had been so long neglected that they took it on, partly out of charity. If the venerable Serafina did not have the cash for taxes, she certainly did not have the money for maintenance. So it sat empty for ten years, letting the roof leak. Everything had needed work.

"She had meant to leave us this *hacienda*," Nicasia began, and the men pulled knowing faces. "Instead, all we have now is this map to the gold and the diamonds from years past buried in the walls here."

"She left more than one map," Procopio interjected.

"She said it was for my sons' Catholic education at the Christian Brothers College."

"Just that?" Michael asked. The map in his shaky hand seemed to breathe. It sounded so utterly simple. "How much does St. Michael's College cost? I mean, it can't be more than maybe eighty dollars a year?" As he spoke, he recalled that except for Procopio and Flora, whom they paid monthly, so few of the locals seemed to have any cash on them.

"She has two boys, *Señores.*" Procopio stood between them, insistent, interrupting and uneasy. The men nodded to each other. To them this was not an impossible sum, and doubled, it still did not require a buried treasure. "They are very fine boys," he added, and with a smile he bowed toward Nicasia. "We have high hopes for them."

"Everybody says your auntie was a saint. How did she get this gold you say she buried? Don't saints take a vow of poverty?"

"It wasn't her treasure. She would have given it to the poor if she'd ever found it," Procopio said.

"The coins are supposed to be all gold?" Richard asked, knowing that Mexican and Spanish trade coins had been silver, not gold. "And how do you account for the bag of diamonds as well?"

"The Empress Carlota was one of the richest women in both Europe and Mexico. They say she had jewelry and old Mayan gold."

"And I suppose she'd taken it from Montezuma himself?" Michael chuckled. "Incredible how none of you Hispanics ever pay attention to the laws! You don't pay taxes; you stuff things in the walls. If it's there, that gold belongs to the heirs of people long dead."

Nicasia's face relaxed. These were the same men who had ripped Adam and Eve to shreds, but now they smelled evil. The devil. They were smart enough to see that so she smiled at them.

"What doesn't figure is that your Tia Serafina was a saint, married to a guy who supplied moonshine to maybe that speakeasy up there on the mountain—what was it called?" Michael paused, jutting out his chest as he recalled the wild stories. "That's right, the Elks Club. I don't find that consistent."

Nicasia leaped up from her chair to protest, and Procopio raised a hand to object, so Michael assumed his mask face for the jury. "May I suggest that the gold was never legally theirs?"

Richard tracked the reaction to these observations and felt Michael was too harsh. "Really, Michael. She said—didn't you, Nicasia?—that your saintly auntie wanted you to give it to the Christian Brothers? Now, that's not an unsaintly act, is it? She just liked hiding her money from the tax department."

"No, she never found it," Procopio interrupted. "This is what my niece is trying to tell you." He had latched onto the perfect cover for his early theft, if it could be called such a thing—taking what was his from a house that belonged to others.

Nicasia had never denied the gold was dangerous, but these men were attacking her. Outraged, her blood boiled. She spun on her feet to flee from the room and behind her back she overheard Michael say, "There I go again! I've struck one of their sacred cows!"

He still held the map in his hand. She had left without it.

"*Nena*, stop!" Procopio ran after her. "Let me show you out."

If the door had been heavier, she would have shattered the window glass when she slammed it behind her. She was weeping when she stumbled on the *plazuela* bricks, reminding herself that she was to use the kitchen door, not the *zaguan*. "For God's sake, never the *zaguan*!"

"There, there," her uncle said when he caught up with her. "They didn't say no."

"They can just go to hell," Nicasia said. "Why didn't you say something?" She waved her hand at him. "Never mind. Don't even take the time to answer me. You don't stand up to them because you grovel; you just want their filthy money!"

"Please, *Nena*!" She backed away from him, and turning, blurry with tears, she stumbled and began to run.

"*Nena*!" he called out.

She looked back and cursed him. "They might have helped."

Late that night, lying in bed, the conversation replayed in her head. She now hated her uncle. He was weak. She knew, too, where the gold rested, festering. She had been near its blistering presence. Her heart quickened. Surrounded by the slow breathing of her sleeping men, she fell back to dreaming. She awoke to a slippery whisper, like rivers moving between warm rocks. "When gold speaks, families break apart. Men kill."

She respected the danger. If she wanted to save her husband and her family, she would have to take a risk. And then it was crucial that she hand the gold off.

Unable to sleep more, she got out of bed before it was light.

After all, the *dueños* had not said no.

CHAPTER EIGHTEEN

Procopio told the legend of the treasure on the cart with the gold-wrapped wheels, as he understood it, from the beginning, and by the end, after answering their repeated questions, he was exhausted. "The spokes of the wheels were wrapped in gold?" His *patrones* however, were energized. Just hearing the word "gold" had an effect.

"If anybody, that poor Faustino bastard really could use a bit of luck," Michael conceded. "His boys could do with decent schooling. They might inform their parents that New Mexico is now part of the United States."

"Let's get this over with, then," Richard said, pulling on a sweater. "I'm not exactly giddy about dealing with that numbskull."

No knock at the door, no gentle self-invitation, just a bang as the door swung open, striking against a stool. Three men, Richard, Michael and Procopio, crowded in, demanding Faustino. They were returning the treasure map. Nicasia had no desire to forgive them for insulting her worthy godmother-aunt. This insult had also included Elodio and most of her neighbors. She blamed Procopio as well. Seeing these brutes in her home was a further insult.

"*Faustino no está,*" Nicasia said, moving to close the screen door.

"Do you expect him soon?" Michael asked, obviously prepared to wait.

"He's next door. Sit, please, while I get him." She capitulated, intending not to go out of her way for them. Looking about in the tidy house, the three men settled at the oilcloth-covered table, silent and ready to wait. If they were righteously furious with Faustino for bashing Panky's truck into their wall, she did not care because no one had been injured.

"Help yourselves to coffee," she said, not bothering to untie her apron as she walked toward the door.

"I'll make more if they want some, *Nena*," Procopio offered. He smiled at her, certain their falling-out had blown over; she had always been like a daughter to him. His recent beef was only with Faustino.

"I hope we don't have to stay here all day," Michael said as the three men sat waiting in the small house, windows curtained against the magnificent landscape of the high desert outside.

When Nicasia pushed Faustino through the doorway before her, he greeted the three men like a convict facing a jury. He knew them to be stubborn, and now she knew them to be cruel. Faustino drew himself up, wanting to tell them he was an honest man, an honest man but a fool. He was prepared to make amends. He was ready to confess everything and ask to be allowed to repair what he had broken. And he hoped that Michael's temper could be contained for the present. Nicasia had nothing to say to any of them.

"Faustino, '*Mano*, these excellent men are here to help you. You need help." Faustino stared when Procopio spoke. Did these men want to check him into the Sunmount Sanitarium and play Chinese checkers all afternoon? Did they think he was mad? Sick?

"*Qué*?" he said, coughing.

"Please sit down," Richard said quietly, pointing to the fourth chair. "We know about your map. We know about all the maps, and we're here to help you. Here, we brought yours back." He gestured to the center of the table where it lay.

"It's hidden," thought Faustino as he edged closer to the Blessed Mother in the *nicho*. Any so-called copy of this map was a delusion, and he gave a wary glance to its hiding place.

Nicasia suddenly interrupted, "It's here on the table, Faustino." Faustino gave her a wild-eyed look. He had put the map under the Virgin's carved foot and not on the table. "We brought you the map," Michael said.

"How did you get my map?" Faustino's resentment surged as he passed his tongue across his teeth and stared at Michael. He could not forgive Michael for his outburst of lies against Mother Church.

"They have come to ask you to explain the map," Procopio said. Faustino again calculated that Procopio believed he knew all there was to know about the map he had never seen. Refusing to speak, Faustino looked around the small room.

"Do you know what these squares mean?"

A strangeness shuddered through Faustino's wiry form. He refused to cooperate with these three men. This refusal compacted around his spine, and he took on the narrowness of a snake. He grew so slim in his mind that he felt unseen. Only a stem of an invisible man, he shuddered like an aspen. "No," he said. In the silence that followed, the word echoed. "No."

Nicasia watched how the stupefying demand affected her husband. She pulled up a fifth chair and sat. "What good will the map do you?" she asked the men, hoping to prompt Procopio to snatch it from the table. "This one is the false map, the phony lead." She lied. Her mother would have lied. Tía Serafina certainly lied often about it.

"There was more than one," Procopio said, and for a long moment all four people watched him, waiting for more information. None came.

"I have the only one. Abran Ulibarri had no right to it." Faustino spoke softly. And while the two patrones waited for Procopio to speak, the percolator began its incessant pop-pop-pop, a countdown to more information. The scent of coffee filled the small room.

"If these squares are rooms, then your gold's in the back wall," Richard said, his voice calm. "It belongs to you. Don't worry; we know it's yours." Faustino scanned the gringos' faces, looking to read what they had in mind.

Nicasia stood to break the tension. She wiped her hands on her tiered skirt and pulled her cotton blouse down, moving to get four cups.

Before she could bring them to the table, Richard reiterated, "That gold, if it is found, is all yours."

There was the dull sound of the ceramic cups striking the oil cloth as, again, silence fell. A few percs from the coffeemaker punctuated the darkness, and Faustino gave a faint nod. Standing, he steadied himself against the kitchen wall. Procopio seemed to have no interest in a share of the treasure. Such a thing was unlikely, but he wanted to appear wholly untainted by greed.

Michael accepted a cup of coffee, murky brown with coffee grounds. The color reminded him of damp adobes. He held the cup in his hand, blew on it out of habit, and said, "We can help. If you find it, it's yours. But you have to do most of the work."

Faustino watched him with a serpent's glare. "Why?"

"You are going to need our help, and we are willing to give it." Richard accepted his coffee and took a sip. Nicasia stopped for a moment. Procopio nodded with an assured smile and said nothing more. Faustino took a deep breath and calculated that his uncle was reckoning up his own percentage, not simply reaffirming that the *patrones* were Christ's own *caballeros* as he had claimed. The silence continued.

"They're saying it's okay to hack on what's left of the wall," Procopio said. "It's already a ruin."

"I'm guessing we all read the map in the same way. Michael and I are willing to take a risk that this is correct," Richard said quietly. "Your wife came, and if she's convinced it's there, I'm willing to believe her."

"Nicasia, how?" Faustino said, looking at his wife. He waited for her to speak.

She was unprepared for this turn of events, but, as she reminded herself, "They did not say no." So without responding to her husband, she addressed the men. "Why, *Señores Patrones*?"

"Why don't we want to take your gold? Is that what you are asking?" Faustino said, "*Sí*."

"That's a valid question. We know we live in your old auntie's adobe. It needed a lot of work, which we did. We are grateful to be living in it." Richard looked squarely at Faustino when he spoke. "The real truth is, I'm lucky to be alive, and we have always aimed to leave this world a better place. It's being what you people call a '*vecino*.'"

"Your wife told us the gold belongs to your family," Michael said. "From the looks of it, you need it, don't you? Like she said, it's for the boys' schooling."

Nicasia was barely able to hold her head up. She had been overcome by the same exhaustion she'd had after giving birth to her sons, an exhaustion like none other coupled with a collapse so complete she could not move. She was too enervated to absorb their offer. If she could smile, it would not be for herself.

"So, let's open up that map one more time," Richard said.

Michael nodded. "That map."

Faustino closed his eyes; he could not move. Nicasia burst into tears and spread it open on the table, moving the cups aside. "It is in the *dispenza* wall," Faustino said as he pointed, "here at the *X* in your powder room."

Leaving their coffee cups on the table, the men stood and filed out of the shadowy room. Nicasia tried to rise while Faustino slumped in his wooden chair, staring at his own dried-out hands. As they left, he raised his head, nodding to them and not bowing. For the moment, he was too confused to continue his courtesies.

"Thank you very much," Nicasia said to her uncle and possibly to all of them. "I don't know what else to say." She had forgiven her uncle for pandering to the gringos when he came around to defend all of them, including Doña Tia Serafina. But she no longer liked him as much as she had before. She couldn't step into the same river twice.

After the three walked off, Nicasia cleared the cups and, weak legged, returned to her chair. She and Faustino leaned over the table on their elbows, lost in their own thoughts. Faustino was gratefully recalculating the Church's teachings on morality while Nicasia was summoning the strength to scorn the offer. In the distance they heard the barking of the dog pack when the three rounded the corner to cut through Paco Gurulé's yard. If he'd even been roused from his sleep, Paco would have come running to Nicasia to report the gringos' walking among his apple trees and not driving their shiny cars. Once the barking calmed, the couple sat again in the dim silence, weighing what they had been given.

Nicasia was wary, if not actually frightened, of the nearing treasure, while Faustino was consumed not with the treasure but again with his neurotic outrage over Michael's denunciation of the Holy Bible, his unnatural sins and now his rich-man's condescending charity. He envisaged Michael's boasting of his so-called saintly act, while Procopio would be busy grabbing credit for protecting the García legacy, for keeping it in their family hands. Again, no words passed, and the adobe home sat solemnly waiting for a burst of vitality when the boys banged home from school.

Procopio had insisted the *dueños* were charitable men. Allowing him to dismantle then rebuild their wall was a kindness Faustino García could accept while still maintaining his vow never to enter their house. Vows were serious business. "*Son buena gente*," Nicasia muttered.

"*Sí*," Faustino said. His agreement came hard. In the back of his mind, he saw Procopio crowing, "I told you so! They are very fine men." He'd heard this for more than eight years, yet he could not trust them, nor could he trust Procopio.

"How," Faustino asked himself, "could any good come out of corrupt motives?" After some time, he capitulated again to his mission, surrendering to the wooden Virgin's demand for gold. "I humbly submit to your will, Virgin Most Pure."

Nicasia rose to turn on the single light over the table when the boys clattered back into the house. After giving each boy an embrace, she finally spoke. "Faustino, please tell the *muchitos* what the gringos have said."

And then, as slowly and carefully as possible, he told his sons about the generosity he had just been offered. As he spoke, tears streamed down the side of his face.

Both boys were terrified that the gold would be found and they would be thrown into the Christian Brothers School. "We don't want to speak Latin," they said. Their eyes pooled.

"After school, you are to help your father rebuild the wall, of course," she said to her silent sons.

"I will make the adobes myself," Faustino said. They would pour the mud at night and leave them to bake in the sun during the school day. "I expect both of you to work on weekends, too." Nicasia watched Faustino's moods fluctuate as he lived through the possibilities this gringo generosity presented. By late night, he had gathered his forces surrendering to their offer.

"I will be working alone," he told Nicasia. "First, I will take down the weak wall and then build it back with new adobes."

Faustino grew to understand the gringos; more than riches, they sought to be admired by other gringos. Like children, they had a deep need for approval. Spud was the first person Michael told about the map and the gold; his large glasses magnified his excited twinkle over the story. "What fun! Even if no gold is found, you'll have wrung more value from that García fellow's so-called treasure than even Dorothy Parker could drum up at her most amusing New York black-tie dinner." And he trotted off to relate Michael's story to a group of Fred Harvey's friends at the La Fonda bar.

That night, Michael dazzled their dinner partners with the story of the map, the gold and the crumbling wall. "If anyone looked in need of some lost gold, that skinny dog, Faustino, does."

Amelia White shook her head with delighted surprise as she heard of their allowing Faustino permission to quietly dismantle the standing wall of the old *hacienda* and enlisted Witter Bynner to write up "a little drama" they could all act out. The story of the lost treasure enticed Will Schuster, who insisted that Michael come for dinner the next night and relate the story "from the beginning." God's Mother-in-law, Mary Austin, thoroughly approved of the venture, nodding her head while requesting permission to use the story in a volume on cultural peculiarities of the region. "It is *exactly* the sort of tale I need to show what life is truly like here."

And, Mabel Dodge Lujan, the self-declared grandest dame of them all, let them get halfway through the much-elaborated story before she interrupted with her own long story about helping the widow of her miserly neighbor in Taos search for gold under her fireplace bricks.

"There is buried gold all through these old *haciendas*! Tony can tell you even more stories," Mabel Dodge exclaimed and asked for another drink. Over the weeks, more wondrous stories surfaced to titillate the revolving houseguests. For weeks, the gossip centered on the treasure, and the story was reworked a short fortnight later, ending up as a witty piece on the White sisters' stage called "A Nose for Gold."

The Anglo contingent raved about Michael and Richard's fine, fair play and called it a fable even as the entire town began tapping on their walls. The search for the treasure had caused such a hullabaloo that even Father Sebastiano dropped his fascination with adultery to focus on "crossing your treasure from Canyon Road to the safety of heaven."

Mary Austin wrote to Willa Cather suggesting that she insert a new diversionary episode in her novel about Bishop Lamy and his insubordinate priests. Even the artists began to put more tinges of gold-hued yellow into their *plein aire* studies of the Ranchos de Taos buttressing.

Crowds gathered across the street from Faustino's project, and when the school down the street let out, the lemonade sales flourished. The bighearted gawkers, when interviewed, agreed that they'd honestly and sincerely be thrilled to hear that Faustino (who happened to be a close relative to everyone in town) had found his gold, and they were certainly interested in fondling an uncut diamond. "Just once!"

The Santa Fe New Mexican printed a front page photo turning Faustino into a local star, and the radio gave morning reports that everyone followed with excitement.

It was not working out as envisioned. Michael said, "He'll take it home silently, stuffing it in his pockets and we'll never know if he found anything at all!"

"He'll spoil the fun, I can guarantee it," Richard insisted.

"You simply have to insist that he show you anything that turns up!" Mary Austin was adamant. "He can keep it, of course. Only after you photograph the stash. It has great historical value."

"Of course, it would be fine with me if he just registered everything that might be of interest at the library," Richard suggested. "I suppose the library is the proper institution. He could leave the pictures for them to catalogue."

"Why don't we offer to buy the damn treasure?" Michael said, blurting out. "Then we can give it to whomever we damn well please."

Everyone agreed that the map strongly conferred the responsibility on whoever had the good fortune to own it to allow the public to examine what treasure was uncovered. "We agreed to leave it with Faustino, and we'll stick by our principles," Richard insisted.

Procopio listened and reserved his opinion for later, waiting with enormous dignity. Some of it might certainly be due him as well, but if nothing turned up, he did not want his early greed to be broadcast.

Barely a week later, Faustino hit the ceiling when he was told of Spud's published essay on the treasure in which he was described as a wretched woodcutter with an even more wretched burro, living on beans and rice while his wife hawked *empanadas*. Who else but the homosexual Freethinkers with their notoriously phony Christian values had fed Spud these stupidities? Where were Sodom and Gomorrah when Faustino was being ravaged in this way?

On the other hand, these men had relinquished their claim to the gold in their walls, which, Faustino admitted, was a decent act. As he prepared to begin his excavation, he was called for another meeting.

"Faustino, please bring that map inside," Richard said. Faustino hesitated. He had vowed never to enter the house, on one hand, but on the other, he was not going to hand over the map. He must either surrender his honor and his convictions or let go of the map. Finally he went.

Procopio, Richard and Michael sat on their *portal* studying the *X* on Faustino's map, further weakening the torn fold. They followed his calloused finger as Faustino explained what he knew in English. "This small room is the *dispenza* wall, the part wrecked by the powder room addition."

"That's what you said before." Richard straightened his collar and stared off, trying to recall just what he had razed when he turned that small, dingy pantry into the luminous, marble-tiled powder room off the kitchen—not the most convenient place for their guests. He remembered its being claustrophobic and cramped, dark, crowded and lined with old stained wooden shelves.

Faustino was insistent. This map was correct: "It's right here."

"If indeed this was the designated wall, old Elodio would probably have sat on a small stool and chipped an opening right about here," Richard said. "Then he'd need to enlarge it." Both Procopio and Michael nodded and agreed that this spot was exactly where Elodio had buried his stash, stopping short of the real treasure as he died.

"How large did you say the treasure is?" Michael asked.

"Small but heavy," Faustino said. "A few hundred gold coins and a leather pouch tied with a thong." He was uncomfortable with this committee.

"No," Procopio insisted. "In a box, a wooden box." Faustino shook his head that this was wrong. Procopio hopped on his soapbox again to loudly proclaim, "The hand-carved wooden box is itself of great value."

"Not true! Pouches, wrapped in the cloth. No box," Faustino said. "Small."

Procopio held his ground: "It was made of cedar, or it could have been imported sandalwood."

"Says who?"

"I've heard it for years," Procopio said, looking to the *dueños* for approval.

"The treasure is not that large," Faustino said, wishing Procopio would go away. "Everyone thinks it's bigger than it is. Bigger and richer." To end the discussion, Faustino caved in. "Have it your way, then. The box might be the size of two bread loaves."

Procopio interrupted, "And not too close to the floor, but a little higher, say, perhaps behind the second shelf from the bottom with those herbs and remedies." He was showing far too great an interest in the treasure's rescue.

"*Basta*, Procopio," Faustino spat.

"No, no. I believe he's quite right," Richard intervened. "Our man here has a good head on his shoulders." All three men nodded with satisfaction. Faustino wanted to spit.

"I'll leave it in your hands," Michael said, hoping to retreat to his studio. "I hope these squares are room. It's much too vague. You should figure out where the dirt floor was before we had everything redone," Richard said, hoping to return to his reading and leave both men wearying the fading *X*.

Faustino visualized saturated and sopping wet leather pouches entombed somewhere in this undermined wall at about the height of his knees. He was sure that the first cut should be direct and straight where the midline of the wall had been. He saw the crowded shelving burdened with herbs, some almost a century old, gathering dust and evaporating potency to the very air. Who did not remember the musty smell of Doña Tía Serafina's medicines?

"It should be right about here." Faustino tapped the wall, but Procopio disagreed. Faustino's skin prickled; Procopio had illicitly taken one cache of coins and was meddling himself into another. Even if he'd told the *patrones* of this early theft, they'd not believe him over Procopio, so he turned abruptly to escape through the kitchen door out onto the street.

There, in the shadow of the monolithic wall, the double-adobe wall with no windows, a crowd was forming, fed with well-informed interest. Fury choked him. Procopio and Flora had been regaling everyone with stories of the map and the treasure.

"Goddamn you; you've told everybody!" He could barely get the words out as he yelled back through the side door into the kitchen.

Procopio came to the doorway. "As I told you, it was never a real secret."

"It was always a secret!" Faustino looked helplessly at the gathering of local *vecinos* and shrugged his shoulders in defeat. "The only secret left is how much you've already filched."

"I'm talking about the great hoard from years back. We've all known that there were maps and that there was a treasure hidden somewhere," Procopio said, never considering the wider value of bringing honor and dignity to the faithful colonists, to the Garcías. Seeing their excitement over finding what Carlota tried to keep, the Virgin, too, knew that only

Faustino could be trusted to understand how these jewels were to be used to restore the Divine Right of monarchs.

Faustino had been given a vision in which both of his sons, their swords upraised and glinting in the sun, stood before a cowering Roosevelt, crying, *"Dios y Santiago!"* To them would be given the credit for reversing New Mexico's statehood and returning her to the Mexico of her forefathers. Imbued with the power of the gold, he would carry on the fight himself until his boys came into their own manhood and restored order to the world.

Again, he stared at the expectant crowd on the opposite side of the dirt road and threw his hands helplessly in the air. With a long face, he walked back into the *hacienda*, stumbling as he went.

"This is now a goddamned *fandango*!" Faustino rushed in shouting. The two *patrones* were startled in their wicker chairs under the *portal*. In clear, unaccented English, he screamed, "Next they'll all come with their own pickaxes."

"You are right; it has turned into a sideshow," Michael said, basking in the limelight on his bighearted stance.

"If I take down the wall, the kitchen will be open to the street," Faustino said. "You'll be exposed to the weather and to uninvited visitors."

"Let's get a good fence," Richard offered. "Or sell tickets and let the whole town join in."

Michael leaned back in his chair. "We should ask Procopio what to do."

Faustino wept for sheer frustration. "No!" Everything that could have been right had now been ruined. The long justice of his legacy would never be restored. "No! Please stop always asking Procopio!" Faustino stomped out.

In their version of compassionate goodwill, these two men innocently hoped that the gold would be found and everyone would live happily ever after. Now they saw that charity and good works might take a toll. Michael exclaimed, "This could go on for months!"

Faustino slammed the *zaguan* door behind him.

"They're so emotional," Richard said, wincing.

"At first, it looked easy," Faustino confessed to Nicasia when he fled home in defeat. "But now, both of the *patrones* say they're getting Eusemio to put up a fence."

"*Son muy buena gente*," she repeated. Their word is their honor.

CHAPTER NINETEEN

Faustino was now a warrior patrolling the fenced, double-adobe wall. When he was not assaying the mud, he was stationed on a wooden chair from predawn throughout the day, remaining late until the last weary bystander had given up and left. Even with his stern pose, Nicasia claimed that her husband was again genial—on those rare times he was at home. Eusemio's eight-foot-high Anchor chain-link fence safeguarded the excavation and protected the patient *patrnes* who had more than proven themselves patient as well as fun-loving and charitable. And the Anglos joined n on the fun.

The White sisters' butler left off one of the canvas scrims from El Delirio's theater to festoon the chain-link fencing and to give Faustino some privacy while Paco volunteered to sacrifice a few of his barking dogs as night guard.

When the whole arrangement was complete, Faustino rocked back on his hard chair, contemplating being able to chip away with no one breathing down his neck. Still, he was shaken over the gnawing rumor concerning additional maps. Procopio continued to excite crowds, touting himself as expert on these maps which, Faustino confirmed, he had not physically touched. He could not certify truthfully that they were identical, or if they pointed to the same prize. "Damned Procopio!"

If his own map were false, Faustino would be mortally disgraced. Often during the early hours, he contemplated the unbearable humiliation he would bring on his family. The ridicule! Several times this past week he had thrown himself to his knees before the Virgin's flickering shrine, praying for comfort.

"My child, your map is the true map," Mother Mary, Queen of Heaven, reassured him again. "Bring me gold. I will shower you with honor and pride."

"I beg you, Mother Most Holy, guide me."

"Turn your life over to me. I will not forsake you." In the frightening silence of night, he prayed for greater faith. At Mass, away from Her gaze, he held the Host on his tongue until it disintegrated, asking the sacrament for a sign that his statue's guidance was infallible. In Her presence, he purposely flattered and assuaged Her by calling Her "Queen," pledging his undying loyalty. But kneeling here at Holy Mass, the Host, the body of his Savior inside his mouth, he allowed his secret doubts to rise; waves of anxiety coupled with pangs of disloyalty left him depressed and confused. The stakes were high: if She were to see how he hesitated, She could withdraw her favors at any moment. He realized that Her wrath alone could easily turn his map into a false lead. In the cathedral, doubts pierced him like St. Sebastian's arrows.

Jorge, the now-exonerated plumber, had come and gone and the resoldered broken pipe had been left exposed so that Faustino might avoid puncturing it. The water service had been restored now hours into the night, Faustino was free to lock his tools inside the ruined powder room, satisfied that the house and the *dueños* were safe behind their metal fence. Faustino thought of nothing but the treasure and how it called to him, like orphans seeking their true mother, like stolen goods longing for their owners.

At first, he thought the gold had a slippery voice, warm with the sunshine, leading him on. Later, he attributed the voice to the Virgin, his Queen. Mingled in and with no melody or beauty came impatient taunts from the *dueños*, urging him to hurry and get out of their lives. Faustino's sleep was shattered by Michael's voice accusing his ancestors of theft and murder.

"And you *conquistadores* took this Mexican gold from the Indios. They have cursed it. It is theirs."

Faustino tried to goad them: "Indian lovers, Indian lovers!" Then the vision dream wandered off into a cave and was lost. He forced himself to follow, but, out of breath, he was too slow.

Reluctantly coming back from the deep, longing never to breathe again, he found himself once more under the lampshade's circle. From the nightmare, he understood that Richard and Michael never wanted to keep the treasure for themselves. Why neither man risked touching it. They believed what Nicasia believed; the gold was cursed.

"*Una pesadilla*; a bad dream," Faustino muttered, disturbed. He presented the Madonna with a question. "Why did Serafina make more than one map?" But he knew that part of the answer was that there had been more than one hiding place. But she was silent.

"Procopio," he demanded, "were Elodio's savings in the walls of the old *dispenza*?"

"He left them for me, yes. In the *dispenza* Elodio's body was found."

"And your map, the one with your wedding photo, led you right to it?"

"Serafina and I were very close; I told you that she wanted me to have the savings."

"Your map looks like my map," Faustino pressed.

"My map showed only one room, the *dispenza*."

"May I please see it to compare?"

"As I said, La Doña Serafina and I were very close. Yes, if you must, stop by the house."

When Faustino parked his battered truck outside Procopio and Flora's *casita*, he entered the house willing the maps to be identical. Wanting his map to be a copy of the first, but it was not. As Procopio had said, his map showed one small room with shelves and an X on a corner where one shelf joined another. One room, no more.

On Faustino's map, the X was at the right-hand end of a series of rooms.

Eusemio Johnson's sturdy metal fencing allowed Faustino to be both the wall's protector and its assailant. He became a local star; he was the Knight of the Adobe Wall and should have worn a costume. This quest was now public; it was a grand theater with money wagered on the outcome. The odds were even-steven and the speculators were fixed to the ground across Canyon Road, allowed to come no further. A burly stranger peered through the steel knitting, threading his fingers through one of the fence's loops while Faustino, the lion, paced within his safe confine around the perimeter of the silent house.

"Hey, buddy," the gringo began. "Want some advice?" He spoke slowly. Texan, Faustino thought.

"*Suéltame.*" Faustino squinted at the man's several turquoise and silver bracelets, noting his expandable watchband set with turquoise. "Stand back," he ordered and picked up an axe.

"No, listen, buddy, I'd be glad to give you a hand in this. If you hit what you're looking for, you'll..." The *tejano* had two *concha* belts, more silver and more turquoise and this set Faustino's blood boiling. Whom was he mocking? Faustino had never clapped eyes on the jerk. He was new in town.

"I know what I'm doing," Faustino shot back.

"No, look, my friend, let me save you a mess of problems. See?" Again Faustino cut the interloper off.

The *tejano* cleared his throat to begin once more. "Metal detectors. We use 'em back home."

"Stand way back. I mean it." And he lifted the axe above his head and let it fall on part of the chewed-up wall where the treasure should have been. The rest of the wall still stood; it had been buttressed years back because of the extra weight of the counter and the marble sink. Faustino figured, and apparently the gathering crowd concurred with him, that the treasure lay in the desiccated dirt, that older, dried-out earth from the 1600s original house.

The decked-out gringo showed no respect for the rules. "Stand back," Faustino warned him again.

"Yer jess spinnin' your wheels here," he said and turned slowly away.

Faustino, fueled by his intense irritation with the meddler, continued to pound the wall with his pick even more angrily than before. To him, his work represented the dignity of a *padre familial*, the head of the family nobly unearthing what was his, working to restore their titles and wealth. He landed the pick more forcefully on the newer adobes, letting out a grunt. Behind the intimidating groan was his own growing regret that his boys absolutely refused to attend the Christian Brothers College. He wanted his sons to tell the gringos to scram—in Latin! New Mexico always belonged to Old Mexico, or better stated, the two Mexicos belonged together.

He gave an adamant thrust of the pick, wondering when he might finally work through the newer bricks. He raised the pick again and slyly glanced over his shoulder. The crowd, used to talking and calling suggestions to him (suggestions that he steadily ignored), had turned away from watching him. Faustino paused midswing to investigate and found that the silver-studded tourist was back and passing out bottles of iced beer.

He laid his pick on the ground; his shoulders ached, his arms throbbed. Spinning around to face the swarm, he regretted that most were relatives. Some were women returning from the Plaza with their shopping bags. All were now chatting and the men were amiably swigging cold beer from Gormley's store up the hill.

"Have one on me, *amigo*," said the stranger, waving a beer on the end of a long arm.

Faustino was too beat to turn down a beer. "Where are you from?" he asked.

"Dallas, Texas," the man said, nodding, bobbing. "It's real hot there." More and more of these Texans had been coming here to stay at La Posada. It had a swimming pool.

"I go back home by November when it gets cold here. But I want to talk to you about…"

"You come here alone?" Faustino's question was heavy with resentment.

"No, I bring my family, my friends. We love it here." And he took a deep draught of his beer, sighing with satisfaction. Faustino stared at the man.

"You believe in Adam and Eve?"

"You kidding? Of course I do. Why'd ya' ask me that?"

Just then Michael came out of the house and addressed Faustino. "I like what I see," he said, surveying the site. "A good clean work spot."

"Can I get ya'll a beer," said the Texan. But Michael shook his head. The Texan was quick to add, "If ya don' mind me sayin' it, there's an easier way to do this."

Michael stopped, interested. Faustino looked up, studying the man's leathery smile.

"I've been watching awhile, ya know," the *tejano* said. "I know a real easy way to find what's in that wall." Faustino stared at the stranger when he heard those words—words from the Virgin. "An easy way."

"We want him to take this wall down," Michael pitched in. "Then he'll put up a new one. A better one."

"I heard there's leather bags with diamonds in them. A metal detector won't help with the diamonds, but it sure can pick gold out fast."

Michael took a deep breath and said, "I guess you guys in Texas know what you're talking about when it comes to stuff like that? Minerals, I mean."

"I hope to tell ya!" Closing in, the Texan continued, "Mussolini, you know him? He used a metal detector at the bottom of a lake to get the gold belonging to Emperor Caligula, if ya know who I'm talkin' about." Faustino continued to stare at the men.

Michael nodded, suggesting he knew both men intimately. He was now interested enough to accept a beer from the chatty stranger.

"So you heard of President James Garfield? You know he was shot, see, and he called in Alexander Graham Bell (this was before your time), and they used a metal detector on him to find the bullet where he'd been shot through the chest." Faustino paused and listened. From his expression, it was clear that Michael was impressed.

"They get the bullet out?" Faustino asked.

"No, sorry to say. No." Michael gave the Texan a what's-the-point-of-this? shrug. "Bedsprings," the Texan continued. "The electric radio beams went wild with the metal bedsprings." Both men stared at the Texan thinking the same thing: The guy is smart.

"How did they find the bullet then?" Michael asked, wondering why this stranger was telling stories like this.

"No need; they left it in. He died from a heart problem. But if I was you, I'd get a metal detector and forget tearin' walls down and ruining the whole house."

"How much do they cost?" Faustino despaired. He had no money.

"How much is the treasure worth to ya?" the Texan shot back. "I'd reckon a couple of hundred'll buy you a detector. Might could be I have one back at my place in Dallas."

"And you'd bring it along?" Michael saw a benefit to this. "When you come back?" The quicker the gold came out, the quicker the ugly fencing could be removed. "I'd not mind renting it awhile and getting my garden back in shape for spring."

"Yeah, late spring's when I'll be back. You can check your newspaper; when it gets over eighty-five degrees in Big D, I pack my wife and kids up and we hit the road. One stop in Lubbock and Bob's your uncle." Faustino watched the strange man carefully. His voice was loud.

"So what do you think? Shut it all down until Buddy here gets back with his gizmo?" Michael's suggestion of closing down the search made Faustino apprehensive. He had no desire to shut down the quest. If he could continue chipping away and found the treasure, there would be no need for the metal detector. The wall would be restored and the fence could be taken down because the house would then be secure.

"I'll find it well before spring," Faustino said.

"With the metal detector, you won't have to keep looking. You'll go right to the spot!"

"True," said the Texan.

"Of course, I will do as the *patrones* wish." Faustino began bowing.

"You are doubly sure that your treasure is in this wall?" Michael pointed to the excavation. "Positive?"

"Yes, *Señor. Sí*," Faustino replied, looking at the Texan—but in the back of his mind danced Procopio's map of Elodio's savings. Did his map show where the treasure was *not*? Did this mean that the Virgin was toying with him, simply amusing Herself? If so, his humiliation and disgrace would be enormous.

"Are you dead sure?"

"*Sí, Señor Patrón*, I am positive the gold is right here," Faustino said. He swallowed, looking into the man's pale blue eyes.

Michael's fleshy cheeks trembled. "*Bueno*," he replied and turned to the Texan. "If it is not too much trouble, can you throw that device into your luggage when you come back here? Just in case?"

"Happy to do it. And no charge. No charge at all."

Faustino ended his day then and there. He had uncovered nothing, and if his *X* marked Procopio's take, his own enormous treasure might even be in the *gran sala*, a room he'd never be allowed to disassemble. Plus, he could not protect the treasure until the Texan returned.

"You know how you keep saying that gold brings death?" he said to his wife.

"It certainly brings me misery."

"I trust you, Faustino. I trust you'll get what you want," she replied. It's a huge sum, or so I've been told by everyone."

"The Virgin said to make a medallion, a holy medal of her."

"*Bueno*, if that's that she said."

"The boys' school. We'll buy some land. Land with water. Sheep, too."

"You want to buy back the stolen land?" She paused; as she touched him, his back rose to meet her warm hands. "Pay for it with the gold?"

"For our sons and their sons, sons of the *ancianos fundadores*. For the *vecinos*."

"*Bueno*," she said. In her mind, the devil's grip loosened

CHAPTER TWENTY

Behind his barrier, as Faustino continued his maniacal work sifting through the detritus of his excavation, the Texan returned with his gizmo. Just as he had promised, he rode into town with his entire family and announced himself. He could be heard at a distance.

"He talks so loud." Flora had said. "That *gabacho* does everything loud!"

"I said I'd bring it in the spring, so I brung it," he announced as Procopio answered the *zaguan* door one April afternoon. Hearing his hearty drawl, Richard rose from his chair under the *portal* to greet him, returning his robust handshake as best he could. He was pleased to see he'd brought the metal detector with him. "This'll do the trick."

"Procopio, give the gentleman a hand here with his machine," Richard said, ushering the congenial man across the *plazuela* now filled with the alert tulips of early April. "Come sit. Have some ice tea," Richard insisted, indicating that he should sit at a small table next to a wainscoted wall.

Flora peered out and with a practiced nod, pulled back into the kitchen to bring a second glass of iced sweet tea after Procopio lugged the machine to set it down inside the house, near the *sala*. The newfangled detector was made out of heavy metal and easily weighed thirty pounds. A silk-bound electric cord was casually curled around the sturdy handle.

"I don't know how to thank you," Richard said.

"I'm delighted, delighted!" the Texan told Richard, accepting the cold glass. And he was even more delighted when he was invited to return that evening with his mannerly family to be served drinks in this "historic Canyon Road *hacienda*."

"It's the real thing, I guarantee ya!" the Texan carried on as they dressed, splashing themselves with Old Spice and Shalimar. Six o'clock on the dot that evening, Navajo jewelry chinking, the Texan arrived to demonstrate how the magic do-whatchee, thingama-doodle worked, leading his wife and daughter. Michael, however, was not ready to sic "the gold finder" on the walls under the Texan's watch, so he saw that they were plied with whiskey and beer while Richard flattered his wife and daughter.

Drinks in hand, Michael led the three into his studio. He waved his hand and said, "Please take one of my paintings here for yourselves. You know, for your help with the so-called treasure."

"No need. No need at all. If truth be known, we collect big scenery paintings mostly with a horse or two. We're horse and cattle people." His broad smile wrinkled around his eyes so they almost disappeared. Michael shot a glance at Richard and they led the summer people through the rest of the fine old adobe house, exaggerating its most historical aspects. "This grand sala used to be four bitty rooms," he announced.

The Texans were mighty impressed, they said. In the blue-tile kitchen, Richard pulled back a heavy canvas curtain they'd put up to keep the dust down from Faustino's never-ending excavation. "Everyone thinks he'll find his gold and silver right here, but so far, nothing."

"In one form or another, he has been at this close to a year now," Michael said. "We hope your machine works and this whole thing comes to a swift end. He won't stop until he finds it."

"I rue the day we gave him permission to dig out his legacy," Richard said.

"Honey, these gentlemen have allowed that poor devil to work here for almost a full year, now. Why, you'd have lost your fine mind if some fool had torn your house into pieces," the Texan said to his wife with a huge smile.

"Don't you just know it!" she replied, jiggling the ice in her bourbon and coke. "Y'all be sure to tell us how this comes out, now!"

"It's just so romantic!" his daughter said, swooning as she followed through room after room in the old house. "I'd just love to find a secret treasure!"

After they'd left, Michael poured himself a stiff drink, downed it and made ready to crank up the metal detector, beginning close at hand in the *sala*. He danced with delight when he was led to a spoon wedged under a sofa cushion. Later, arms aching, with the metal detector screaming, he pulled up a ladder-back chair and yelled for Richard. Something half buried in the interior wall was facing him; there was evidence of an old lintel that had once opened into a closed-off storeroom now accessed from the *plazuela*. By the time of Serafina's household, the recess for the door had been filled with a dilapidated armoire, which Richard had had removed. Because the space was large, deep shelves for his Indian pot collection were installed, and not much thought had been given to the rough plastered back.

"Wasn't that room back there one of the birthing rooms once?" Michael had asked Flora years back. He liked the idea that this home brought new lives into being; it had launched his own new existence. Michael's recovery was a form of birth. It really was.

"Don't ask me," she said. "I wasn't even alive back then."

Facing the shelves, he realized that what everyone believed the map indicated was a pantry or a closet could reasonably be a part of this walled off birthing room. The machine screamed that something was concealed in the deep alcoves behind the shelves. Stretching to feel with his hand, Michael ran his fingers over a rough spot on the far right side, along the thick adobes of the doorframe.

"Richard!" he called out again. "Bring a flashlight, goddammit!" What he had come across was so probable that he silenced the machine and called again, "Richard, I found it!"

Richard had been at his desk describing the Texan visitors in his weekly letter to his family in the East. Slightly irritated, he ambled into the room holding a four-battery flashlight.

"I believe I've found it," Michael said. "Look here!" When he put the light on the rough patch, not disguised but unseen behind artifacts, he said, "Why didn't we catch this in the beginning?"

"Remember that ratty armoire?" Michael said. "It has always been stuck behind the stuff we collected." Together, they took the pots off the shelves and set them safely aside. He felt the sandy plaster patch above the second shelf, touching it once, twice and then tapping with his fist, listening. "It could be the treasure."

"So...the map was wrong!" Richard said, pulling up another chair.

"No, who knows what the map meant?" Michael tapped the side of his head. "If we'd just used our heads, we didn't really need this thingamabob at all!" The rough patch was waist high and pointed to the thickest part of the double-adobe wall.

"Serafina never found it. She didn't know," Michael said thoughtfully. "She was the type who'd give it all to the archbishop anyway."

"But she knew where it wasn't. She drew a map to the wrong place." Michael shook his head in amazement.

"She never moved the furniture. I can't really believe that treasure is still in there."

"If the thingama-doodle screams again, it is." Michael turned it on. When it shrieked, he switched it off quickly. "Sorry. Loud, isn't it? But, according to it, there is a lot of stuff right here."

"There's a problem now. You promised the Texans that we'd show them what we find," Michael said.

"What is best is that no one see what we find here. Not Procopio, not the Texans." Richard was pensive. "It would be for the best."

A half hour later, with a small chisel, Michael had removed the shelves and chipped out the plaster patch to reveal the disintegrated sides of a carved wooden box, buried inside the dry earth of the wall. "Procopio said it was supposed to be in a wood box."

Richard reached in to touch it. "It's wood, all right." The silk cloth bundling was shredded and fell apart in his grip. The sides of the box were disintegrating, so Michael reached in to pull it out with a steady force. When it was out, a sifting of sand and pebbles fell to the floor.

"Careful!" Richard cautioned. "It's coming apart. It'll spill out all over the place. Here, put it on the colonial table over there." He trembled with anticipation.

"Don't yell at me like I'm a child." Michael shuffled across the room to the refectory table, working to hold the heavy box together. When he placed it squarely on the table, Austrian gold pieces tumbled out. They both gasped.

"Look, there's more!" Richard yelled. Inside the dark hiding hole, Richard spotted the splintering side of yet another box and there they found the promised gold coins with several bars of bright yellow gold, plus the loose diamonds the legend foretold. They were not uncut, but they were rough cut. When Michael weighed them in his hand, he felt they were more than a pound, perhaps even two pounds, of diamonds the size of roadside pebbles. There were doubloons as well and a collection of jewelry.

"Fit for a queen." Richard gasped, dizzy from such a sight as this.

"This calls for a toast," Michael ordered. "I need another drink to get me to gather my wits enough to turn it over to that damned Faustino. I don't want to have that madman come in here to get it, for godsake! We'll have to take it to him."

"He'll have to begin rebuilding the south wall," Richard said. "He'll be back tomorrow like clockwork. We don't have to rush."

"Spare me all his tedious bowing and scraping. That and his unbearable "*Señores patrones*." The two men reluctantly raised their glasses to Faustino and proceeded to polish off the French champagne. "With a fortune like this behind him, he'll become really insufferable."

"Bottoms up. Don't let it go flat," Michael chirped. "Let's count the take. I can't wait another minute."

Richard held up his hand. "First, another bottle of bubbly." So they cracked open a fresh bottle of scamper juice, distracting themselves with it, debating about turning everything over to Faustino. "It would be in very good hands if we kept it." They poured more champagne and sat at the table, not wanting to share this astounding find with anyone else.

"You realize how enraged everyone would be if we did that? Amelia, Mary, Spud—all of them understand that this was never ours to keep. We made a bloody point of being good citizens."

"But, what if we keep half? We didn't think we'd uncover a true king's ransom here. Now that we can see the extent of it…"

"It's the principle of the matter. If what we had found was a small sock with a few coins, you'd have no hesitations." The two men toasted again, took a deep breath and bent to tally the glorious find spread before them on the table.

"Oh Carlota!" sighed Michael. "If you'd just let us keep this safe for you…"

"My god," Richard whispered. "I love this stuff." His hand trembled as he swept first-found coins into a pile, making order by stacking the Austrian coins by fives and tens. He was hypnotized by the perfectly stamped gold pieces with their Imperial Hapsburg eagles, claws holding onto proud flags of the old empire. "Any of these coins could be jewelry!"

"There's so much more here," he added, sweeping across the table with his elbow to clear a new space. When Richard looked up, he found Michael's hands overflowing with the collected wealth of the Hapsburg Empress. Standing out in the piles of rings and jewels set in enameled broaches were heavy, gold medallions of the Virgin Mary. "These came out of another pouch."

The second box was packed in with gold coins, less from Europe now but more worn coins, booty no doubt pulled from shipwrecks and Indian mines.

"The sad Empress could have bought her husband's freedom with these riches," Richard said. He remembered learning that the Mexican insurgents had shot Maximillian and that the Empress spent her long, lonely years mourning for him. "She might have saved him with all of this."

"The revolutionaries would have taken the money for guns and shot him all the same. Too, don't overlook the fact that Maximillian always knew Mexico was rich in silver and gold. He'd have stayed home otherwise."

"Revolutionaries are as bad as the rest," Richard said. "This cache, then, would have gone away bit by bit to small gun dealers, to black-market crooks. It wouldn't be here now."

"Still, I hate to turn it over to that numskull," Michael said, "when it belongs in a museum."

"It's not ours, remember?" Richard was the one who had nearly died. He felt his life had been spared and he needed to show his gratitude.

"Mary Austin is going to keel over when she hears about this. It breaks my heart to have to say it."

"Drop it," Richard replied, never lifting his eyes from the treasure.

"But, it's a goddamned crime to give it to him."

"You'll like yourself better when you do what you know is right," Richard told him, preparing to rewrap the treasure. "I'm going to need a dishtowel or something like that to wrap this stuff in."

Michael stood, turning on lights as he left for the kitchen. Richard was hesitant to leave the stash unguarded, so he waited for Michael's slow return before he hurried off to find a valise.

"Did you notice the musty odor of the silk wrapping?"

"Smelled fine to me. Like the rank relics of King Philip's socks!" Michael paused and bent to finger the disintegrated silk. "I'm glad that saintly old lady never got her hands on this loot. The Archbishop was rich enough."

"She sure as hell wouldn't have paid any taxes with it. Let's have another toast!" Richard suggested. "Bottom's up. I'm not lugging this stuff to Faustino sober."

Drinking, they lingered, delaying. "I wish we could give this stuff to the Metropolitan," Michael lamented.

"You just want your father to eat his hat when he sees your name under the display case," Richard said, holding up his glass. "Chin-chin, bottoms up. Get your coat."

"We're off!" Michael said with a sigh. "Mad Carlota grieves in her grave over what we are about to do. How did we get the idea that Carlota's stuff really does belong to Faustino and his wife anyway?"

"It's out of our hands," Richard said. "Bring the car."

The drive was a short one and now dawn was only three hours off.

A narrow moon lit the short walk to Faustino and Nicasia's door. In the dim light, everything slept; the houses, the humans and their animals were all quiet. No radios scratched, the crickets' sawing was turned off, and the roosters held their heroics waiting for the first light. Michael cut the engine of their new 1935 Lincoln Zephyr in front of the quiet García adobe, still debating whether to hand over the fortune.

"Does it make any difference that someone told me this gold is cursed? I forget who."

"All the more reason to give it back," Richard said. Slowly, they walked to the door together and Richard set the valise down on the step before he knocked on the door. Michael stood behind, waiting.

At first, there was no response. He banged again, which started Olivia María braying and set off Paco's seven dogs' furious barking.

"They make me feel like we're thieves," Michael said with heavy melancholy. "Let's get away from these horrid dogs!"

Nicasia awoke first, hearing the ruckus. She rose in her nightgown, padding across the uneven floor to the unlatched door, shocked to find Richard pulling Michael into her house, away from the dogs. She jumped back. "*Señores Patrones?*" she exclaimed, slapping her hand to her mouth.

Alerted, Faustino crawled out of bed and pulled on his pants, bowing to his statue of the Queen of Heaven as he passed into the main room. Next, the boys awoke in the next room, nudging each other, holding their breath, eavesdropping to listen more closely as they picked out the rising and falling of whispers. They heard the sound of chairs scraping and water running and occasionally a statement of disbelief. When Melo's curiosity overcame his hesitancy, he tiptoed to his bedroom door and through the hinged crack, he saw that Nicasia in the kitchen had thrown her arms around Richard's chest, clutching at him until he carefully disentangled himself from her and turned to the valise set on the center of the table under the single light. The crack was not large enough to allow him to see more than just that.

Michael reached in and pulled out a handful of gold. "Here, this is all yours," he said as stray pieces rolled across and some fell to the mud floor. A large gold disk wobbled and settled on the oil cloth covered table.

Nicasia was unable to speak; she stared.

Faustino called out, "The medallion! Here's the gold medallion with the Holy Mother Virgin!" and grabbing it to himself, he took it immediately to the *nicho* and placed it at the Virgin's feet. "Thank you, my Lady," he said, weeping and falling on his knees.

Michael watched this and continued to arrange the gold and jewelry on the table, lingering. Nicasia turned away to shake off what felt like hypnosis. She felt pulled into gold's lure. Not able to ignore what was on the table, she moved off to do something, anything.

"Coffee?" she asked.

No one responded. The gringos were mesmerized, moving the coins across the wooden tabletop, totaling the stacks. They coughed and cleared their throats, almost forgetting to breathe, each still overcome with feelings of enormous gain and wretched loss. The two *dueños* were torn turning this splendor over to a man so disfavored by the twentieth century. A primitive man who refused to read more than the Bible. They turned to find Faustino on his knees before the wooden statue, his head bowed.

To Faustino, the gold itself was insufficient to buy back his people's God-given and bountiful *mercedes*. He sensed that this gold had been paid for with soldiers' blood. It might have been taken from Jezebel as she danced half naked. His loss, and his people's loss, had been so enormous that this yellow metal and these baubles were unequal to the purchase price. He saw the enormity of needed ransom and grieved that this was inadequate.

Nicasia, her back turned, feared her own greed in desiring the gold. Even if it were used for good, she refused to touch it. Treasure of this sort was known to cause wars.

Before they left, she turned to Richard and Michael. "We want you to choose a coin."

"No, no." Both men shook their heads. "We're going back to bed. It's yours."

"How did Tia Serafina get all this?" Melo asked when he crept out of his room after the *dueños* had gone.

"It was never hers," Nicasia said, still facing away.

"But it came from somebody, didn't it?"

"It was lost by that German Empress."

Later, Nicasia recalled that at the time, she had been overcome with a giddy sense that she had been crowned, and her beautiful crown was heavy with gold and sapphires. But she never wore it without her *vecinos* spurning her and throwing rocks.

For weeks afterward, when her heart stopped pounding in her ears in the dark of night, she considered that for the gringo *patrones* the incident was trivial, a footnote in their lives. They were rich men and did not need to steal what was not theirs. Like all men, even these two were proud, too proud to keep back even one coin for show.

"We would never take it for ourselves," Richard had said. "It is yours." Faustino argued that the two unnatural men had squandered far too much of this legacy already: the *hacienda*, the true Church and the grace and loveliness of the colonial past.

As dawn was breaking, Nicasia reburied the great wealth under the *nicho* in her kitchen. For her it was a great burden and she would have to lie about having it. "I don't know how they are going to explain what they found to Procopio."

Faustino waited reverently for his Virgin's next visitation. "She will tell us Her next step."

CHAPTER TWENTY-ONE

Although times had never been easy, by the 1930s, the economy in Santa Fe had plunged. The rest of the country slowly edged itself out of the Great Depression by shifting into the industries of the Second World War. But this fix not only bypassed New Mexico but also drained off her able-bodied men by offering out-of-state work for a dollar an hour, four times the set wage back home. Route 66 had been siphoning restless workers to the coast since 1926, reallocating a whole population into the orange groves of California. Fortuitously then, the labor force was in place for the burgeoning wartime factories on the West Coast.

"Just another of their Yankee double crosses," Nicasia said, waging a bold protest against her men leaving their centuries-old community. The slightest mention of California, that golden state, had been causing all three boys, Franque, Melo and Senio, to have impatient dreams of sunshine and riches. Nicasia put her foot down, saying that her boys were not, nor would they ever be, factory workers.

Fortunately, Franque and Melo began to hang around the New Mexico National Guard stables at Fort Marcy, draping themselves over the fences to admire the horses. Men and horses had always belonged together, especially young men and fast horses.

The National Guard paid eighteen dollars per month. With Nicasia's encouragement, Franque swaggered into the recruitment office on his sixteenth birthday, and to demonstrate his skill, he threw his leg over an unsaddled horse and cantered off. He was immediately enlisted and issued new boots and a khaki uniform. His younger brother, Melo, was burning to mount those horses and lied about his age. His best friend, Senio, lied as well, and they were both immediately inducted. Proud of themselves, they were told that dozens were turned away.

Horses had always been a way of life for young men hot with wild Iberian blood. Working with horses hardly seemed like work, so the cavalry was a perfect fit for any son of the early *hidalgos vaqueros*. Franque, Melo and Senio were now paid to canter and gallop at the parade grounds, showing off their inborn elegance inherited from Oñate and his *hidalgo caballeros* in the 1500s. In those days, *conquistadores* spent day after day in the saddle, parading their small, rugged Spanish Barb horses, herding their *churro* sheep and cattle, searching for riches, converts and good pasture.

Fifteen generations later, the stock sired by horses such as Don Fructoso de García's Relámpago continued to stir up clouds of dust just as they had when the astounded Indians beheld their first glimpse of horses and horsemanship. The way these men seated high on their mounts could cover vast distances quickly added unanticipated dimensions to the lives of every native across the landscape. In time, the *antiguos pobladores* taught the natives to feed and care for these marvelous creatures, but curiously, when the Spanish fled for their lives during the Indian Revolt in the seventeenth century, the Pueblo village warriors ate the horses. Any raiding band of Apaches, Comanches and Navajos would have ridden off with all the livestock. Not the Pueblos.

When the first American cowboys and their herds of cattle arrived from Texas in search of new grazing lands, they met up with the matchless Hispanic cowboys, the *vaqueros*. To their amazement, they discovered men who could rope anything from a saddle, outshining them completely as horsemen. *Vaqueros* set the style, and even though the *tejanos* dressed like them, in their chaps and large hats, no one ever equaled their style or dexterity.

Growing up, Franque, Melo and their friends grabbed any chance to join the small weekend rodeos, jumping on bucking broncos, trying their hands at barrel racing and roping. These events were capped by the traditional *matanza*: a butchered goat cooked under the night's star-spray, a potluck followed by singing to guitars. Aping the *vaquero's* hospitality, the cowboys' barbecue was "beef or nothin'."

Because of her sons' horseplay with the National uard, Nicasia's fears of losing them were allayed. Both boys rode mustangs, small horses that were strong and hardy. Hombre was issued to Melo, while Cervantes, darker and faster, was Franque's mount. Senio rode Chief, a gelding,

"I see you love your horses," Nicasia commented with a smile as the boys drank coffee before sunrise, ready to walk down to the National Guard stables. "I wish we'd given you horses when you were growing up. But look at how you've gotten them for yourselves."

"I still love Olivia María, though," Melo said. "She's getting old."

"Think we could run her out to Panky's land in Villa Nueva? Let her graze there?" Franque knew this idea would suit his mother.

"If that burro left, I'd have some peace." She looked up to see Faustino coming in from the outhouse. Some neighbors were getting indoor plumbing, but Faustino thought it indulgent. "If the *muchitos* get married and move out, maybe..." was all he'd promised his wife. She agreed that "that smelly business" should stay outside, like the burro. "Out of range."

"Still talkin' about Olivia María? If it's not Hoover and Roosevelt around here, it's the burro." Faustino took a chair and was handed his blue and white coffee cup. The number of chips set his apart from the others.

"Panky's got a bunch of acres on the Pecos river," Franque said. "I'm thinking to haul her out in the pickup and let her roam." Faustino's mouth fell open, but no words came out. "You don't need her to haul wood anymore, Papa."

"Most people have dogs. I have my burro. Guards the house," Faustino managed to say between blowing on his cup and taking sips. "Maybe she guards the outhouse better than this place? A man feels safe out there."

"Faustino," Nicasia began. "The time has come to put her with Panky. Franque says he'll get her out to Villa Nueva."

"What did Panky say about it?" Faustino asked. Pancracio, Paco's brilliant cousin, landed forty acres on the river selling his faded truck to Faustino. So there he was, thirty miles east of town and no transportation. No phone either.

"Got to ask Panky; he'll likely say yes." With this, Faustino had agreed to abandon a faithful friend.

"He'll say yes," Nicasia said. "I'll send out some *tamales* with her."

"So how's it going riding Hombre and Cervantes?" Faustino asked his sons. "Sure are pretty. Wish you could bring 'em here."

"They should give you the horses," Nicasia said. "Tell the guard you'll take horses and no pay." She hated their pay; money alienated her boys from real life. It opened glimpses into the worthless, wider world: clothes, beer, movies, cars and girls. "A horse is for life, or for a good chunk of life."

They paid no attention to her. "*Mamá*, I have pesos," Melo said, chinking coins in his pocket. In the vernacular, a peso was a dollar. It was the same thing.

"I said, if they gave you the horse, I'd say, fine. That would be good," she said. "I spit on their pesos."

Melo ignored her stubborn cant, managing to dodge any further lectures on money.

"We need our forest back." She turned to look up from the kitchen sink out the window, observing scattered clouds cross her deep sky. "Not their pay."

In the beginning, the pay was her only grievance, but neither she nor Faustino had anticipated the disaster brought on by their boys' joining the National Guard. Indeed, it was worse than the pay. It was part of a grand trick: dazzling them with their pomp and bravado on the National Guard parade grounds. These parades were especially grand on the Fourth of July, when the depleted US Military eyed these riders for their cavalry.

"Do not take their pay," she told her sons. Had she said this often enough?

"Aww, *Mamá, no me hables así*; how can you say that?" Franque said, his hand in his pocket, fingering his dollar bills. "Shoes, I can buy you shoes."

"I've *got* shoes," she said. Her still sturdy shoes, waxed and repaired, would last past her requirements. "We have always had everything we ever needed."

Nicasia was not stupid; she had seen how money poisoned families, severed their neighborly ties. Before Uncle Sam, the *vecinos* built the community. Money now corroded their Catholic decency and ruined the small, mountain towns, calling the young to abandon their elders.

"You took the money the *dueños* paid you for your *empanadas*," Melo reminded her.

She was quick to snap back that her pesos went directly into the Cathedral's poor box—a ridiculous lie. She turned from the sink and shook the rinse water off her hands. Drying them on her plaid skirt, she faced her youngest son, trying to reason with him, to warn him.

"*Mamá*, you are really old-fashioned! Everything is different now from when you and Dad were young," Melo interrupted. "I mean, take how you and Papa are now buddies with Michael and Richard. Even Dad has eased up on them."

"What about them?" she challenged him. Michael and Richard were like family now. "We all owe them a debt." Now she called them true Christians; Melo was right. "They have shown us great kindnesses." And so saying, she watched his eyes, and she saw a still impressionable child parroting words he'd heard here and there. Words not his own. She scanned his face and found that he had begun to look like a man, his upper lip a shadow of black, downy hair. Suddenly she was overcome with clarity, realizing that he'd indeed not tricked the recruitment sergeant at the National Guard into believing he was of age. It was the other way around; he was tricked! They all knew he was underage. He'd been lured, trapped by paper money, pinned like a bug in a biology lab. Now the *muchitos* hung out in pool halls; their friends had cars. Melo, with his manly courage, was incapacitated by being forced to obey senseless orders. Franque as well.

Melo continued, "So, remember that night when Richard and Michael came over with the treasure?"

"Who could forget it?"

"They woke Franque and me up. Just after the new room was built, remember?"

"Yes. Richard banged on the door in the middle of the night, getting us out of bed."

"It wasn't really that long ago," Melo said. "We heard you whispering loudly and all the chairs scraping. We spied you throwing your arms around Michael, sobbing. You were crying, *Mamá*."

"They turned out to be real fine gentlemen," she said in English. "They stood back and let your father make a mess of the back of their house, and they were the only ones who never wanted a share."

"So, they're rich; what do they need money for?"

"They let your father hack down their outside wall, and they even put up a chain-link fence, and all the time, your father called them *hotos* behind their backs."

"So when did Dad decide fairies were okay by him?" Melo wanted to make his point. Times could change fixed attitudes.

"Their kindness humbled him. He's physically affected...can't talk about it," she said. "You know how he hates the Freethinkers, but he knows these men are good men."

"O, *Mamá!* You still think they're going to hell?"

"Maybe not. Only God can judge. They are good people, but they are frivolous. Even if they are *muy buena gente*, they are still not wise." She shook her head and shrugged her shoulders because the argument should not be about the two *patrones*. It might be about Faustino's taking money when he didn't need it, but it was really about being touched by the gold's curse. "But in the end, they did not do us any good," she said, which made no sense to Melo. "Things turned gringo. You have turned gringo."

"Like how? We're living in the twentieth century now, we have electricity, radio. We've even got a pickup." Melo paused. Counting their blessings made him grin. "We have our family, our home."

"We've gone crazy for stuff we don't need," Nicasia said, her voice stepping up an octave, note by note. "We've gone mad paying for what is ours by royal decree."

"Like?" Melo challenged.

"Water. We sweat for cash to pay taxes on a house the Garcías built with their own hands. Uncle Sam, the same fiend who took our land, is going to take you away. All the time, the gold is here plastered in the wall, saying, 'Get some more!'"

"Don't blame the Devil, *Mamá*. You guys are out of step. We live in the greatest country in the world; we won the Great War so there can't be wars anymore. Uncle Sam is good! We have telephones, movies and things we never had before." Nicasia looked into her son's defiant eyes and sorrowed. "I'm grateful to be an American," Melo went on. "I'm loyal."

"Tell me this, *Hito*: what makes you loyal to President Roosevelt? Just tell me why?"

"I was born here. This is my country."

"Just because you were born here? You don't even remember being born." Nicasia's face was stern, her eyes tightening as she pictured poison coursing through her boy. Its color was gold.

Before she collapsed onto her bed in the darkened room, she told him, "The Devil and his gold are going to throw your heart to Uncle Sam's dogs."

"Oh, *Mamá*, don't get that way again."

"I'm telling you the gold is cursed. The *patrones* would not touch it." Proudly historic, the vixen gold lay quietly festering, feigning to be harmless and unimportant. Sleeping. No longer did people speak of it.

Nicasia had forfeited her last chance to save herself and her family, she thought. She should have turned the pieces over to some museum or to the Catholic Church for the poor instead of suggesting that they rebury the fortune in her own kitchen wall. Her three men were alive, strong and able in that time before the war. She should have rendered them 4-F for the next great war-to-end-all-wars. They could easily have shot off their own fingers, uncomplicated for resolute men, men easily strong enough to support the pain. She should have shot them off herself.

Always the voice in Nicasia's ear: "Beware of the gold!" Had she heard this, or had it been a dream? Faustino claimed to hear messages from the unblinking wooden carving, yet their lives were quietly turning for the worse. And Faustino had no inkling.

Her boys had been numbed. They pocketed the dollars, drank beer and wore store-bought clothes. Melo got a girlfriend, LaBelle Rodriguez, who loved beer as much as she loved him. She had landed in town down from Trinidad, Colorado, on the train, looking for excitement in the closest big town. When the population of *La Villa* fell and adobe houses had been boarded up, a girl as savvy as LaBelle easily stepped into the Five and Dime to serve Frito pie on the Plaza. And not just because she was a dish herself, a real dish; the town hurt for workers.

For a year or more, the quiet town ignored world news, oblivious to the impending war. Nicasia suffered a jolt when Faustino's sidekick, Justo, came alone one morning to explain why he had joined the US Army. "After Maribel, you are the first to know." Saying this, he found it impossible to look at her square in the eye.

Of the three inseparable *pegados*, only Justo had ever actually left town—to return time and again, disheartened. The three childhood friends had married within a year of each other, always living close by. Justo had fathered seven bright children, one after the other, which everyone agreed was God's blessing. Such richness, he said, forced him into the same work as his father had taken in the Eastern Colorado sheep camps, until the rains failed and the lands desiccated. Before Faustino's own father had died from a heart attack, he'd returned home, pockets empty, to report that the dust from Oklahoma had buried the stock under drifts; there was no more work. Ranches were in foreclosure, so he worked for the railroad for a time. Now, Justo had stopped by to announce he'd signed up for the 200th Army Artillery, ready to do basic training at Fort Bliss, Texas. "After basic, I'm counting on Paris," he said, but he was not turning his back on his best buddies. After one stint, he'd be right back as a *vecino* and a *compa*, for sure. "Count on it. You know I'd never leave here."

Justo's wife, Maribel, wept and tore her hair, begging him, pleading with him not to abandon her, but he insisted that she'd be fine now that his two eldest sons were both capable of taking on a man's work. He insisted his family needed the pay, not to mention the benefits, and he was joining up to support them. "Besides," he told Faustino, "the recruiting sergeant said something about being an American goodwill ambassador to the far-off territories." Faustino stood to add more percolated coffee to his cup as Justo explained, "Over there, I can do some good."

"Your wife needs you here. She can't run an outfit the size of yours by herself." He referred to their *acequia*-watered compound, the *milpas* of standing corn, the fields of *chiles* and the tethered goats the same way the Navajos spoke of their homesteads; he called it an *outfit*. A good term, Faustino thought to himself. Justo is *patrón* of an important outfit and a growing family. "Do good by staying home," Faustino added. "They need you."

The two friends were the same age, thirty-six and strong, weathered, responsible men with families. "What can they show you that you don't already know?" Still standing, Faustino hoped to face Justo down, but he finally accepted that any argument would now fail. Justo was about to make the same mistake again that he had made over and over: leaving. And one day, he'd not return.

"They need me," Justo replied. The 200th Army Artillery now had the reputation for being the best antiaircraft regiment in the whole army. "I heard it's tanks and antiaircraft. Not like the old days when men rode horses with *huevos* like the old *caballeros hidalgos*." He paused and picked up his blue and white cup from the saucer. "They told me I have a steady hand and an excellent eye."

"So, what's new? Everybody already knows that about you here." Faustino turned his back on his buddy and stomped out of the house.

"See the world," Justo quoted the sergeant. "Get paid and take a break." But just for a short time, though. A one-time stint. He repeated, "One time only."

"So don't go," Faustino called over his shoulder. "You're going to be homesick as hell."

The *vecinos* threw a *despedida*, sending Justo off with a loud farewell. Happily drunk, he wildly promised to write every day, to tell them all what he saw and how he slept. Channy and Faustino gave speeches filled with reluctant advice, and when they had finished, they took Justo by the arm and whispered some private admonitions. His children milled around, confused about how they should feel. Certainly, since their father had said he was leaving, the fights between their parents had grown unbearable. Neighbors stood around insisting that he'd be right back in town with money falling out of his pockets. "Let him go!"

Once he was there in the Philippine Islands, Justo lied about his homesickness in his letters, bravely writing Channy, his other *compapegado*, that he liked the travel part well enough, seeing new places. One early letter spoke only of how, while drinking beer after beer, he felt he had personally discovered the legendary lost islands of Coronado's futile search. That first explorer claimed huge areas of barren land for Spain. He sought more than gold; he urged his men over each new horizon, past Arizona, praying to find the fabled inland shortcut across America to the Pacific Ocean and on to China's riches. "And now," Justo wrote, outside of Manila, "I finally understand that the riches Coronado wanted are still waiting for him and for me right here."

Channy read the last part aloud: "I am proud to stand where Magellan stood when he claimed these islands for Philip the Second."

"Lucky stiff," he commented. Channy was truly amazed.

When Faustino read the passed-around letters, he didn't buy that Justo was a new Magellan. Certainly the Philippine Islands were the glorious Spice Islands where the Spanish had traded Mexican silver to the canny Chinese traders for their embroidered silks and the famous blue and white porcelain. But so what?

Justo had barely been in the Philippines a week when he wrote that just standing on these fabled islands gave him a new reverence. And, he said, he had found the true end of the rainbow and sent lovely silks home to his wife, imploring her to stop weeping. But she claimed his departure was a betrayal. Maribel knew she had been abandoned.

His letters arrived home on airmail parchment (no postage necessary, return address c/o FPO San Francisco), telling long stories. These letters were passed around and read aloud. The first batch related how when the first battalion of the *nuevomejicanos* arrived in their

247

sister colony by transport ships, they were welcomed and celebrated as prodigal cousins, a bond cemented by the glue of their antique language, the same spoken Spanish left in the mountain colony by Oñate and the conquistadors.

Justo, hunched near a single bug-battered light, soothed his feelings of strangeness at night by writing long, florid letters, reminding himself, "These Filipinos are our long-lost brothers." To Franque, he wrote, "The villages surrounding the base are like a fantasy. They are filled with easy girls; boys, too, if you want. They got aphrodisiacs, like *balut*, that fetus-filled duck egg. I tried it once. At night there's the moon, and radios scratching out love songs, and beer, and mold and pig roasts. They warned us of malaria, dangerous animals and poisonous insects, too." Justo added, "VD's on the list, so if you come, I want you to be real careful." Another letter was passed around.

To Maribel, he scratched, "It's like summertime all the time." Polishing small things bright, he added, "I haven't gotten malaria like half of the others have."

She wrote back, "Go AWOL. You won't be the first. Come home, please. Your boys need you bad. There's no men left in town unless you count Paco Gurulé."

Justo wrote to Faustino and asked him to check up on his outfit. He meant that Maribel was cracking up again.

When Faustino stopped by, he found that Tino, Justo's eldest son and named after him, had enlisted. "The others are following," he wrote back. "Maribel can't run the place without them."

"None of the men from Santa Fe will ever return," Maribel predicted.

"*Amor*," Justo wrote to her. "Wait. I ask you just to wait. You know I'm coming home to you. They're gonna discharge me in twenty-six months, five days and six hours from now."

Meanwhile, he was there with a whole colony of long-lost cousins.

"Dear Franque: You can get almost anything you want for a pack or two of cigarettes from the PX, even silks and hardwood carvings, like the giant Igorot spoon and fork I sent back last month. When I say anything, I mean everything!"

"Dear Maribel: You know I can't come home yet. I'm a goodwill ambassador, helping train the Philippine Scouts and pitching in for General MacArthur."

For three months, Justo continued to rave about Manila and their Filipino hosts; meanwhile, privately to his *cuates*, he sobbed that he was homesick. "Always rice. The hot *chile* has no taste. Our *chile* tastes of the earth in Chímayo and Socorro."

In less than four months, the novelty of the place had solidly worn off, and Justo longed to come home to his family in the high desert, where the dust from a single rider could be seen for fifty miles.

"Keep this under your hat," Justo wrote. "Swatting mosquitoes and flies, sweating through the dry season, and waiting for the rains, I feel like New Mexico is thousands of miles away."

It was. These islands were on a shadow planet, green and leafy, warm and humid, named for King Philip the Second by the same Charles the First of Spain who had christened *La Villa Real de la Santa Fé de San Francisco de Asís*. But here they were battered by typhoons, flooded during the rainy season by too much of the water that parched New Mexico fought over.

Channy read this as a cry for help. Faustino agreed that his buddy needed them bad.

Growing more and more frightened, Justo wrote confidentially to his *cuates* that under the dog-sized jungle leaves, he was beginning to feel cramped and crowded.

"In a place like this, a gang of armed men is invisible, and you can't hear 'em, either, because of the rustles and crackles of the swaying vines in the matted plants. Even the bugs make noise. Standing guard at night, I hear a million strange sounds." The hairs on his arm stood on end as he cradled his rifle. Had that one been just fruit falling, once, twice, more? Were those tappings another secret signal spread on the bamboo telegraph? "Twice on my four-hour watch, they've stolen equipment. I figure if a bird blasts up from the jungle, it's a warning. I think I'm going crazy here. I am scared I'm coming down with malaria. I got dysentery, but if I leave, it's desertion. Dishonorable discharge. I could be shot."

Procopio sucked his breath in and said, "I feel real sorry for the *pendejo*. Real sorry."

"I told that *vaquetón* not to go," said Faustino. "Don't tell Maribel he's sick."

Paco hitched up the tail of his work shirt and, leaning against his warmed, south-facing adobe wall, scratched his belly. At his feet, three of his eight yellow dogs lay sleeping in the dirt. Occasionally one of the dogs would twitch, or a dreaming foot would race as the dog flew through the forest after a jackrabbit, his eyes squeezed shut, his tongue parting his lips in a smile. Paco smiled as well, recalling the descriptions of the Philippine Islands in Justo's letters and dreaming of trading cigarettes for cold beer. Santa Fe was so slow-paced and quiet; any letters from the Fleet Post Office fueled lively new dreams. So now, Paco dreamed of being young. With a gun. On an island. Trading for gold. Three willing girls.

In the high altitude, the autumn sun was butter-warm, pouring sweet sleep over his dried bones. His fruit had been harvested and canned, his sister's mason jars were finally stored in dark places, and Paco deserved his rest. Last month, he had picked and pitted his apricots, small prune-sized fruits with orange centers said to cure cancer and other maladies. These small fruits had been spread out on a horsehair screen to dry in the soft afternoon sun. Once they were dry, Paco could be counted on to spend the moon-roaming night cracking open the pits. But now, as he slept, the apricot stones and their medicine kernels waited in a bucket on the table for him to bend down and sort them under the hanging kitchen light, next to a bottle of beer. *Thwap-thwap*. It was the soft kernel that healed.

Dropping off his pot of pinto beans the night before, his sister had badgered him again to get to work on this. "It's time you did something for yourself!" She slammed the wooden door as she left. He noted wistfully that she was getting old and looked tired. Time had passed slowly in the mountains, and Paco knew that *he* did not look old and certainly did not look tired; he did not have a mirror.

After his simple dinner, Paco sat with his beer, a hammer and a board, with the bucket of apricot pits on the floor at his right. *Thwap-*

thwap. Once the pit was cloven in two and he had picked out the soft seed from the center of the pit (by whatever means—his crusty fingernail, for instance), he placed it in a bowl. The longer he worked at this, the fewer small kernels he collected...or was it just that working addled his brain? As he lowered the hammerhead once more, the *thwap* was louder than before and each new *thwap* became a growing symphony of percussion, with muttered curses piled on his bossy sister for making him do this. Because of her, he occasionally bludgeoned his own left thumb.

As he bashed another pit in half, the strike resounded inside and outside his skull with a ghostly *thump*. He stopped short, listening for more eerie sounds, but there was only hollow silence; a cricket sawed in the corner of the room. There was no refrigerator to pulse and just one silent, bare light over the table. *Basta*, he said to himself and leaned back on the straight wooden chair.

Suddenly, from nowhere, he heard a rhythm of echoing thuds. Forgetting to drop the hammer on the table, he hit himself with it as he clapped both hands to his temples to silence the sounds in his fogged brain. A deep pounding resounded from his wooden door. With his left hand, he rubbed his throbbing temple and hefting the hammer on the table, he bellowed, "I don't have no lock on the door." He was, as always, disappointed to see Faustino slumping in.

For the past years, his stock greeting for Faustino remained, "Still depressed?" He turned back to his dangerous task without taking the time to examine his neighbor's face. Had he done so, he would have seen Faustino looking more darkly ominous than ever.

"They're taking the *muchitos*." Faustino could say nothing more than that. The New Mexico National Guard had been federalized. "Uncle Sam says the boys are his. They are going to the Philippines. Court-martialed if they don't go."

Paco gave a solid bang without looking and hit his thumb. "*Oww!*" Sucking his thumb, he tried to interrupt with, "It's work, at least. They are fine boys."

Faustino sat on a chair, put his head down on his arms and wept. "They took our lands, they took our language, and they are taking my boys."

"Well, Justo's already gone, and Channy's talkin' about it. They been saying it's like one huge fiesta over there. I even tried to sign up, too, but the sergeant said I was too old." Paco was frustrated, as always, with Faustino's gloom. "I don't look old."

Faustino choked. "It's beer and cigarettes, but Justo's got island fever now, and they still won't let him come back."

"So you told Franque and Melo they can't go?"

"Tried."

"Let 'em go, then; let 'em have their fun. I wish I was younger."

"If they go, I go."

Paco stared at his crazy neighbor and shook his head. He was what? Not even forty years old, and he looked like he was sixty 'cause his hide was like a worn-out boot. He never smiled. "They won't take you. You can't do nothin'."

"I can drive a truck. I can skin a goat."

"You're crazy," Paco said, weary of trying to cheer his neighbor up. But Faustino looked up, and his determination shone through his watering eyes. Paco understood Faustino's deep tie to his sons, the pride he took in them, and how Faustino's stern life held a glimpse into an eternity of sons begetting more sons on down the line 'til the Second Coming. The *muchitos* made Faustino's stay on earth worthwhile.

Paco rubbed his eye with his wrist, thinking about how he'd never have kids after his wife ran off. He wondered if she'd ever married again and if she felt bad about it, and he hoped she knew it was bigamy.

"It's a long boat trip," Faustino said. "Three weeks, they say. More, even."

"Nicasia's gonna say no."

One letter that young Franque kept for himself said that the brown-skinned Filipinas were tiny—barely five feet tall, teeny. You could almost put 'em in your pocket, although they couldn't lift much, being so little. But they liked to dance and they laughed all the time.

Laughing was good, Franque agreed, interested in meeting these happy girls. LaBelle, Melo's *novia*, was anything but giggly and petite.

"I could eat them Filipino girls for breakfast," she thundered.

Franque only half liked LaBelle, so he said, "I'm fixing to trade a carton of Camels for a moonlit night and a pretty girl," hoping to egg her into exploding again.

"You better not come home with the clap!" LaBelle turned away, clearly interested only in his brother. For a year, she and Melo had been hot and heavy, making out behind the shed, on the Plaza benches, going all the way in the back of Senio's dad's car. But only once. After Melo staged out, she moved into his old room to wait out the war, "till you get back home."

Nicasia liked LaBelle fine, but she took up enough room for two. She was well-meaning but loud. But when Nicasia's father, Nando Larrañaga, died in his sleep, LaBelle was solicitous. She cooked, served and helped Nicasia through the funeral. After that, her presence was unquestioned, and Nicasia made space in her heart for LaBelle.

Slowly, Justo's miserable homesickness took a U-turn, and his letters reflected how he had begun to buck up when the scuttlebutt hinted that the men were going to be shipped off this bug-infested island to Paris, France, to fight the Germans. Justo's reports gnawed on Channy, who felt that life was passing him by. He was spinning his wheels, losing hair, becoming useless in the closed-off forest, living in a small town.

Justo said, "Paris!"

Meanwhile, Maribel continued to lament in her tearstained, onionskin paper letters that she was half crazed now that Tino was in the PI. And to make it worse, now that the National Guard in Santa Fe had been federalized, Melo García and Senio Lujan, with one thousand eight hundred other National Guardsmen from New Mexico, would soon be shipped out to reinforce MacArthur's Scouts. Her letters accused both Justo and Tino of abandonment. She complained that Nicasia and the other women were being left without their men, young girls were losing their *novios*, houses stood empty and the fields were untended.

When Justo's lively letters described the Philippines like a beach vacation, Channy got to thinking about tropical nights as he worked his feet inside his boots, trying to bring circulation to his frozen toes. He needed new boots, and his socks were worn thin. It was close to Thanksgiving in 1941, and his plump, laughing *suegra*, his mother-in-law, had been knitting more socks for Christmas. Always the same color, each a different size. "Feet are never the same; one is always bigger than the other," she insisted. No matter how she measured and concentrated, she was unable to produce any two the same size. The smaller wore out before the larger.

Moving his toes like a pianist at his scales, he muttered, "I missed the signs." Signs that trying to buy this National Forest was a waste of his time. Signs that things had been tightened up. Police stopped him, asked if the gates had been double-locked, questioning. The very air spat change, inviting Channy to join Justo, Melo, Franque and Senio to support the brotherhood of Spanish soldiers.

Channy wanted the *gente* to take back their mountain. "We could have bought the whole damned mountain with the gold. 'Give it back to our people,' Channy pleaded. "We could have pulled down the fences, culled the elk, fished for the plentiful, shimmering trout and gathered the *berro*, the spicy watercress clogging the quiet tributaries. We want it all back. We have the money. We want to give the water away like before, free."

Faustino said it made sense to him, and he'd ask the Virgin.

It was a great idea, but even She knew it wouldn't work. For more than twenty years, Channy had opened the gates in the dark for woodcutters. But he was spitting in the wind in a near-vacant town where even the CCC camp went empty, a few gates sagging on their hinges, a door here and there open to the wind. The government pulled the relief workers out and said it was over. The National Guard came to walk the fences.

War was in the air, German War, a poison gas war, a war with planes overhead to devastate their lives. Nazis. Nazis targeted water. Channy was ordered to tighten security of the Santa Fe watershed: "Double, triple-lock those gates and fences."

He took his name tag off of his issue jacket. "Johnny Vargas," it said. It should have said "Juan María de los Angeles de Vargas," a direct descendant of the founding *hidalgos*. He was not Johnny; he was always Channy. Anglos thought it sounded the same. He held the name tag in his hand and looked at it, scratched as it was, then let it fall into the dirt.

Feeling that he served no purpose under this new administration, Channy climbed into his truck, gunned the engine, and stopped short of the metal gate. Once the padlock was sprung, the unlatched gate swung downhill, stopping with a lurch as it settled open. He removed the hand brake and let the truck roll in neutral downhill through the gate. As he got out, pushing the gate closed and relocking it, he felt more and more certain that he had a manly calling, a mission and a purpose. By the time he pulled up at *Los García*, he had it all worked out.

"Hey," he called out to Faustino, who came to his doorway, beckoned by the sound of the truck's engine. Faustino nodded, smiled too faintly for detection, and pointed toward the back of the truck, where, heralded by several interested flies, a quartered doe lay covered by burlap. Channy nodded solemnly and motioned to Faustino to collect what was his.

"I can't take it no more," Channy said, one arm out of the open window. "The mountain is our mountain. If we can't buy it back and give it to everybody, then I don't care if the Nazis come over. I can't stop 'em by myself."

Faustino interrupted, "My boy, Melo, is packing to go. I told him no."

"You should tell him yes. It beats doing nothing here in this town; this town is broke." Channy climbed into the bed of the forest service truck, grabbed hold of the quarter elk, using the burlap as a grip, and pulled it up onto his shoulder, waiting for Faustino to open the door of the shed. Olivia María brayed a warning, bringing Nicasia to the doorway to watch the two friends move the carcass into the shed. "We tried to give 'em enough to save their asses, but nobody speaks money here."

"Hold on," Faustino said as he lowered a hook to hold the chunk. "Don't go."

"This here is the last, so this meat better be good," Channy offered. "I quit. This time, I mean it for sure."

Faustino was confused. "Why quit? The mountain is still ours even if we can't buy it from the government. You control it, and for sure, we need you to get us in there. Forget the ransom; there's holes in the fences."

"You can't fool the goddamned government. We've been watching the CCC build roads into the forest, roads to nowhere, just to build roads.

Then we watch the artists painting pictures on the post office, painting on all the walls just to paint and people taking photographs getting paid by Roosevelt just to take pictures. Now they've brought in men from the National Guard in El Paso paid just to lock up the gate every night. You can still get in, but you got to pack your kill back out. I can't haul it for you anymore."

"But, *Cuate*, this place is shit without you," Faustino said in English.

"No, man, I've been squeezed out of the *floresta*. Rubes, high school dropouts, they're dropping rolls of eight-foot chain-link along the sides. Laying track to drive army trucks. If we can't just use the mountain and run free on it, I'm long gone. I want to do something good. Something to make my kids proud of me."

"We are all proud of you, and you don't have any kids anyway. You're up there to protect the old ways, how we all used to live."

"*No más*! I still quit. I'm thinking to sign up and fight."

"Fight? For what, goddammit?"

"The Germans are back doing what they've done before. They move in and take over all the other countries, empty their banks, take the farms."

"Sounds like what the *americanos* done to us here, robbed my land, took everything, taxed the rest. If you go, they're killing the *floresta*. Don't go to war to help any Roosevelt or the rest of those bald white men," Faustino said.

"I'm thinking to go down to the Philippines with the rest of the men here. Melo, Franque, Senio. They'll be on their way soon, being paid to have a hell of a great time." Channy hoped he'd not have to say it again. "I'm throwing in the hat."

"You don't owe Uncle Sam a dime. Don't do it!"

"Thought I'd just go down there to see. You come too. Stay together like always, the three *cuates*."

Put that way, it almost made sense. That Melo and Franque were there was the pull for Faustino, stronger in fact than his hatred for Uncle Sam over the lands lost. Stronger than staying back to sabotage the ten-foot fencing on the mountain.

"No, Faustino. No," Nicasia said, standing at her cookstove that night. "I need you. My papa's gone now. We need a man here. I can't run sheep by myself with no help."

"I'm just a skinny old goat, and they sure don't need me—but Justo is there, and Channy leaves for boot camp soon. Both of our *muchitos*..."

"You and Channy want a big piece of the old grant. You said you were going to buy up land. You have to stay here and run it."

"Land can wait. I have to follow my sons."

"It's a snare! Another brainchild to destroy families."

In the *nicho* in the corner by the door stood two framed photos of the boys in brown uniforms, their thick, black hair shorn; they looked almost like prisoners of war. Their portraits stood upright fronting the Blessed Mother.

Because of them, and only because of them, Faustino enlisted to defend his oppressor, the bully United States. He joined to be with his sons, who would be welcomed by their commander, General Douglas MacArthur, with these scathing words: "These are not men; they are Boy Scouts."

"It's just the usual chickenshit they hand out," the draftees mumbled. "Soldiers learn to take it." Melo was just sixteen and Franque eighteen years old.

Even before Faustino was loaded into the back of an army personnel carrier, Nicasia felt his death. She shredded her colorful, cotton skirts and stripped them into braids for small rag rugs to catch the last dirt from mudded boots. She consigned her blouses to the scraps and threw in shawls and scarves. By the time Faustino left, she had shrouded herself in widow's black, finishing what she'd started when her sons were shipped out to Fort Bliss for basic training. She rent her tablecloths and towels. Nicasia knew her husband would be killed. She had no doubt.

CHAPTER TWENTY-TWO

When the two boys had completed basic training, they came home on their last leave before shipping out to Manila. The combined García families requested a special Mass for Franque, Melo and Senio followed by a huge *despedida*, the same good-bye party they'd thrown for Justo when he was assigned to the far side of the wildly spinning world.

Arriving home in high spirits, the two boys swung off the Deuce n'half to be greeted by a dirge-like Nicasia, wearing a soiled apron over her black dress and a black *tápalo* over her shoulders. LaBelle had not finished curling her generous, long hair and would rush in typically late.

"*Mamá*, we're home. Stop acting like we're already dead," Melo said. Franque added, "We'll be back home in eighteen months. Tio Channy says it's great over there."

"The Philippines are warm. Tropical! Just imagine it," Melo said, anxious to get there but not looking forward to the rough, three-week Pacific crossing when he heard how all the GIs from New Mexico got seasick.

"I brought all of this on myself," Nicasia said slowly, covering herself with blame. She condemned the *americanos* for their lies and empty promises. She blamed the gold, the horses and the pay.

She suspected the Virgin was double-crossing her, too, by speaking only to Faustino.

She had failed to act; now the unavoidable doom was in place. She was not strong enough to have destroyed the map at the first sight of it. The treasure now buried in the wall under the *nicho* festered. "Yes," she said, and she threw herself down. "It was the treasure's evil. It fouled her men. The Devil had taken over the Virgin's statue."

But lifting her gaze from the wall, she caught a glint flashing from one of the statue's glass eyes, and she stared at the Virgin in horror and screamed, "Who are you?"

The saint did not speak a name; Nicasia saw only a stranger.

"Whose side are you on?" she demanded from the statue. In her bones, she mourned the future.

On the day of the *despedida*, the special Mass was held. Nicasia was too drained to attend it, and LaBelle stayed back with her, waving Franque and Melo off. "Hurry, you'll be late!"

Maribel, Justo's abandoned wife, arrived early, hollow-eyed, leaving her five younger children to mill about on the street, impatient for the *despedida* to get underway. The sawhorse tables had been set up with an assortment of stacked plates, leaving enough space for everyone's potluck dishes. Procopio and Flora had dropped off twin *cazuelas* of green *chile* and pork: "Plenty for all the pretty girls who want to come."

Right after Mass and waiting for the guests to come, Melo and Franque sat on the front steps, reminiscing. A pack of dogs bounded in, followed by Paco lugging his contribution to the feast. Under his arm he carried two tender, young goats raised by a cousin in Nambe. They were wrapped in burlap, skinned, trussed and dressed ready to roast in the dug-down pit. When he spied the *muchitos*, he dropped both carcasses on the ground.

"Franque, Melo," he called out, "give me twenty push-ups!"

"Tio Paco!" The boys wrapped their strong arms around their crusty neighbor, giving him repeated *abrazos* and then soundly pounding him on the back. Paco would miss these genial boys. They were the sons he wished he'd fathered. "You both look wonderful!" His delighted grin revealed his last teeth.

"*Qué guapos!*" he called out, but stopped midbreath to say, "I hear your *mamá's* not doing too good."

"Yeah, she's takin' it hard that we're going. But me, I can't wait to get out of here," Franque admitted.

Nicasia was indeed having a nervous breakdown and refused to come out into the yard. Everyone commented how broad the boys' shoulders were after basic, and Paco gave them a few more admiring punches before he kicked his dogs away from the *cabritos* he was delivering to Nicasia. Later, he kicked himself for not remembering how she loved goats and detested burros. He should have skinned Olivia Mária.

She stood motionless in the doorway, blocking any passage. Her dark clothes swathed the grieving woman within, swallowed the light, shadowing her face. When Paco approached her with his meat, he hoped she was looking at him. He could not tell.

"Nicasia, *querida*, I brought these for the feast. *Les gustan? Son suficientes?*" Paco displayed his two butchered goats.

She stifled her sobs with her sleeve and gasped. "*Son muertos.* They are dead!"

Paco searched her face, wondering what she meant. But he knew, they all knew, that she was reeling between grief and fury. "I brought these for you."

She shook her head no. After a moment, her bare hand pointed to the open pit in the far corner of the dirt yard. His gift turned into a desecration.

"*Allá. Póngalos allá.*" It was almost too late to start cooking them

"Please, Nicasia. They'll come home safe. Stop worrying." Her grieving frustrated Paco, and he fled, carrying the carcasses to be piled onto the heated rocks with the young pig. Hoping for a beer, he stole off to look for Faustino, who was avoiding her as well by reliably manning the trick spigot on the keg.

"*Una copa?*" He needed a drink.

"Here, give me a hand," Faustino said. "You hold the glass and I'll pour." Paco picked up a jelly jar and saw that Faustino, too, was a wreck. At least he was outside with his boys and not haunting the house, staring ghostlike out the windows.

"Is Nicasia gonna be okay?" he asked.

"She has to come around; she's strong," Faustino whispered. "I've never seen her like this."

Filling his glass, Paco moved off, shaking his head. *Despedidas* were meant to be bittersweet but not tragic. Nicasia was making everyone miserable as she moved farther inside the darkened house, watching from the corner of a window during the hour the boisterous García relatives and neighbors filed in, greeting and admiring her sons. The boys stood tall in their khaki uniforms. Even taller, with his back straighter, was Melo's sidekick, Senio. They were all shipping out together.

Indeed, the town turned out, crowding in to admire Senio Lujan and the García boys looking smart in their uniforms. Flocks of weepy girl cousins walked in arm in arm to wish them safe travels, bringing their friends along. The small yard was jammed, especially around the keg of beer under the apricot tree, ever conscious of Nicasia's spying eyes and how her heart was broken as she mourned her sons' departure. The men heading for the beer felt watched, and the women arranging the buffet kept glancing at the house while the children ate first. Everyone wished she'd come out. María Elena, Maribel, and others tiptoed inside to talk to her, but she shook her head, forcing them back into the yard.

"Leave me alone."

Faustino asked to have the music stopped when the guitar struck up, and he tried to muffle the conversations. When he put his finger to his lips to quiet any laughter, Melo stepped in to put a stop to this tension over his mother.

"Music, please! This is a fiesta, everyone! Come on, everybody!"

The guitar started up again; three little girls had practiced singing, "De Colores" for the handsome soldiers. Accompanied by the guitar player, their thin voices promised the men that the lovely, bright world was waiting for their return.

"*Aplausa*!" Senio called. "Give the little girls a big hand!" The ice was broken and conversation picked up, but the guests were too nervous to laugh aloud because if a window curtain moved slightly, it was Nicasia, watching.

"Go on, punch me in the gut," Melo told the small boys. "Harder!" The new US Army recruits held the day, looking brave. When LaBelle strode onto the scene, pushing into the cluster around Melo, the party picked up.

"You want someone to punch you in the gut?" LaBelle called out, and ready with her right arm back, she took her stance facing her lover. "I'll show you what a fist can do!"

"Oh, Mother of God, save me!" Melo bellowed, laughing, cowering behind his fists. "Help! Save me."

"Save him, save him!" the children called out.

"You damn well better be afraid," she menaced him, her threats ending in a slobbery kiss. "I pack a wallop..."

"*Novios, novios!*" the children chanted, pulling them apart. "Sweethearts!"

"Quiet, quiet please!" Faustino stopped the music to direct everyone's attention from their *cabrito* and beer to the late summer sky, now shot with the blood red of their mountain preparing for the night. The diners stopped, midconversation, to observe how the descending sun set up a background pageant honoring the three departing soldiers, reminding the guests of their sorrow. Melo took LaBelle's hand and held it to his heart. Slowly, a golden light broke through the silver clouds and washed over the small mountain town.

Behind the curtains, Nicasia sobbed. The red sky signaled that innocent blood was at stake. She had warned them. She had done everything possible to block them from pledging their lives to bumbling Uncle Sam. They had rushed headlong into the monster's craw. Only more evil would come of this. She had warned them to stay clear of Uncle Sam's domination spreading to the lands beyond the western sea. She had tried.

Colored red from the sunset, the upturned faces were resigned; it was too late to undo the wrongs. By taking their loyalty oaths as soldiers, these boys had pledged to follow orders, just as Oñate's soldier-conquistadors had signed away their rights to abandon the rump colony for home. Once given, a soldier's loyal oath could not be broken: for those who tried to leave, Oñate had ordered death by strangulation in 1599.

When he was faced with the massive second mutiny, he called for the traitors' swift decapitation. The history of Oñate and his Franciscans defined the absolute weight of all God-invoked vows. And because his sons had made unbreakable oaths, Faustino felt he had no choice but to follow them. His place was with them.

Nicasia was now thirty-five years old, but her black hair was fading and her bright eyes were swollen and yellowed. Finally she recovered her composure enough to come outside; she stood glancing across the heads of her relatives and then retreated into the brooding shadow on the east side of their adobe. She was thin and looked prematurely aged as she clutched the fringe of her *tápalo*, hovering in the shade and avoiding the food. Next to her, almost twice her height, stood LaBelle, wearing her new gingham skirt and an alluring, open shirt.

LaBelle, tall, hefty and frighteningly fertile, dared men to take her. She had been in Santa Fe over a year now. There were men in town who desired her, but she had set her cap for Melo, the one lover who had been the most awkward with her. Even so, he had never taken his eyes off her breasts, fascinated by her breathing. She knew he needed her and staked out his bed. "I will stay here while you are away and take care of your *mamá*. I will cut the wood and feed Olivia María." Her breasts took four short, industrious breaths for punctuation.

"I want you," he said.

"Never leave me," she demanded. Overwhelmed, he promised he'd marry her when his overseas duty was over. This promise she held prisoner in the house; it was a pulsating desperation waiting four years for his return. "If you come back with VD, I'll hack off your *cojones*."

"*No te preocupes*," he insisted. "You have nothing to worry about, *mi amor*. We will be married the minute I am discharged."

On this last night of home leave, Melo peeled off his favorite shirt and covered his face with it, breathing in his own familiar sweat now mingled with hers. The shirt held the bouquet of piñon smoke and the simmering pork, beans, garlic, *chile* and coffee. As he let it drop to the floor, he fixed it in his mind; it was the distillation of all he'd known, of the home he was leaving behind, and he vowed never to let go of the memory even as he contemplated the untamed pleasures lying in wait for him when he got to the Philippines. Justo had promised him continual sex.

"I will write you every day," LaBelle said. He knew she would.

The next morning, the Deuce n'half arrived to take them to the train station in Albuquerque.

Faustino enlisted in the army that afternoon. He took the Virgin's medallion with him.

The day her husband was loaded onto a personnel carrier truck, Nicasia took her butcher knife to the wall under the Virgin's *nicho* and hacked away the plaster to rid her house of the gold's reeking curse.

"*Mamá*! What is this mess? What are you doing, for God's sake?" LaBelle took the frail woman in her arms. "*Mamá...*?" she crooned. From the start, Nicasia had been her *mamá*.

"It is evil," Nicasia whispered.

LaBelle counted one by one as coins fell to the hardened floor, spilling out from the disintegrating pouches. "*Mamá*?"

"The gold has brought us only suffering. Child, do you see how lonely we are now?"

"Oh yes, we are lonely," she said, rocking her future mother-in-law. "Yes, *Mamá*." She rocked the woman while saying nothing more.

"If I throw it in the river, it will blacken the water."

"No, *Mamá*. Don't throw it away."

"If I bury it, maps will be drawn and more men will waste their lives pursuing it. It cannot be destroyed." Nicasia looked at the young woman. "Tell me, how can I unbury the evil? Where can I hide it?"

"The gold can give us the house next door for Melo and me and land for Franque. Give it to me, trust me."

"Faustino had his eye on a way to buy back the stolen land, and I said it was insane to pay for what was always ours. Like buying water, buying air. Channy had the right idea—get the forest back, get everything back—but we didn't try hard enough."

"I heard the gold was stolen from the Indians in Mexico."

"Stolen land for stolen gold?" Nicasia's fist rose to her head. "Of course! How blind could I have been?"

"Melo said it was hidden and nobody had a map."

"I hate the gold."

"I've got an idea. Are you okay with me selling it, if I can?"

"Thank you, child. Sell it to the Devil."

Rehearsing her pitch to the *patrones*, LaBelle knocked on the zaguan door. She knocked again and again until Procopio finally came.

"*Qué?*" he called, pulling the small insert window open. "Oh! La Belle, *si?*"

"I'm Melo's girl," she said to remind Procopio how they had met. She wore the same alluring open shirt to jog his memory along. "You remember me?"

"*Si*, but you must telephone first. I was in the far back when you started banging on the door. It upsets the *dueños* when I can't get here right away."

"Sorry. We don't have a phone. I didn't know."

"The gas station has phones. The number is in the book." He said, pulling the large door open wide enough to admit the girl. "What are you looking for?"

"I want to talk to your bosses. Privately."

"About what? They don't like to be interrupted when they are painting."

"Private, like I said." She stood her ground. "They will tell you if they choose. Only if they choose." Procopio looked at her heaving breasts and a vision of angry bulls came to his mind.

"They cannot be interrupted," he replied. "I will request a time when they can see you but when you come again. Please do not wear rodeo clothes, come dressed as a lady."

"I have all day, I'll wait right here, she said, looking around for a chair."

"If you want the favor of the *patrones*, you must have manners. Were you raised on a farm?" Procopio was indignant.

"Yes, as a matter of fact, I was," she said.

"I will let you know when you can return, if you are given an appointment."

LaBelle flushed with anger and threw her nose in the air. "They'r likely in there counting their money. I'll wait on the front steps for them to finish up." She turned and walked out the big door, leaving it open behind her so as to be seen. Procopio hesitated before he quietly closed it and left her outside on the steps.

"I don't know what she wants," he informed his *patrones*. "She's Faustino's son's *novia*."

"I smell trouble," Michael said.

Richard looked stricken as well. "If we ever did right by anyone, we did right by him. Be sure you tell her that."

"Yes, sir," Procopio agreed.

"Let me deal with this," Michael said, standing to walk to the *zaguan*. "That family has a healthy respect for my temper."

When he returned from the front steps five minutes later, he had a wonderful smile across his face. "How much money do we have?" he asked Richard. "Cash?"

"Depends on what you need it for," Richard said.

"We're making a grand donation to the Metropolitan museum in both our names."

"Oh no," Richard said. "You can't mean it. My uncle will sing up there on his heavenly cloud!" He shook his head. "Such a surprise. I want to see your father's face when he opens an engraved invitation for the reception honoring our display. He is going to keel over! The Empress Carlota's treasure. We *are* splendid, are we not?" More champagne was popped that night. "No good deed remains unpunished," he added. "We almost could have owned it for nothing."

"We thought about it..."

"Wait 'til Mabel Dodge hears this!"

When she returned to Los García, LaBelle smiled as well. "They didn't say no," she announced.

"That's how they talk," Nicasia said. "*Son muy buena gente.*"

That night, late, they rapped on the door, bringing their sturdy valise. Nicasia took a hammer to the wall and pulled everything out. Faustino had taken the Virgin's medallion to war, but everything else was out to be counted.

"When this war is over, the whole world will thank you for keeping Carlota's riches intact," Richard said. An account was opened at the First National Bank in her name; deposits were made into it.

The US Forest Service again refused to sell the side of the mountain to Nicasia, saying, "The land already belongs to the American people. It is yours and it is mine! Seems to me you were in here before. You friends with Channy Vargas?" The man wore a National Guard uniform; he stood when ladies entered his guardpost.

"It belongs to us; we want it back. Vhanny wants it back, too. Tell us how much you want for it. Just name your price."

"It doesn't have a value, it can't be sold. It was overgrazed, and the river supplies water for the entire town."

"But you locked us out! There were homesteads there, farms up there; people got their game there, their trout, their firewood. The water is ours; it belongs to all of us, and we want it back. It's always been our our mountain." Nicasia's face was stern.

"So, how much?" LaBelle went on. "I've never known of anyone refusing to sell when offered good money."

"It's government land, ladies. It already belongs to you."

"So, take down the fences. We're ready to make a deal. Give us the word." LaBelle said she knew how to talk to men.

After they had walked out exasperated, one officer turned to the other and said, "I should have sold them the Brooklyn Bridge."

"They'll be back. I've seen 'em before. Bonkers. As if that old dame had a million dollars in her pocket to buy the whole damned watershed. Cut me some slack!"

With LaBelle's help, Nicasia bought the horses the National Guard put up for sale, Franke's Cervantes and Melo's Hombre. Senio's horse was thrown in as well and taken to Panky's forty acres along the Pecos.

Borrowing back his old truck after Faustino shipped out, he was ready to haul hay and maybe find a wife.

Next, LaBelle eyed the house next door, but it was not for sale, either; it was a García house for Garcías. It was Melo's if he needed it. One for Franke, too. All in due time.

"What good is it?" Nicasia wanted to know. "The money just stays in the bank."

"Melo and I could run a farm outside of town. A good place for the kids."

"You'd move away?"

"Yeah, if we had a farm, like Panky has."

Nicasia held her tongue.

At night, alone in her marriage bed, Nicasia envisioned how the earth would celebrate her men's safe return from the Philippines. And she prayed every day. But the war wore on, unending and tragic.

For three-and-a-half years, LaBelle, more and more desolate, wrote every day. She had learned with the *vecinos* that the Japanese Imperial Army had overrun the Philippines and that Melo, Franque and Senio had been cornered. They surrendered and were imprisoned in the worst defeat the United States had ever suffered. Faustino had arrived there in time to join Channy and to console Justo when his discharge was cancelled. He had just been reunited with his sons when he, too, was captured. No one knew how many had survived, if any.

When the news leaked out about the Bataan Death March, Nicasia put her hands to her mouth, choking on an agonized scream. She did not wish to survive this report. She was impaled; her pain was unbearable. Too faint to stand the next day, she saw this march as a perversion of their own founding myth, that initial thousand-two-hundred-mile walk along the unforgiving *Camino Real* from Mexico City so far from here to the *Tierra Adentro*, the land of empty promises, land with neither gold nor riches. In 1598, they had named it the *Jornada del Muerto*, the Death March. Now the brave horsemen from the New Mexico National Guard were loaded on ships. Within the year, out of supplies, food and medicines, they met a new brutal Death March—ninety miles from

Bataan without food and water. Five thousand Allied soldiers were left to rot on the route, unburied, their dog tags gathered by their commanding officers.

In her mind's eye, she saw more men leaving their women for the dead lure of the far away. It was in their bones, this leave-taking. Sons and fathers, arms around each other, gathering up their *despedida* gifts: here a sacred talisman, there small bags of medicines, *tisanes* against liver and kidney infections, powders for lung infections, salves to sooth the skin. They could not take much away with them, trying to jam small pouches inside their canvas fatigues, those clothes yet to soften, jackets with uncut ends of thread reeking of overheated sewing machine oil. They wore St. Christopher medals hung on chains with their dog tags, praying to him for protection on the journey and to the Blessed Virgin to keep them safe on land. Faustino wore the Virgin's gold medallion.

They promised to be faithful and true. They promised to eat vegetables and fruit, to drink little beer and no whiskey. They promised as men will do to ease this leave-taking.

The women would have thrown themselves in the path of the army truck to stop this *despedida*. But their men had orders to leave for the unknown as goodwill ambassadors, like Oñate bringing Christ to the Indians. LaBelle would have crawled into the reaches of the densest jungle to bring Melo home if she had just known he was still alive. The women did not weep; they mourned howling, keening their misery into the deepening sky.

Their rage called for blood.

The lovely, empty mountain town echoed with ceaseless mourning.

Nicasia fell to ranting—shoving furniture around, slamming doors—until finally she accused the Blessed Virgin's statue of causing her misery. Kneeling before her shrine with the military portraits of her men, she glared into the glued, glass eyes of the dressed-up statue. The Mother of God, Guardian of the Hearth, Queen of the Heavens stared back, saying nothing.

"Speak to me," Nicasia demanded. "Look at me!"

The Virgin stood mute, Her eyes downcast.

"It's true," Nicasia said. "You spoke only to Faustino. You poisoned him, a gullible man, with false desires!"

Nicasia saw the vacuous eyes close, and she took up her position on the floor beneath the *nicho*. A silent hour passed as she glared at the carving.

"You are not the Blessed Mother! You are no one!" Nicasia stood and shoved the doll-saint deeper into the shrine, spilling the hot candle wax from the votives, those daily prayers for her men's safe return.

The framed portraits of her three men in uniform clattered to the floor.

"Who are You, in God's name?"

At last, the two-hundred-year-old wood *bulto* spoke; Her voice was low. "You know me; you gave me my name."

Nicasia clenched her teeth. She yanked the idol from her *nicho* and shook her. "I believed you were good. I believed that Tia Serafina made you holy!" Enraged and screaming, she slammed the whispering Virgin against the wall.

"Who are you, Deceitful Virgin?" Nicasia's hands trembled from the sheer force of her violence. She grabbed a handful of matches and set the statue's wax-spilt blue brocade robes afire; her hand blistered from the heat.

"You are not the Blessed Mother!"

The fire leaped and, rising to her fury, burned through the fine-stitched silks. Laces and adornments quavered and then leaped to cremate the antique carving, the fire calling for wood.

"Speak to me!" Nicasia wept for her own obstinacy. If the Virgin had betrayed her, she had doubly betrayed herself.

The answer was loud: "I am your invention. You made me."

The tongues of fire reflected in those glass eyes, but the heat could not blacken that fixed stare. Her eyes hardened in the heat. Fixed.

Nicasia dropped the flaming doll on the dirt floor. "You are a liar! You are the Devil's whore!" But the statue had no feeling. Her body blazed darker, and impassive because She felt no pain, She calmly bore Nicasia's wrath.

"I mirror men's desires, only that," She pronounced. As the dress melted, Her face peeled to a scoff.

"You poisoned our home. It was You who desired the gold," Nicasia screamed. Blaming the statue did not lessen her own misery.

"I delayed," Nicasia cried out, sobbing. "I was wrong, weak."

The time for rescue had passed and was gone.

"I kept the gold inside my home, eating us up," Nicasia said, howling. "My family is marked for slaughter, like fat-marbled goats for a funeral feast."

She was not alone. All the *vecinos'* hearts had been crushed; hardly an adobe home was not missing its sons. After four centuries of courage and survival, the heart of Santa Fe, that noble *La Villa Real de la Santa Fé de San Francisco de Asís*, was picked clean.

"I am you," the statue gasped, falling into smaller fires. Faint breaths of woody incense rose as the figment died.

Nicasia told LaBelle, "She was false. I was forced to burn her."

When Roosevelt's two $10,000 death gratuities (sic) arrived wrapped in tight triangulated flags, government checks to pay for the lives of her husband, Faustino and her son, Franque; she burned them as well.

www.ingramcontent.com/pod-product-compliance
Lightning Source LLC
Chambersburg PA
CBHW060527260626
47161CB00003B/790